False Negatives

R Gregg Miller

This book is a work of fiction. Any reference to historical events, real people, or real places is fictitious. Other names, places, and events are products of the author's imagination, and any resemblance to actual events or persons, living or dead, is entirely coincidental.

ISBN: 0692668608
ISBN 13: 9780692668603

Acknowledgements

WITHOUT SUPPORT AND encouragement from so many people, *False Negatives* would not have been published. While I can't begin to thank everyone by name, I have to mention a few: Tony Manente, Teri Goodwell, Tom Chevolek, Antonio Lee, Dave Hayman, Mike Roth and all the member of my Ventura County Writer's Club critique group.

For Rachel

1972
Seal Beach, California

1

THE WORK LIGHTS on the catwalks of the American Oil refinery waver ghostlike in the fog. It is always murky on the graveyard shift, but the soup pouring ashore tonight is especially thick. The roiling mist even mutes the floodlights at the main gate, turning the normally penetrating white lights astride the guard shack into milky pools of ecru radiance.

Inside the sparse aluminum enclosure, an ebony twig of a man in a security guard's uniform shivers against the cold as he struggles to stay awake. Startled by the roar of a V-8 engine, the great-grandfather's eyes open wide to the sight of a full-size sedan charging toward the gate. The thumping inside the old man's chest abates when he recognizes the two-tone Buick Electra 225 as Jake "Cannonball" Kramer's sled.

The deuce and a quarter's front bumper stops just inches short of crashing into the gate. The big Buick is still bobbing on its suspension as Jake cranks down the driver's window. But before the fox-haired, forty-year-old Texas transplant with an off-center face of porous concrete can speak, the guard's mottled lips stutter, "What cha doing here...this early, Jake? Lose another fight wit' da...old lady?"

The haltingly uttered queries make their way around the tooth-pick in the guard's mouth, but not around Jake's sensitivities. "Fuck you, Lamont! Hit the button to raise the damn gate. With this fog, if I wait till the regular time, I'll never get to Bakersfield."

The guard hits the button and watches as Jake's eight-cylinder behemoth accelerates into the yard, leaving only exhaust in the damp night air. The security guard shakes his head and says to himself, "Poor bastard. He ought'a *dee*-vorrzz the bitch."

• • •

Parked in the employee lot, Jake gathers his lunch box and portable cassette player off the floorboard. Long hauling in his own rig for a decade, he resents needing to drag his tunes to a company rig every morning. It's more than an inconvenience; it's a reminder that American Oil Company owns the trucks. They just rent drivers like Jake.

Though he hated to admit it, his wife had been right every time she nagged, "You can't be a husband and a father when you're never here." Long hauling had left him home only a couple of days a month. During those few days, he felt like a stranger in his own house. The final straw came when he realized his next-door neighbor knew more about his son's exploits on the baseball diamond than he did.

So Jake sold his rig and took a job with American, hoping to make a fresh start with his wife, Brenda. There wasn't much left over after paying off the loan. Before they even got the check, it was already spent on a new dinette set and floral print drapes for the living room. But more time at home only brought more of Brenda's whining, more arguments, and more nights on the couch. Jake pines for the refuge of his own rig. He has to settle for the temporary shelter of a company truck.

After signing the dispatcher's paperwork, Jake struts to his assigned rig. He stuffs one of his prized snakeskin boots into the bottom rung of the cab ladder and propels himself into his domain. His gnarled finger presses play on his portable cassette player. Firing up the diesel, he grabs the thermos from his gray metal lunch box and pours himself a cup.

Jake lectures the empty passenger seat as he maneuvers the eighteen-wheeler through the yard. "They give me a ration of shit for leave'n early but bitch whenever I'm late deliver'n. Fuck'm!" The feel of the steering wheel on his calloused hands, the throb of the engine beneath his seat, and the hot black coffee soothe him. Working the gears to the rhythm of the country tune, Jakes releases a sigh. Just like the load of one hundred thousand gallons of unleaded premium gasoline, Brenda's bitching is behind him—out of sight and out of mind.

They don't call him "Cannonball" for nothing. Despite the limited visibility, Jake is making time as he sings along with his favorite country star.

> I'm ride'n the white line
> Put'n my troubles behind
> Gonna forget the past
> To find love that'll last...

• • •

Jaime is passed out on the bench seat of his ancient pickup truck parked on a fog-shrouded East LA side street. An eruption from his sour stomach rousts the middle-aged, fat-faced Sinaloa native to semiconsciousness. Too much tequila—too much chili. His thick tongue scrapes the unfamiliar rough edge of a broken tooth as he works his jaw. The bile in his mouth only adds to his misery. Somehow these maladies must all relate to last night, but a wall of alcohol still obstructs the details. Then it comes to him. "Si, requerdo." Somebody had objected when he tried to walk out on a side bet at the cockfights.

Pulling heavily on the steering wheel, Jaime draws his bloated torso into an upright position. Instinctively he reaches for the ignition and grinds the flathead V-8 to a hesitant start. The groans of the tired engine reluctantly coming to life are instantly joined by overamplified mariachi music from the ill-fitting speakers in the kick panels. With the engine running, gasoline fumes add to the assault on Jaime's senses. His truck gathers speed as the moist chill swirls through the missing wind-wing. Although the cold air makes the cab feel like a freezer, it helps dissipate the gasoline smell.

Color fades. The forest-green sign at the entrance to the Golden State Freeway is only a patchwork of gray floating unnoticed past Jaime as he accelerates northbound into the fog. Normally it only takes about thirty minutes to get back to Pacoima. "Pero, con la neblina?" Contemplating how long before he can pass out in his bed, Jaime's bleary eyes don't notice the white dashes as he drifts across three lanes. Awareness strikes suddenly at the sight of the double yellows. Instinctively he jerks the wheel to the right, just in time to avoid colliding with the center divider, but not in time to avoid the unseen debris from an earlier highway catastrophe. With a metallic clang, an angular piece of steel wedges itself into the engine compartment, shorting the electrical system.

"*Dios mio!*" Disbelief suspends time. Everything electrical is dead. No headlights. No dash lights. Adios, mariachis! Jaime pumps on the gas pedal while profanely exhorting his pickup to keep going. "*Chinga tu madre! Andele pendejo!*" His shouts, his mashing on the gas pedal, and shaking of the steering wheel do not alter the pace of deceleration. He cranks the wheel farther to the right in an attempt to reach the relative safety of the shoulder. Its energy spent, the dark balky contraption comes to a dead stop straddling the right two lanes.

• • •

Despite the limited visibility, Jake "Cannonball" Kramer is true to his motto, "Haul'n ass—Haul'n gas." The beads of moisture running across the red, white, and blue American Oil emblem don't penetrate the cab where Jake's raspy voice accompanies the singer on the cassette tape...

> Hard-hearted man on a melancholy highway
> Forlorn and forgotten, resigned to his fate
> Lost control of his soul so long ago...

As if conjured by a demon, the dark outline of Jaime's stalled pickup materializes out of the fog. "*Shit!*" No time to maneuver. Stomp the brakes. The screeching of tires is overwhelmed by the brutal din of steel crushing steel. There is a blinding flash, a radiating shockwave, followed by the roar of the explosion. Silhouetted by the inferno, the twisted wreckage wavers in the heat. Giant flames flail skyward, their tremendous energy being silently absorbed by the limitless cold and dark of the night.

Glendale, California

2

AFTER HOURS OF shifting in the sheets, I finally slip into slumber...

What the hell is that racket? A cruel reality registers—that irritating rhythmic clamor is my alarm. I stare in disbelief as I reach for the Baby Ben on the nightstand. *Why is my alarm going off at quarter after midnight?*

As I strangle the alarm, my sleepy brain makes an unwelcome discovery. The *hour hand* is on the three. The *minute hand* is just past twelve. Instead of quarter after midnight, it's a couple minutes past three.

I swing my legs over the side of the bed as I run my hand on the wall. *It has to be here somewhere.* When my hand finds the light switch, my eyelids slam shut. Fumbling like a blind man, with one hand shading my eyes and the other waving in front of me, I find the bathroom. It's quite a feat, considering I only moved in yesterday.

After relieving my bladder, I make my way to the kitchen for a quick breakfast of instant oatmeal and Tang. My orders are on the counter. "All recruit officers shall report to the gymnasium at the police academy at zero-four-thirty hours wearing appropriate business attire..."

My suit and tie will no doubt meet the LAPD's appropriate business attire standard. That's not what I'm worried about. Appearances have never been my problem, except maybe for a few cases of mistaken identity. Like that woman on a flight from Chicago who thought I was one of the actors who played in *Deliverance*. I told the woman I wasn't that actor, but she kept asking for my autograph. It took the stewardess to get the starstruck passenger back in her seat. I would have thought flying coach, not first class, should have been evidence enough. Still, I don't expect anyone at the police academy will ask me for a souvenir signature.

My concerns are harder to describe. Imagine a thousand people spread out in a freshly planted Nebraska cornfield. I'd be the one struck by lightning. Yeah, I'll admit sometimes it's my fault, but most of the time shit just happens.

"About as subtle as a train wreck." That's how my high school English teacher described me. More than my forthright verbal manner, maybe it's my mischievous sense of humor that pisses some people off. Whatever the reason, I've got to dial it down a notch. I just want to go unnoticed, remain anonymous, and stay in the middle of the pack.

Out the door an hour early, I'm enveloped by the musty shade of gray that invaded while I slept. The fog has even seeped into my apartment's underground garage. Rivulets of condensation cascade down the driver's window when I insert my key in the door. Breathing into my hands, I wait for the engine to warm up and clear the windshield.

The fog-shrouded streets are nearly deserted. Heading toward the freeway, I'm trying in vain to adjust my windshield wipers to keep time to the Motown tune on the radio. *What is that orange glow?* Before I see the highway patrol car that blocks my onramp, the source of the mysterious glow becomes apparent. A jackknifed tanker is sprawled across the highway, engulfed in fire. The huge flames silhouette the twisted wreckage against the veil of moisture.

The only way I know to get from my new apartment to the academy is via the freeway. A few minutes ago, I was second-guessing my decision to leave this early. Now my abundance of caution looks more reasonable. I take a residential street south, but it ends after only a couple of blocks. I make a left at the T-intersection, then a quick right as I try to zigzag my way closer to the academy.

At a divided boulevard, I have no choice but to make a right. Ornate concrete guardrails tell me I'm on a bridge. Miraculously, the bridge spans not only the river, but the freeway, too. My good fortune ends on the other side, where the topography steepens, and the visibility drops to near zero. My right thumb presses against the selector on the dash and confirms it is on defroster. Despite the whoosh of air from the vents, my curled index finger tugs on the fan switch, but it is already on full blast.

When the road veers to the right, back toward my apartment, I make a left turn onto a residential street. I plan to make the first left to get back on track toward the academy, but the side streets aren't cooperating. The tangled roadways rise and fall as they curve around the steep terrain. Each stretch of asphalt ends, either at the edge of a ravine or the base of a cliff. I have to turn around again.

Straining to see through the heavy blanket of moisture, I have lost my sense of direction. With each glance at my watch, my stomach twists a little tighter. *I can't be late to the academy. Not on the first day. Even juggling three part-time jobs in college, I was never late to work!*

Everything beyond my windshield is a shade of gray. At any moment, I expect to hear Rod Serling's voice. "Next stop *The Twilight Zone.*" Finally, I stumble upon a frontage road that leads me to where I would normally exit the freeway.

My orders were explicit: "All recruits shall park on Academy Road, not in the parking lot." There isn't time to search for a closer spot. I pull to the curb at the end of the long line of cars. My sport coat can't keep out the cold as I walk toward the foggy aurora of lights in the parking lot. Maybe it's nerves, too, but by the time I reach the main gate, I'm thoroughly chilled.

My only previous visit to the police academy was for the physical agility test. I had to leave for work right after the test and didn't get a chance to explore the iconic facilities originally built for the 1932 Olympics. *How do I get to the gym?* At this hour, I don't even consider the door adjacent to the dark offices. I eschew the stairway on the left, opting instead for the service drive on my right. Quickly beyond the reach of the lights in the parking lot, I move cautiously amid the foul odor of Dumpsters. Finally, I find a door, but it's locked. In near total darkness, I feel my way along the cool concrete wall. Finally, I find another door. This one yields.

The tiny muscles in my eyelids quiver as my dark-adapted eyes squint against the gymnasium's bright lights. My footsteps blend with the muffled conversations echoing throughout the cavernous space. Crossing the basketball court, I detect the distinctive odor of aged hardwood covered in years of lacquer varnish. The smell reminds me of my grandparents' home in Chicago. In addition to the slightly sweet smell of old school varnish, there is the metallic scent of artificial heat. Looking up, I can see rows of blue flames inside a natural gas heater suspended from the ceiling. By the time I make it to the other side of the gym, the initially welcoming warmth begins to stifle.

I resist the urge to take off my jacket. I don't want to draw attention to myself. Likewise, I keep my distance from a guy in a lime-green leisure suit.

At precisely 4:30 a.m., four members of the academy staff in perfectly tailored Class A uniforms scream at us to fall in. As soon as we assemble in ranks, two instructors begin to circle the leisure suit like a pair of cheetahs stalking a lame zebra.

The cheetahs pounce. "Who the hell are you supposed to be, Mister? Soupy Sales or the Good Humor man? Get down and give me twenty."

In my peripheral vision, I can see the guy in the pastel outfit assume the position. He wearies after only a couple of push-ups.

One of the cheetahs speaks, his gravel voice dripping with sadistic sarcasm. "Gentlemen, none of you has to be here. But as long as you are here, you will *all* work together. Since the Good Humor man can't seem to give me the push-ups I require, I'll get my push-ups from all of you! Everybody assume the position!"

My academy experience began less than ninety seconds ago, and here I am in the push-up position, my imported silk tie sweeping specks of dust off the varnished maple floor with every repetition. As we struggle to give twenty *good ones*, the instructors meander through our ranks and spread the word. Any of us can stop at any time. Just say you want to leave, and it will be that easy. No more yelling. No more push-ups. No more standing at attention. Just quit.

• • •

The Good Humor man was the first to take their offer. No one ever saw him again. Although he was the first, he wouldn't be the last. In the next four months, I'll admit there were a couple of times I was tempted, but something inside me knew I would never quit. I really wanted to be an LA cop. Besides, I wasn't going to give the bastards the satisfaction. I don't know where it came from, or how it got into my head. I just know it became my mantra: *They can kill me, but they can't eat me.* It is amazing how much it helped.

3

EVERY DAY AT the academy will start with an inspection. Although we are dressed in civilian attire, today is no exception. The staff methodically proceeds from recruit to recruit. No one escapes criticism. Standing at attention, my eyes front, I hear an instructor question a recruit somewhere to my right.

"What did you use to shave with this morning, Mister?"

Clearly puzzled, the recruit hesitates. "A shaver...Sir."

"An electric shaver?"

"Yes, sir."

The instructor says loudly enough for everyone to hear. "Gentlemen, every one of you limp dicks shall shave with a blade every morning. You can give back the electric razor to your sister who gave it to you for Christmas. She can use it to shave her legs. In the LAPD, we shave with cold steel. Do I make myself clear?"

"Yes, sir," we shout.

"I can't hear you."

"*Yes, sir!*"

This time our response hammers off the walls with enough force to satisfy the instructor, who is now inspecting the man on my immediate right.

"What you looking at? You queer for me, boy? At attention, you keep your eyes front. You hear me?"

"Yes, sir."

"What did you say?"

"Sir, yes, sir."

"Get down and give me twenty!"

After a shuffle of feet, the instructor is in front of me. Trying to avoid looking at someone when his face is only inches away is difficult. When the man screams at you, it is especially hard not to twitch your eyeballs in his direction. Fortunately, the officer in front of me is short, and the top of his head is below my eye level.

He sniffs the air like a Yorkshire terrier. "You smell like a French whorehouse. This is a police academy, not a bordello."

Whatever is tickling the instructor's nose isn't coming from me. All brands of *smell-well* give me a headache. Of course, my sensitivity to personal fragrances is immaterial. The instructor thinks the odor is from me. Fortunately, he doesn't make me do push-ups for it. I'll take my due, but don't punish me for someone else's screwup.

When the lead instructor continues down the line, the second member of the inspection party takes his place. This instructor is taller, and I have to concentrate harder to keep my eyes from following his movements. Even under the best of circumstances, it is uncomfortable when people stare at you. It is particularly unnerving when they're looking for imperfections. After all, no one is perfect.

Finished with the inspection, they call the roll. Two names don't answer. I figure the Good Humor man is one. As we file out of the gym, the other name shows up. I hope he's in shape. I bet they make him do a million push-ups.

It is still dark as we march across Academy Drive to a modular building adjacent to the track. The plaque on the wall says the floor space was donated by Jack Webb, the producer and star of the *Dragnet* TV show.

Seated at one-piece desks, we are set upon by a series of bureaucrats, each with stacks of forms for us to fill out. After almost an hour, we are down to the one document that really matters, the oath of office. We stand in unison, face the flag, and lift our right hands as we repeat the oath: "I, Jacob Maximilian Stoller, do solemnly swear..."

Immediately after we are sworn in, we get the welcome aboard speech from the commanding officer of Training Division, well-rehearsed remarks from a cardboard cutout.

"The training here at the academy is extremely rigorous. I make no apologies for it. It has to be tough because the streets of Los Angeles are tough. Just as a sword's steel is tempered in a forge, then sharpened to a razor's edge with an abrasive stone, so LAPD officers are fashioned by a demanding regimen here at the academy into the strongest and the sharpest officers in the world. While the training is demanding, the whole process is fair and just. The standards are high because they have to be high to keep the LAPD as the finest law enforcement agency in the world. Look around the room, gentlemen! More than half of you won't be here come graduation day." He points to the badge on his uniform. "Only the best of the best will graduate and wear this badge."

I take a quick glance around the room and wonder who will be with me at the end.

The captain continues, "Our equipment is the best, having been selected and approved only after extensive research. All the manufacturers, from weapons to vehicles, strive to have their products selected by the LAPD.

"Gentlemen, this next one is really important. The LAPD is corruption-free. Unlike the police departments in New York, Chicago, and Detroit, the Los Angeles Police Department is totally devoid of corruption. Regrettably, in many American cities, it is standard practice to put a twenty-dollar bill in your wallet behind your license. In those cities, when you get stopped, the cop takes the twenty and gives you back your license.

"We don't tolerate that in the LAPD. Just the other day in Rampart Division, a man visiting from New York tried to hand a motor officer a twenty to get out of a ticket. When the officer told him to put his money away, the violator offered another twenty. The man kept offering more, thinking the officer was just trying to negotiate a higher payoff.

"When the violator refused to sign the ticket, a sergeant rolled to the scene. The New Yorker ended up going to jail for trying to bribe his way out of the ticket, but not before he offered the sergeant a hundred dollars. The moral of the story is clear—you can't buy an LA cop!"

The captain takes a practiced pause, scanning his captive audience. "Work hard, keep your nose clean, and you can be chief someday. Promotion in the department is based on merit. You have to take written and oral tests to promote. There is no room for nepotism, favoritism, or politics in the LAPD."

My eyes grow misty and goose bumps rise on my forearms. Finally, I've made it to an organization that values integrity and honors your accomplishments—not your connections. I don't care how tough things get. I won't quit.

At the break, I mingle with my classmates. We all went through the same selection process: written exam, civil service interview, physical agility test, medical exam, psych exam, and background check. While some of the guys look familiar, I don't see anyone I spoke with during testing.

Most of the guys are from blue-collar backgrounds and have only a high school education. An exception is the recruit who was late, Dick Logan, a tall, handsome blond. He makes a point of telling everyone he has a bachelor's degree. For some reason his salesman's smile reminds me of my dentist telling me to open wide.

About half of my classmates have prior military experience. All were enlisted, except Jackson Davis who was a lieutenant in the Marine Corps. Davis is five foot eight, the minimum height for the LAPD, and he has the classic fireplug build. Everything about him, from his crew cut to his accent, says he's from a traditional southern military family.

Nearly everyone is white. There are only a few black guys and about twice that many Hispanics. There is one obviously Jewish recruit, Jerold Silverstein. If the actor who played Tevye in *Fiddler on the Roof* had a son, he'd look like Silverstein.

Nearly everyone is in his early twenties. The age standout is one of the black guys who looks like he's forty. Of course, he can't be over thirty-four, the upper age limit. His graying close-cut hair, atop a weathered brass complexion, conjures the image of a semi-jacketed forty-five-caliber bullet. Some of the guys are already calling him "Bullet-head" behind his back. To his face, they call him "Pops."

There is no way I can call the guy those nicknames. He reminds me too much of Scatman Crothers, the voice of the Scat Cat in Disney's animated hit *The AristoCats*. I met the Scatman when I worked the parade crew at Disneyland. Mr. Crothers was the grand marshal of the Christmas parade the year the film was released.

While my classmate bears some resemblance to the actor, it's more a question of personality. Like the celebrity, he has an infectious, wry, if not raunchy sense of humor. I guess that is why my classmates feel comfortable calling him by a moniker on the first day. I make a point of calling him by his surname, Booker.

Back in the classroom after the break, we are beset by a battery of standardized tests. Contemplating trick questions and filling in the little circles with the number two pencils provided, turns my brain to mush. I make myself a promise—tomorrow I will to have a better breakfast than instant oatmeal and space-age orange juice.

Before our instructor dismisses us, he admonishes us not to be late returning from our thirty-minute lunch break. I take his words to heart and hurry to the Academy Café. The eatery is a classic 1950s-style diner, LAPD's version of *Happy Days*. The stools at the counter rise on chromed steel cylinders bolted to the floor. Everything is trimmed in stainless steel and upholstered in red vinyl. The countertops and tables are white Formica, the kind speckled with little pink squares. Sepia photos of LA cops, standing in formation, and other police memorabilia decorate the walls.

I grab a spot at the counter between a uniformed instructor and some old guy in civilian clothes. Fortunately, the breakfast crowd is gone, and the lunch rush has yet to arrive. My waitress fills my water glass as soon as I sit down. I quickly scan the menu and order a tuna melt combo on wheat with lemonade.

It is only a few minutes before my attentive waitress slides my plate in front of me. I munch the fries and nibble on the dill spears between bites of the sandwich. Although it is just generic coffee shop fare, it tastes delicious.

When the waitress drops my check on the Formica, I glance at my watch, happy I opted for the counter. En route to the cashier, I notice a couple of tables jammed with my classmates who are still eating, or worse yet, still waiting for their food. Dick Logan, the same guy who was late this morning, is one of those having a leisurely meal.

A classmate at Logan's table looks at his watch. "We better finish quick. They said be back in thirty minutes."

"Don't sweat it!" Logan says. "Look at all the instructors in here who are still eating. We've got plenty of time."

4

I LINE UP with the others who have made it back from lunch on time.

The instructor immediately perceives our ranks are deficient. "In the LAPD there is no such thing as being fashionably late. Thirty minutes means thirty minutes. So...while we wait for your classmates to return from their lunch, we will pass the time with a little PT. Assume the position!"

Lecturing and punishing those who show up on time for the sake of those who are late, has never made sense to me. Yet here we are, those of us who came back on time, suffering in the push-up position awaiting the arrival of our tardy classmates. As I hold myself parallel to the ground, I wonder how I'm going to put up with this crap for another sixteen weeks. Time lingers as I struggle to keep my back straight.

The instructor's gritty sandpaper voice accentuates his sarcasm as he continues his harangue. "Gentlemen, this isn't the LA City College. In case any of you don't realize it, let me set you straight. This is the Los Angeles Police Academy. Being late is not acceptable. We don't accept notes from your mommy. Don't even think about trying to give me an excuse. As the saying goes, excuses are like assholes—everybody's got one! And no one needs more than one—especially not me!"

An instructor meanders through our prostrate ranks. He stops next to a recruit who is shifting his weight in an unsuccessful attempt to mitigate his distress. "Any of you can leave at any time. All you have to do is say the magic words. All you have to do is say, 'I quit.'"

The recruit stands up and is whisked away. His ordeal is over.

By the time Logan and a throng of others show up, my shoulders are trembling and my back feels like it's on fire. I never thought I'd be so happy to hear someone shout, "A-ten-*hut.*"

Back on my feet, my upper torso relaxes. I'm anxious to return to the Jack Webb building and give my stomach a chance to digest the food I just tossed down. But instead of marching into the classroom, our formation heads uphill on Academy Drive at double-time. The tuna fish, french fries, dill pickles, and lemonade are definitely percolating now.

When we reach the combat range, the asphalt makes a sharp left turn and the slope goes from steep to stairway steep. Although I am in good shape, pushing up this acute incline with a stomach full of fried food is a chore. By the time we get to the top of the hill, my stomach is pretty sour. We head back down, only to turn around and ascend again.

I am really surprised nobody has puked yet. For my part, I am swallowing hard, trying to keep the bile out of my mouth. I definitely don't want to draw attention to myself by being the first guy to vomit. Thankfully, the next time down the hill we continue past the firing ranges and end up back inside the Jack Webb building.

My shirt is wet with perspiration. My silk tie is ruined. It isn't long before the initially refreshing air becomes a chilling distraction.

A recruit raises his hand. "Sir, could you back off the AC a little?"

The instructor doesn't hesitate. "Listen up, all of you. The temperature in here is LAPD perfect! If it is too hot or too cold for you, that's your problem. It's a case of mind over matter. *I don't mind, and you don't matter.*" He looks over the room. "Besides, any of you can leave at any time."

We spend the remainder of the day getting outfitted. In addition to our police utility belts called Sam Brownes, we are issued handcuffs, batons, recycled riot helmets, a hardcover copy of the California penal code and a softcover version of the vehicle code. We get gray metal name plates already engraved with our last names, black polyester clip-on ties and quarter-inch tie bars made out of the same pewter-colored metal as the name tags.

The strangest items come in a small manila coin envelope, four metal buttons shaped like miniature acorns with an eye extending from the point at the bottom. Each button has a tiny flat washer with an oval opening to accommodate the eye and a miniature cotter key to attach the assembly to the uniform. Until today I hadn't even noticed these adornments on the LAPD uniform.

We are issued our duty weapons: blue steel, four-inch, .38-caliber revolvers made by Smith and Wesson. Along with our pistols we are each handed a cleaning kit and a dark-green canvas bag containing fifteen hundred rounds of wad cutter ammunition.

We learn that recruits don't wear the dark blue wool LAPD uniform until the final phase of the academy. During our first three months we will wear khakis. Our khaki uniforms must be purchased today at our own expense. Because a freshly laundered and pressed uniform is required every day, it is *highly recommended* we purchase five sets. The minimum we can possibly get by with is three. We also have to buy physical training gear. Altogether, we need to come out of pocket with around four hundred bucks, about half a month's salary.

Not to worry, the LAPD has the answer. This morning we all signed up with the Los Angeles Police Credit Union. Being a member of the police credit union, we are automatically entitled to borrow up to four hundred and fifty dollars to pay for uniforms and equipment.

• • •

Later I would learn this is by design. The brass wants every cop to be financially strapped. Management's thought process is simple—they control the purse strings. The more dependent cops are on their paycheck, the greater control management feels they have. Most cops are very obliging, since like most people, cops tend to live from paycheck to paycheck.

I never liked to owe anybody money. I financed my first car on a three-year contract but paid it off in a little over a year. Although it just about emptied my bank account, I wrote a check for everything. I am one of the few who didn't begin my LAPD career indebted to the police credit union.

5

THE NEXT MORNING I keep my promise to eat a better breakfast. I whip up a cheese omelet and top it off with a big glass of real orange juice. The fruit juice tastes great compared to yesterday's powdered orange drink, appropriately named for its bite.

Today my good clothes will stay in the closet. I've finally found the perfect occasion to wear that hideous paisley tie Aunt Miriam gave me for my twenty-first birthday. I'm not leaving an hour early, either. My on-ramp should be open. Just in case, I scouted a couple of alternate routes on the way home yesterday.

I'm at the academy in twenty minutes. After stashing my PT gear, some toiletries, and my lunch in my locker, I head upstairs to the gym via the internal stairway. Not coming in from the darkness, I'm not blinded by the bright lights. I see Booker telling tales of his amorous feats as a young sailor in the navy. A crowd surrounds Davis as he recounts his days at OCS (officer candidate school). I don't see Logan. I wonder if he will be late again.

Even before we fall in, I can see our numbers are significantly smaller than when we left yesterday afternoon. I can't blame anyone. It is better to avoid embarrassment and end an abbreviated stint as a cop with a little bit of decorum than to give up in front of the class.

After inspection, they divide us into four squads. Officer Robles, the squad adviser for the third squad, calls my name, and I head to his corner of the gym. Robles looks to be about thirty-five. He sports a meticulously trimmed jet-black mustache that points down at the edges, accentuating his frown. He is the epitome of the handsome mustachioed Mexican gentleman. Replace his frown with a smile, and he'd be the perfect ambassador to represent some regal product of Mexico. But he doesn't smile.

I want his frown, not because it is attractive, since certainly it is not. I want the expression etched into his face because it's a manifestation of measuring up to what the mean streets of Los Angeles dish out.

Officer Robles is sparse with his words. His lips barely move when he speaks, like he's practicing to be a ventriloquist or something. "For now, I will put you in order from the tallest to the shortest. The tallest will be your squad leader. But that is just for now. Later, I'll assign the best man for the job."

Guess who is the tallest in third squad? Me.

Officer Robles gives us a shorthand version of the obligatory pep talk. He ends with a succinct summation. "If you have what it takes, I want to help you graduate. But this job isn't for everyone. Most of you will know pretty quick. But dig this…if you have to ask me if this job is right for you…then it isn't."

Before anyone can pose a question, we've been dismissed. That's fine with me. The other advisers jaw with their squads a lot longer. When the others have finally finished, Sergeant Sinclair announces he's chosen Jackson Davis as our class DI. The fireplug marches us across the street to the Jack Webb building. That is fine with me, too.

In the classroom, we get our orientation to MILES, Multimedia Individualized Learning and Examination System. I could have sworn Officer Robles said MILES stood for Multimedia Instruction for Law Enforcement Studies. Whatever the acronym stands for, I understood

Robles's meaning when he described MILES as a lame attempt to stamp recruits into cops on a self-paced assembly line. He cynically categorized it as another progressive LAPD program carried like a torch by a captain lighting his career path to commander.

Under MILES, the traditional curriculum at the academy has been divided into modules. Recruits check out a study guide and videotape for each module. In most cases the video is just a recording of a lecture from the days when live classes were the norm. After reading the study guide and watching the video, the recruit heads to the testing trailer for a Scantron multiple-choice exam.

Sergeant Sinclair personally gives the MILES orientation. The barrel-chested former marine's megaphone-voice demands attention. "If you fail any examination three times, you fail out of the academy. That means if you fail a test the first time you take it, you'd better be pretty damn sure you know the material before you take it a second time. There are no exceptions. If you fail a test three times, you are out!" He scowls at us. "Obviously, gentlemen, there will be a lot of pressure on you to pass these tests. Some of you will be tempted to cheat. *Don't!* The penalty for cheating is *termination*."

The veins in Sergeant Sinclair's shaved head begin to pulsate, and a thin sheen of perspiration forms on his face. "A recruit who has failed a test twice, knows he is out of here if he fails again. He might just think he has nothing to lose by cheating. You might even be tempted to help. *Don't!* Giving answers is as bad as asking for answers. It is cheating! And the penalty for cheating is *termination*! Have I made myself clear?"

"Yes, sir."

"*I can't hear you.*"

"*Yes, sir!*" we shout.

"Gentlemen, the captain has to hear you...and his office is across the street. *Have I made myself clear?*"

"*Yes, sir!*"

After lunch, we report to the range. Although I've never shot a pistol before, I'm not exactly a novice when it comes to firearms. I first learned to shoot a .22 rifle with the Boy Scouts at a small range tucked among the factories just the other side of the railroad tracks. The cost of the program was low enough that I was able to participate along with my best friend, Mike, whose dad had a well-paying job. Mike had an eagle eye. He could look downrange and see where each of his rounds landed. It had been a source of pride to me, and an annoyance to Mike, that although I couldn't see the holes my bullets punched in the paper, I could put my rounds in a tighter group.

Still, I'm nervous about my lack of experience with pistols, and I'm not the only one. A classmate who was an MP in the army is giving an impromptu lecture. As his audience grows, my confidence sinks.

"Shooting a pistol is much more difficult than shooting a rifle," the former MP crows. "Unlike a rifle, with a pistol there is no sling to steady your grip. It is even worse because the LAPD uses revolvers, and the trigger pull on a revolver is really long." He shakes his head. "On the range at MP school, it looked more like birds learning to fly than soldiers learning to aim a handgun. More guys flunked shooting the Colt Nineteen-Eleven and had to be reclassified Eleven Bravo than for any other reason."

There is one of those unexplained lulls. In that awkward moment, someone looks around and sees Officer Noble, our firearms instructor, calmly taking in the scene.

"Fall in!" our DI yells.

We are literally bumping into one another as we assemble into ranks. I'm certain we will pay a heavy price for our inattention. But instead, Officer Noble tells us to fall out and gather around him.

While the rest of the cadre at the academy wear the regular blue LAPD uniform, the shooting instructors wear khakis. Unlike the starched and pressed khakis of the recruits, it is obvious Officer Noble's cotton shirt and trousers have never been near a commercial laundry. His shirtsleeves are crumpled and folded back to his elbows, exposing his freckled forearms. His eyes are a lively shade of blue, belying the gray that graces his temples. His soft, yet masculine voice is filled with authority when he inquires, "How many of you have fired a pistol before?"

A few hands go up.

Officer Noble takes his time and asks the name of the recruits with raised hands. After he has memorized the name of each recruit with prior pistol training, he says, "I'm glad there are only a handful of you who have bad habits that I will have to break. As for the rest of you, let me assure you there is nothing difficult about firing a pistol. It's easier than aiming a rifle. Pistol shooting is based on pointing, and everyone has been pointing since they were babies. Of course that is not all there is to it. Safety is most important. But rest assured, if you apply the techniques we teach, you will become a safe and proficient shooter. That does not mean you will be able to shoot proficiently without practice. But with practice, there is no reason why any of you should fail. And believe me...you will all get plenty of practice."

• • •

Firearm training wasn't limited to shooting. We spent hours drawing and holstering our revolvers *by the numbers*. Drawing my weapon became as natural as zipping and unzipping my fly. I would have loved the shooting no matter what, but because the firearms instructors treated us like human beings, it was the only part of the academy I can honestly say I enjoyed.

6

THE LOCKER ROOM is filled with the odor of the black indelible ink used to stencil our last names on our sweatshirts. It reminds me of that new-car smell. While not a particularly pleasant aroma, once it's gone, it's gone. This artificial smell will soon be replaced by something more organic.

We are standing at ease outside the locker room when Jackson Davis shouts, "A-ten-*hut!*" The approaching instructor doesn't have the same buzz cut as the rest of the PT staff. While his scalp is visible on the sides, he has about three-quarters of an inch of brownish-blondish hair on top, combed in what my barber calls a boy's regular. Despite his slightly more conventional haircut, he's a muscle machine like the rest of the PT staff. The veins in his neck are visible as he speaks, but his voice carries naturally, not exaggerated like so many of the cadre.

"Welcome aboard! My name is Officer Turner. I'm your physical training instructor. Today you will take your first PFQ, physical fitness qualifications test. The exam consists of six exercises: overhand pull-ups, push-ups, sit-ups, burpees, obstacle course, and a one-point-two-five-mile run. There is a minimum qualifying score for each exercise. If you fail any one exercise, you fail the whole test. It doesn't matter if you max out every other event; if you fail to attain a passing score on even one exercise, *you fail your PFQ*! Is that understood?"

"Yes, sir!"

"I can't hear you."

"Yes, sir!"

"Mr. Davis, double-time the class to the chin-up area."

At every stage of the application process we were admonished to get into shape. Not everybody heeded the advice. Some of the guys who look like they're in shape aren't. Conversely, there are a few guys who do much better than I would have anticipated. Booker, the old guy everyone calls Pops, rips off about twenty pull-ups like it's nothing. Of course the instructor only gives him credit for nine or ten. Pops's performance stands out. It is more impressive when I watch a bunch of the young studs who can't even do one.

We are called to exercise in alphabetical order. Silverstein is ahead of me. He looks a little soft, but I hope he will surprise everyone like Pops. He doesn't.

I hear the murmurs from a classmate standing somewhere behind me. "The Jew-boy ain't going to make it."

"Stoller!" An instructor's voice rings out.

I jump up, grab the bar and make certain my body is *quiet* before I raise my chin above the bar.

"One!" the instructor counts.

I do another rep.

"No kipping! Still one!"

I make certain my body is completely still before I begin my next rep.

My effort is rewarded. "Two!"

Although my next pull-up is just as clean, this time the instructor says, "Chin not all the way above the bar. Still two."

On the next one I hold my chin well above the bar, and the instructor gives me credit. Although my next pull-up is a carbon copy of the last one, this time the instructor says, "Elbows not completely locked. Doesn't count. Still three!"

Pull-ups have always been hard for me. If I can just get past this event, I know I'll at least meet the minimums on everything else. While I have actually done fourteen pull-ups, I am officially credited with seven. At least I pass.

I drop off the bar and head to the next event, push-ups. I already know this instructor's last name is Lance. The coal-black hair on his head is only slightly longer than the whiskers on his close-shaved face. From his ongoing commentary with the other instructors, it is obvious he is a born-again type who wears his holier-than-thou, evangelical religion on his sleeve.

The scowl on Lance's face becomes a sneer as I get into the push-up position in front of him. Officer Lance gets down on all fours to scrutinize my movements. His face is only inches from mine. As soon as he gives the command, I start pumping them out. He doesn't give me credit unless I go real slowly.

. . .

"You didn't touch down. Still twenty-three!"

I lower my chest to the ground more slowly.

"You didn't lock out. Still twenty-three!"

I struggle to lock out...

"Twenty-four!"

My triceps are full of lactic acid. Just lowering my chest to the ground is agony. It feels like gravity has tripled. My arms are shaking.

"Twenty-five!"

Down again until my chest touches the dirt, my brain is commanding my arms to push, push, *push*!

"You didn't touch down, still twenty-five!" The arteries in his thick neck are pulsing. His saliva showers my face as he rages, "*You worthless piece of crap! How the hell do you think you can protect the citizens of Los Angeles when you can't even do a few push-ups? You're so weak. You can't even protect yourself. Get out of my face.*"

I recoil from the self-righteous prick. I use my sweatshirt to wipe my sweat and his spit from my face as I jog to the next event. *What the hell is wrong with that guy? You'd a thought somebody told him I raped his sister.*

Thank God I draw someone else to count my sit-ups and burpees. The obstacle course is easy.

7

THEY GIVE US a get a chance to use the restroom before we double-time in formation to the lower field. We fold our sweats and place them on the grass at our feet before we break ranks and head to the street. The intersection of Academy Road and Stadium Way is the starting and ending point of the one-point-two-five-mile run.

I ran the mile in high school, so I know finishing in under nine minutes is not going to be a problem. That doesn't mean I don't have prerace jitters. When Officer Turner drops his hand and shouts, "Go!" I accelerate to the front of the pack along with Logan and another recruit. I let Logan set the pace. Our trio quickly opens a gap on the rest of the field as Academy Road begins to incline.

A couple of members of the PT staff have jumped into a police car to monitor the run. I can hear them yelling at the throng of recruits behind me. In addition to the jeers and cajoling, one of the instructors issues a more ominous message: "Don't even think about trying to cheat!"

After almost a half mile, Academy Drive crests, and our trio picks up speed on the slight downhill. The easy speed ends when we turn right at Solano Canyon and start up the steepest part of the course. We're all breathing hard as we approach the locked gates that guard the entrance to the Dodger Stadium parking lot. After whipping around the steel pole in front of the gate that marks the halfway point, our strides lengthen and we gain momentum on the steep downhill. The rest of the class is headed uphill toward the gates. As our trio passes the recruits struggling uphill, the instructor's warnings about cheating suddenly make sense.

I'm still on Logan's heels as we turn onto Academy Road, but I'm not worried about him. Something in his stride tells me he is beginning to fade. Running third behind the other guy would have been better. At this point, it doesn't matter. I'll make my move at the crest of the hill and kick the rest of the way to the finish.

Logan must have read my mind. He's already pushing the pace. Worse yet, he no longer looks tired. As fate would have it, I spent five days in bed last week with the Hong Kong flu. I have to hope Logan will falter.

As per my plan, I pick up my pace when the asphalt bends downhill. At first, Logan's lead recedes with every stride, but then he shifts into high gear. I'm still gaining, but not by much. My brain is calculating the rate at which I am gaining against how far we have to go. I shouldn't have let him open up a lead. If Logan can hold this pace, he is going to beat me.

I know that telling my legs to move faster won't do any good. My track coach taught me that concentrating on my arms could put a little extra speed in my gait. That's what I'm doing when Logan turns his head. It is just a furtive glance, but it tells me I have a chance. My lungs are on fire, my legs ache, but I keep the pedal to the metal. My quarry's movements are no longer smooth and coordinated, and his looks back are not furtive glances anymore, either. As I eat up his lead, my thoughts turn to the guy behind me.

After blowing past Logan, I fight the urge to glance behind me. Adrenalin enters my system as I push for the finish line. Of all the physical gifts God has bestowed on me, natural speed is not one of them. The man behind me has run the perfect race. He has more natural speed. There's nothing I can do as he pushes past me at the finish line. Although I finished second, I am proud of myself. I beat Logan.

I see a glimpse of approval in Officer Turner's face. The look from Officer Lance makes it clear he still thinks I'm a worthless piece of you-know-what. I congratulate the guy who won. The name on his T-shirt is Vaughn. It fits. He could be a double for the actor who played Napoleon Solo in the farcical spy show, *The Man From U.N.C.L.E.*

Logan has faded to a distant third. He might even end up fourth or fifth. When he crosses the line, I reach out my hand to congratulate him, but he turns away without a word.

I'm shouting encouragement to my classmates. "You can make it! Push! You're almost there." Officer Turner is calling off the time. Pops is grimacing. I know he won't pass the finish line in time, but I keep yelling, "You can make it, Booker!"

Silverstein is well behind, lumbering side by side with the biggest guy in the class, Sean Edwards. They look like a couple of dinosaurs trudging through an invisible primordial swamp. Eventually the only contests are recruits fighting their own weariness. At this point, there are as many walking as running. Curiously, some of the walkers are moving faster than the joggers.

After the last man has crossed the finish line, Officer Turner orders us to fall in on our gear. As we don our outerwear, Officer Lance replaces Officer Turner at the head of our formation. Officer Lance brings us to attention and begins to pace with his hands behind his back. He snarls with venom in his voice, "You are undoubtedly the worst excuse for a class of police recruits I have ever seen."

What is wrong with this guy? I'm watching him strutting back and forth. *He isn't playacting; he's fucking serious.* I snap my eyes front before any of the PT staff notices my faux pas. I can no longer see Lance. He is somewhere behind me, meandering through our ranks continuing his harangue.

"My grandmother could meet the minimums on every part of the PFQ. And yet out of this whole class, only three of you passed: Davis, Stoller, and Vaughn. And those three just barely passed."

His voice tells me he is close, and still somewhere behind me.

"Gentleman, this isn't kindergarten. This is the LAPD! Normally after a PFQ we let you go home...but this ain't normal." There is a lull in his diatribe. Suddenly he is screaming in my ear, "'Cause *you* ain't normal. You make me sick! Push-up position, move!"

I drop to the ground and comport my body into the unnatural position, my palms crushing the grass. I'm craning my neck to look forward. Busting my butt cost me my anonymity. I should have stayed in the middle of the pack. *Why is Lance yelling in my ear? Why not Vaughn or Davis? Or better yet, one of the guys who failed the PFQ?*

I was only five years old when my parents changed our last name and moved to California. The name change was plainly evident on my birth certificate. I had assumed nobody in the police department cared. *Had someone figured out why? Did Lance know?*

A different voice yanks me back to reality. "Sit-up position, move!" Officer Turner is in charge again. After only ten reps, Turner brings us to our feet. He gives the right face command, and positions himself at the front of our column. "At double-time...forward, march!"

The command was double-time, but we aren't much over a walking pace as we make one slow circuit around the lower field before heading for the showers.

8

ALMOST EVERYONE GETS gigged during our first inspection in khakis. Those not singled out for deficiencies at the inspection don't miss their opportunity to exercise. Before we are dismissed, the whole class is made to do push-ups.

At the morning break, Silverstein slides up next to me. One of the other smokers immediately pulls out a Zippo and lights Silverstein's cigarette. His hand trembles a little as he takes a long drag. He bends his head backward to exhale the smoke. He introduces himself. "Jerold Silverstein. My friends call me Jerry." He reaches out his hand.

I shake his hand and return the favor. "Stoller. I go by my middle name, Max."

"Want a smoke?" he asks.

"No thanks." Genuinely curious I ask, "Where you from?"

"The Valley." He gives me the same question. "How about you?"

"Orange County. Anaheim. You know...where Disneyland is." I always say that. Most people don't know Anaheim, but everybody knows Disneyland.

Silverstein shakes his head. "Driving in from the Valley is bad enough. You must get up real early coming in from Orange County."

"Naw, I rented an apartment in Glendale."

Jerry eyes me curiously. "You look like a natural at this. Your dad on the department or something?"

"No. When my dad works, it's in tool and die. How about you?"

"My dad's in real estate. My parents want me to be a doctor or a lawyer. I graduated from CSUN. Got accepted into law school. But I wanted to try something, you know...different."

"I can relate. My mom wants me to be a doctor or an airline pilot." I laugh. "She likes to travel...she says if I were a pilot she could fly for free."

My remark brings a laconic smile to Jerry's face. Finished with his smoke, he stoops down and snuffs out his cigarette on the asphalt, and then field-strips it just like he was taught on the first day of the academy. He tosses the filter in the red coffee can with "BUTTS" stenciled on the side. He stands up and looks me in the eye. "On the other hand, the something different I had in mind wasn't Officer Lance screaming in my face."

"Amen, brother. I heard that!"

I'm studying a MILES workbook when I get the word to report to my squad adviser. My gut tightens. In the LAPD lexicon, when a recruit is told to report with his cap and books, the recruit is never heard from again. It's a throwback to the days when live lectures were the norm at the academy. Hopefully my classmate who delivered the message didn't just forget to mention the *cap and books* part.

I double-time to the squad adviser's trailer and find a slab of wood bolted on the wall adjacent to the door with generic instructions on how recruits are to present themselves. I read the instructions, swallow hard, and take a deep breath. *Here goes.* I pound on the wood three times.

"Sir, Recruit Officer Stoller requests permission to enter, sir!"

"Enter!" Comes the reply from inside the trailer.

I pull open the door, remove my hat and march inside, assuming a braced position of attention with my hat against my left trouser seam.

"Speak!" the instructor bellows as loudly as when I was outside the door.

"Sir, Recruit Officer Stoller reporting as ordered, sir!"

"Report to Officer Robles." He directs me with a wave of his hand.

I make a left face and march to Officer Robles's office. After a repeat of the formalities, I'm admitted to my squad adviser's office. My eyes focused on the wall, I hear him rock back in his chair.

"At ease, Mr. Stoller. How do you like the academy so far?"

I hope I haven't hesitated too long. "Sir, it's…good, sir."

"That's *good* to hear, Mr. Stoller."

Through his pronunciation and emphasis, it is clear he is mocking my choice of adjectives.

"A couple of days ago I made you my acting squad leader."

I relax a little. Officer Robles is just relieving me before announcing his permanent choice for the job. When Officer Robles stands up, I turn for the door, but catch myself in time to see he is offering what looks like a cuff link box.

"Congratulations! Now you are not acting," he says with a smile.

I grab the box with my left hand, somehow managing to keep hold of my hat. I make eye contact when we shake hands, and halfway expect to get rebuked for it. Instead, Officer Robles comes out from behind his desk and shows me the proper way of pinning the chromed diamond-shaped insignia on my collar.

Back behind his desk he says, "I told everyone I would choose the right man for the job. I don't like to be wrong." His eyes pierce mine. "Don't let me down. Don't let yourself down." He lowers his eyes for an instant. When he raises them again, he says, "Remember, I can take the job away just as easily as I gave it to you."

I never wanted the position in the first place. But now that I have diamonds on my collar, I can't countenance the thought of losing them. In my exuberance to get out of the office, I almost run into an instructor.

"*Make a hole and make it wide!*" the instructor yells.

The trailer shakes as I slam my back up against the wall to let the instructor pass. As soon as my route is clear, I sprint out the door.

9

THE NEXT DAY we report for PT wearing our Sam Brownes over our sweats. Although our holsters and ammo pouches are empty, we are otherwise fully equipped with handcuffs and batons. I'm glad to see Officer Turner step to the fore when we arrive at the lower field.

He gives us the at-ease command and begins his spiel. "The physical training program here at the academy has been scientifically designed to achieve maximum results in a minimum amount of time. It has been designed not by members of the PT staff like us," he looks back at the other PT instructors who are milling around behind him, "but by exercise physiologists and physicians from Medical Services Division." He holds up a blue three-ring notebook. "So while it might sometimes appear as if we are just making it up as we go along, let me assure you we are not."

Turner paces with the deliberate gate of a caged predator. He makes eye contact with us as he speaks. "I will perform every repetition of every exercise with you. If at any time you think you can't, or don't want to perform any part of this training, you are free to quit. You do not need to explain anything to anyone here, especially not me." The sinewy lines in his jaw flex as he growls, "I don't want to hear it.

"I am not asking any of you to do anything that I am not doing myself. If you can't hack it, or don't want to hack it, just walk up the hill to the office. By the time you get there, your resignation paperwork will be ready for you to sign. Gentlemen, be advised, if you walk off this field, you can never come back. You come here as a class, and you leave here as a class. The only way you can leave without your class, and still be able to return, is if you are carried out of here on a stretcher. I'm not kidding. I assure you, before this class graduates, more than one of you will leave this field in an ambulance." He stops pacing, and ends his soliloquy with a modulated tone. "The more you sweat here—the less you will bleed in the street. That's not just a fancy saying; it's a fact."

At a certain point, PT shifts from pure exercise to the so-called self-defense training. Except for the baton moves and kicks, this invariably involves working with another recruit. On command, the first and third squads turn to face the second and fourth squads. I'm facing Sean Edwards, the squad leader of the fourth squad. While Sean is a good guy, there is a downside to having him as my self-defense partner—he is the biggest guy in the class. We will repeat physical grappling techniques every day. That means I'll be trying to manhandle a two-hundred-and-thirty-five-pound gorilla every day. Worse yet, this gargantuan animal will be body slamming, twisting, and choking me every day.

Our workouts always end with a run. Like we do everything, we run in formation. As squad leader of the third squad, I'm right behind Officer Turner. I lock my eyes on to the back of his neck and put the rest of the universe on hold while our formation snakes through the streets of Elysian Park, past lovers in cars, the US Naval Reserve Training Center, and an old sanatorium. On our return to the academy, Officer Turner slows the pace so the stragglers can catch up. He tells Davis to give us a cadence.

Davis chants, "Everywhere we go-*o*."

We repeat in unison, *"Everywhere we go-o."*

Our footsteps magically fall into unison as we continue to repeat the DI's cadence:

"People want to know-*o*."
"People want to know-o."
"Who we are-are."
"Who we are-are."
"So we tell them."
"So we tell them."
"We are the PD."
"We are the PD."
"Mighty mighty PD."
"Mighty mighty PD."
"Mighty L A P D."
"Mighty L A P D."

There is something mystical about running in formation and shouting cadence. Pride and a sense of belonging well up inside of you. It may sound trite to those who have never experienced it, but there is a physical sensation, too, and it is as real as the warmth of the sun's life-giving rays on your face.

• • •

Nowadays I can't always remember where I put my car keys, but just the mention of the academy triggers vivid images in my mind. I see the back of Officer Turner's neck. I hear the trample of feet mixed with the jangle of metal keys and plastic whistles rattling against wooden batons. I can even smell the spicy scent of Chavez Ravine's eucalyptus and pines.

10

THOSE WHO COULDN'T adapt to the boot-camp style are gone. Each morning, we check one another's appearance in the locker room before going upstairs for inspection. In the vernacular, we are squared away.

No matter how squared away we are, the staff never fails to find reasons for us to do push-ups, eventually focusing on the minutia. We respond to their scrutiny, even scouring our khaki uniforms for *Irish pennants,* the derogatory term for threads protruding from seams or buttons. I marvel at the irony. Our holsters are empty except when we are on the range, but we are never without nail clippers, the weapon of choice for excising the near-microscopic offenses created by the tailor's less-than-perfect sewing.

Our instructors eventually resort to lifting up the flap of our shirt pockets to see if the adornments are affixed in the prescribed manner. A world of hurt opens up to the recruit who has secured one of the little acorn buttons without the washer, or heaven forbid, using a small safety pin in lieu of the regulation cotter key. Even when no actual deficiencies are found, the staff is not above manufacturing some.

After inspection, we march to the classroom. Most of the academic curriculum is like in any other school. A lot of department policy doesn't make sense. It is just a matter of memorizing the rules. Only a few wash out on these exams, but almost everyone runs into difficulty with the law modules. If the study guide and videotaped lectures were all I had to go on, I would have been lost, too.

When I was a freshman in college, and all the daytime electives were filled, I enrolled in an evening criminal law class. The instructor wasn't a college professor. He was a practicing defense attorney. I don't know how good the man was in court, but he was a great teacher. Consequently I started the academy with a firm understanding of the legal concepts, probable cause, *stare decisis,* and the exclusionary rule.

I guess it shows because my classmates keep asking me to help them with the law modules. It makes me nervous. I remember Sergeant Sinclair's admonition: "Giving answers is as bad as asking for answers. Both are cheating, and the penalty for cheating is termination."

I'm always careful to explain the legal abstractions based on the MILES study guide. I augment the explanations based on what I learned in college, while scrupulously avoiding any reference to the specific questions on the exams. Who has the faculty to grasp these concepts is akin to who was physically in shape at the first PFQ. Some of my classmates who I expect would struggle, quickly internalize the concepts when presented with a few examples borrowed from my college course. While others I thought would catch on quickly, seem positively incapable of understanding.

• • •

Dissolving days become weeks. Except for PT, the academy isn't that tough. But I dread PT more than two-a-days at the beginning of the football season. It isn't the push-ups, sit-ups, or burpees. It isn't the kicks or the baton moves, either. It's the control holds. Half the time

I play the cop, and Sean plays the suspect. On command, we switch. Basically we are beating the shit out of each other every day.

The first control holds we learn are the so-called pain compliance holds, twist locks and wristlocks. These techniques, as their names imply, require keeping the suspect in pain.

Without warning, an instructor will yell, "*Suspect, get away!*" The recruit who is acting as the suspect is supposed to try his best to get out of the hold. Although Sean and I have made many a pact to take it easy on each other, adrenalin and testosterone keep us pushing things to the limit.

It's not hard to spot the ones who are faking it. Chavez is always goldbricking. But the staff never does anything to Chavez or Logan. Instead, certain instructors focus on their habitual targets. It's disgusting. Silverstein would make ten times the cop Chavez would.

A favorite form of punishment is to send recruits to run up a steep dirt incline at the edge of the lower field. Silverstein and Booker are frequently ordered to "*hit the hill!*"

They dutifully struggle against gravity up the extremely steep hill, and then they risk serious injury as they careen back down the slippery surface. But when Chavez is caught faking for the thousandth time, instead of ordering him to hit the hill, Officer Buckler leans back, puts his hands on his hips, and calls, "*Chavez, give us a growl!*"

Chavez opens his smirking lips and issues an irritating high-pitched whining sound that matches his peevishly insolent Chihuahua face. If he had a shred of dignity, he would quit. But the little lapdog has made it clear he can't be shamed.

By the second week, we are introduced to the primary control techniques, the choke holds. Properly applied, these techniques can render even the most violent suspect unconscious in a matter of seconds. While the need to practice them is obvious, willingly submitting to being choked is an unnatural act. Maybe I'm claustrophobic, or maybe it's just my survival instinct. Whatever it is—I hate getting choked.

With Sean's arm around my neck, cutting off the oxygen and/or blood to my brain, I can't say, "Hey, Sean, lighten up a bit." No, if the hold is being applied correctly, it's impossible to speak. The prescribed protocol is to slap our hands together to signal we are about to lose consciousness. It's bizarre.

The hazing, exercising to exhaustion, pain compliance holds, and getting choked, are a royal pain in the ass. But the worst of all is the *combat wrestling*. It's brutal. Of course we don't jump right into combat wrestling. The first couple of days we do collegiate-style wrestling where the goal is to pin the opponent. It's actually fun. They keep changing the rules until it's basically a street fight. In the end, there are only two rules—no biting or gouging the eyes. The PT staff picks two recruits and the rest of the class encircles them. It doesn't end until one guy is either unconscious or submits.

Many of my classmates get seriously injured and have to be *recycled*. That means they have to wait until they are medically cleared, and start all over again with another class. One afternoon two of the bigger guys, Sorensen and Grissom, are paired off. As usual, the fight quickly goes to the ground with both guys crabbing for an advantage. Sorensen has worked his way behind Grissom, trying to get a choke hold. Somehow Grissom is able to reverse Sorensen's hold and throw him over his shoulder. The expected thud of Sorensen's body as it crushes the turf is accompanied by an unnatural popping sound. He screams out in pain, and the PT staff literally dives onto the combatants to stop the fight.

Sorensen's arm is obviously broken. They put him on his back and immobilize his mangled limb. One of the PT staff tells Chavez to run up to the office and have someone call an ambulance. When the RA (rescue ambulance) arrives, it drives right out on to the field. Obviously this isn't the first time they have responded to the academy for an injured recruit. As soon as Sorensen is in the capable hands of the LAFD (Los Angeles Fire Department), we go back to combat wrestling.

As the ambulance starts to pull away, Officer Buckler shouts, "*Wait!* Don't leave! I know there's room for one more in that thing."

At first, I'm thinking it is a joke. But the ambulance doesn't leave until we've finished combat wrestling.

Most of the time, I'm matched up with the bigger guys. One day they put me in with Simpson. They tell me to get down on all fours while my opponent gets a grip on my waist, collegian style. As soon as they shout, "Fight's on!" Simpson is on my neck. I can't believe how fast and strong this little son of bitch is. I tuck my chin to my chest to keep him from getting his forearm across my throat. With my head in the grass, I'm scooting around in an attempt to dislodge the wild animal from my neck. Suddenly the PT staff members blow their whistles and jump on both of us. When I sit up, Officer Turner is holding my head with a palm on each side of my face. There is something warm and wet in my eye. It is blood, my blood. Officer Turner picks up a bloody shard of green glass. Fortunately it only cut my forehead, and it looks worse than it is. A few stitches, and I'm good to go.

I have a newfound respect for Simpson. He might be on the small side, but he exemplifies the old saying: *It's not the size of the dog in the fight—it's the size of the fight in the dog.*

● ● ●

Ten years later, Simpson would be the first to come to my assistance in a hellacious fight with a PCP (phencyclidine) suspect. For all his strength and courage, Officer Simpson didn't even make twenty years. He died of cancer. The rate at which police officers die of cancer is higher than any other profession. Of course the city denies there is any connection to the job, because they don't want to pay workers' comp. But it makes sense. Police are usually first at the scene of structure fires, vehicle fires, and other HAZMAT situations. And street cops don't have breathing apparatus or protective suits, either. Add the stress of the job together with exposure to carcinogens, and the high cancer rate shouldn't surprise anyone.

11

OUR LUNCH CROWD is perched on the stone wall at the front of the academy. Today is our long run day.

"How far you think we're gonna go?" Grissom asks.

"A ten K anyway." I shrug my shoulders. "All depends on how Officer Turner feels...I guess."

"Didn't you hear?" Sean asks me.

"Hear what?"

"Officer Turner has gone back East for a death in the family."

"Too bad for him," I mumble with genuine compassion.

"Don't you get it? That means somebody else is going to lead us on the run today. I hope it's Officer Buckler. He hates to run. But Officer Montana or Officer Baxter would be OK—just not Lance. Anybody but that prick."

The Crazy Scot, Jim Rutherford, who amazes me by smoking a pack of cigarettes a day and drinking a pint of whiskey a night, says, "A hundred bucks to anybody who'll shoot Lance's mom...so we get rid of him for few days."

"He ain't got a mother," Grissom says.

"He's gotta have a mother," Booker insists. "Everybody has a mother. But offing his mom wouldn't work anyway. That asshole would pass on his mom's funeral if it meant miss'n one minute of fuck'n with us."

Silverstein adds his voice of reason. "Why go after his family? They probably hate him, too. I'll give a hundred bucks to anybody who'll shoot Lance. That way, we'll get rid of him for good."

We laugh so hard we have tears in our eyes. But our festive mood doesn't last long. Guess who is taking Officer Turner's place in PT today?

Instead of an abbreviated set of calisthenics to warm up, Office Lance leads us through three sets of every exercise. We do more repetitions of our baton moves and kicks than ever. Fatigued before we start to run, Lance sets a brutal pace.

It doesn't take long before Sean is hurting. I put my right hand in the small of his back and push as we climb a hill. By the time we get to the top, Vaughn is the only one who is keeping up with Officer Lance. It isn't like he and Lance are out in front of our formation. There is no formation. Guys are strung out for a half a mile. Officers Baxter, Montana, and the remainder of the staff are trying to gather the flock, yelling for everyone to catch up. Officer Buckler is behind the last guy, Chavez, of course.

After we crest another hill, Lance slows the pace. Most of us catch up within a minute or two. Our legs are pumping up and down, but we are making little forward progress as we wait for the stragglers. When Officer Lance picks up the pace, our class quickly becomes an ant trail again. My hand is on Sean's back again.

"I just can't!" Sean says. His face is bright red. His legs are moving, but his forward progress is limited to what my pressure brings.

"Don't stop!" I yell at him. "Whatever you do—don't fucking stop!"

On the next downhill, Sean gets his second wind, so I drop back to help Silverstein. Our class is like an accordion as we traverse one hill after another.

While it helps the guy who is getting pushed, it really saps the one doing the pushing. Usually running is easy for me, but the combination of a faster pace and pushing these behemoths has taken its toll. I'm exhausted, and Sean is fading again.

Officer Lance is running backward. "Close it up. Where are my squad leaders? Form up on me...*now!*"

To hell with Officer Lance. To hell with my position as squad leader. With one hand on Sean's back and the other on Jerry's back, I keep pushing. My unfocused eyes fixed on the asphalt a few yards ahead, I repeat my mantra—*They can kill me, but they can't eat me.* I no longer have any idea where I am.

• • •

Finally something feels familiar. I look up and recognize we are close to the academy. We aren't a class. We are a ragtag line of individuals strung out for well over a mile. There is no cadence. There is no pride.

Officer Lance brings us to the lower field and shouts, "Exercise formation, *move!*"

I'm too weary. I cheat on the push-ups, doing maybe half the repetitions and those with my knees on the ground. I even cheat on the sit-ups. I'm lightheaded, but somehow conclude that if I just keep moving, I won't pass out. *Something must be wrong with my eyes.* It is like I'm looking through a kaleidoscope.

Finally the stragglers show up. Chavez is last, but Logan is only a few yards ahead of him.

I don't remember double-timing to the ramp and being dismissed. Awareness only begins to return as I undress in front of my locker. My sweats are just that—soaked in sweat. They weigh a ton. The wet cotton adheres to my skin like papier-mâché, and my arms shake as I fight to pull my T-shirt over my head. I have never been this tired in my whole life. As I'm walking to the showers, I hear guys telling Chavez he has to try a little harder.

Chavez is recalcitrant. "I was keeping up with my squad leader. What more do you guys want?"

Revived a little by the shower, I get an idea. Instead of saying something to Chavez, I decide to encourage Logan to get on board. I head toward Logan's locker. He is already dressed in his street clothes. I feel a little self-conscious wrapped only in a towel, but I'm committed.

Logan faces me with a smirk on his face.

I give him my best aw shucks look and say, "We gotta all work together. The rest of us were dying there at the end—"

Logan squares his shoulders and juts his chin toward my face. "*Fuck you!* I don't have to do anything more than what I've been doing. Just because you're too stupid to see how easy it is to skate through this shit."

Initially surprised by his virulent response, I'm quick to match his hostility. My fuse is burning fast when an octopus of tentacles wrap around me.

"Don't do it, Stoller! He isn't worth it. You'll get canned."

Boy, have I been stupid. Fortunately, my classmates keep me from doing something really stupid. I'm back at my locker getting dressed when Officer Buckler saunters into the room.

"Anybody got a problem?" he asks, as he walks the length of the locker room, barely pausing at each row.

Nobody says a word.

I know the academy is a game. I'm not that stupid. The whole idea is to play together. Teamwork is the key to winning. No one is asking anyone to do more than his best. Those who can't hack it—can't hack it. Logan's physical conditioning is as good as anyone's. His God-given athletic ability is greater than most. He could have kept up today. He probably could have helped others. If he doesn't want to help anyone else, that's fine with me. What pisses me off is that Logan is happy to have a worthless piece of shit like Chavez in the class. As far as Logan is concerned, the slower Chavez goes, the better.

That night I have trouble sleeping. The next morning it is clear I'm not the only one. Some agree with Logan—the best way to get through the academy is to scam everyone, including your classmates. Most think it is better to work together. Most believe every man has an obligation to himself *and* his classmates.

12

I PUT THE locker room scene behind me, content to believe Logan has done the same. Still, I'm a little surprised when Logan sidles up to me a couple of weeks later.

"Vaughn is kicking ass on the academics," he says through his salesman's smile. "Sergeant Sinclair told me that anybody who finishes all his qualifications early will be sent to the field and only have to come back for graduation ceremonies."

"No shit?"

"Yeah. In the past, some recruits have been sent out to a division as much as a month before the rest of their class."

"Maybe I better step it up," I say, thinking out loud.

Logan interrupts my musing. "My squad adviser showed me the list. Vaughn has got a lead on everybody in the academics race. I'm in second place. I'm sure you could move up if you pushed it."

I didn't want a fight with Logan in the first place. If this is his olive branch, that's fine with me. Getting out of here even one week early would be worth the effort. I thank him and take my leave.

The next day it's like nothing ever happened between us. Yep, Logan and I are best buddies. He seeks me out during the morning break and asks if we can talk privately.

"You were right, Max." The look on his face is serious but not hostile.

I hold up my hand to stop him from saying any more. "I'm sorry if anything I said pissed you off. That wasn't my intention—"

Logan cuts me off. "You're right. We need to work together." His mug brightens. "I'd like to take a little of the load off you. You know. Help tutor guys on the law questions."

I'm trying to think of who hasn't passed the law tests.

Logan doesn't miss a beat. "It's just that a couple of those questions can't be answered based on what's in the study guide. You know, like the one about searching the trunk, and the one about stopping the guy on the street with the bags. How do you explain those to the guys?"

I've barely lapsed into my often-repeated explanation when he interrupts.

"Yeah, yeah. I know all that crap about probable cause being *that set of circumstances leading a reasonable and prudent man with similar training and experience to believe there is criminal activity afoot*, but that doesn't help answer the questions."

He is right. Memorizing the definition doesn't help much. Besides, there are different levels of probable cause. One level justifies stopping a person; another is necessary to arrest. The legal threshold relating to searches is even more complex. Probable cause is subject to interpretation in every case, and is literally argued daily in the halls of justice from the lowest trial court to the Supreme Court. Because each decision can set precedent, determining what constitutes PC is the ultimate moving target.

The import of cops not understanding the law hasn't even crossed my mental horizon at this point. I just don't want to be accused of cheating. Up to now I have scrupulously avoided the particular questions on the exams. *What is the harm? Logan must have passed these tests a long time ago.* I am about to explain how the legal principles given in the study guide can be applied to each of the test questions when Silverstein runs up to us.

A little out of breath, Jerry says, "Officer Robles wants to see you ASAP."

"Shit! What happened now?" I ask.

Silverstein shrugs his shoulders.

My law conference with Logan will have to wait. I hustle to the adviser's trailer. I'm standing at attention in front of Officer Robles's desk, staring at the imaginary spot on the wall when my squad adviser tells me to stand easy.

In a subdued voice he says, "They are just now telling Davis. It's a good thing his wife spoke to a member of the staff first." Robles comes out from behind his desk and rests his hand on my shoulder. "Davis's mom died unexpectedly this morning. I'm sure he's going use his three days bereavement leave and go back to Alabama for the funeral." He purses his lips. "I know this isn't what you want. But it's not about what you want. For the record, while I know you can handle it, this wasn't my decision." He looks me in the eye. "You're the acting DI for as long as Davis is gone." He lets his hand drop away. "I'm not going to tell you not to let me down. I know you won't."

Officer Robles is right. I don't want the job. But being assigned as the temporary DI isn't what is weighing on me. It's Davis losing his mom. That hits too close to home.

13

DURING LUNCH, SILVERSTEIN starts needling me. "I wasn't sure you were going to eat with us lowly recruits. Now that you're *the DI*."

I can't resist giving it back to him. "Yeah, I wasn't sure if I was going eat with you pukes, either, but then it hit me. I'm just *acting DI*." With a haughty pretentiousness in my voice I tell everyone, "But you can bet your booty, if I were the *full-time DI*, I'd be taking my afternoon repast with those of better breeding, more appropriate to my station in life."

"Keep talking like that, and I'll kick your *mo-fuck'n, act'n di ass,* right off this wall," Booker bellows.

Everyone roars.

Silverstein segues, "So Logan has finally come to you for the answers to the law questions?"

"What do you mean?" I don't realize Jerry has changed the topic.

"What...I...mean...is." Silverstein draws out his words like he is talking to someone who has trouble understanding English. "Logan is so desperate, he has finally come to you for the answers to the law questions."

Still uncertain where Jerry is coming from, I hit him with the obvious. "Logan has been bragging from the beginning how easy this stuff is compared to college. He passed the law modules a long time ago. He's right behind Vaughn in the academics race."

Silverstein looks me in the eye. "Suppose you can't remember if you passed a particular test? Where do you go?"

What is Jerry doing? I dodge his question with sarcasm. "I don't have to look up which tests I've passed, *because I don't forget.*" I'm smiling as I lock onto Silverstein's gaze, trying to read him. He is not returning my smile.

"Next time you are in the testing trailer, look for the clipboard on the wall under our class number. It's there so you can check to see which tests you've passed and which ones you still have to take. *Everyone's* testing history is there. Do yourself a favor. Look up Logan's."

Our thirty minutes for lunch is almost up. There isn't enough time for me to check on Logan's test history now. I can't go after shooting, either, because as the DI, it is my job to report to the PT office prior to formation. There is no way I am going to risk being late to the PT office. Stories of hazing in the PT office are legendary. Once they made a DI get in the push-up position between two desks. The staff kept loading stuff on the poor recruit's back. When the DI's back was piled high with office supplies and he was still hanging in there, they decided the only thing left to stack on his back was a member of the staff. I have visions of Officer Buckler climbing on my back as I am stretched out in the push-up position between two desks. It isn't a pretty picture.

After shooting, I hurry to change into my workout gear and run down the hall to the PT office. I pound three times on the wooden plank next to the door, and announce myself in a loud voice. There is no response. *Shit! If they're in there, they have to have heard me. If they aren't, I have missed them. Either way, I'm in deep kimchi.* I try again, pounding so hard the windows rattle and debris falls from the acoustic ceiling. For a moment, I think the wooden sign over the door engraved with the saying, "The more you sweat here—the less you will bleed in the street," is going to come crashing down. It doesn't. There's still no response from inside.

My Herculean pounding arouses a geek who works in the captain's office down the hall. Apparently, over his fear that the world is coming to an end, the pencil-neck bean counter peeks around the corner. Just as he opens his mouth to chew me out, Officer Buckler's voice blasts through the door. "Enter!"

I march into the lair of the beasts, leaving the captain's bun boy in the hall. The squint doesn't dare confront the PT staff. No doubt he will skulk back to his office to complain, confident the commanding officer will bring us ruffians in line.

At a braced position of attention, I fully expect to be ordered into the push-up position with my hands on one desk and my toes on another.

Instead, Officer Turner is matter-of-fact. "The Prison Gang Unit of OCID (Organized Crime Intelligent Division) caught some ex-cons watching us training on the lower field. We've found more broken beer bottles down there, too. The suits from downtown think those same assholes are responsible. So, until further notice, we're going to be working on the upper field." Turner indicates the blue three-ring notebook on the shelf to my right. "Get the binder and have the class at the upper field."

"Yes, sir."

I grab the notebook and do an about-face. Reaching for the door handle, I hear Officer Turner laughing. "And relax, Stoller, we aren't gonna eat ya. You don't have enough meat on your bones."

• • •

The next day I am in the testing trailer before the morning break. The two-hole clipboard is right where Silverstein said. Normally my sense of propriety would prevent me from prying into another man's business, but I have to know. My vague disquietude from violating my own ethics evaporates when I reach the page I'm looking for. *I'll be a son of a...*Logan has failed two of the law modules, twice. If he flunks either of them again, he'll be history. I issue a silent whistle. *He's got to be stressing.*

Then it hits me. He isn't at the front of the pack academically. He is closer to the back. He isn't sorry for the incident in the locker room. He isn't trying to help me tutor law, either. He is scamming to get me to give him the answers to the test questions. *What an asshole!*

At the morning break, I half drag Silverstein onto the track. I grip his shoulders and blurt, "Thanks, man. I checked Logan's records this morning. You were absolutely right. How did you know?"

"It wasn't hard. I saw a lot of his kind in college."

Still incredulous at my own stupidity, still excitedly shaking Silverstein, I tell him what he already knows. "Logan was lying to me from the get-go. I don't know how to thank you enough for setting me straight—"

Silverstein interrupts. "Hey, man, it's no big deal. Like you told him that day in the locker room, we all gotta work together."

At the time, I didn't know it, but that would be the last day I would see or talk to Silverstein. I had never thought to get his address or phone number. *Why should I? We saw each other every day.* The following morning he just wasn't there. I guess he just had enough.

My three days as the DI stretch out to a week. Things go smoothly, too smoothly. When Davis gets back, I'm surprised how many guys are rumbling they want me to continue as DI. But it wouldn't be right. Suggesting Davis lose his job because his mom died, is just plain wrong.

What surprises me even more is what Officer Robles tells me. He says Officer Turner and several others approached Sergeant Sinclair about keeping me as the class DI. Sinclair wouldn't hear it. Robles doesn't elaborate, but he makes it clear that Sinclair's objections are not out of loyalty to Davis.

· · ·

Today the infamous Los Angeles smog is at a minimum. The down-town skyline provides the backdrop as we brown-bag on the stone wall. With Silverstein and Sorensen gone, our group is smaller. The regulars still include Booker, Grissom, and Rutherford. Chomping on my dry homemade sandwich, washing it down with grape juice, I'm bitching about the prospects of another day of torture on the PT field.

The Crazy Scot, Jim Rutherford, makes light of our situation. "Just think...in four weeks we're all gonna to be getting fat eating dough-nuts and drinking free coffee. All this academy bullshit will be noth-ing more than a memory."

Booker chips in, "My wife jest as soon my training lasts a long time. She likes having me home ev'ry night and off on the weekends, too."

If I were married, maybe I'd see things the same way. It's just when I'm dead tired and that idiot Lance is screaming in my face, even a few seconds seems like an eternity. Putting up with jerks like him is not the kind of challenge I had in mind when I joined the LAPD. I'm tired of wrestling with my classmates. If I'm going to get into a fight, I want it to be with a real criminal.

14

WE ARE FINALLY in our last week. The hazing is behind us. Morning inspection in our Class A uniforms is a formality. Even PT is just for show. After graduation, we will no longer be recruits. Of course we will still be P-1s for eight more months, and some of us aren't going to make probation, but that battle starts next week.

About a month ago we listed our top three choices for assignment after graduation. I made Rampart Division my first choice based on Officer Robles's recommendation. He pointed out that Rampart is not only one of the most active divisions in the city, but it is also one of the most diverse. Geographically it encompasses the area west of downtown. He explained the northern portion includes the Silver Lake District with million-dollar homes and movie stars, while the southern portion is poor and black. In between there is most every other type of neighborhood. I'm excited to be heading for the same streets patrolled by Officer Robles during his time in the field.

Our last week won't be spent studying MILES modules. Instead, we get a series of live lectures on a single subject—officer survival. All the speakers bring multimedia adjuncts to their presentations. One instructor shows us crime scene and autopsy photos of LA cops killed in the line of duty. After projecting the disturbing images on the screen, the instructor circulates eight-by-ten glossies to make sure everyone gets an up-close and personal look. The images of dead cops with horrible wounds, frozen in grotesque positions, surrounded by pools of their own blood, are sobering. In nearly all the cases, the officers were working in uniform when they were killed, the same uniform we are wearing.

The instructor says, "Fuck up in the field, and this can happen to you. If any of you think I enjoy showing these photos, you're nuts! I don't want to ever put another photo in this collection. As much as I don't want to add any more pictures, I know I will." He pauses and scans the room. "So what's my point?"

Booker raises his hand and is recognized. "Don't fuck up in the field."

"Exactly! You don't want *me* to have any photos of *you!*"

For those of us who are not visual learners, our next instructor plays a recording of a probationer screaming into the microphone after his training officer has been shot. Although the actual incident is history, my chest tightens and my stomach muscles spasm. Just listening to the nightmare captured on tape causes my adrenalin to flow. I'm surprised at the intensity of my visceral response. I yearn to be the first on the scene, save the downed officer, and kill the bad guy. There is just one problem—the boot (rookie) has no idea where he is. Because the probationer can't give his location, no one knows where to respond. During my *ride-alongs*, just like the young officer on the tape, a good part of the time I had no idea where I was. With gritted teeth I vacillate between pity for the boot and a fierce desire to strangle the incompetent son of a bitch.

All the instructors mention the case of the probationer who was killed on his first day in the street. One presentation focuses exclusively on this tragic case. We hear the call being broadcast, a "four-fifteen man with a gun." (415 is the California penal code section for disturbing the peace. Pronounced four-fifteen, it is not only part of the official LAPD radio nomenclature, but integral to LA *copspeak*.)

We hear the deceased probationer's voice as he acknowledges the call. We learn the route the officers took to the location. We see photos and diagrams of where the training officer parked the car. We are given details about the suspect, including his name, his criminal record, and a complete description of the gun he used.

The instructor shifts from facts to conjecture as he looks around the room. "No one will ever know why the young officer walked right up to the address in broad daylight. Maybe he didn't realize which house was which. Maybe he was trying to impress his training officer with his bravery. Maybe he thought it was another routine incident where the caller had just said there was a gun involved to get a quicker response. Maybe he was daydreaming about a woman or sports."

The instructor ends his speculation. "Whatever the reason for his mistake—it would be his last." He points at the center of his chest. "He caught a round in the ten ring. The bullet severed his aorta. Had there been an operating room next door, it would not have made any difference. He was a dead man the moment the bullet entered his heart."

Evidentiary photographs bear a case number; the first two digits indicate the year. A strange sensation creeps down my spine. It wasn't long ago the dead officer was in this classroom, probably seated at one of these desks.

Other presentations alert us to other concerns. We hear stories of training officers who drink on duty. We hear about TOs (training officers) who leave their boots in the car while they have sex with some sleazy whore, and then expect the boot to cover for them when the sergeant shows up. The incongruity with the captain's speech on the first day has me wondering. *How can that happen in the corruption-free LAPD?*

• • •

Officer safety is the justification for all the maltreatment at the academy. The brutality in PT is excused as being necessary to prepare us for danger in the street. I do not quarrel with the premise. However, I take issue with staff members who use this legitimate purpose as convenient cover to carry out their own agendas. I decry those who satisfy their sadistic yearnings by punishing those they judge as less than worthy. I say *convenient cover* because the point where harsh treatment crosses the line from training to abuse cannot be judged solely on the conduct involved. The pivot point is the instructor's internal thought process. When the motivation moves from professional to the personal, it is no longer training and no longer justified. Since no one can ever really get inside another person's head, a certain amount of leeway must be permitted and has to be endured. Therein lies the problem.

The LAPD is filled with rules, rituals and traditions. It is more like a religion than a job. The academy is like the seminary. In the late sixties and early seventies, the academy was extremely rigorous and purposefully designed to eliminate all but the strong. A washout rate over 50 percent was the norm.

Did the academy get rid of those who were weak? Or did it just get rid of those who were different? I did not know enough to even ask such questions back then. I only knew I was headed to the street, and I couldn't wait. Later I would discover the perils of questioning any of the rules, rituals, or traditions that comprise the LAPD theology.

15

I'VE BEEN ASSIGNED to *morning watch*, LAPD's euphemism for the graveyard shift. About the time I would normally be pulling down my bedsheets, I am pulling into the lower-level parking lot at the rear of Rampart station for my first shift as a street cop. If I wasn't so nervous, I'd be sleepy.

I park in the employee lot and grab my gear. As I walk past rows of police cars parked on the lower level, I feel like a thief in the night. But unlike a burglar absconding with the loot, I'm hauling my uniforms and equipment toward the rear entrance. Fortunately, there isn't anyone in sight when I reach the solid steel door. I put down my cardboard box to retrieve my *999 key*. I twist the *do not duplicate* key in the lock and pull. It takes serious effort to overcome the tension of the closing mechanism and open the heavy door.

With my foot holding the door open, I pick up my cardboard box and step inside. I'm relieved to find the hallway is empty except for the smell of freshly waxed linoleum. With my uniforms draped over my shoulder and my big box once again tucked under my arm, I head toward the locker room. A step and a half down the hallway, the bulletproof door returns to its secure position. The heavy sound shatters the silence. *So much for stealth!*

Fortunately the closing door's abrupt announcement of my arrival is short-lived. By the time I enter the locker room, the quiet has returned, and the rush of air from the overhead vents is the only accompaniment to the beating of my heart. I find the locker with the same number as the key they gave me in the penultimate aisle. A quick peek down the last row assures me I'm alone.

I balance my cardboard box on the narrow dressing bench, and insert the stamped sheet metal key in the locker. A half turn releases the latch, but the handle doesn't yield. I pull harder, but more force only brings a chorus of groans from the hollow steel enclosure. I get a better grip and yank. This time the balky mechanism gives way. The handle slams against its stop with a loud clang and the door whooshes open, wobbling on its hinges.

Hanging my uniform on the door stops it from shivering. After arranging my gear inside my new locker, I sit astride the wooden bench to spit shine my leather gear. The tedious process of rubbing a slurry of black boot polish and water in small circles with a rag from an old T-shirt, numbs the mind. By the time my shoes and Sam Browne are suitably lustrous, not only has my anxiety melted, the silence has given way. I'm no longer alone.

Conversations echo throughout the locker room. Mixed with the usual talk of sports and women, there are anecdotes from the street. I hear a cop say: "I lit up this deuce last night. When he finally pulled over, he hit the curb so hard the right front hubcap came off and went rolling down the sidewalk. This guy was superwasted. So I gave him my patented, superwasted field sobriety exam. I asked him if Mickey Mouse was a dog or a cat. I guess he thought the answer was written on my forehead. The fool almost fell over backward looking up at me. When I told him to put his hands behind his back, the drunk slurs, 'Mickey Mouse is a dog.' When I told him he was wrong, he started screaming, 'Mickey Mouse is a cat! He's a cat!' My partner was laughing so hard, I thought he wasn't gonna to be able to put the bracelets on him."

I stick my police ID card, driver's license, and a five-dollar bill in my breast pocket. Before I close my locker, I give my .38 a final check. I eject the rounds into my cupped right hand, visually inspect the barrel and cylinders, and then reload the six rounds of 158-grain roundnose lead ammunition. The crisp metallic sound of the cylinder closing is reassuring. Still, force of habit takes over. As I pull back the hammer with my right thumb and rotate the cylinder with my left, I hear my firearms instructor's voice in my head—*A round of ammunition with a high primer will turn your pistol into a short metal club.*

I put my hat on my head and gather my stuff. I grab my baton, flashlight, ticket book holder, helmet bag, and three-ring binder. Stuffed with policy guides and exemplars, the binder is as unwieldy as it is heavy. I'm happy the roll call room is only a few steps down the hall. I wouldn't want to haul all this stuff upstairs.

An extra-wide wooden desk sits centered on the raised flooring at the front of the assembly room. It is the perch from which the watch commander reigns during roll call. A blackboard behind the desk, flanked by an American flag, gives a classroom feel. But in lieu of individual desks, there are rows of narrow laminate tables bolted to the floor. Behind each table, metal seats rise at regular intervals on steel stanchions also bolted to the floor. The unpadded seats are rigid, except for a few degrees of squeaky, side-to-side swivel. Maps of the division, sprinkled with colored pins, adorn the walls. Fluorescent light fixtures suspended from the acoustic-tile ceiling round out the institutional ambiance.

In the LAPD, time on the job it everything. It even dictates the seating arrangement in roll call. The back row is reserved for those with the most hash marks on their sleeves. Being on probation, I know I have to sit in the front row. Even if I wanted to turn around, the rigid, concave seat makes it difficult.

The sharp sounds of batons, saps, revolvers, and heavy metal flashlights landing on the laminate tabletops, punctuate the jargon-laced conversations. Behind me, I hear a cop say, "Yeah some asshole tried to beef me for calling him an *asshole*. The sergeant agreed with me that the guy was an *asshole,* but he said I couldn't call him that. Man, this department is getting really chickenshit. You can't even tell the truth anymore..."

The cacophony tapers off when the watch commander enters the room. By the time Lieutenant Price sits down, it is quiet enough to hear the hollow timbre as he scoots his chair across the raised flooring. The LT is a gaunt man in his early fifties. His Dracula hairdo is streaked with gray, the same color as the ashes drooping from the cigarette in his ever-frowning lips. His blanched skin and sunken features make him look much older. The LAPD uniform hanging on his emaciated physique looks out of place.

"All right, listen up! *Roll call.*" His voice is what I expect a cadaver would sound like if it could talk. He starts by reading the assignments. "Adam-one, Russell and Stoller."

"Here, sir!" I answer.

The aging Dracula glances at me over his readers. "Welcome aboard."

I nod my head to acknowledge the lieutenant's formality before cranking my neck to catch a glimpse of Russell, who answered up from the back row. Of course, it's too late.

16

ROLL CALL ENDS when the LT growls, "All right, let's get out there and relieve PM watch."

As I gather my gear, Officer Russell walks past. He tells me to check out a shotgun and meet him in the parking lot. Being the most junior boot, I am relegated to the last spot in line. When I reach the window of the kit room, the desk officer hands me a shotgun with one hand and pushes four rounds of double-aught buck ammunition across the counter with the other. I print my name and serial number on the sign-out sheet before stuffing the rounds between my Sam Browne and taut stomach.

Holding the shotgun by the pistol grip, careful to keep the barrel pointed upward, I squat down to grab my notebook off the linoleum. I wedge my three-ring binder under my arm, slip my fingers through the straps of my helmet bag, and stand up. Thank goodness someone has propped open the heavy steel door.

The parking lot that was so quiet when I arrived, is alive now. Car doors slamming, a momentary chirp of a siren, the metallic clicks of pump-action shotguns, all are magnified by the late hour. The voices of the female dispatchers from the speakers inside the cars compete with the male voices of the officers bantering among themselves.

The discordant chorus reminds me of an orchestra tuning up prior to a performance.

I look over the rows of black-and-whites and spot my TO engaged in conversation with the sergeant, who is checking in the night watch. I try my best to look professional, but I can't stop my helmet bag from smacking my knee as I walk. *At least my uniform is squared away.*

As I approach my TO, he shifts his weight to his right foot and leans that direction. He exaggerates his stance by canting his head sideways, and scrunching his face as he stares. After an uncomfortable pause, he slowly draws out his words. "You...sure...look...pretty...Question is...can you fight?"

I'm caught completely off guard.

"You don't have to answer, kid. I wouldn't take your word for it anyway. Besides...we'll find out soon enough."

My training officer would never be selected as a poster boy for the LAPD. If he stood up real straight, he might reach five ten. Pushing forty, he sports a pronounced paunch. The cigarette hanging from his pursed lips accentuates his unhealthy morning-watch pallor. Unfriendly is an understatement for the worn, disgusted look on his face. Despite his outward relaxed appearance, there is an invisible bowstring tension about him. But his most remarkable feature is his eyes. They are black holes.

Pointing to a police car with the trunk lid raised, he says, "Throw all your stuff in there. Thataway, your hands will be free to preflight the shotgun."

Fortunately, I can perform the five-point safety check in my sleep. I say fortunately, because I know my TO's black holes are going to track my every move. Like a lot of police recruits, the academy was my first experience with a shotgun. Some of the other guys were intimidated by it. Not me. I loved *the tube* from the start. For most of my career, we will use the Ithaca twelve-gauge pump shotgun with a barely legal eighteen-and-three-quarter-inch barrel. Although somewhat antiquated, it's a great weapon.

I begin by checking both visually and with my fingers that the weapon is empty before backing off the knurled knob at the end of the magazine to remove the barrel. I look through the barrel like a telescope to be certain it is free of obstructions, and I tuck it under my left arm to free up my right hand. My fingers check the extractors to ensure they are sharp and have spring tension before I turn the weapon upside down and rap on the stock. Visually and with my fingers, I verify the firing pin remains recessed, and then pull on the trigger to test the safety. Finally, with the safety off and my finger over the exposed bolt, I pull the trigger to be sure the firing pin strikes my finger with enough force to dent the primer.

After reassembling the shotgun, I close the action and switch on the safety before feeding the rounds into the magazine. I snap the weapon smartly to port arms and make eye contact with my training officer. He nods and tells me to secure the weapon in the car.

The commission that investigated the 1965 Watts riots concluded that vertical mounting systems for shotguns in police cars were offensive, particularly to members of the minority community. Consequently, the LAPD designed a rack that secures the weapon parallel to the floorboard. To stow the shotgun in this unorthodox rack requires kneeling on the front seat. After I've locked the shotgun in the rack, I back out of the passenger door and find myself face-to-face with my training officer.

"I'm Ron Russell. Welcome aboard." He extends his hand.

"Stoller." I say as I shake his hand. "My friends call me by my middle name, Max."

My TO brushes off my attempt at familiarity and goes into his spiel. "I know you made it through the academy, but I'm not going to assume you know anything. Besides...the way we do things in the field is a lot different from what they teach at the academy."

I circle the car with my TO as he explains we are looking for fresh damage. We also check that all the lights work, including the reds and ambers in the *tin cans* mounted on the roof. All the other police departments have long ago transitioned to light bars that provide three-hundred-and-sixty-degree visibility. Ron opens the rear door and lifts the backseat to look for contraband or evidence a suspect might have dropped. Nothing so far is different from what they taught us at the academy.

When we finally settle into the front seat, my TO shoves the key in the ignition, but he doesn't start the car. Instead, he removes his field officer's notebook from his breast pocket. He glances at me and asks, "What's your horsepower?" When I don't immediately respond, he rewords the question. "What's your serial number?"

I rattle off my number.

"You sure that's your serial number?" Ron snickers. "Sounds more like the national debt."

Most people think your badge number is your police department identification number. Some places it is, but not in the Los Angeles Police Department. In the LAPD, the badge number is just that, the number on a piece of equipment. Unlike the badge that can be reissued, your LAPD serial number is unique, and it's what counts. It is like your LAPD tattoo, largely invisible to outsiders, but indelibly marked on everything inside the department. A lower number means more time on the job. And in the LAPD...time on the job is everything.

The other cars have all left, and the late-night quiet has returned. We are alone except for the static-laced radio transmissions from the speaker on the floorboard of our cruiser. I lift my chin, draw in a deep breath, and steel myself for my first foray patroling the mean streets of Los Angeles.

My TO returns his field officer's notebook to his breast pocket but not his pencil. Instead of reaching for the ignition, he pivots toward me as he leans back against the driver's door. He holds up the pencil with two fingers.

"See this pencil?"

"Yes, sir."

"If you fuck up with this end, you just turn it around and erase your mistake with this end—no real harm done. If you fuck up in a tactical situation, you just might get yourself killed. There's no eraser for those kinds of mistakes."

"Yes, sir."

"Why do you think I am telling you this?"

"Ah...well, I guess you don't want me to get killed."

"You're part right," my TO slides the pencil into his breast pocket, "because I definitely don't want to go to any more cops' funerals. But the real reason is...if you fuck up and get yourself killed, there is a good chance you might just get me killed right along with you." My TO throws his right arm across the back of the bench seat. "While getting yourself killed would not be good...getting me killed would be an *unpardonable fucking sin!*"

Is this guy serious? How did I get assigned to him? Was there any design to it? Or was it random bad luck?

My TO isn't finished. "Why do you think so many guys hate boots?"

He doesn't give me time to time to answer.

"It isn't 'cause they hate you. They don't know you. Out here, we have to depend on one another. When you are new and don't know shit...no one can count on you. Despite your best intentions, instead of being helpful, you are just as likely to get somebody hurt. Don't take it personal...'cause it ain't."

Ron pulls a cigarette from a pack of Marlboros tucked in the visor and lights it with his Zippo. "I'm telling you up front. I'm going to ride your ass about everything you write. Why? 'Cause everything we write out here in the field is reviewed about a million times by pencil-neck geeks. Not just the water closet here at the station. This fuck'n department has got more guys than you can shake a stick at sitting on their sorry asses downtown at Parker Center, trying to find something wrong with what some poor street copper wrote. That's those assholes' whole job—looking for some mistake we might make."

He takes another draw on his smoke. "When one of those squints finds something wrong with something we did, they get their rocks off by kicking it back. Now if the water closet kicks it back...it's no big deal. But when some jerk-off from downtown kicks it back, it comes down the chain of command, starting with the commanding officer. Trust me, you don't want that, and I don't want that. So I'm going to check and double-check everything you write."

Holding his Marlboro in his lips, he brings his arm back from its resting place behind the seat, and pivots into a driving position. "In the end," he glances at me, "fuck all the paperwork. What is most important is that we go End of Watch every night in at least as good a shape as we started." He fires up the engine. "Officer safety first... everything else second."

17

RON DRIVES UP the sharply curved and inclined ramp that leads to Temple Street. He tells me, "OK, kid, you can clear us now."

I hope he doesn't see my hand tremble as I reach for the microphone hooked on the dashboard. The tan hunk of metal, tethered by a curly cord to a radio mounted on the floor, is exactly like the ones I used at Disneyland. It is the same as we practiced with in training. But this is not the academy. And it sure as hell isn't Disneyland. In more ways than I can appreciate, I've graduated from Fantasyland to Realityland.

Hoping my voice doesn't betray my anxiety, I say into the microphone, "Two-Adam-one, clear." (Two indicates Rampart Division, Adam indicates a basic car, one is our beat, and clear means we are available for calls.)

The radio telephone operator (RTO) immediately inquires, "Verify, that's two-Adam-one clearing?"

When I don't immediately respond, Ron grabs the mic. "Roger, it's two-Adam-one. We're clear."

"Two-Adam-one, clear," the RTO repeats.

Ron replaces the mic and explains, "You have to listen to be sure no one else is talking before you key the mic. Someone else was broadcasting when you were trying to clear. When that happens, both transmissions get garbled. The girls do a great job, but some-times they can't make it out. Although she thought it was us, she had to be sure."

My TO glances my way. "Some cars have a *cheater*. That's another radio that lets you hear the other units broadcasting. When you can hear both the RTOs and the cars talking, it is much easier to avoid stepping on someone else's transmission. But this car doesn't have a cheater, so you're gonna have to pay close attention."

"Yes, sir," I say, promising myself as much as answering my TO.

"We're a north-end car," Ron says. "Technically we have the north-west part, and A-3 has the northeast part of the division, but we don't sweat that. By staying north of Sunset Boulevard, none of the stupid-visors are gonna give us any grief." Ron is tapping the notepad between us.

Is this another of his nervous habits like his wince?

Ron picks up the microphone. "Two-Adam-one, verify the address?"

Shit! It wasn't a nervous habit. He was trying to draw my attention.

After he has acknowledged the call, my TO points to the pad again. "Write the type of call, 'code thirty' (burglary alarm), then the address." He repeats the numbers.

After I've jotted down the address he says, "Put down the time we got the call, and draw a box around it. No confusion with the address that way."

"Sorry, sir."

"Don't be sorry. Just pay ah-fuck'n-ten-shun. I know this is your first night. It takes a while to tune your ear to the radio, but your ear won't tune itself. You gotta work at it. OK?"

I'm looking out the passenger window, trying to catch an address.

"We're almost there," Ron says, throwing me a quick glance. "Most of these alarms are false, but every once in a while we catch a burglar. So stay with me and watch your ass."

Ron turns off the lights and guides our cruiser to a stop about two car lengths from the call. He puts the car in park, sets the brake, and slides out of the driver's door. Even doing all this and coming from the driver's side, he is already walking up the sidewalk by the time I get out of the car. I hustle to catch up, still putting my baton in its ring.

Ron's right hand is gripping his holstered .38. Because his *clamshell* holster rides low on his hip and swivels, his shoulder remains in a natural position as he saunters up to the call. Unlike my partner's holster, my *breakfront* holster sits high on my hip. I have to raise my shoulder and awkwardly bend my arm to grip my pistol as I traipse after my training officer.

The doors and windows at the front of the body shop are secure. A six-foot chain-link fence interrupts access to the rear. Ron tells me to slide my baton into the woven metal fence a couple of feet off the ground and hold it with both hands. He steps on my baton like a rung of a ladder and makes his way over the fence, dropping heavily on the other side. I return my baton to its ring, stuff my spit-shined shoe into the chain-link fence, and scamper after my TO.

While the front of the business is well lit by the streetlights, there is only a single low-wattage bulb over the rear door. The beam from my partner's light is narrow and weak compared to the column of light coming out of the chrome Coleman I picked up in the camping section of Zody's for less than two bucks. *I'd have thought a veteran like Ron would have a better light.*

"Looks secure to me." Ron says.

I again put my baton in the fence to help Ron vault the chain-link fence. I'm halfway over the fence when I see a police car approaching at a full throttle. Ron holds up four fingers to signal code four, no further assistance required. The black-and-white hits the brakes and makes a U-turn.

When we've settled into the front seat of our car, Ron dictates word for word what I need to write in each box of the Daily Field

Activity Report (DFAR), the log. Then he tells me precisely what I have to say on the radio. Finally, he admonishes me to wait until the air is clear so I don't step on anyone again.

Mentally I repeat what I have to say a couple of times. When I think the frequency is clear I begin, "Two-Adam-one, ah...Show a code four." I give the address. "Ah...No outside evidence four-five-nine" (459 is the California penal code section for burglary).

The RTO comes back immediately. "All units show a code four on the code thirty...No outside evidence of four-five-nine. Two-Adam-one, are you clear?"

I grab the mic. "Two-Adam-one is clear."

I'm mentally congratulating myself when Ron interrupts. "You need to get a good flashlight. Most guys carry one of these." He hands me his well-worn heavy metal flashlight. "They're strong and have a lifetime guarantee. They also make a hell of a club...that's how come everybody calls them kill lights."

I want to tell him Stevie Wonder can see my flashlight is five times brighter than his, but I don't. Instead, I say, "Mine gives out a pretty good light, and it was really cheap."

"Yeah, well your really cheap light is gonna break the first time you hit somebody with it...leaving you standing there with nothing but a scrap of chrome-plated tin in your hand."

"Doesn't department policy forbid using a flashlight as a weapon?" I regret it as soon as the words have left my lips.

"Yep, but that's because the assholes who write policy don't work the street. Ninety-nine percent of the time, when the suspect you're talking to decides he's gonna clean your clock...the only thing you have in your hand is your flashlight. At that moment, how bright it is doesn't matter. How strong it is does."

"They cost over a hundred bucks. I haven't got that kind of money right now." Actually, I could probably scrape up the money. I just don't want to spend it on a flashlight.

"Kel-lites are pricey. I'll give you that. But your camping special is chrome plated, so even in low light…it's impossible to miss. That makes the person carrying it impossible to miss."

"Yes, sir. I see your point." I hurry to change the subject. "We practiced a lot with the baton at the academy, but they never showed us that chain-link trick."

"The baton is a good tool. You can do a lot with it. The chain-link-step technique is just one. For instance, the baton is your best defense against dogs. A good smack across the chops sends 'm running. And if you gotta break out a window, don't use your flashlight. It's too short, and the glass'll cut you. Use your baton instead."

Ron glances at me to be sure I'm paying attention. "Just don't hit anybody with the baton. If you hit somebody with the baton, I gar-an-fucking-tee you will get a beef, and you will take days."

Stopped for a red light, Ron turns in my direction, his black holes sucking up the light between us. "If you hit somebody with your baton when you are working with me, I will personally kick your fucking ass." His black holes again aimed outside the car, Ron accelerates through the deserted intersection against the red and continues his lesson. "There is only one time you can hit somebody with your baton. I got a ton of stick time in the Watts Riots and nobody said shit. But other than a riot, leave your baton in its ring."

I can't believe this guy. First he wants me to get a club for a flashlight, and then tells me he will kick my ass if I use my baton to hit somebody. We spent untold hours in the academy practicing baton strikes by the numbers, and learning under what circumstances these techniques are approved. *I wonder if I can request another training officer.*

Ron continues our tour of the northern part of the division. Despite my best effort, I can't get a mental picture of the area. The streets run every which way as they bend around the topography. One minute we're heading north, the next we're heading east or west. Every couple of minutes I'm near panic, searching for a street sign. Trying to listen to my TO and to the radio, reading the street signs, and looking for bad guys all at the same time is overwhelming.

I miss our call sign again and again. A couple of times, I see Ron's finger tapping the notepad and write down the call. But just as often I am looking for a street sign or something else, and Ron has to grab the microphone. The technical term for my condition is *sensory overload.* Polite words cannot soothe my ego. More importantly, semantics don't alter facts. I know this is unacceptable.

We respond to a couple of burglar alarms that prove to be false. The disturbance calls we get all turn out to be disputes. I just stand there while Ron soft-soaps the people. Back in the car after our last call, Ron tells me to hold off clearing.

It's time to eat," he says, as we pull into the parking lot of a twenty-four-hour coffee shop..."if they will let us."

I request code seven. In less than a minute, the RTO gives us permission to eat. I am quick to pick up the mic and acknowledge, "Two-Adam-one, roger, OK, seven."

I didn't feel hungry a minute ago, but walking into the restaurant, I am suddenly starved. Good tactics dictate we sit in the back where we can see the cash register and the door. I can't say I'm relaxed. But compared to the car, this is heaven.

After we order breakfast, Ron says, "You always have to be polite to the girls on the radio. It's more than just good manners. They hold our lives in their hands."

"Yes, sir." At the academy they told us that pleasantries are to be avoided on the radio because they waste airtime. *Besides...when was I impolite?*

"Next time when we get OK, seven, be sure to say thank you. It's not a big thing...but it's important."

"Yes, sir."

Before we have finished eating, our waitress drops our checks on the table. Out of habit, I pick mine up and turn it over. "LAPD" is written diagonally across the face in big block letters. The total price of the meal has been divided in half. In the academy, we were warned that half-price meals are considered a gratuity and strictly forbidden.

"Sir, ah...I see they cut the price in half. In the academy, they told us—"

"Look, kid, I don't give a shit what they told you in the academy. I ain't made out of money. So like every other street cop I know, I eat at places that give me a break. When you are the car commander, you can go any damn place you want to eat. Until then, just be sure you have enough money to cover it, just in case they don't pop."

After breakfast, the air is dead and the streets deserted. While Ron patrols at soporific speed, I struggle to stay awake reading street signs. The sun has been up for a while when Ron tells me to put us "out to the station." Ron reads me the ending mileage as we pull into the station. He looks over my log. I only have to make a couple of corrections.

As we unload our stuff, Ron asks, "So what did you think about your first night?"

"I'm an idiot. Four months in the academy didn't teach me a damn thing I need to know out here."

"I agree with you on the academy, but in my book," he hauls his helmet bag out of the trunk, "tonight was a good night because we're going EOW in as good a shape as we started. Try to get some sleep, kid. See you at roll call."

18

ON MY WAY home, I stop at a hardware store and pick up a roll of black plastic electrician's tape. I wrap my *camping special* so the only chrome left visible is the thumb switch. At a glance, in the dark, someone might mistake it for a Kel-lite.

Happy with my camouflage job, I crawl into bed, but the sunlight seeping around the curtains conspires with memories of last night. Until the sun goes down, the best I can manage are stints of semiconsciousness. When I finally drop off, the sleep is delicious, but short-lived. I wake with a start. The Baby Ben on my nightstand is telling me I've got to get out of bed. I'm hungry, but dinner doesn't appeal. I make a big breakfast and devour it with gusto.

. . .

It feels like a continuation of last night. Right out of roll call we get three calls. Ron says we'll take the four-fifteen man at a bar on Sunset first. En route to the call, my TO gives me the plan.

"Bars are a tactical bitch. A little better in this case 'cause the place is small. I'll go in and try to bring the problem outside. You wait at the door. If the shit hits the fan, run to the car and call for a backup, then haul ass back to help me out."

"Yes, sir."

The boulevard is busy. The only space at the curb not jammed with cars is the driveway of a closed business about two hundred feet away. I expect Ron to park in the driveway, but instead he deftly squeezes our black-and-white onto the sidewalk and drives right up to the call. He parks on the sidewalk a car's length from the entrance to the neighborhood watering hole.

"Be sure to leave the mic outside the window," he says as he gets out of the car.

Ron may have his idiosyncrasies, but years working the street have taught him a trick or two. As soon as Ron steps inside the bar, I take up a position in the doorway under the red neon cocktails sign. I stand with one foot inside the bar and one foot outside on the sidewalk. My left hand automatically grabs for the grommet of my baton in the stance they taught us at the academy. I watch Ron make his way to the rear of the bar and turn his back to the wall. When our eyes meet, I let go of my baton.

Ron is talking to the bartender, but between the jukebox and the customers' alcohol-raised voices, I can only guess at what is being said. The bartender points to a longhair wearing a faded army OD (olive drab) field jacket and hip-hugger jeans. After some animated coaxing by the proprietor, the unkempt patron rises to his feet. Ron points to the exit with his flashlight. Initially the suspect holds his ground, but when the problem child glances at the door and sees me, the change in odds brings a change of heart. The hippie shuffles toward the door with Ron close behind, his flashlight at the ready.

Outside on the sidewalk, we keep the suspect between us. Ron tells the suspect to turn around and put his hands behind his head. The inebriated man's unsteady pirouette leaves him facing me. Ron grabs the suspect's hands and begins his cursory search. "Lots of people carry guns nowadays, so I'm gonna check real quick, just to make sure you ain't pack'n."

"Man, I'm a flower child...peacenik. You know...nonviolence, Ravi Shankar, and all that shit. I ain't got noth'n."

"What's this here?" Ron pulls an eight-inch-long folding knife out of the guy's right-front pants pocket. After slipping the weapon in his waistband, my partner continues his search.

"That's just for protection, man. You know...some niggers try to take me for my bread...what am I gonna do? You know you pigs ain't never around when I need ya."

Ron's retort is immediate. "Yeah, I was born with a bad sense of timing. But at least my parents taught me some manners." Finished with his pat down, my partner lets go of the suspect's interlaced fingers and pushes off. That sends the hippie staggering my direction.

Out of reflex my muscles stiffen. My hands come up, and I get deeper in my stance. Fortunately the suspect pivots back toward my partner, who is telling him to come up with some ID. When the suspect faces my partner, I start to breathe again.

The pig comment was a mistake. I just can't tell if this guy's brain is functioning well enough to realize it. Judging by the neglect of his personal hygiene, there is little reason to believe he has taken any better care of the thinking organ ensconced inside his skull. When Ron has enough info, he stuffs the FI (field interview) back in his breast pocket and tells the suspect to put his hands behind his back. That's my cue. My hand trembles as I open the flap of my handcuff case. I hope the suspect can't tell I'm more nervous than he is.

As soon as he's cuffed, the guy starts chipping, "You fuck'n pigs! You always hassl'n longhairs for no reason. Man, I was just have'n a beer, minding my own business, when you pigs come in and roust me for no reason."

Ron has the FI out again and is recording more details as he rebuts the punk's ridiculous assertion. "Yeah, right. Like we got nothing better to do than walk into this dive to roust a fucking faggot flower child. Think again, dickhead. The bartender asked you to leave half a dozen times. Two hours ago he called the cops. All you had to do was get your dumb ass out the door before we showed up. Know what that makes you?"

The question rattles around the guy's mostly empty cranial housing group for a while. The best he can come up with is, "I know I ain't no fuck'n pig."

"It makes you felony fucking stupid, Ron says.

Walking him to the car, my partner pulls at the suspect's dirty field jacket and squeezes the ripstop material. "What have we here?" Ron says as he extracts a dime bag of low-grade marijuana from the lining of the flower child's jacket.

The guy is felony stupid—literally. Sitting in back with the suspect en route to the station, I get a much greater appreciation of how poor his personal hygiene really is. I'm happy to put the suspect behind Plexiglas and steel while Ron runs him for warrants and gets booking approval.

As we escort our grungy suspect from the holding cell to our cruiser for the short trip downtown, the suspect asks, "Where you taking me?"

"Jail," is Ron's one-word answer.

"Yeah, but which one?"

"The glass house."

The exterior of Parker Center is predominately glass, prompting the criminal element to refer to it as the *glass house*.

I stay as far away as possible from our ripe prisoner, thankful for the wind generated by our speed down the freeway. When we arrive at the jail, the lot is full. Fortunately, a couple of cops are walking down the ramp. We grab their parking spot when they pull out.

I remain a few paces behind as Ron walks our prisoner past the misdemeanor entrance. We make a right turn and follow the concrete walkway to the jail's rear entrance. When Ron hits the buzzer the solenoid slams the dead bolt open. We pass the GCIs (breath-testing machines) and continue down the corridor to a special elevator that serves the felony jail on the second floor. After securing our weapons in the gray metal gun lockers, Ron presses the call button.

When the elevator doors part, Ron marches our prisoner to the rear and tells me to hit the button for the second floor. I push the button, but nothing happens. I'm about to push it again when the car lurches upward. The elevator car bangs against its tracks as it slowly ascends to its only destination. As suddenly as it started, the elevator stops, and the steel doors part to reveal the felony booking cage.

Two patrol cops and a jailer stand by as a young Hispanic gang-banger is checked into LA's gray-bar hotel. Two more blue suits wait in the corner with their arrestee. Ron grabs our suspect by the arm and wheels him out of the elevator.

Our flower child lifts his shoulder, and tries to pull away. "Man, you ain't gotta grab me."

Ron tightens his grip and forcefully yanks our self-proclaimed peacenik into an unoccupied corner. With his face uncomfortably close to our stinky prisoner, Ron gives our suspect the facts of life. "Until you're booked into this fine establishment, you're my responsibility, and I'm gonna make damn sure nothing happens to you. After you're booked, you can bitch to the rest of the dirtbags in here about your bad treatment at the hands of the LAPD. Till then...*shut the fuck up.*"

Behind a waist-high wall of concrete, topped with wire mesh that extends to the ceiling, a civilian jailer is typing the paperwork on the eighteen-year-old being booked as an adult for the first time. Without looking up from his IBM Selectric, the typist asks the same question he has asked a million times before. "Who you want notified in case of emergency?"

"No one." the punk responds defiantly.

Instead of looking at the civilian behind the counter, the arrogant arrestee faces off with the middle-aged man in khakis. The neophyte prisoner affects a badass-street-hoodlum pose, tilting his head back as he stares. The punk is too busy playing Sal Mineo to notice the badge on the man's khaki uniform is a three-digit policeman's badge worn smooth from years of daily polishing.

Except for the stub of an unlit cigar stuffed into the corner of his mouth, the tenured policeman's face is placid. When the middle-aged cop uncrosses his arms, I see a globe-and-anchor tattoo on his forearm. At the end of his muscular forearms are giant paws where his hands should be. His teeth clenched to keep his unlit cigar in place, the veteran cop instructs the prisoner in a low, almost grandfatherly voice. "There is no need to feel embarrassed. Everybody has to do it. Just take off your clothes and hand them to me one piece at a time. It's no big deal."

"Fuck you, man. I don't take my clothes off for nobody 'cept my bitches—"

The hiss at the end of bitches is still coming from the punk's mouth when a meaty palm collides with the side of his head. Unconscious before gravity has pulled him to the rubber flooring, the gangster goes down like a latex bowling pin. I never saw it coming. Neither did he. Obviously the punk expected his treatment in the men's felony jail would be similar to his experiences at the hands of the social workers at juvenile hall.

The Marine Corps veteran chews the cigar in the corner of his mouth as he waits for the hoodlum to regain consciousness. To hurry the process along, one of the arresting officers cracks an ampoule of smelling salts and waves it under the prisoner's nose. When the gangster starts to come around, the jailer resumes in the same low tone. "This is my house. When you're in my house, you follow my rules. Take off all your clothes and hand them to me, one piece at a time."

My partner points to a process room and tells our prisoner we will wait our turn in there.

"Yes, sir," the flower child replies.

It is a miracle. The negligence in our prisoner's upbringing has been retroactively improved.

• • •

When we get back to the car, I find my flashlight took a tumble on the drive downtown. The lens is broken. En route back to Rampart, I peel back the tape, twist off the head, and carefully remove the pieces of broken glass. Screwing the head back on to the flashlight, I can hear small fragments grind against the metal. I have my doubts, but when I press the switch, the bulb lights. I try to rewrap the tape, but it doesn't want to hold. I'll have to use some fresh tape when I get home.

Even though my TO dictated every word in all the reports, he still checks everything before he drops the stack on the water closet's desk. Lieutenant Price picks up the paperwork and leans back. The spring in his swivel chair groans as he peers through his readers.

"This isn't like you, Ron." The LT looks up from the reports. "A humbug dope bust on a busy night?"

"I'd a just kicked his ass out of the bar, but this asshole would have been back as soon as we left. You know I don't like nobody else having to come back and clean up my mess. If the asshole had warrants, that would a been faster and easier, but I gave him a worldwide check and came up with a blank."

"Why not just book him for drunk?" the LT asks.

"Yeah, I could have cut him some slack, but the asshole talked me out of it."

"All right. Get out there and clear. Communications is giving calls to outside divisions."

19

AS SOON AS we clear, the RTO gives us three more calls, including one we sold back a couple of hours ago after we popped the flower child. Most of the incidents are stale and have handled themselves by the time we get there. For example, we arrive at a liquor store where the complaint is a four-fifteen group. The store is closed and the area deserted. The clerk who called is probably home asleep by now. We go to a code thirty ringer. Instead of the usual mind-jarring racket, the circular bell only issues a syncopated rattle, punctuated by an occasional metallic clang when a piece of the broken clapper falls against the enclosure.

Ron parks a couple of doors from a family dispute call. Leafy branches of mature trees block the streetlights. I stumble in the dark on the buckled sidewalk before catching up to my partner, who has paused at the short chain-link fence that encloses the front yard. He shakes the gate and whistles softly. He turns to me and whispers, "Good way to check to see if they have a dog is to shake the gate or whistle."

The gate creaks as my partner opens it and slides through. The house is dark. There isn't even the glow from a TV. Standing on the porch we can't hear anyone inside. Gently opening the wood-framed screen door, Ron taps lightly with his flashlight. When there's no response, he lets the screen settle back softly and then writes something in pencil on the doorjamb. He waves me off the porch.

Back in the car I ask, "How do I log this?"

"Yeah, normally I would have pounded on the door. And if nobody answered, we would request further. That is what the book says. But you gotta use your head out here. The call wasn't coded, and it's at least three hours old. Obviously the couple solved their own problem. The last thing they need is for us to wake them up." Ron looks at me for a second. "Think about it. If you had called the cops four hours ago and they never showed up...then after you finally get to sleep, the cops start pounding on your front door...how happy you gonna be?"

"I see what you mean. But I can't put that in the log."

"No, for the dispo, just put down, 'No evidence of four-fifteen family dispute—No answer.'"

"Yes, sir."

Ron lights up a smoke and expounds a little more. "Ninety-nine out of a hundred times this won't happen, but let's just say tomorrow morning the old lady is still pissed and calls the station to beef...says the cops didn't even bother to show up. I wrote the date, time, and my serial number on the doorjamb. So when a sergeant goes out to interview the old lady, he should see my writing. That's our proof we were there. Police work isn't rocket science, but you gotta use common sense...and always cover your ass."

"Yes, sir."

The arrest that started our shift seems like it happened a week ago. We've been chasing the radio ever since. A few minutes in the coffee shop and something to put in our stomachs would be great, but there's no chance. Every car that has requested code seven has been rebuffed with *continue patrol and handle* followed by three more calls.

What a bizarre job this is. I thought I would be spending most of my time trying to catch bad guys who were stealing or hurting somebody. In reality, we spend most of our time being directed to where people are not getting along. We drive from trouble call to trouble call, trying to solve people's problems. We respond to neighbor disputes, business disputes, landlord-tenant disputes, and family disputes. The calls are for problems we can't solve and are usually not criminal.

Like the call we just left. Ron is right. The couple is undoubtedly asleep, probably with a gap of angry linen between them. Perhaps their anger has subsided and they are entangled in a lovers' embrace.

The thought triggers images and sensations of the last time Katarina and I made love. After we were spent, she fell asleep nestled under my arm. I didn't want to miss any of that beautiful time. I fought dropping off and combed my fingers through her silky—

Ron's angry voice yanks me from my reverie. "You had your head up your ass again, and it's locked!" He is in no mood to bail me out this time. "Have the RTO repeat the fucking calls."

Standard radio procedure requires beginning every radio transmission with your call sign. In my haste to recoup from my error, I grab the mic and simply say, "Could you repeat our calls?"

The RTO comes back immediately, "Two-Adam-one, are you the unit requesting I repeat the calls—*again*?"

I realize I have fucked up—*again*. My jaw is so tight, my mouth hardly moves. "Two-Adam-one, roger. Could you please repeat our calls?"

As I write the info on the notepad, I avoid looking at Ron. He's right. I did have my head up my ass.

We chase the radio right up to EOW. As we walk across the parking lot after emptying out the car, Ron says, "I'm off for a couple. If you don't get yourself fired, killed, or quit...I'll see you when I get back."

20

THE NEXT NIGHT, both of my training officers are off. Lieutenant Price is off, too. When the assistant watch commander, Sergeant II Arman Arnhardt, reads off the assignments, I learn I'm working with an officer named Morales. After roll call, the heavyset P-2 with hollow eyes and a pockmarked complexion approaches me in the hallway.

Fiddling with the keepers on his Sam Browne, he snarls, "Check out our shit and meet me at the car."

"Yes, sir."

I find Morales sitting in our black-and-white with the engine running, his fingers drumming on the wheel. I place my helmet bag on the ground outside the passenger door and throw my notebook on the front seat. I wedge my ticket book between the dash and the windshield. I quickly preflight the shotgun. After securing the shotgun in the rack, I back out of my side of the car and ask for my set of keys so I can unlock the trunk. Morales tosses the keys in my general direction. They jangle as they ricochet off the kick panel of my open door.

I scoop the keys off the concrete like a shortstop fielding a ground ball. With my helmet bag stashed in the trunk, I'm back at the passenger door, sliding my baton into the radiator hose bolted to the inside of the door. My butt has barely landed on the seat; I haven't even shut the door when the car lurches forward.

"Fuck'n loootenant knows I hate the north end. Unless we get a call, we ain't go'n up there." Morales doesn't take the ramp that leads to Temple Street. Instead, he circles around the parking lot and exits on Benton Way, heading south.

I need the starting mileage, my partner's serial number, and his initials for the log. I am about to ask when I notice the info is scribbled on the notepad. From his serial number, I can see that Morales has only been off probation for about a year, making his old-salt imitation all the more ridiculous. He pulls to the curb in front of a dingy storefront that peddles cheap booze and tobacco to the down-and-outers who call MacArthur Park home.

He tells me, "Wait here and listen to the radio, kid."

I scrunch up my nose against the persistent odor of urine that hangs in the damp air, and adjust my side-view mirror to keep an eye on the transient who is panhandling on the sidewalk behind me. In front of me, more drunks try to hide their short dogs (slang for a small bottle of cheap fortified wine). Across the street an old woman drags her wire-frame two-wheel shopping cart behind her. Wrapped in a scarf and huddled in an ancient overcoat, she looks like my *bubbie* back in Chicago coming home from the A&P. I hope she makes it to safety before we leave.

The female voice of the RTO on the radio is suddenly replaced by the male voice of the link, a tenured officer at Communications Division. "All units on all frequencies stand by. Eleven-Adam-eighty-nine is in pursuit. Eleven-Adam-eighty-nine, your location?"

I can hear the voice of the officer in the pursuing unit through the link's open microphone. "Eleven-Adam-eighty-nine is in pursuit southbound Marmion Way at Avenue Forty-Five."

Morales comes out of the liquor store. "What we got?" he asks as he stashes a bottle wrapped in a paper bag in the trunk.

"A pursuit in Northeast," I tell him.

The link's voice is calm. "Eleven-Adam-eighty-nine, your location now?"

"Eleven-Adam-eighty-nine, southbound Figueroa Street from Marmion Way." The siren is audible in the background as the officer's voice modulates with excitement and the wild ride.

"They're coming our way!" Morales exclaims as he fires up our cruiser and blasts from the curb.

My knowledge of the city is limited, but from just a couple of trips on the Pasadena Freeway, I know the pursuit is a long ways off. There has got to be a least a dozen units closer than we are. At the moment, the pursuit is heading our direction, but there's no reason to expect that will continue. My thoughts are interrupted by the pursuing unit's broadcast.

"Eleven-Adam-eighty-nine, suspects have T/A'd, Figueroa and Avenue Thirty-Seven, requesting assistance."

That didn't take long. The bad guys already crashed.

Morales is driving like a madman. We have not even reached the Hollywood freeway before we hear, "Code four—suspects in custody."

Morales pounds the steering wheel. "Shit, I was hoping to get some stick time."

With the frequency no longer on standby, the RTO gives us three calls: A four-fifteen man, a business dispute, and a burglary from motor vehicle (BFMV) report. I mentally note the type of each call as I write the addresses on the notepad. I'm pleased with myself. I don't have to ask the RTO to repeat anything.

Morales doesn't say a word. Ron would have told me right away which call we were handling first, so when I acknowledged the calls I could tell the RTO. As Ron would say, airtime is a precious commodity. I look at Morales to prompt a response, but either he is ignoring me or doesn't notice.

Eventually I ask, "What should I tell Communications?"

I'm about to repeat my question when Morales snorts, "Tell her we'll handle the four-fifteen man first." Instead of driving to the call, Morales parks in the red zone a few feet from the entrance to another neighborhood store. Again he tells me, "Stay in the car, kid, and listen to the radio."

From my vantage point, the only part of the store's interior I can see is a section of shelving adjacent to the door. *I wonder if Morales planned it that way.* Perhaps it's the neighborhood, or maybe it's because this little convenience store sells liquor. Whatever the reason, the scene looks a lot like our last stop. The sidewalk and doorways are filled with the same strain of street urchins. Some are doing their best to look pathetic as they panhandle. Others try to look menacing as they size up potential victims. As the legitimate customers navigate the gauntlet, the unsavory characters cast furtive glances my way. It is like an impromptu contemporary dance with the police radio as the music. It strikes me that I'm not just watching the show; I'm part of it.

What is keeping Morales? How long can it take to get another bottle of booze? The more time that goes by without any sign of him, the more nervous I get. I want to go inside, but he told me to wait in the car. I know I'm supposed to do exactly what my senior officer tells me. On the other hand, we aren't supposed to be here. I don't have to listen to the radio, because Communications Division thinks we are on a call a couple of miles away. *What if a sergeant sees me sitting here all by myself?*

This isn't really a tactical situation, but it was drummed into my head in the academy, never split up, always keep a visual on your partner. *What if my partner walked in on a robbery? What if the suspects got the drop on him like in the Hettinger and Campbell case?*

The hell with it! I'm not going down in LAPD lore as the dumb-shit probationer who just sat in the car while his partner got murdered. Not me! I lean forward so my left hand can reach the radio on the floorboard. My left forefinger rotates the volume to full at the same time as my right hand yanks on the door handle. Pushing the door open with my right elbow I step out and grab my baton from its holder in one fluid motion.

It's almost comical. Caught off guard by my rapid movements, the street people stiffen. Only when it is obvious I'm headed for the store, do they resume their pretexted casual roles. Even from the doorway, I still can't see much of the store's interior. I grab my holstered revolver as I step inside.

The Asian kid behind the counter looks way too young to be hawking booze. *Shit! Where the hell is Morales?* My lips are forming a question to the youngster when I hear steel sliding on steel. My heart hammers inside my chest as I turn toward the sound. My eyes focus on the dingy orange curtains in the recessed hallway at the far end of the store. Morales is pushing the dirty drapes aside with a bottle of booze wrapped in a brown paper bag. I exhale, and the pounding inside my chest begins to abate.

Morales comes out from behind the counter. He doesn't miss a beat. "A pack of Winston soft," he says to the adolescent behind the counter, "and another for my partner here, too."

Without taking his eyes off Morales, the kid reaches under the counter and grabs two packs of cigarettes. With obvious disdain he stacks them on the counter and slides them forward. Morales grabs them on his way to the door. "What we got?" he asks.

"Just those same three calls. I saw a sergeant drive by and didn't know what to say if he stopped. You know…where is your partner? What are you doing here? Stuff like that." I expect Morales will be pissed off. But my lie about seeing a supervisor has had the desired effect. Morales doesn't even give me the stink eye.

"Which sergeant was it?

"Dunno."

"How do you know it was a sergeant?"

"Just one guy in the car."

"It could a been the U-boat. You sure it was a sergeant?"

"He had three stripes. I know that."

21

WE HANDLE OUR three calls. That is to say we drive by the locations. We don't actually talk to anyone. We never even get out of the car. Morales tells me to dispo all three calls as GOA-UTL (gone on arrival—unable to locate), and then tell the RTO we are out to the station. I do as I'm told.

Morales pulls into the lower lot and stops near the back door. "Go get yourself a cup of coffee. I'll meet you at the watch commander's office in a little while."

I dutifully head upstairs, even though I don't drink coffee. I'm alone in the breakroom. Uniform cops don't use this room, and there's no one else in the station at this time of night. I put a quarter in the hot drink machine and push the hot chocolate button. The vending machines look just like the ones in the employee break areas at Disneyland. No wonder, the little stickers at the bottoms of the machines show they're operated by same company.

Down to the last sip of my hot chocolate, I figure it is time to end my exile. I use my key to reenter the nonpublic confines of the station. Still, I don't feel like I belong to the fraternity in blue. My baton hanging from my Sam Browne adds to my sense of isolation. Real cops don't wear their batons in the station, except if they are on their way to their cars to start their shift or making the opposite trip at EOW.

I had grabbed my stick out of reflex when Morales dropped me at the back door. Now it is just another indication of how boot I am. For a moment, I consider putting it back in our patrol car. The problem is, I don't know where Morales parked it. It could be in the upstairs lot, the downstairs lot, on the street in front of the station, or even in the employee lot.

I find Morales in the watch commander's office schmoozing Sergeant Arnhardt. He has a notepad scribbled with orders in one hand and a wad of one-dollar bills in the other. When Morales sees me, he stuffs the bills in his pocket and makes for the door.

As I follow Morales down the hallway toward the back door, Sergeant Arnhardt calls after us, "Hey, Sticktime, I see you're training your boot right. Even got him carrying his baton in the station."

"Gotta train'm early," Morales says over his shoulder.

We are on a chow run for the station to a fried chicken place in Echo Park. The fast-food joint is in the parking lot of a twenty-four-hour grocery store that serves as a hangout for the Echo Park cholos. The gangsters are conspicuous with their hair overdosed on pomade and wearing baggy khaki pants, white T-shirts, and bomber jackets. As we pull to the curb, the delinquents are already disappearing into the ready supply of shadows.

Morales leaves me with the same admonishment I have already heard too many times tonight. "Stay in the car, kid, and listen to the radio!" Then he adds, "When I give you the high sign, come help me carry the stuff."

There's no reason for me to be in the car listening for our call sign. But at least I can see my partner, and I know our errand has been blessed by the AWC (assistant watch commander). The fried chicken smells delicious. Eating always makes me feel better.

Morales is at the window chatting up the night manager when a cholo comes out of the shadows. The gangster crosses the street and gets in the line with the customers. Something tells me the gangster is high. *Why should I care?* My gastric juices are already flowing. *I'll feel better with something in my stomach.*

Our order must be ready because Morales is impatiently motioning for me to get out of the car. *I might be a boot, but I'm not a slave. I might have to do what he says, but I'll be damned if I am going run over there like a—*

Just as Morales turns around to gather up the food, the gangster steps out of line and kicks Morales in the back. Caught completely off guard, Morales crashes headlong into the counter. Just as suddenly, the punk's bravado deserts him. He is picking them up and laying them down pretty good for being high. The suspect has opened a substantial lead on Morales, who is running after him with his baton in hand.

I'm twice as far behind the subject as Morales. I lose sight of the gangster when he veers behind the chicken stand. My instincts developed years ago playing outside linebacker tell me to go left behind the restaurant to cut him off, but I don't know the layout of this playing field. Rounding the restaurant, I find my path is blocked by a Dumpster and a loose-top chain-link fence. I grab the fence with both hands and wedge my shoe into the mesh. When I try to vault over the top, the woven metal buckles. Straddling the springy mesh, wobbling several feet off the ground, I glance at the fleeing suspect in time to see him turn his head to look back. He trips and lands heavily on the asphalt.

I tumble off the fence, tearing my uniform and bruising my elbow. Back on my feet, I see Sticktime trying to live up to his nickname, but the gangster has rolled onto his back and is effectively blocking the baton blows with his legs.

It's over before I get there. Between the foot chase and excitement, Morales is out of gas. Red-faced, bent over with his hands on his knees, the portly officer struggles to gulp oxygen. The subject is exhausted and looks up at me in resignation. I roll the gangbanger onto his stomach and handcuff him just like I'd done to Sean a thousand times in the academy.

As we walk the punk back to our car, it is apparent the arrestee and my partner are not strangers. All the way to the station, like an elementary school kid on the playground, the punk keeps repeating his taunt, "Morales is a peen-chee pussy. Morales is a peen-chee pussy."

The subject's name is Jose Antonio Gonzalez. Too bad he's seventeen, still a juvenile. I was looking forward to the welcome this little prick was sure to get from the cigar-chewing policeman who works the felony-booking cage.

At the station the gangster continues his harangue from inside the holding cell. Nearly every cop recognizes him. I'm gathering the info I need, when Sergeant Arnhardt comes out of his office and joins my partner in the hallway. They open the holding cell and escort our arrestee down the hall. I catch up to them just as they turn in to the unused jail. Sergeant Arnhardt bends his thick neck to look at me. "Get lost, kid. You might see something you don't wanna see."

The sergeant's meaning initially goes right over my head. When it hits me, I realize how boot I really am. From the deep recesses of the jail, I hear the subject's profane taunts turn to pleas. The violence visited on the asshole in the street was well deserved. Morales's use of the baton under the circumstances was definitely within policy. Whatever is going on in the back of the jail, that's another matter.

● ● ●

I'm in the report writing room when Morales comes in and flops down on a chair. He lights up a Winston and tells me I'd better get started. I can't believe it when he tells me the reports will make no reference to his use of the baton.

I protest this lunacy. "I just graduated from the academy. I know the latest policy. In a situation where an officer is alone confronting a suspect after a foot pursuit, a suspect who just moments before launched a completely unprovoked attack on the officer, and who is kicking and resisting arrest—there is no question—the use of the baton is definitely in-policy. "

"Just write the report exactly as I tell you. The subject's injuries came when he fell, period. That's the way AWC wants it, and he is the one who is going to sign everything. Is that fucking clear?"

"Yeah, but that doesn't make any sense."

"It makes sense to the boss, and it makes sense to me. Just do like you're told."

The whole episode is insane. The subject's rap sheet shows he has been booked fourteen times on charges ranging from runaway to attempted murder. It's not like a court cleared him on any of his arrests, either. The disposition on every case, even the attempted murder, shows *petition sustained,* the equivalent of a guilty verdict for an adult. This jerk is living proof the revolving door of justice is spinning at high RPMs.

I'm amazed at the extra paperwork required to book juvees (juveniles). No wonder cops are so reticent to book minors. Morales is no help. I have to do the fingerprinting and photographing in addition to the crime and arrest reports. Fortunately, Sergeant Arnhardt orders a day watch unit to transport the subject to Eastlake Juvenile Hall; otherwise, we would be OT (overtime). It's not the trip to juvenile hall I'm anxious to avoid. I don't want to spend one extra minute with Morales.

Taking off my uniform in the locker room releases my emotions. Jose Antonio Gonzalez richly deserved the baton blows he got prior to my cuffing him. I don't know what went on back in the jail, but if it was what I think it was, that was just plain wrong. Thank God Sergeant Arnhardt was wise enough to make sure I was neither a witness nor an accomplice to any of that extracurricular stuff. But to insist the arrest report contain no reference to the use of the baton is beyond stupid. Worse yet, it locks me into complicity. Covering up a completely justifiable use of force is insane.

All thoughts of stopping by the uniform store to buy a police flashlight have vanished. The last thing I need is to waste a hundred bucks on an aluminum flashlight. I can't wait to go home and climb under the covers. When I accepted the appointment to the police academy, I promised myself no matter what happened, I would not go back to Disneyland. Getting back into college won't be a problem, but what will I do for a job?

22

I'M SITTING IN my usual spot in the front row at roll call wondering who I'll be assigned with tonight. *Please not Morales...anybody but that prick.* Things quiet down a bit, but I still hear some snickers. Usually a drop in decibels signals the imminent arrival of the watch commander and his entourage.

What's burning? It doesn't smell like tobacco. *Heat! Why do I feel heat? Holy shit!* I look back to see flames licking up at my seat. I jump out of my chair. Someone put a good-size wad of loosely scrunched up newspaper under my chair and lit it on fire. I'm still stomping out the embers when the LT and two sergeants stride briskly through the door.

The sergeants are smiling as they take their seats. The LT remains standing, and the expression on his face shows he isn't pleased. The ferocity in his raspy cadaver voice catches me off guard. "I told you assholes—no more fire in my fucking station! If the brooms (janitors) can't get the scorch marks off that linoleum before our annual inspection, I'm gonna find out who did it this time, and I am gonna burn your ass for destruction of city property. Is that *fucking clear*?" The room goes completely silent as the LT's emaciated figure settles in his chair.

After roll call, my partner introduces himself. "Hi, I'm Aaron Beeman." He offers his hand and a big smile. "I'm the other P-3 on the car. I'll help you check out our equipment."

Officer Beeman is about my height but with a stockier build. His face shares the same pasty complexion as Russell. Maybe it's the contrast of his coal-black facial hair with the blanched color of his skin that makes him look like he needs a shave, or maybe he just stood a little too far away from the razor today. With a stubbled boyish face on a man's body, he is a study in incongruity.

"That little newspaper trick is not unusual. Don't sweat it. It was worse when I was a boot back in sixty-eight." He gives me a schoolboy's grin. "So you worked with Ron your first two nights?"

"Yes, sir."

"A little rough around the edges but a great training officer. You're lucky to have him as your primary TO. Who'd you work with last night?"

"Morales."

"Sticktime? That must have been educational."

I respond with a tight-jawed glare.

Officer Beeman's smile dissolves. "OK. Last night you learned what not to do. Tonight we'll teach you the right way." Reaching the kit room window, my partner grabs the shotgun. "You got enough to carry. I'll get the tube."

Turning his attention to the policeman behind the counter, Aaron says, "Hey, Smitty. The PM watch got a body and gonna be OT. We need a car." (Normally we use the same car as the shift we're relieving, and get the keys from the officers going off duty. We only sign for the car at the kit room.)

The gray-haired permanent light-duty desk officer grabs two sets of keys from one of the cup hooks in the cabinet and slaps them on the counter. "It's a piece of shit, Aaron, but it's the best we got left. Just came back from an A check, so everything should be working."

"Thanks," Aaron says, grabbing the keys. He stuffs one set in his Sam Browne and hands the other to me. I stash my set in my belt and follow Aaron to the parking lot. The already familiar routine of pre-flighting the car and equipment doesn't take long. In a few minutes, we are turning onto Temple. I tell the RTO we are clear.

The unseasonably warm temperatures of the last few nights are gone. Maybe it is the chill in the air. Maybe it's the new moon. Or maybe something inside of me has sped up. It seems there is just enough time for Aaron to walk me through everything.

In between the police work, Aaron's easygoing banter doesn't stop. "I took the last two days at the end of last DP (deployment period) and the first three days at the start this DP. That gave me five days off in a row. Drove the wife and kid up to Oregon to see my in-laws. Had to...couldn't afford to fly. You married?"

"No, sir."

"I got married right after I got back from 'Nam. My daughter was born about a year later." Aaron pulls a photo from his breast pocket and hands it to me.

"She's real pretty," I say. It's my standard response when guys show me photos of their kids. I can't see myself as a husband, much less a father. A wayward emission from a streetlight glistens in Aaron's eye as he slides the photo back into his left breast pocket.

"I got another on the way...made for an interesting drive. Pregnant wife had to go to the bathroom every few miles, and my five-year-old kept asking, 'Are we there yet?' I'm almost glad to be back at work." Aaron tosses a smile my way. "Almost."

"So, I'll be working with Ron most of the time?" I ask.

"Yep. There are supposed to be two P-3s and a boot assigned to every basic car. Only one of us is supposed to be off at a time. Not only does that keep the car covered, it keeps a P-3 with the boot every night. On a night when all three of us are working, you'll be partnered with Ron, and they'll assign me elsewhere...usually to fill in for another A car where both the P-3s are off for some reason. That's what should have happened last night. They should've put you with a P-3 from another car."

Beeman is right, more right than he could know. They should've assigned me with anybody but Morales. I'm starting to realize that working the street, there is a considerable gap between what happens and what is supposed to happen.

When the stream of radio calls slows to a trickle, my partner recites the patrol cop's credo: "A ticket a day keeps the sergeant away." He explains, "Recapping a couple of cites on a slow night, means you don't have to sweat squeezing in a ticket on the busy nights. Besides, you need to learn how to write tickets...not that it's rocket science. Hell, if motor cops can do it, anybody can."

Aaron pulls to the curb facing a four-way stop. He turns off the lights but leaves the motor running. "This is what is known as an *orchard.*" he says. "You could write a whole book of tickets here in no time. Think of it like going into a peach orchard. You wouldn't just grab the first one you saw. You would look around awhile and pick a really sweeeet, juu-ceee one. We'll wait for a real juicy violation."

"Yes, sir. I get it."

Aaron outlines the plan. "I'll approach and get the info from the driver...come back to the car and help you write it. Then you can approach and get the violator to sign. OK?"

"Yes, sir."

Aaron is right. Nobody stops for the stop sign. It only takes a couple of minutes before a late-model Pontiac blasts through the intersection at about forty. Aaron doesn't wait for me to say anything. He flicks on the headlights and smokes the tires accelerating after the violator.

Although Aaron has it floored, the empty stretch between the Pontiac and us is diminishing slowly. We're upward of seventy miles an hour before we really start to gain on him. Our rate of closure increases as the driver of the sedan backs off the gas for a sweeping left turn. Not us. I'm pressed against the door as the tires register their complaint. Closing on the violator, Aaron calls out the license plate. He is almost shouting to be heard over the wind noise.

I repeat the plate as I'm writing it on the same notepad we use to record our calls.

"Check the hot sheet. Maybe we got a roll'n stolen."

I check the list we got at roll call, and tell Aaron it's not there.

"Just 'cause it's not on the sheet, don't mean it ain't hot." Aaron hits the reds and high beams simultaneously. Crimson light floods the interior of the Pontiac.

The driver's head snaps a look in the rearview. The brake lights come on as he heads for the curb.

"The cross street is Scotland," my partner says as he jams the gearshift in park.

I repeat our location out loud, thankful for the critical info. It's almost second nature to turn the radio to full volume, grab my flashlight, and throw the mic out the open window. As I pull my baton out of its holder and step out of the car, something strange happens. It is like I'm having an out-of-body experience watching myself. The surreal effect ends when I reach the right rear quarter panel of the Pontiac Skylark.

The words I heard so many times in the academy echo in my head—*It's the hands that kill you.* My eyes track the driver's hand as he reaches for the glove box. When the only thing he retrieves is the registration, I let go of my holstered revolver and relax a little.

After a brief conversation with the violator, Aaron joins me on the curb next to our car and gives me the driver's story. "The poop-butt says he stopped at the stop sign for three minutes. Says he knows it was three minutes 'cause he was looking at his watch. Says he's good friends with Mayor Sam and is having lunch with him tomorrow at city hall."

"You think he even knows the mayor?" I ask.

Aaron laughs. "I don't believe that story any more than I believe he stopped for the stop sign and looked at his watch for three minutes."

Aaron tells me to take my time filling in all the boxes. He dictates the short blurb that describes the violation. After checking the ticket for errors, he reminds me which copy to give the violator and clears me to approach the driver's window. Again it feels like I'm observing from outside myself. I hear my voice explaining to the violator that his signature is not an admission of guilt, only a promise to appear. I'm surprised how effortlessly my words flow. To my surprise, the violator signs the ticket without hesitation.

After I hand him his copy of the cite, I give him back his driver's license and vehicle registration. The driver smugly drops the paperwork on the seat next to him and tells me, "You just wasted your time, officer. I'll have this ticket fixed tomorrow."

"Thank you for your cooperation and drive safely," I say. Aaron is right. This isn't rocket science.

Aaron heads to a different orchard where he gets his ticket. When we return to patroling, Aaron returns to his storytelling. "Before I came on the job I was working part-time in a grocery store and going to school on the GI Bill. Money was tight, but my wife always found a way to cover our obligations. We were sure my full-time LAPD paycheck would make it easier, but after all the deducts, and without the GI Bill, my wife was finding it even harder to make ends meet."

I'm surprised how comfortable I feel in the police car tonight. The warm air from the heater is easily keeping pace with the cool air encroaching through the open windows. While I don't know the names of the smaller streets, I have memorized the majors, so I'm never in a panic to read a street sign.

Aaron continues, "My wife insisted on tagging along when I went to get fitted for my two city-issued uniforms. She told me she wanted to make sure they fitted me right. But I think she really wanted to be sure I didn't spend money we didn't have." Aaron smiles. "When she saw the price of the metal flashlights, she almost fainted. We both knew we couldn't afford one of those." Aaron looks my way to see if I'm paying attention. "My wife was proud of me graduating from the academy, but I think she was almost more proud of herself. She couldn't wait to show me the flashlight she found at a discount store for only a few bucks. It had a white serrated ring on the head that changed the focus of the beam. Pretty cool actually...the problem was it was made out of bright red plastic. It looked like a big piece of candy."

My partner rubs his left hand through his hair and massages the back of his neck. "If you think they are giving you a ration of shit here in Rampart, you don't know the half of it. The coppers in Seventy-Seventh Division were brutal. They ragged on me something fierce about my candy-red plastic flashlight. At first they called me the Candy Man, and then they shortened it to Candy. Of course that led to another word frequently being appended. Yeah, sometimes I wonder how I made probation with a moniker of Candy-Ass." Talking more to himself than to me, he muses, "A roll of black electrician's tape would have saved me a lot of embarrassment—"

The radio interrupts. "Two-Adam-one of the PM Watch, roger, out to the station."

Hearing our call sign grabs my attention, but I'm befuddled. I haven't broadcast anything, and we're not out to the station.

"Confusing, isn't it?" Aaron gently directs me to a greater state of awareness. "That was the PM watch going EOW. Good that you recognized our call sign. This time of night I still sometimes miss a call. Lots of guys do. Not Ron. Even in a dead sleep, snoring like a lion, he'll somehow hear it. That guy's incredible."

Aaron starts another story. "One night when I was still on probation, my training officer and I stopped a really clean sixty-five Chevrolet Impala with four male usuals in it. It wasn't on the hot sheet, but we had gone code six, since it was obviously more than just a routine traffic stop. We had everyone out of the car in the wall search position...we were still using the wall search back then," he says as a parenthetical aside. "Anyways...just as I go to pat down the driver, the suspects come off the wall like the Fearsome Foursome on a blitz," Aaron turns toward me with a grin on his boyish face, "and yours truly was the QB."

As Aaron expertly guides our cruiser around a car parked haphazardly on a narrow residential street, he continues, "I tried to hold on to the driver, but after the stampede, the only thing I still had a grip on was his torn shirt. My training officer was yelling at me to stay with the driver, who, due to my efforts, was bare from the waist up and trailing the other three. My TO was putting out a foot pursuit broadcast, and the whole world was en route. Of course, I didn't know that at the time."

I wish Aaron were my primary training officer.

"Anyways, the suspects turned into an alley. I rounded the corner just in time to see the driver's bare back disappearing over a wooden fence into somebody's backyard. I grabbed for my flashlight, but the only thing in my pocket was the remnants of the plastic case and two D cell batteries. I jumped the fence. It was even darker in the backyard than in the alley. I couldn't see shit. I heard tires squealing and fumbled my way out front. I got there just in time to see a couple of coppers handcuffing my shirtless suspect in the street."

I can see Aaron is reliving the moment.

"The two cops were none too gently stuffing the shirtless suspect in the backseat of their patrol car when an air unit showed up. The pilot came in at full throttle and pulled into a tight orbit about two hundred feet off the deck. I guess the slapping of the rotors and whine of the turbine had me flashing back to 'Nam. Later, back at the station, everyone wanted to know why I was crouching. When I explained, they thought it was funnier than shit."

Aaron glances my way before continuing his story. "I came out of my crouch when the helicopter's Nightsun lit up the street like a major league ballpark. Just that fast, the air unit's dazzling light shifted from the street to the backyard where I'd been. Despite the roar of the chopper circling well below minimums, I heard sirens and figured somebody must have put out a help call."

I am jolted back to the present when Aaron hits the brakes. A mangy mutt, startled while rummaging the contents of an overturned trashcan, had scampered into our path. My partner's quick reactions are impressive, especially at this time of night.

Aaron continues, "One of the cops who caught my suspect was an old-timer named Nelson. He was a big man who measured up to his nickname, Full. When he recognized me, he got a big shit-eating grin on his face and grabbed the microphone hanging out the window of the nearest police car to put out 'code four—missing officer from the foot pursuit located.'"

I interrupt. "So that's how you came to get your Kel-Lite." I want Aaron to realize the moral of his story hasn't escaped me.

"Yeah, but that's not the half of it. The air unit had shifted its light to the backyard because officers had found another one of the suspects hiding in the bushes back there. A few feet from where they found him, they found a .32 auto."

"Holy shit!" The image of Aaron motionless in the backyard with the suspect aiming the weapon at him from the shadows, gives me a chill.

"Yeah. That's what I said. It turned out the car was a West LA stolen, and University Division robbery detectives later tied the car and the suspects to a two-eleven (robbery) of a liquor store on Santa Barbara Avenue. All things considered, I was really lucky. The very next day I was at the uniform store to buy a Kel-Lite. I didn't know how I was gonna pay for it, but I knew I couldn't afford to be without it. The guy at the uniform store said I could pay him a little each payday. At first I thought he was being nice because of what had happened." Aaron makes eye contact with me. "But I found out they will make the same arrangement for any officer on the LAPD."

The eastern sky is no longer as dark as on the western horizon.

In the station at EOW, I'm en route to the second floor to drop our log in the watch commander's in-box when Aaron stops me in the hall.

My training officer reaches out his hand. "Give it here. I gotta go to court this morning, so I can't go home anyway."

"Thanks." I hand him the paperwork and reverse course toward the locker room. After a couple of steps I do another one-eighty. I call after Aaron who is already at the bottom of the stairs. "Thanks, Aaron...thanks for everything."

"You're welcome," he says over his shoulder, heading up the stairs. "See you tonight at roll call."

23

AFTER ANNOUNCING THE assignments and marking the time book, the watch commander will typically spend fifteen to twenty minutes keeping us abreast of crime trends, wanted suspects, changes in procedures, new regulations, etc. The prescribed repository of this type of information is a clipboard that rotates with the shifts, earning it the descriptive name, the rotator.

The department manual specifies the watch commander shall read each item in the rotator three days in a row. The rationale is to ensure every officer, even those who might have been off for two days, hears the information. A corollary to this imperative is that the majority of cops in roll call are sitting through a recitation they've already heard at least once before. Except for the wanted suspect notices, most of the stuff is the routine nonsense generated by the department's bureaucracy. *Special Orders* are a prime example.

Special Orders are the LAPD's method of disseminating changes to the department manual. Like the policy guide itself, the updates are written in a wearisome style, seemingly designed to defy comprehension under the best of circumstances. When repeated aloud to street cops, especially morning watch cops, the stupefying effects of the genre are magnified substantially.

While a young police lieutenant might labor under the false notion the troops are enraptured by this drivel, Lieutenant Price is under no such illusion. He recognizes the trance-like state of his audience as the inevitable result of reading bureaucratic bullshit to the sleep deprived.

After reading the last of the *Special Orders*, Lieutenant Price departs from his monotone. "All right, listen up. *This is important.*" Instead of reading from the page in front of him, he gives it to us in his own words. "There are a couple of Hollywood Division coppers who are lucky to be alive right now. Seems the assholes have devised a new way of trying to kill LA cops. Last night they put a pipe bomb under a police car while the officers were inside a restaurant having code seven. The bomb squad says the pipe was filled with enough explosives and barbed roofing nails...had it gone off, it would have literally torn the officers to shreds, and killed a bunch of civilians in the restaurant as well."

The sound of guys collectively readjusting their positions in the unpadded chairs segues the LT's description of the particulars. "The trigger for the device is an ordinary clothespin with wires attached to thumbtacks stuck in the pincher ends. The suspects attach the clothespin to the underside of the car. When the clothespin is dislodged, the thumbtacks come together and whammy. Last night, when the officers backed out of their parking spot, the clothespin twisted as it came loose. It twisted just enough so the thumbtacks missed touching." He holds his forefinger and thumb an eighth of an inch apart. "We came that close to having two dead cops, and who knows how many civilian casualties."

The room is awash with profanity as the watch commander continues, "So...from now on we're going check under our cars every time we return to them. I'm not just talking about coming out of code seven. If you've been away from your patrol car for any reason, check under it when you come back. Use your flashlight. Last night the assholes disguised the device by placing it inside one of those large plastic trash bags. If you see anything under your car, a trash bag or anything unusual...back off and call the station. Remember, don't use the radio. It can trigger the device. Landline L ninety (the station's call sign) and we'll get the bomb squad out there ASAP. In the meantime, we'll clear a one-block perimeter around the thing."

The lieutenant lights up another Pall Mall. "This goes for the station, too. Check your car every time before you get in. Desk personnel are going to be checking all the unassigned cars on a regular basis. And don't forget...the assholes know the cars in our lots belong to cops, so check your personal vehicle at EOW before you head home this morning. Not just today, from now on. Check it every time." The LT ends with his usual, "All right, let's go out there and relieve the PM watch."

My first official act with my new flashlight is shining it under the police car, looking for a bomb.

Ron quips, "Finally got you a kill light, huh?"

"Actually it's a Prolight. I would a got a Kel-Lite, but they were out."

"Can I see it?"

"Sure." I hand it to my TO.

He hefts it in his right hand, and then smacks his left palm. "That'll work."

Compared to Aaron, Ron has not exactly been a Chatty Cathy, except for his ramblings trying to keep himself awake. His communications are usually direct, and job related. Blunt is more like it. Still, he has his moments. We aren't even out of the parking lot when Ron asks, "Know why they call this a radio car?"

Before I can say anything, he answers his own question. "Because we handle radio calls. Mostly anyway. Oh yeah, occasionally we handle station calls, usually for things like death notifications, bomb threats, and sensitive stuff they don't want to go out over the air."

Where is he going with this? I know I didn't miss a call because the frequency is on standby while A-89 runs a suspect for warrants.

Ron continues, "What do we call it? Working uniform? Working a black-and-white?"

Realizing his questions are rhetorical, I relax a little.

"We call it working patrol. That's because when we're not chasing the radio, we are supposed to be patroling our area, looking for the bad guys." He glances my way. "Notice how slow I go when we're patroling? Know why?"

He answers his own questions again. "Because any faster than twenty-five...you can't see shit! You won't believe the number of times cops have driven right by a crime in progress. A few years ago I handled a robbery at a mom-and-pop on Beverly Boulevard. When we got there, we found the clerk bound and gagged on the floor. As soon as I pulled the duct tape off, the clerk started asking why we had waited so long."

Ron lights another cigarette. "The clerk had seen three police cars pass by while he was tied up on the floor. He thought we were all a bunch of cowards for not coming in sooner. I kept telling him we were the only car on scene, but he was so pissed off he wouldn't believe me. I understood his frustration, especially considering the robbers had pumped a couple of rounds into the owner before heading out the door." Ron takes a drag on his Marlboro. "Shit. If I'd have been the clerk, I'd have been seriously pissed off, too."

Ron groans a little as he readjusts his position behind the wheel. "Of course nobody admitted to driving by the store during the robbery. Not that I blame them. Hell, if it had been me, I wouldn't have said shit, either. Imagine how all those cops felt? They didn't see what was going on because they were driving too damned fast and/or not paying a-fuck-n-ten-shun. So why am I telling you this?"

Ron glances at me as he answers his own question. "Because you are going to be driving soon." His eyes are outside the car again. "And when you do, I am telling you right now, unless we are responding to a call, or we have some other damn good reason, you shall keep your speed below twenty-five miles per hour. Is that clear?"

"Yes, sir."

At around 4:00 a.m. the radio dies, and a quiet comes over the streets like an invisible snowfall. Even the normally well-traveled avenues are nearly empty. I'm struggling to stay awake. I'm glad Ron is driving..

Ron is fighting to stay awake, too, and decides we should get a cup. He doesn't have to worry about stepping on anybody because the frequency is dead. He just grabs the mic and starts talking. "Two-Adam-one requests Adam-forty-three meet us on tac-two."

The RTO's voice shows she is as bored as we are. "Two-A-forty-three, meet two-A-one on tac-two."

The frequencies are marked on the radio, but it is always better to keep your eyes outside the car. Ron switches the center knob on the radio all the way to the left, then back one click. This is the position for tac-two, the tactical frequency we use to talk car-to-car. Ron arranges to meet the other car for coffee.

I expect we are en route to a Winchell's or some generic version thereof. But when we arrive, all I see are two police cars with four officers standing in the typical jaunty street cop pose, one hand resting on a service revolver and the other holding a cigarette or cup of coffee. Ron parks on the sidewalk. He gets out and heads toward a stainless steel cart on a concrete pad adjacent to the street corner. Despite the cold temps, the paunchy proprietor behind the cart is wearing only a sleeveless T-shirt and a dirty white apron. Fortyish, unshaven, with mussed hair, he looks like he just rolled out of bed.

"What'll it be?" the swarthy, disheveled man asks my partner.

"Coffee."

"How you take it?"

"Like my women...hot and black," Ron replies.

The man pours.

My partner grabs the Styrofoam cup filled with dark steaming liquid and heads toward the group of blue suits.

It is my turn.

The scruffy proprietor demands, "What'll it be?"

When I tell him hot chocolate, he shakes his head and calls toward the group, "Hey, where'd you get this guy? He's asking for hot cocoa."

He turns his attention back to me. "Kid, all we got here is coffee."

"That'll be fine."

Being careful not to spill the hot black liquid, I join the others, feeling like a fifth grader in short pants walking into the senior prom. I take a sip and scald my lips and tongue. *Shit! I didn't know you could get water this hot.*

A burly P-3 nicknamed Wrap directs a remark to my partner. "Hey, Ron. Remember Billy Sears...he's work'n the bomb squad now. He says the SLA (Symbionese Liberation Army) are the assholes responsible for the pipe bomb. Says they've been ambushing cops and blowing up shit in the Bay Area for years...Guess they got tired of the dreary, depressing San Francisco weather. Thought they'd take themselves a vacation in sunny Southern California." He takes a noisy sip of his java. "And figured they'd keep in practice by trying to blow up a couple of LA's finest."

A young P-2 everyone calls Samolian chimes in, "Fucking cowards! Come down here and try to kill us with bombs instead of facing us straight up with guns."

Reynolds's response is immediate. "The Black Panthers tried that shit a bunch of times with LAPD. They came out second best every time...and you know what they say about coming out second best in a gunfight."

The laughter subsides when one of the officers with P-3 stripes, but only one hash mark, changes the subject. He asks my partner if he ever worked anything other than patrol.

"I've spent my whole career in uniform," Ron says. "But technically not all of it in patrol. I worked traffic and rode motors for a while, too." He takes a drag off his cigarette. "As the saying goes, there are just two kinds of motor officers...those who have gone down, and those who haven't gone down *yet*." An involuntary wince scrunches up his face. "I didn't stay in the second category very long." This brings another chorus of laughter.

Ron is in his element. "Although riding motors was a lot of fun, after the second time I went down, I realized it wasn't for me. I need four wheels to keep me healthy." After a quick sip of coffee my partner continues, "It was a great assignment though. I especially liked working deuce watch. My partner and I had our own booking policy. If they were drunker than we were, then they were going to jail. And believe me, we never booked any hummers. I never once had a low blow (cop slang for a DUI whose breath test isn't over the legal limit). Everybody we hooked up was good and drunk."

Sam Samolian remarks, "I wish I had a little something to fortify this coffee right now. I can't wait for EOW. I think I'll hit the Short Stop (a dive of a bar frequented by cops) on the way home."

"No shit, Sam. It would be news if you *didn't* hit the Short Stop."

Back in our cruiser after our coffee break, I remark to Ron, "I figured out Reynolds's nickname."

"Yeah, Reynolds Wrap is a natural."

"Why do they call that P-2 Sam Samolian?"

"Samolian is slang for a buck. If you ever go drink'n with him... Sam will tell you he only has a buck on him."

I couldn't even imagine going to a bar after working all night, but there are lots of guys like Sam Samolian who do it almost every day.

When EOW finally rolls around, I just want to go home and get in bed. But as I grab my helmet bag from the trunk, the sergeant checking in the watch tells me I'm to report to Sergeant Wilson before going home. Everyone knows Sergeant Wilson. He's the beef sergeant, the one who handles most of the complaints. He finds me in the hallway on my way to the locker room and tells me to meet him in his office after I've changed.

Everyone in the locker room is giving me advice.

"Don't say shit!"

Another cops says, "Don't roll over. "

"And remember...you can't remember!"

Sergeant Wilson leads me into a small interview room, tells me to have a seat, closes the door, and sits down across from me. Pulling out a yellow legal tablet, he says, "First of all, let me explain this is formal one-eighty-one stemming from an arrest you and your partner made the other night." (Bureaucracies like the LAPD can't just call a form by its name. They have to number the piece of paper, too. The personnel complaint form in those days was numbered 1.81. In the LAPD lexicon of the day, the entire complaint process was most frequently referred to as a one-eighty-one.)

Sergeant Wilson continues, "We are only concerned with the arrest. We will not be investigating the circumstances surrounding your being at the chicken stand, as there are no allegations of an unauthorized code seven or gratuities."

I hope the sergeant doesn't see my emotions boiling over. As pissed-off as I was at Morales that night, I am even angrier now. Sergeant Wilson begins with the preliminaries. He establishes my identity, my assignment, and my partner for the evening. He hands me a copy of the report, then quickly gets to the meat of the matter.

"Do you recognize this arrest report?"

"Yes, sir."

"Do you recognize the handwriting on the narrative of this report as your writing?"

"Yes, sir. It is my writing."

"OK, so let's get to what happened. Did you see the subject, Jose Antonio Gonzalez, kick your partner?"

"Yes, sir."

"Did you see any provocation for the subject kicking your partner?"

"No, sir."

"OK. So what happened after the subject kicked Officer Morales?"

"The subject started running away."

"And did Officer Morales give chase?"

"Yes, sir."

"And what did you do?"

"I went in foot pursuit of the subject, too."

"OK. So you kept your partner and the subject in sight?"

Up to this point, I've been pissed-off because Officer Morales and Sergeant Arnhardt put me in a position where I'm going to have to lie about seeing Morales hit the subject with his baton. But now I face a moral hazard of my own making. I made the tactical decision to veer to the left of the restaurant in a misguided attempt to cut off the subject. It was a violation of a tactical doctrine drilled into me at the academy—*never split up from your partner*. It was my mistake and my mistake alone. If I'm going to lie about seeing the use of force, why not simply lie about my own violation of policy and avoid the repercussions?

My delay prompts Sergeant Wilson to repeat the question, and emphasize the policy implications for me. "So you followed your partner's path as you joined the foot pursuit."

"Initially...yes. But when I saw the subject and my partner disappear behind the restaurant, I thought I could cut them off by going around to the left of the fast-food place."

"I see. So even though you knew policy requires you stay with your partner, you elected to separate."

"I didn't see it as splitting up from my partner, I thought I was actually going to join up with him sooner. I didn't realize there was a Dumpster and chain-link fence behind the restaurant. Believe me, I now have a much deeper understanding of the wisdom of the policy."

"OK, so what did you see after you got over the fence?"

"I saw the subject on the ground with my partner standing over him."

"Did you see your partner strike the subject?

"No, sir."

"Did your partner have his baton?"

"Yes, sir."

"Did you have your baton?"

"Yes, sir."

"Did you at any time strike the subject with your baton?"

"No, sir."

"Did your partner have his flashlight with him?"

"I don't know."

"Did you see your partner hit the subject with his flashlight?"

"No, sir."

"Did you have your flashlight with you?

"No, sir."

"Why not...ah, strike that. OK. So when you caught up to the subject and Officer Morales, what happened next?"

"I used a felony-prone technique to securely handcuff the subject's hands behind his back."

"Did you strike the subject at any time during the handcuffing?"

"No, sir."

"You were not driving, correct? Your partner drove. So, you rode in the backseat with the subject, correct?"

"Correct."

"Did you strike the subject while en route to the station?"

"No, sir."

"OK. So I guess we should sum this up. Did you strike the subject at any time during or subsequent to the arrest?"

"No, sir."

"And you don't have anything further to add...correct?"

"No, sir. Ah...nothing."

"OK. You are free to go, but I'm giving you a direct order not to discuss this case with anyone other than me or another supervisor investigating this matter. Specifically, you are not to discuss this matter with your partner that night, Officer Morales, or any of the other officers, including your training officers. Is that clear?"

"Yes, sir."

Walking out of the interview room, I'm fuming. The last person I want to talk to about this is Morales, but I would like to run the whole thing by Aaron. Actually I would really like Ron's insight, but regardless of what the sergeant said, I could never approach him on this.

On the way home, I keep going over the whole scenario. It was stupid of me to have copped out on myself for my tactical mistake, but strangely I feel better about telling the truth on that part.

A lot of other things come into focus as I lie in bed trying to fall asleep. The interview was carefully crafted to avoid the extracurricular stuff that went on back in the jail. And by not mentioning the chow run, the issue of getting food at a discount in violation of department policy was neatly avoided, too. A whole bunch of people would get roped into that one.

Then it hits me. Morales had collected money from everybody, but he never handed over any cash for the food. Morales ripped everyone off. Damn! He is even more of an asshole than I thought. He isn't just a heavy-handed, lying SOB…he's a thief!

24

AFTER ROLL CALL, Ron tells me that he's keeping books tonight. At first I think he is joking. I've only been out of the academy two weeks. Normally it's at least a month before a boot gets behind the wheel. I'm not ready. But my self-assessment isn't part of the equation. My TO says I am driving—so I'm driving. Still, I'd be a liar if I said I wasn't stoked. Just the prospect of piloting this 1972 American Motors Matador with its 401 cubic inch V-8 bolted to a Torque-Command transmission, is exhilarating.

As I'm preflighting the car, Ron says, "Driving a police car isn't the same as any other kind of driving, and it's not something you can learn sitting in the passenger seat. Besides, I can't drive and sleep at the same time." He gets a wry look on his face. "And me driving every night is cutting into my beauty sleep. That's something I can't afford." His smile disappears. "Although I'm keeping books, that doesn't mean I'm doing the writing. Except for the log, you will write all the reports. I don't need practice…you do. And remember what I told you; unless you have a damn good reason, keep it under twenty-five."

To this point in the shift, things have gone well. Ron has only yelled at me to slow down a couple of times. I'm on the brakes almost stopped at a red light when I see a car coming downhill from the right. The light is yellow for him, and it's obvious he isn't going to make it. With his speed and momentum, there's no way he's going to be able to stop, either. The sixty-three Chevy bottoms out and is trailing sparks as it barrels through the intersection against the red.

I want to hit the gas immediately, since the light is now green for me, but it is green for the opposing traffic, too. My right hand fumbles to find the toggle for the emergency lights. The delay is critical. As soon as my hand finds the switch I'm on the gas, but so is the car on the opposite side of the intersection. *Shit!* I jam on the brakes and bring the wheel back to center just in time to avoid a collision. The bewildered driver of the other car turns his head and stares at me as his car passes within inches.

Safely past the other car, I hammer the accelerator and the 255 horses respond. The violator's taillights are getting small in the distance. I am surprised the guy hasn't made a run for it, or at the very least, made a couple of quick turns.

When I close the distance and hit the reds, the driver obediently pulls to the curb. Parking our black-and-white in the offset position behind the violator, I slam the gearshift into park. My eyes stay focused on the violator as I grab my flashlight and baton while throwing open my door. Our bright lights make it difficult for anyone in the car to see me as I approach. I can see the upper portion of the interior, but everything below the level of the windows is obscured by darkness. From the movement of his shoulders, I can tell the driver is doing something. I can't see his hands.

When my partner taps the right rear quarter panel, the driver turns toward the sound, and away from me. I take the opportunity and approach to where my flashlight beam can penetrate the shadows. When I see there's nothing in the lone occupant's hands, I relax my grip on my pistol.

"Driver's license and registration."

"Sorry, Officer. The hill…I couldn't stop. I'm just coming back from my girlfriend's place and it's late…and I gotta work tomorrow—"

"License and registration," I repeat.

My eyes follow the violator's hand as he retrieves the registration from the glove box. After he gives me the paperwork, I tell him, "It'll just be a few minutes."

I know the adrenalin tremble in my fingers hasn't escaped my partner's notice. To everyone else I look like any other cop standing on the sidewalk with my flashlight tucked under my arm writing a ticket. After the violator is on his way, I park at the curb so Ron can log the citation. As he writes, he says, "Ain't as easy as it looks."

"You're right, sir."

"Of course I'm right. Had you T/A'd...your ass would be grass. You'd probably have to find a new job, and I'd have to answer for why I let you drive after only a couple of weeks. But you didn't. Keep it that way."

"Yes, sir."

Since the radio died about an hour ago, I've been meandering through the side streets to further familiarize myself with the area. I haven't heard a peep out of Ron for a while. When I glance at my training officer, he is wedged between the passenger door and the bench seat with his arms crossed and his hands buried in his jacket. His eyes are closed and his chin is on his chest.

I make a right turn onto the main drag from the residential street. Suddenly things don't look familiar.

Ron's voice asks, "Did you get a transfer?"

I take another quick glance at my partner. His eyes are still closed.

"Why we are patroling Hollywood Division?" he asks.

"My mistake, sir."

I flip a U-turn, trying to figure out how he knew. To avoid accidentally leaving the division again, I decide it is better to avoid the residential streets and spend more time on the major streets. But keeping it under twenty-five driving on the wide thoroughfares presents its own challenge. The tendency is to keep up with traffic. Without realizing it, I'm doing forty. A blow from Ron's baton causes my right hand to retract from the wheel. Ron's baton continues smacking the steering wheel.

"Slow the fuck down!" Ron grumbles. "I told you not over twenty-five unless you have a damn good reason!"

My hands dance on the wheel to avoid Ron's baton. His one-handed drum roll doesn't stop until we are at idle speed. I knew my TO was a little *rough around the edges*, as Aaron would say, but this is bullshit. He is completely out of his mind—100 percent psycho! Rubbing the back of my right hand on my pant leg to ease the soreness, I've made up my mind. If he tries that shit again, we are going to the mat.

Barely over idle speed, my eyes have too much time to just watch traffic. I see a dog slink under a chain-link fence, and freeze. What's moving the slider on that porch? Could it be the wind? There is no wind. A cat springs off the slider, scurries across the yard and disappears. Mystery solved.

• • •

It's somewhere after four in the morning, a time when the temperature is at its lowest, my mind is at its slowest, and there isn't even a hint of the dawn on the horizon. I'm only slightly more awake than my partner, who is snoring like a lion. The last time I was in bed, I managed only a few fitful hours of sleep by draping woolen blankets over my apartment's windows.

I'm idling northbound on Stadium Way, a wide stretch of asphalt just around the corner from the police academy. The excitement of my first night driving a police car has long since dissipated. I'm struggling to stay awake.

"Turn right at the next intersection," Ron says.

Is he talking in his sleep? My sluggish brain tries in vain to come up with a reason he wants me to turn. Have I missed a radio call again? I glance at the note pad where we write down our calls—it's blank.

My partner's eyes are still closed. Even if they were open, he couldn't have possibly seen anything up in the hills, not in the dark. He has surprised me before with his powers of observation, but he always says something. *Why hasn't he said something this time?*

My preference would be to stay on the wide, well-illuminated lanes of Stadium Way and not venture onto the narrow, dark environs of Elysian Park Road. Yet it never crosses my mind not to do as I'm told. I make the turn. The headlights splash in an arc, briefly illuminating the oleanders and weeds that mark the boundary of the pavement. I have barely straightened out the wheels before I'm again cranking hard right to stay on the crumbling stretch of asphalt as it marches up the side of the ravine. After we crest the hill, Ron tells me to turn off the lights.

Shit! My weary eyes are already aching from the strain of trying to see. *How the hell am I supposed to drive on this inky twisting path without lights?* Still, my left hand automatically extends and punches off the lights.

"Pull over there and stop," my partner says, directing me to a dirt apron off the side of the road with an unobstructed view of downtown. Our cruiser is not completely stopped before Ron has rolled himself out of the passenger door and is walking up to the edge. With the same well-practiced ease as he alighted from the vehicle, Ron has unzipped his fly and is happily pissing over the side. The view is phenomenal. I get out and join him in relieving myself over the cliff.

"This is one of my favorite piss spots," Ron muses. "From here I can piss on city hall."

I have to admit it certainly feels like it. In the cool predawn darkness, the brightly lit city hall dominates the scene. Its classic shape stands out in relief against the dark montage of old and new Los Angeles. For years, earthquake regulations limited the height of buildings, and kept city hall as the tallest structure in Los Angeles.

Eventually building technology advanced, and skyscrapers were permitted. But from here, all the higher, more modern buildings are in the background. Not only are the taller structures in the background, the lighting of the modern glass-and-steel buildings is demure compared to the exterior floodlights reflecting off the concrete tower that is city hall.

It is nothing short of surreal. When I was only five years old, sipping cocoa in the living room of my grandparents' house in Chicago, that same image filled the small, almost oval black-and-white TV screen at the beginning of every episode of the *Dragnet* TV show.

Standing on the edge of Chavez Ravine, the same tower that dominates the cityscape glistening on the badge on my chest, feels like destiny.

25

THE NEXT NIGHT I'm back to keeping books. I figure Ron realized I'm not ready to drive yet, but to my surprise, he says from now on we will alternate. Right out of roll call, Ron heads for his favorite taco joint to get a Special Quesadilla and a cup of coffee. Unless we have a priority call or have to back somebody up, this is our routine. My partner is as interested in a lady working the counter as the food.

A police car is a pretty intimate environment. Despite Ron's authoritarian style, I have already learned a lot about him. His wife suffers from depression. She has even been confined a couple of times. Working the overnight shift isn't just a preference for Ron. It's more like a necessity. Morning watch usually finds him home in time to get the kids off to school. On the other end, he doesn't have to be out the door until after his kids are supposed to be in bed. *No wonder he drinks.*

The woman working the window of the fast-food joint flirts with my partner. He eats it up, and I don't mean the food. It can't be the way she looks. She is in her midthirties, short and substantially overweight. To my eye, her face is generic Central American with a mottled complexion. Of course, my crusty TO isn't exactly a dashing figure, either. The sleep deprivation inherent in all these years on mornings has multiplied the effects of aging, entirely erasing any remnants of youthful attractiveness he once possessed.

While normally I would think poorly of a married man acting this way, knowing the reality of his home life, I don't begrudge him this simple pleasure. I'm content to stand outside our police car listening to the radio and sipping my 7-Up while they share each other's entreaties with some amount of privacy. My mind has just started to wander when the link comes on the air with a hotshot.

"All Rampart units and two-Adam-one, two-Adam-one, a four fifteen gang fight with chains and knives, approximately thirty involved, handle code two." There is no address given, just an intersection. I only recognize one of the cross streets.

I grab the mic and acknowledge the call. I start to write the particulars on the notepad as I slide into the passenger seat. Although my partner was pretty engrossed in his conversation with the quesadilla lady, by the time I'm done writing, he's back in the car.

"What we got?"

I repeat the call verbatim.

"Sounds like someone's been watching too much *Westside Story* on late-night TV," he says as we lurch out of the driveway.

The RTO's voice blares through the speaker, and my hand strikes like a viper at the volume nob. I forgot to turn down the radio. "Sorry, sir."

Ron doesn't comment on my boot mistake. Instead, he explains the call is in Frog Town, a narrow strip of land bordered by the Golden State Freeway on the south and the Los Angeles River on the north. It gets its nickname from the frogs that come out of the river and invade the place every spring. Just another piece of trivia I picked up from Ron during those slow predawn hours spent trying to stay awake on patrol.

"I wonder where A-3 is," Ron muses out loud. The call is in A-3's area. If they were on the air they would have been assigned. With

A-3 off the air, and because Frog Town is geographically isolated, it is very unlikely anyone else will be rolling.

Ron accelerates to about seventy miles an hour before he is on the binders to make the ninety-degree right turn onto Riverside Drive. He gets back on the throttle out of the turn. Soon he has to stop accelerating, not because the turns are tight, but because the roadway is a washboard.

This portion of Riverside Drive is comprised of oddly shaped sections of concrete, framed and finished one at a time by hand during the Depression. Not only are the cement blocks slightly uneven in height, the slabs have migrated over the years, leaving some substantial gaps. Filling the spaces with tar may stop the weeds, but it does little to moderate the rough ride. The car's suspension struggles to dampen the jarring impacts. The vibration enhances the sensation of speed.

Approaching a red light at Stadium Way, I'm watching for cross traffic. "Clear right!" I shout to be heard over the wind noise and staccato sounds of our tires as they pound the roadway. These words are not of my own choosing. There have been some horrible accidents when the passenger officer's choice of words to describe the traffic conditions led to confusion. The classic is when the passenger said, "No!" but the driver thought he said, "Go!" Consequently, policy requires you either say, "clear" or "not clear."

Ron is back on the throttle as we pass under the Golden State Freeway. Ahead is another light for traffic exiting the freeway. Although the signal is green for us, I'm watching the off-ramp.

Ron brakes at the limits of traction. At the last second, he lets up on the brake pedal and cranks the steering wheel to the left. Back on the binders, he extinguishes our lights as we enter the housing tract. Down to about ten miles per hour, he disables our brake lights, too, by keeping pressure on the toggle switch below the left side of the dash. It's spring-loaded as a fail-safe to prevent officers from inadvertently driving around without brake lights.

"That's it up ahead," Ron says.

I broadcast we're code six and adjust the radio volume so I can just barely hear the RTO when she acknowledges we are at scene.

The rock roof houses that line the street are all dark, and the cars on both sides of the street are covered with dew. Everything is eerily quiet. Ron tells me to put out a four. Still scanning the scene for anything out of the ordinary, I pick up the mic. "Two-Adam-one, show a code four. No evidence of four-fifteen group. Requesting further."

In this case, my code four tells other units who might still be rolling that they can cancel their response. Requesting further is the LAPD's terminology for someone at Communications Division to call back the phone number to see if they can contact the PR (person reporting) for more information. (There was no caller ID in those days.) While we wait on our request, my partner continues patroling the area, still blacked out. He explains he is avoiding the streets that dead-end at the river.

Since we received the call, I have been envisioning arriving on the scene to find thirty or more suspects actually fighting with chains and knives. When we got here and found nothing, I was both disappointed and relieved at the same time. I give whispering voice to my thoughts. "I still can't believe how many calls are just the result of some weirdo's hyperactive imagination."

"Yeah, most of these bullshit calls are just some sick son of a bitch getting his jollies by jerking off the cops, but some are setups."

Setup is the police vernacular for an ambush. Militant groups like the Black Panthers, the Weather Underground, and the Symbionese Liberation Army have been ambushing law enforcement for years. Their usual tactic is to lure officers to a particular location by stiffing in a phony call. While officers from other agencies have been killed in these attacks, to date every attempt against LAPD has failed. One of the most famous failed attempts occurred in Wilshire Division. Several Black Panthers tried to assassinate two young cops. Surprised, outnumbered, and outgunned, even after being wounded multiple times, these two valiant officers kept fighting until they had killed their assailants in what remains one of the LAPD's most heroic triumphs.

Realizing some dedicated hate monger might be eyeing me down a gun barrel at this moment makes the damp night air feel colder. While the danger quotient is potentially very large, there are too many unknowns to solve the equation, which limits our options for mitigating the risk. Keeping our heads on a swivel, avoiding the dead-end streets, while staying in motion—is about all we can do. What surprises me is my attitude. I'm less concerned about my personal safety than I am about disgracing myself. I'd rather get shot, even killed, than to let down my fellow officers, especially those who have paid the ultimate price.

The RTO puts a familiar finish on the situation. "Two-Adam-one, there's no answer at the call back. No further."

While we raced to the call, my body secreted the same hormones as when I was lined up on the football field for the opening kickoff, but tonight the ball was never put in play. Without that first tackle to dissipate the tension, my nervous energy remains. Slapping my notebooks shut after completing my log entry, I am surprised at the exuberance in my voice. "I can't believe they are paying me to do this shit!"

Ron takes a drag on his Marlboro. With a knowing, almost evil smile on his face, he snickers. "Don't you worry, kid. You'll earn your pay...this fuck'n city doesn't give noth'n away."

26

WE HANDLE A couple of additional routine radio calls, but instead of clearing after our last one, Ron tells me to put us out to the station. He parks under the overhang near the gas pumps and disappears through the back door, saying something about a sergeant, a transfer, and Harbor Division.

I double-check all my log entries to be certain I have my abbreviations right. Yes, the anal retentive LAPD has its own list of approved abbreviations. If a supervisor finds an unapproved abbreviation in my log, he will kick it back. I double-check my reporting districts, too. Like most cops, I've enclosed a copy of the divisional RD map in plastic and taped it onto the flap of my notebook.

I'm pretty satisfied I have all my paperwork in order, when my partner plops back into the driver's seat. Still curious about his comment, I ask what he meant about transferring a sergeant to the harbor.

"I had to take a shit," Ron says.

I can't help but laugh. Rough around the edges is an understatement; probably a functioning alcoholic, irreverent as hell...but he has his moments. As soon as we clear, we get a call, another family dispute. I've probably handled more family disputes than any other type of call, and it's the only type of call I'd just as soon not get.

Officially, our mission on dispute calls is to "keep the peace." The book answer sounds easy enough, but in reality, the protagonists usually await our arrival before really laying into each other. So instead of having a calming effect, our presence usually does just the opposite. Besides, what the heck am I going to say to these people? I'm only twenty-two years old and never even been married.

The address is an old redbrick apartment complete with sash windows and black wrought iron fire escapes. Ron parks in the red zone, which he describes as "police parking." This time of night, it's the only part of the curb not jammed with basic transportation vehicles. We lock our car and head up the concrete steps toward the entrance. When Ron pulls open the door, a warm rancid odor contrasts sharply with the cool outside air.

Ron explains, "Even if the building has an elevator, it's best to take the stairs. Being stuck in an elevator is a tactical nightmare. Too many cops who were too lazy to climb the stairs have died in a barrage of bullets when the elevator doors opened. It happens more back East where there are a lot of multiple-story apartments. Still good tactics are good tactics, and the price of bad tactics is too high."

This place is a walk-up, so we don't have a choice. We head up the stairs en route to apartment 214. The smell of the mildewed threadbare carpets, stale urine, rotted food, embedded cigarette smoke, and other noxious odors is stifling. I can't wait to get out of here.

We deploy to either side of the door and wait. We are still listening for signs of a struggle inside the apartment, when the door of the unit behind Ron opens slowly. An older woman in a tattered nightgown and a headscarf beckons with her hand and a whisper. Ron motions for me to stay put while he takes a few steps down the hall.

After he returns from his hushed conversation with the neighbor, Ron brings me up to speed. The neighbor is the one who called. The woman who lives in 214 had come to the neighbor's apartment earlier in the evening, telling the usual tale of domestic discord. When the yelling started up again around three, the older woman decided to call.

Apparently, the busybody feels entitled to watch and keeps her door ajar. Ron scowls at her and orders her to close her door. Only after the PR finally acquiesces, does Ron direct me to knock. Standing on the right side of the door with my flashlight in my left hand, I'm about to rap on the wooden door when I notice Sergeant Shaw emerge from the stairway. I know he isn't here to see how well my veteran partner handles a family dispute.

Eventually, the door opens a crack, and a mousy woman in her midtwenties leans around the door. As she is telling us she didn't call, we hear a man's slurred voice snarling in the background, "Tell 'em go away."

When Ron pushes the door open, we can see the woman is plenty pregnant. Her dirty brown hair covers her face as she hangs her head and explains her husband has been "drink'n and fuss'n at her all day." Questioned by my partner, she says there is no one except her husband and their kids in the apartment. Asked if there are any guns in the house, she shakes her head no. It's business as usual.

The living room is to the right of the entrance. On the other side of the short entry hall there's a bedroom. Straight ahead is the kitchen. After a quick check reveals no one in the bedroom, Ron starts to talk with the wife in the kitchen. He directs me to get an FI on the husband, who is slouching on a filthy brown sofa in the living room.

The inebriated husband leans back on the middle cushion of the corduroy couch muttering obscenities under his breath. He eye-fucks me as I enter the room. A couple of empty beer cans are scattered on the floor. A partially consumed can of Brew 102 sits on the cheap skinny-legged coffee table in front of the husband. Condensation on the outside of the can shows how much is left.

Next to the partially consumed sixteen-ounce can of beer is a large ashtray overflowing with cigarette butts and a few half-eaten strawberries. Next to the ashtray is a dinner plate with a depleted mound of fruit. The remaining strawberries are littered with ashes and cigarette butts. Obviously the drunk confused the plate of fresh fruit for the ashtray more than once.

I assume the "position of interrogation," facing the suspect across the coffee table. I keep my left leg forward to keep my gun hip away from the suspect. Behind me, in a set of bunk beds, three kids pretend to be asleep. The stale odor of beer and the musty smell of cigarettes mingling with the sweet smell of the strawberries put a bad taste in my mouth. Worse yet is the disgusting sight of several cockroaches scurrying through the strawberries. I imagine the kids brushing the ashes and cockroaches off the strawberries before eating them.

I pull a field interview card out of my breast pocket as I ask the husband, "You have a driver's license or other ID?"

"I ain't bother'n nobody. She din't call. So what the fuck you gotta hassle me for?"

"I just need to see some ID."

"She din't call. What the fuck you here for?"

"A neighbor called. We are here now...so let's just see some ID."

The thin, thirty-something Caucasian is wearing a tan plaid shirt and dark brown pants. Like his wife, his dirty limp hair falls in his face when he bends forward to look under the sofa cushion on his left. When he raises the cushion, I can see a wallet. For some reason, instead of retrieving the billfold, he lets the sofa cushion back down. Maybe he can't see because of the hair in his face. Or maybe he's too drunk. When he leans back, his eyes meet mine and he again curses me under his breath. "Motherfucker."

"Just get your ID out of your wallet. The sooner I get your ID, the sooner we get out of here."

He leans forward again, but this time he grabs the cushion on his right.

Just like he confused the ashtray with the dinner plate, this guy is too drunk to remember where he stashed his wallet. Still, it strikes me as strange that he is using his left hand to lift the cushion on his right side. He bends forward a little more trying to look under the cushion. When he lifts the worn corduroy sofa cushion higher, I see something under the cushion. He starts to reach under the cushion with his right hand.

Holy shit! He's reaching for a gun. In an instant I'm in my two-hand shooting stance with my arms extended, the barrel of my revolver pointed at the suspect's chest. My finger is exerting smooth steady pressure on the trigger. A fraction of an ounce more will drop the hammer.

"Don't move! Don't fucking move!" I shout.

The man's filthy hand stops just inches from the pistol. He straightens up a little as he turns his head to look at me. The kids in the bunk beds behind me are screaming, "Don't shoot my daddy! Don't shoot my daddy!" I'm not taking my eyes off the guy's hand, but in my mind's eye I can see my partner and the sergeant are near panic, convinced the boot is going to kill a poor drunk son of a bitch in his own living room, just for lipping off. The inebriated husband apparently thinks better of it and starts to withdraw his hand.

I take my finger off the trigger as I bring my revolver to my right hip. Still pointing the weapon at the suspect with my right hand, my left hand is free to grab the suspect's gun. I shuffle forward. Just as I extend my left hand to grab the gun, the asshole makes another move toward his pistol.

Without a thought, I shove the coffee table forward with my left leg. The sharp edge of the table digs into the man's shins and distracts him long enough for me to snatch the .22-caliber Hi-Standard Western-Style revolver from under the sofa cushion. When I step back, Ron is there to grab the suspect's gun from my trembling hand. I holster my revolver and take a deep breath.

The husband continues to curse me in low tones. All he wants is to know how I knew he was going for the gun. He's oblivious to the enormity of the situation. Either that, or to him it really isn't that big of a deal.

Things quickly calm down. The kids go back to pretending to be asleep. My partner renews his conversation with the wife, but with some added skepticism, since she clearly lied when she said there were no guns in the house.

I get the husband's identification, and the sergeant goes downstairs and runs him for warrants via the police radio. We can't run a gun via the radio, so the sergeant uses the neighbor's phone to call the station.

It's definitely this asshole's lucky night. He didn't get shot. He doesn't have any warrants, and the gun is actually registered to him. There is nothing left to do. Sergeant Shaw pulls me aside and tells me I did a good job. He tells me he's going to write it up in his log.

The sergeant is already in the wind as Ron and I retrace our steps to our patrol car. I open the passenger door and stuff my baton into its holder. I'm about to slump into the passenger seat when my training officer calls to me over the roof of the car.

"Hey, partner."

It's the first time he has called me partner. Facing him across the roof of the police car, I watch his lips grab a cigarette from his soft pack of Marlboros. His dark eyes lock on mine. In one motion, Ron flicks open his Zippo and turns the friction wheel to ignite the fumes. His eyes divert from mine just long enough for the flame to lick its way up to the tip of his cigarette. The glow from his cigarette illuminates his face as he inhales deeply. Snapping the lighter shut, my partner's black holes reset on mine. He is wearing the same knowing smile as earlier in the shift.

With smoke streaming from his mouth, he snickers. "Feel like you are earning your pay now?"

"Yeah. Now just get me the hell out of here."

I collapse into the passenger seat and roll down the window. Ron fires up the engine and accelerates from the curb. The rush of cool night air, the smell of burning tobacco, the vibration of the road through the seats, are all more real to me than ever before. I feel alive, and it feels good. Up to this point, I would have never dreamed of telling my training officer to do anything...much less "get me the hell out of here."

I'm on probation, *lower than whale shit*, as the expression goes. While I'm still a boot and Ron is still my training officer, there's been a shift. Curiously Ron isn't pissed at my insolence. He's almost joyful as he says, "People watch those cop shows and think they know what it's like out here. Truth is...they don't know diddly shit. A guy almost killed you, and you almost killed him. In fact, it would have been a damn good shooting if you did. Yet we couldn't even book the son of a bitch. Nobody in Hollywood would ever fuck'n believe that."

The rest of the night is pretty uneventful, relatively speaking. We go EOW on time. After turning in our shotgun at the kit room, I head upstairs to turn in our log. I fold it twice to hold the night's citations and FIs before dropping it in the watch commander's in-box. I've done the same thing every night.

Up to this point, I always felt somehow out of place, more like I was acting, playing cop. My uniform was like a costume. I felt like an interloper in the locker room. I tried not to listen to the conversations, as if they were talking about something I should not be privy to.

I no longer feel like an actor playing a part. My uniform isn't a costume. I'm not a Disneyland ride operator or a college kid anymore. I'm an LA cop. Although I haven't admitted it to anyone, up to this point, I wasn't sure I had what it takes. Tonight answered that question. I belong here.

27

ON THE WAY home, I feel strangely at peace. The nonspecific anx-
iousness and fear generated by self-doubt have evaporated. Whatever
happens, I'll deal with it. This recognition acts as a sedative. I sleep like
a slab of granite nestled in a distant pine forest until the afternoon
sunshine beckons me awake.

I don't have to work the next two days. After a quick shower and
face scraping with the razor, I jump into my fire-engine-red Camaro
and head south on the Golden State Freeway. Cruising with the windows down, the air swirling around me feels especially refreshing.
Colors appear more vibrant, and the throaty dual exhaust resonates
more powerfully. Even the *Supremes* on the radio sound more soulful.

I'm replaying the events of last night in my head, but for the life
of me, I can't remember reaching for my weapon, unsnapping my holster, and drawing my revolver. My grip, stance, sight picture, breath
control, and trigger pull—everything happened without conscious
thought. It was a reflex, like blinking my eye. I saw the man reach for
the gun, and my next conscious thought was an acknowledgment of
a decision I had already made—if he touches the gun, I'm going to
shoot. The weapon was just there at the ready, testimony to the qual-
ity of my training. My decision making had been just as automatic.
Up to that moment, I wasn't sure how I would react when faced with

a life-and-death situation. Yeah, I'd told everyone I could do it, but I wasn't really sure.

Maybe everyone questions his or her emotions after surviving a dangerous encounter, or perhaps it's my introspective nature that has me questioning my joy at being alive. It's disconcerting because entwined with the intense elation is an enigmatic sadness.

• • •

Over the years, I have looked back on the incident many times, eventually identifying the source of the desolation mixed with the *joie de vivre*. I have concluded the anguish was for my lost innocence. Like a child who learns Santa Claus is not real, it's heartbreaking to confront the truth—there is a baser side of humanity. Knowing there are people who will scratch you from the list of the living without a second thought brings an abiding sense of despair. As disturbing as that is, realizing under certain conditions I could also take a life, almost without conscious thought, still fetches angst from the depth of my soul.

28

ALTHOUGH IT IS the better part of an hour, it seems like only minutes before I'm pulling into the worn asphalt driveway of my folks' house in Anaheim. There's no answer to my knock on the door. Although it feels somehow unnatural, I use my key. As I close the door behind me, I see my mom step out of the kitchen.

"Sorry, I didn't hear you," she says.

"That's OK. I used my key. How are you feeling?"

"Oh, I'm OK. I go back to the doctor for more tests next week. They changed the dosage again on my medication. The doctor says he wants to try some new drug."

My mom has lupus erythematosus. It is an autoimmune disease where the body fails to recognize its own antibodies as friendly and attacks them as foreign invaders. I was only fifteen years old when my mom got really sick. She was near death in the hospital, not responding to the treatment for leukemia. After a lot of yelling and screaming, a young upstart internal medicine man replaced our longtime family physician. Despite negative test results, the young internist began treating my mother for lupus. Her response to the treatment was dramatic. Twice more the tests for lupus came back negative. While eventually the results came back positive, my mom's new doctor said the lab work was just confirmation. My mom's response to the treatment was the primary reason for his confidence in his diagnosis. He explained some diagnostic tools are plagued by high rates of *false negatives.*

One thing is clear; my mom would not have lived long had this young doctor not taken over. Still, it remains a struggle to keep the disease under control, and control is the best-case scenario since there is no cure.

Sitting at the dining room table in my usual spot, talking to my mom, nothing has changed. The green sculpted carpet, the light-gray tint on the walls, and the awful paisley drapes are the same as when I lived at home. It's equally evident I don't fit here anymore.

My mom is looking at me like she did when she thought I got some girl pregnant in high school. "So how is everything going?"

"Fine. Everything is fine—"

"Has anyone said anything?"

I'm a little slow on the uptake.

"You know...called you any names or anything?"

"No. There were a couple of instructors at the academy...but mostly they focused on Silverstein and the black guys.

"How about where you are now?"

"At Rampart?"

"Yeah. Anybody like those academy people there?"

"It's fine."

Either satisfied, or resigned, my mom lapses into normalcy. "You want to stay for dinner? I don't know what I am going to make, but you are welcome to stay for dinner."

"No thanks. I'm going to get my hair cut and then catch up with Katarina. We'll get a bite and catch a show or something." As soon as I mention Katarina, I know it is a mistake.

My mom goes on her usual rant. "What are you doing with *that* girl? You should have married Sylvia. She was such a nice girl."

"Mom, it wasn't like that. It wasn't up to me. Sylvia went off to Notre Dame and converted to Catholicism. She married a Catholic guy—"

"You could have kept her from going. She was a wonderful girl. You'll never find another like her."

"You're right, Momma." I stand up from the table. "I gotta get my hair cut."

"Your hair looks fine. Just get a trim. You know I've never liked short hair on you."

"I know, Mom. But you know how they are at the police department, and I'm still just a rookie. I gotta follow the rules real close." My mom is on my heels as I cross the living room, heading for the front door. She stops just inside the doorway as I head to my car.

Holding the screen door open as if her words won't pass through the mesh, she shouts, "Be careful. There are some crazy drivers out there."

"I will, Mom. I promise. I'll call you later." Considering the events of the last twelve hours, I can't help but smile.

Turning the key in the ignition engulfs me in the comforting sounds of horsepower mixed with rock and roll. I back into the street and head to John's barbershop. I've been getting my hair cut at John's since I was in the third grade. Even when I was in the academy, he had been the only one to cut my hair. From the parking lot, I can see two guys getting their hair cut and two waiting. *That'll work.* I park in the far corner of the lot. A short walk is a small price to pay to avoid a door ding.

As I approach the barbershop, I can already detect the familiar odor of John's favorite brand of professional tonsorial products. John acknowledges me with his usual slight nod of the head. I settle into one of the chrome-and-vinyl benches facing the barbers' chairs and grab an issue of *Popular Mechanics* from the stack on the table.

An old codger in John's chair is venting about a traffic citation he feels he didn't deserve. John is trying to redirect the conversation to a safer subject, but the man is not taking John's cues. My barber continues his efforts at diplomacy while he makes a pretext of trimming some of the few remaining strands on top of the guy's blotchy scalp.

I glance over the top of my magazine at the old-timer as he continues his harangue. His wrinkled and soiled linen shirt is so thin I can see his ribbed sleeveless T-shirt underneath. I can almost read the warning label on the pack of Pall Mall cigarettes in his breast pocket. His complexion betrays his penchant to overindulge in alcohol.

"You've seen'm, John. They're always at Winchell's drinking coffee and eating free doughnuts. They only leave the doughnut shop long enough to give a poor old guy like me a fuck'n ticket."

"There's not that much going on here in Anaheim," John says, "It's not like LA."

I've seen John deftly steer his customers' conversations many times before. I actually enjoy watching his considerable skill at redirecting his patrons' discussions to safer topics. I'm confident he has done it again. No doubt John's tact will bring at least some small acknowledgment from the aging malcontent that the venerable LAPD is not like these small-town cops. It's the seventies and the LAPD is universally acclaimed to be the finest law enforcement organization in the world. The *Adam-12* television show brings a glorious vision of the LAPD into living rooms of millions every week. The central characters of the show are the absolute embodiment of virtue and valor.

The guy's next comment reveals he is not a fan of the show. "LA cops aren't any better. Hell, they let the niggers burn down half of Los Angeles."

I put my head back into my magazine. It is all I can do to keep from bursting into laughter. While I know I can suppress my laughter, I also know I can't remove the silly smirk on my face. I'm not hiding my smile from the old bigot. I don't care what he thinks. It's John. While my barber probably agrees with the guy, he's embarrassed for having failed to gingerly disarm this customer with his usual inimitable aplomb.

After the crabby old man has paid and walked out of the shop, it's my turn in the chair. John says something like "better to keep quiet and let people think you are a fool than to open your mouth and remove all doubt. "

I stop John short, and mimic his diplomatic style. "If I held you responsible for all the stupid stuff your patrons say, then I'd be as big a jerk as your last customer."

Running a comb through my hair, John asks how things are going at the academy. When I explain I've graduated already, he asks me how the job compares to the *Adam-12* television show. He pretends to listen as I explain that the uniforms, cars, and radio procedure portrayed on the show are fairly realistic.

After my haircut, I get back in my hot rod and head for HoJo's to meet Katarina when she gets off work. The Howard Johnson's located across from the employee entrance to Disneyland is one of the main social spots for the over-twenty-one crowd who work at the park. Katarina is a perky, black-haired beauty of Czechoslovakian descent who I met at the Inn Between (the employee cafeteria) when I worked at the Magic Kingdom. She is four feet ten inches tall, perfect for her job as Minnie Mouse. The first time I saw her, I was struck by her beautiful porcelain features and flashing dark-brown eyes. We dated regularly when I worked at Disneyland, but we've hardly seen each other since I entered the academy.

I'm sipping a beer in the rear of HoJo's when she strolls in with several other park employees. She wears her hair in a Dorothy Hamill. I love the way it shines and bounces when she walks. The moment she sits down, I notice that the spark that customarily lights her face is missing.

"A lot of kids trying to beat up Minnie Mouse today?" I ask.

"No, actually it was really slow today. Only about eight thousand in-park the last hour."

"You hungry?"

"A little. Let's just...get something fast and light."

"Sure," I say.

To look at her lithe athletic body, no one would ever guess she has a weakness for fried food. I follow her to the little fish-and-chips place just a couple of miles from the park where we used to go pretty regularly. As we share our snack, Katarina tells me I've changed.

I stammer, "You say I've changed. But how? I mean...what exactly do you mean? Is it the way I look? The way I talk? My hair was shorter than this when I was in the academy."

"It's not your hair or anything like that," she says, fingering the sleeve of my T-shirt. "I just knew it would happen."

"Well, maybe you just think of me differently now that I don't work at the Park." What she is saying doesn't make any sense. I'm still good old Max Stoller.

It isn't ugly. It's not because she's hurt. She doesn't want to hurt me, either. She honestly believes I'm not the guy she used to know. In her mind at least, I've changed. And that is that. "Max, we just don't fit anymore."

Standing outside her car it's obvious we are a mismatch in height, but that's always been true. Whenever people pointed it out, I always told them the same thing. "It's not a problem...I just pick her up to kiss her." Now as I put my arms around her, that's what I want to do. But that won't make things the way they were. With my hands on the small of her back, I kiss her gently on the top of her head. The smell of her lustrous hair triggers beautiful memories. I say softly, "If you ever want to talk—"

She hugs me with her head against my chest, then turns and opens her car door without looking up. She hurries to start the engine as I gently close her door. There is moisture in my eyes as I watch her drive away. I don't move until her car is out of sight.

It feels like only a couple of weeks since I entered the academy and pressed life's accelerator to the floor. I lost all sense of time. With my focus on the vanishing point of the track ahead, familiar things whizzed by unnoticed. Katarina's estrangement is like Ron's baton smacking at my hands on the steering wheel. It hurts and forces me to slow down. Suddenly I'm seeing things I've paid scant attention to for the last five months. It's disconcerting because familiar things don't look the same.

At the time I thought the world had changed a lot during those five months. Of course it hadn't. What had changed was my perspective. From a different place, even familiar things can look peculiar.

Katarina was wrong. I hadn't changed. But perspective is relative. Being in a different place not only affected my view of the world, but also how the world saw me. That night, Katarina's changed perspective was the only one I cared about.

29

THE PUBLIC ENTRANCE to Rampart Station features a brick facade with double glass doors. From the lobby a corridor provides public access. The engraved plastic sign above the first door on the left says Watch Commander. The sign across the hall reads Commanding Officer. The secretary's desk sits just inside the CO's door on the right. Straight ahead, the adjutant's gray pedestal desk guards the entrance to the captain's inner office. Sergeant Stoddard mans this post like the Great Sphinx of Giza.

Evelyn, the captain's secretary, is off socializing again, so when the phone rings, Sergeant Stoddard has to answer. Without altering his perfect posture, the adjutant brings the phone to his ear. His East Coast boarding school diction accentuates the formality of the phrase the LAPD manual prescribes.

"Rampart Division, captain's office, Sergeant Stoddard, may I help you?" The prim adjutant immediately recognizes the voice on the other end. After he hits the hold button, the sergeant turns his head toward the inner office and sounds off like an aristocratic butler. "Captain, it's Deputy Chief Callahan on line one. He wants to speak to you personally, sir."

Captain William Wilks curses Stoddard under his breath. Had Evelyn answered the phone, she would have given the deputy chief a bunch of razzle-dazzle sexual innuendos and taken a message. But now, thanks to that idiot Stoddard, Captain Wilks knows he doesn't have a choice. After crushing out his cigarette, he extends a bloated hand. His pudgy finger presses the button for line one. He'll just have to schmooze his boss as best he can, despite his hellacious hangover.

There is no need for the captain to fasten the top button of his shirt and cinch his tie around his Henry the Eighth jowls. The deputy chief can't see through the phone line. Nonetheless, when the captain picks up the phone, his eyebrows flatten, and he is wearing a phony smile. "Good morning, Chief. Nice to talk to you. How is Margaret?"

"Bill, I'm not in the mood for small talk. I'll get right to the point. Next week is Rampart's annual inspection. If your division doesn't score upper ten percent in every category, I'll transfer your ass to the security detail in fucking Lone Pine."

Wilks pulls the receiver away from his ear and extends his middle finger at the phone. Realizing his door is open, he hastily brings the phone back to his ear. The portly captain's smile disappears. His weak lips twist into an insolent sneer.

His boss's loud voice is further amplified by his hangover. "Every one of your coppers better be squared away. I don't care if you per-sonally have to shave'm. No long hair, no mustaches beyond the ver-million, no unauthorized ammo, no patched-up uniforms, no dirty weapons..."

Captain Wilks again angles the phone toward the wall.

When he returns the receiver to his ear, the deputy chief is still ranting. "...all the files in order, all the cars clean, the floors clean, not one gig. You got it?"

"Yes, sir."

"Oh yeah, Chief Davis goes over the Neighborhood Watch statis-tics very carefully. None of my divisions will ever report a decrease in meetings or attendance. I'm not going to give Crazy Ed ammunition against me. Count by twos if you have to. Hell, count by tens. I don't care. But your reported BCP (Basic Car Plan) numbers shall never go down. Is that clear?"

"Yes, sir, we—"

The chief cuts him off. "Good. Now that we have that squared away, I was just checking my calendar." The sound of the chief thumbing the pages of his Day-Timer is audible through the phone as he inquires, "We are still on track for our golfing weekend in Palm Springs with one of your boosters, right?"

"Yes, sir. It should be a nice weekend for everyone. My wife is looking forward to spending more time with Margaret—"

"Yeah, yeah. It'll be OK, I'm sure. But I gotta tell yah…I just got back from a fishing trip off Baja. It's not like I'm really into fishing, but this was my kind of trip. No wives. Plenty of good booze. Lots of great food. This Central Division booster—now this guy knows how to support your local police. 'Fighting those game fish can be arduous,' he says. So he brings special massage therapists on the trip to relieve any stress we might experience." Callahan gives a whistle. "Damn. Those women were gorgeous, with big tits, and man did they know how to…relieve stress, if you know what I mean. Anyway, I gotta go, Bill. Just remember what I told you about upper ten percent in everything."

Before Captain Wilks can say anything, he hears a click that terminates the connection. Wilks opens his desk drawer and grabs the bottle of aspirin, wondering if it is possible to overdose on the stuff. He is tempted to grab the bottle of Johnnie Walker. After a moment's hesitation he spills two of the scored white tablets into his trembling palm. "Stoddard, get me a soda!" he shouts through the open door.

"Yes, sir!"

The captain reaches for a fresh cigarette, and grabs a pack of safety matches. Palming the aspirin, he strikes a match on the cover. It lights on the second try. After an initial drag, he rests the cigarette on the edge of the ashtray and begins to massage the bridge of his nose.

Sergeant Stoddard gives a courtesy tap on the doorjamb before stepping into the inner office. When the sergeant slides the can of Coke across the desk, Captain Wilks stops rubbing his sinuses. "Go find Evelyn and tell her she has to stay put to answer the phones. Then come back in here and close the door." The captain waits until his teetotaler subordinate has left before he downs the aspirin.

After Sergeant Stoddard closes the door, the captain rocks back in his chair and exhales a lung full of smoke. His bloodshot eyes scan his subordinate's face. "It's nice working day watch, banker's hours—Saturdays, Sundays, and holidays off—no more of the unpleasantness of police work. You like being my adjutant, don't you?"

"Yes, sir. I appreciate your choosing me, sir."

Captain Wilks shifts his gaze from the cigarette he is crushing in the ashtray to his adjutant. "Rampart better score upper ten percent in every category on this year's inspection, or you will be working morning watch in the harbor and can kiss your chance to make lieutenant good-bye. Is there anything I have to do to make that any clearer?"

"No, sir. You are perfectly clear, sir."

For the next twenty minutes the adjutant briefs the captain on the status of preparations for the annual inspection. Stoddard has been coordinating with the watch commanders of all three watches, who have been conducting regular inspections of the division's personnel. The adjutant has personally supervised sprucing up the facilities, even arranging for a steam-cleaning firm to *donate* its services. A crew spent two full days scouring the concrete parking lots and walkways.

Listening to the admin sergeant cataloging his efforts, Captain Wilks has to admit Stoddard maybe an idiot, but he's an efficient idiot. Finished with him for the moment, the captain waves his adjutant out of his office.

On his way out, Stoddard mentions, "By the way, sir...Sergeant Wilson says he needs a word with you. At your convenience of course."

"Tell him after lunch. I'm having lunch with the detective lieutenant. He can try and catch me afterward."

• • •

It's late in the afternoon before the captain gets back from his lunch at the Mexican Village restaurant. Wilks is feeling much better after a number twenty-three combination plate and several stiff drinks. Tipped off the captain is back, Sergeant Charles Wilson strolls into the CO's outer office. The sergeant's eyes wander to the cleavage of the captain's secretary. "Nice blouse, Evelyn. Is it new?"

The attractive brunette smiles as she arches her back and pushes out her chest in a well-practiced flirt. "The blouse is new, but what you're looking at isn't."

The captain's voice interrupts their interlude. "OK, Chuck. Stoddard said you wanted to see me about something. Might as well get it over with."

With a nod to Evelyn's bosom, Sergeant Wilson heads into the captain's inner office. He hasn't closed the door before he begins, "One of our frequent customers comes in here with his older sister a couple of weeks ago. Says a bunch of Rampart cops beat him up. He's got road rash on his hands and one knee. Got four welts on his legs consistent with being hit by a baton. He's naming names, everyone from Morales to Sergeant Arnhardt. Says he was minding his own business, just walking across the grocery store parking lot, when the cops jumped him."

"OK. So what's the problem?"

"I get a copy of the report and sit down with him." Sergeant Wilson pulls his chair a little closer to the captain's desk. "Maybe I ought'a back up a little...in case you aren't as familiar with Jose Antonio Gonzalez as I am."

Wilson fires up a smoke and continues, "He's a chronic complainer, not quite an adult..." Wilson stops to pick a tiny piece of tobacco from the tip of his tongue. "He's got lots of gang tats and a rap sheet a mile long. On probation for two-seventeen (attempted murder)."

"Yeah, yeah. I got the picture," Wilks mutters, looking at the ceiling.

"The arrest report shows the asshole kicked Officer Morales in the back while he was on a chow run for the station at that fried chicken place in A-3's area. Anyway, when I confront the punk, he denies he kicked the officer. Says he just called him some names." Wilson exhales blue vapor then taps his ash into the captain's huge ashtray. "So much for his story of getting jumped by the cops while walking across the parking lot minding his own business."

"OK. So what did the witnesses say?"

"They all back up the officer's story. The night manager and a couple of customers say the gangster just kicked the officer. No provocation. Not a word exchanged."

"OK. Get to the point. Where's the problem?"

"The night manager of the chicken stand was really pissed. He wanted to file his own one-eighty-one on Morales."

Captain Wilks interrupts, talking more to himself than anyone else. "Shit! Don't tell me Morales beat the asshole right in front of all those witnesses?"

"No, that's not it. The kid turned tail and ran. None of the wits saw what happened when Morales finally caught up to him. We don't have any independent wits to the actual altercation."

"You're really trying my patience, Sergeant. The asshole had it coming. Under these circumstances use of the baton is clearly in policy. So what's the night manager's problem? He think we should have just let the asshole go? If the prick kicked an officer, do you think he would hesitate to kick the shit out of the customers, or better yet, the night manager? These bleeding-heart liberals have shit for brains."

"No, Captain. The night manager's anger has nothing to do with use of force. Like I said, the manager didn't even see it, and like I said, the complainant's injuries are minor. The manager is pissed because Morales keeps coming in, ordering ten or fifteen meals, and not paying for them." Wilson snuffs out his smoke in the captain's ashtray. "It's a pop spot boss. They normally go half price. But Morales refuses to even pay half price. If Morales was just ordering one meal, the manager could cover it. But he has people to answer to—"

Obviously perturbed, but still leaning back in his chair, the captain interrupts again. "Yeah, OK, I got it. No problem. I would have thought you could've handled this—"

The sergeant is quick to defend himself. "I talked the night manager out of making a formal beef. I skirted that whole issue in the interview summaries on the excessive force complaint—"

"OK, so you just wanted me to know, right?"

"Well, there is a little more to it. Everything would be fine except the arrest report indicates the officers never touched the guy. The report says the subject fell while running away, period. That would explain the abrasions on his hands and knee. But the welts on his legs did not happen in a fall. The marks on his legs are perfectly consistent with an appropriate use of the police baton. If the officers had simply documented the use of the baton, everything would be jake. As it is, things don't add up, and here is where it gets worse. When I confronted the guy with his statement about getting jumped crossing the parking lot, the asshole says he got thumped by Arnhardt and Morales back in the jail before he was booked."

The captain lurches forward. The sudden move is punctuated by the sound of his executive chair slamming upright. "God damn it! I told Arman to knock that shit off." The captain takes a deep breath. Regaining some of his composure, his angular eyebrows are pointing to his receding hairline. "All right, who was Morales working with? Reynolds or Langley?"

"Neither. He was working with a boot, some kid named Stoller, just out of the academy."

"Oh yeah, the idealistic movie-star-look-a-like Jew-boy. A couple of instructors at the academy called me about him." The captain's voice trails off. "OK, we'll just blame the whole thing on him."

"How you gonna do that? Even the complainant says Stoller is the one officer who didn't do anything wrong."

Wilks stands up and points to the corner of his desk. "Just leave everything here. I'll handle this." Before the complaint folder lands on his desk, the captain is already waving Wilson out of the office.

30

TODAY IS RAMPART'S annual inspection. Deputy Chief Callahan and his inspection party have had nothing but compliments. The day watch troops looked terrific. Even the PM watch cops were squared away. The steam-cleaned sidewalks and parking areas look fantastic. The newly painted walls, set off by the highly polished linoleum, make the station look as good as the day it was dedicated in 1967.

That afternoon, there are smiles all around when the deputy chief makes it clear he's not coming back in the middle of the night to inspect the AM watch. He's sending a flunky commander instead. Wilks knows it will be a formality. As soon as the deputy chief and his entourage head back to Parker Center, Wilks takes off for the Mexican Village.

It's after 9:00 p.m. before Captain Wilks is back in his office. Apparently not content with the load he took on at the restaurant, he pours three fat fingers of Johnnie Walker in his coffee cup. Chemically confident, he leans back in his swivel chair as he lights a fresh cigarette. After he takes a drag on his smoke, he calls toward the outer office, "Stoddard, get in here!"

"Yes, sir," the adjutant responds, grabbing a legal tablet from his desk.

"Sit down, Sergeant. We have some time to kill before the commander gets here. We might as well make good use of it. Tonight I'm going to personally fix that complaint Wilson fucked up." He smirks at his adjutant. "You and I are going to interview the probationer."

"Morales is a walking time bomb, sir," Stoddard says. "You want to get the probee to roll over on Morales?"

"Fire Morales? Hell no!" the captain bellows. "I don't want to get rid of Morales. Yeah, he's a heavy-handed son of a bitch...likes to beat people. So what? It's easy to control that stupid, sick SOB. Besides sometimes a heavy hand is just what is called for. Hell, I could fire Morales anytime."

Another sip of scotch whisky warms the captain as he eyes his subordinate. "Sergeant, there is a difference between supervision and management. You need to get a handle on the distinction. Management means managing, not supervising. It means getting what you want out of who you have. I agree Morales can be a supervisor's nightmare, but from a manager's perspective, he's a great guy to have around because he'll do anything I tell him—anything. Why would I want to fire him? Remember all that great stuff we raffled off at the Christmas party last year? Morales got almost all of that stuff. When I need somebody to lean on the boosters, he's just the guy. The beauty of this case is...I can jerk on Morales's choke chain and get rid of that idealistic Jew-boy at the same time. That kid doesn't fit here. He doesn't belong on my police department. Can't you see what's go'n on? The kikes have teamed up with the niggers and are trying to get one elected mayor. Politically I can't touch a Negro, but Hebes are still fair game."

Lifting himself just enough to clear his chair, Sergeant Stoddard sidles sideways. After stealing a glance at the outer office door, ensuring it's closed, he quietly shuts the inner office door.

Captain Wilks takes a noisy sip from his coffee cup. "You know the best part? The Goody Two-shoes can't wait to roll over on his partner. I'll give him the spiel on integrity, and he'll come clean. Once he admits he lied in the initial interview, firing him will be a foregone conclusion. Of course that will be my recommendation. Hell, even if I were to recommend leniency, downtown would kick it back. They'd insist on termination. But you can bet your ass I'd never recommend going light on him." Wilks takes another drag on his cigarette. "I have my reputation as a strict disciplinarian to uphold. I'm just living up to my obligation to keep the LAPD corruption-free."

"Sir, what about Morales? How can you fire the probee and not Morales? I mean Morales is the guy who did the beating, and he is the senior officer. And what about Arman Arnhardt?"

"Oh, Morales is gonna get a couple of relinquished days off, for sure. That's actually not a bad thing. Weren't you paying attention? When I bring Morales in here and tell him how hard I worked to save his job, that will convince him he owes me big-time."

"But, I still don't see how you can recommend firing the probationer and not the training officer."

"Easy. I'm the captain. And don't forget, Morales is not really a training officer. He's a P-2. We'll blame the whole thing on the boot. We'll say the kid wrote the report all on his own. Morales just failed to check it over well enough, because Morales isn't a training officer." Captain Wilks smiles broadly. "And at least Wilson was smart enough to keep Arman's name off the beef from the start, so we don't even have to address that. Remember, too, the boot can't opt for a Board of Rights—he doesn't have any rights. Just watch how well this goes." He takes another swig from his coffee cup. "In the meantime, type up the probationer's resignation. Do the relief from duty paperwork, too. When we put the paperwork in front of him he'll opt to resign. You'll see."

• • •

All my leather gear is spit shined to a deep lustrous black. My weapon is immaculate. There isn't a speck of lint on my wool uniform. Every facet on my badge is without blemish. Just like in the academy, I am squared away.

It's almost disappointing when I realize the inspection is only a formality. The commander is more anxious to get it over with than we are. What puzzles me is the way the captain is looking at me. He's grinning like a Cheshire cat. And it's obvious he's had a couple—more than a couple.

After the inspection, Ron tells me I don't have to start a log. He says he'll check out our equipment. I need to go see the captain in his office. Heading upstairs, I'm wondering what the captain wants with me.

The adjutant ushers me into the CO's inner office and closes the door. After brief introductions, the captain starts, "We are here tonight to talk about the complaint stemming from your arrest of a minor named Jose Antonio Gonzalez. I know Sergeant Wilson already interviewed you on this matter, but I don't think he impressed on you the importance of being scrupulously accurate in your responses. You have only been out of the academy a few weeks, and never been interviewed on a one-eighty-one before. Isn't that true?"

"Yes, sir. That's true, sir."

"Good. That's what I thought. And that is why I am personally taking over this investigation. I have Sergeant Wilson's notes from his interview right here." The captain holds up a couple of pieces of paper. "I'm gonna throw them away." Wilks makes a show of tearing the pages in half, wadding them up and throwing them in the waste-basket behind him. The captain looks me in the eye. "I give you my word; as far as I'm concerned, that interview never happened."

Wilks lights up a smoke and leans back in his chair. "People make mistakes sometimes. I know that. And then there are some people who just don't belong here in my police department. I know you've heard guys say don't roll over on your partner and all that, but the truth is, part of being the best police department is being the most honest." The captain leans forward, teetering over the desk, aiming his substantial bulk in my direction. "When it comes to honesty, let's just say that's the way it has to be, even if it means somebody is gonna get hurt. You understand my meaning, Officer Stoller?"

I'd like to believe the captain, but something tells me I can't. The papers he ripped in half and threw in the trash might have been a *copy* of Sergeant Wilson's notes, but they are not the originals. I wasn't sure at first, but then I remembered Sergeant Wilson used a yellow legal tablet like the one Sergeant Stoddard has in his lap right now. The sheets of paper the captain ripped up and threw away were white. More than that, I have a tight feeling in my gut. Captain Wilks's little speech about honesty is fraught with contradiction. If honesty is so unequivocal to him, how can he be making an exception in this case? He asks if I understand his meaning. I think I do. "Yes, sir."

"Good. That's what I thought. The captain hands me an eight-by-ten enlargement of the booking photo of the subject. "You recognize this photo?" he asks, never taking his eyes off me.

"Yes, sir." I cannot help but think to myself, of course I recognize the photo. It's the booking photo I took. How can the captain not realize that? If he does realize it, why didn't he phrase his question differently?

"And that is a photo of the juvenile subject you arrested that night, correct?"

"Yes, sir."

"And he is the same one who kicked your partner, Officer Morales, that night. Isn't that correct?"

"Yes, sir, that's him, sir."

The captain shows me a copy of the arrest report. "And this is the arrest report that goes with the photo, right?"

"Yes, sir."

"And that is your handwriting? You wrote the report? Correct?"

"Yes, sir."

"Good. So where were you when the subject kicked your partner?"

"I was just getting out of our police car."

"You were parked in front of the chicken stand? Correct?"

"Yes, sir, on the street about fifty feet south of the location."

"And both you and Morales gave chase, is that right?"

"Yes, sir."

"Good, so you and Morales caught up to the suspect in the parking lot, right?"

"Are you asking me what happened, or are you asking me what I saw?"

A hint of the same grin I saw during the inspection crosses the captain's face.

"So you're telling me what you wrote in the report is not exactly what happened? Is that right?"

"I'm saying I wasn't there when Morales caught up to the subject."

The captain is doing his best imitation of a glad-handing Southern Democrat promising prosperity in exchange for a pull on the handle of a voting machine. "You know you cannot separate from your partner, right?" The captain's thin lips turn down at the corners. "That would put you in violation of one of the department's most important safety doctrines."

"Yes, sir. I know that."

"So, you had to be there when Morales caught up with the subject. In fact, you were the one who handcuffed him. Right?"

"Captain, you said people sometimes make mistakes. I made a mistake. In the academy they drummed it into our heads to never split up from your partner. When I saw the subject disappear behind the chicken stand, I was sure he was veering left. I was just as sure I could cut him off by running to the left of the fast-food place. It was my mistake. That is why I wasn't there when my partner caught up to the subject. I'm sorry, sir. I'm just glad nothing bad happened to my partner before I could get over the fence and catch up."

"In the report you wrote the subject tripped and fell while he was running away. Isn't that right?"

"Yes, sir."

"You saw that part, right?"

"That's what Morales told me. It made sense to me, sir. Can't imagine Morales catching up to him any other way."

Sergeant Stoddard is working to suppress a smile until the captain hands me photos of bruises on the subject's legs.

"You see these? They are bruises on the subject's legs. You're telling me he got these bruises falling down?"

"No, sir."

"You're a pretty fast runner, aren't you?"

"I can hold my own, sir."

"Even going around the other side of the fried chicken stand, you couldn't have been that far behind your partner. You couldn't have lost sight of your partner for more than a couple of seconds. And these photos clearly show the subject took four baton blows to his legs. Yet, you sit there and expect me to believe you didn't see anything?"

"Sir, let me ask you a question. In a case where a suspect attacks an officer with absolutely no provocation, where the officer gives chase, is alone apprehending the suspect, and the suspect is resisting…wouldn't the use of the baton be justified?"

The Cheshire cat appears again. "Of course it would. Now do you want to tell me what really happened?"

"I'd love to tell you what really happened. It's just…I don't understand."

"What don't you understand?"

"Why would I lie about seeing a justified use of force? I'm not saying it didn't happen. I'm just telling you I didn't see it. But you don't seem to care about what happened. You're trying to get me to say I stayed with my partner when I didn't. Or I saw something I didn't. Sir, look at the booking photo, there isn't a mark on the subject's face. In fact, the only injuries I saw that night were the marks on his hands and the small tear of his pants at the knee. Those minor abrasions were completely consistent with his falling. I never saw any other signs of injury, so there was no reason for me to question my partner's account of what happened when he was out of my sight."

I see the exasperation growing in the liquored-up captain. The lyrics from a Bob Dylan tune are playing in my head, *when you got noth'n—you got noth'n to lose.* Being respectful as I can, I press my point. "You say those marks on the arrestee's calves were caused by a police baton. I don't dispute it. You're the captain of police. You know the personalities of the people involved, and undoubtedly you've seen these kinds of injuries before. So I believe you when you say the marks on the subject's legs came from a police baton. I just don't understand why…out of this entire episode…you're focusing on me… trying to get me to say I saw something I didn't see, or I didn't split up with my partner, even though you know I did. I'm not covering for Morales here. Believe me, Captain, that's the last thing I want to do."

The captain is about to bust a gasket. The odor of alcohol about him is suddenly more intense. He finally gathers his composure and lapses into a well-practiced phrase. "Being observant is an essential skill for a police officer. Obviously you lack this basic requisite skill, and therefore you are unfit to be a police officer—"

"Sir, my first few nights in the street I was definitely suffering from sensory overload. To be completely honest, I seriously considered resigning. But—"

The captain shouts, *"Well, you can resign right now!"*

Sergeant Stoddard slides the resignation in front of me. I see my name, serial number, and the date are already typed on the form. That strange feeling of watching from outside of myself comes over me again as I lecture the slovenly man in charge of Rampart Division. "Had you put this resignation in front of me after my first couple of nights, I probably would have signed it…but since then…things have changed." My voice is matter-of-fact. "I'm not stupid. I know you're the one who decides if I make probation. But I'm not going to quit and make that decision for you. I'm going to continue doing my best and leave it up to you to do the right thing. From where I sit, I don't see I have any other choice."

Sergeant Stoddard stands up and interposes himself between the captain and me. "I think we all need a break." His voice drops. "I know I do." He motions for me to stand up. I've barely gotten to my feet when he pushes me toward the door.

"Go get yourself a cup of coffee. We'll call you."

• • •

Seeing me exit the captain's office, Lieutenant Price casually strides in and asks, "Well, sir?"

"Well what?" The captain snarls at the lieutenant.

"I'm doing the board for tomorrow. I was wondering where I should put Stoller?" The LT looks down and sees the unsigned resignation. "Giving him a chance to resign, huh?"

A virulent look of hatred comes over the captain's flush face. "I'm gonna fire that son of a bitch."

"What for, Captain?" The old-school LT really wants to know what the beef is all about.

"Unsat performance on probation." The captain sneers.

Confusion takes over the LT's face. "Unsat performance on probation? It's his first DP. Got a pretty good log entry from Sergeant Shaw the other night. His TO says he is doing good. And you know Russell ain't easy to please. Hell, Ron even let the kid drive already. I thought you had something on him."

"No more positive log entries, Lieutenant. *That's an order!*"

"Yes, sir." As he heads for the door, Lieutenant Price stops and looks down at the clipboard in his hands. "The commander singled Stoller out during the inspection tonight. I assume you want me to scratch his name off the commendation list for outstanding appearance at the annual inspection?"

The captain spits his response. "You're damned right I do."

"Done, sir," the LT says on his way out.

31

RON FINDS ME in the coffee room.

"Let's go!" he says.

"Ah...I don't know if I can. The adjutant said they would call me—"

"Hey, the LT told me to get my partner and hit the street. The city is falling apart. We gotta get out there and handle some radio calls."

When we're settled into the police car, Ron tells me, "Before roll call, the LT took me aside and told me to send you up to the captain's office right after the inspection. Said I should just stand by. Said you were probably gonna get fired." Ron winces. "He said if you got fired, he would let me go home early instead of making me work an L car tonight. Now I guess I gotta finish out the shift."

"Sorry to disappoint you," I say, staring out the window, feeling like something a dog left on someone's lawn. Even the steam-cleaned concrete is mocking me.

Ron jerks the car to a stop and looks at me. "Stoller."

I turn my head and meet his gaze.

"Max, I'm fucking with you. I don't know, and you don't have to tell me what happened...if you don't want to."

"They ordered me not to talk about it. They specifically ordered me not to talk to my training officers."

"Big fucking deal. That's standard procedure. They don't want you to get your stories straight with your partner. But in this case it makes no sense, especially now. I can't change what happened. You've already given a statement. What are they afraid of? I'll give you good advice?" Ron lifts his hands off the wheel, looks at me, and continues, "If you tell me what happened, I will give you good advice, even if that means telling you to resign. It has happened before. I had a boot who fucked up bad. When I found out what he did...I told him to resign. I didn't want his kind on the job. He didn't deserve to be here. I want to hear it from you. But, like I said, it's up to you."

Between handling radio calls I tell Ron the whole story. He asks lots of questions. Based on his questions, it's clear he understands exactly what happened. I actually feel much better having told him.

Ron has a lot to say. "Look, Morales is an asshole. He thinks the guys call him Sticktime because they admire him. Truth is...they don't. No one wants to work with him. Why do you think they have him assigned on an A car even though he's been a P-2 for a year? Why you think the LT's got him with two vets like Reynolds and Langley? So they can ride herd on him—that's why. LT tried to put him with me. I told him 'no fucking way.' Hell, if Morales wasn't the captain's bun boy, he'd been gone a long time ago."

Stopped at a red light, Ron turns toward me again. "Look, for the record, the LT did not put you with him that night. It was Arnhardt. He's another one of the captain's bun boys." Ron's face contorts. "Remember your first night when I told you never hit anybody with your baton when you're working with me?"

"Yes, sir."

"You thought I was fucking crazy. Didn't you?" He pauses. "It's OK. You can say it."

"Ah...yes, sir, I did."

"I'm not crazy. Leastwise not about that. Even with the best of intentions...your baton usually connects with the suspect's gourd and leaves some nasty-looking injuries. The department doesn't like that. The department likes pretty. They created this really pretty blue uniform." Ron pans his torso with his free hand. "Everything we who wear the uniform do...has to look just as pretty. When it doesn't, the brass don't give a shit about right or wrong, policy, or any of that crap. They just hammer the copper who did something that didn't look pretty."

When the light turns green, Ron takes his foot off the brake and we start to idle through the intersection. "The irony is Morales wasn't trying to exercise restraint. Hell, if he could have hit that asshole in the head, he would've. But because the suspect was on the ground kicking up at him, and because Morales is fat and out of shape, the most he could do was smack the lower legs a couple of times. The marks on the asshole's legs were textbook. Still, if you hadn't handcuffed the guy when you did, who knows what would have happened after Morales caught his breath. Everything that happened up to that point was completely 'in policy' and justified. Being your third night in the street you were in no position to tell Morales, much less the watch commander, what should or should not go in the report."

"I know one thing. I'm never gonna be put in that position again."

"I believe ya, kid." Ron fires up another Marlboro. "Hell, after politely telling the captain to go fuck himself, telling a P-2 or even the watch commander where to get off should be child's play." Smoke trailing from his mouth, Ron declares, "Experience is a hell of a teacher."

Our conversation is interrupted by the radio. "All units, two-Adam-seventy-nine is requesting a backup, Twentieth and Arapahoe on possible burglary from motor vehicle suspects."

My partner turns onto Alvarado and hammers the accelerator. The location is at the extreme southern edge of the Rampart bordering Southwest Division. Still, at this time of night I know we can be there in less than three minutes.

Ron says, "Unless Communications simulcast the backup to South Bureau, units in Southwest won't even hear it. Likely only Rampart will be rolling."

We hear the RTO announce, two-Adam-fifty-one is en route to the backup. I snatch the mic to say we are en route, too, but my TO cuts me off.

"I know it's tempting, but the RTO and seventy-nine already know they got people rolling. Now it's more important to keep the frequency clear. I've seen it too many times, guys broadcasting they are en route, step on the unit reporting they are in foot pursuit or requesting help."

Our RTO announces, "All units, two-Adam-seventy-nine is requesting assistance, partner in foot pursuit, westbound through the houses from Arapahoe north of Twentieth Street."

We are flying. Ron is braking at the very last moment, approaching a red light. I'm calling out the cross traffic. My partner has his foot back in the carburetor as soon as it's clear. Ron isn't really talking to anyone, certainly not me. It's more like he is praying to the police gods. "Where's the fucking air unit? We could use the fucking helicopter right about now."

Through an open mic at Communications we hear a Newton Division unit. "Thirteen-Adam-sixty-one is code six on the foot pursuit in Rampart."

The RTO repeats the information. "All units, thirteen-Adam-sixty-one is code six on the foot pursuit, Twentieth and Arapahoe."

"You can always count on Newton for backup," Ron interjects as he stomps on the brakes approaching Hoover. When I call "clear right," he is back on the accelerator again.

We are just a couple of blocks away when the RTO broadcasts, "All units, code four on the assistance call, Twentieth Street and Arapahoe. Suspect in custody. All officers accounted for."

My partner slows down, but continues toward the call. While only two units went code six, there are at least five police cars at the scene, their doors still open after being hastily abandoned. Cops are sauntering back to their cars as we idle up to the scene. The scents of burned rubber, hot metal, and scorched brake pads hang in the cool night air. Ron leans over my way and calls through my open window, "Hey, Williams."

A tall African-American cop walking toward a patrol car with "13" on the trunk lid, turns toward us. The big cop looks in our direction. Not recognizing me, he bends down so he can see inside our car. A wide grin accompanies recognition in his face. In a baritone voice he queries, "That you, Russell? I thought you took a pension after drop'n your motor."

"Yeah, they said I could'a got one. Sometimes I think I should'a." Ron winces, and then gets as big a grin as I've seen on him. "You guys are a little out of your area, aren't ya?"

Officer Williams points his finger toward his chest. "Badge says City of Los Angeles. 'Sides, we were com'n back from booking a body at JD...thought we'd poach a little at Juicy Lucy's." (Lucy's is a twenty-four-hour Mexican fast-food place around the corner.) "Figured if we was gonna burn up your pop spot, least we could do was hep you out with your crime problem."

"Much obliged." Ron grins. "You help out any, or jest get in the way?"

Williams is laughing. "Helped a little. Din't take much. The asshole caught hisself. Got over the fence into his own backyard. Thought he was King's X. 'Bout to declare olly olly oxen free when he realized his mom locked the security door. Yeah, that security door worked real good. Kept the burglar outside. All we had to do was hook him up."

Ron and his old partner bullshit for a while. As we are pulling away from the scene, I take out my log.

Ron queries, "Did we go code six?" Before I can answer, he asks, "Did we do anything? See anything?"

"No, sir."

"Officially we were never there. Let's keep it that way. It's not like we need to pad the log. The rule of thumb is, unless you go code six on the air, you don't log it." Ron is in his rhetorical-question-teaching mode. "Why? Because let's just say somebody got thumped on that caper and a beef comes out of it. Everyone who shows at the scene, either on communications tape or on the log, is gonna get interviewed."

My TO lets that sink in a little, then continues, "I'd just as soon not get interviewed any more often than I have to. Then again, maybe you enjoyed your little chat with Captain Wilks tonight."

"Not so much," I say, stashing my books on the seat next to me.

"Normally I would'a flipped a U as soon as it was code four—never even driven by. But I heard the Newton unit going code six, and I was pretty sure it was my old partner. Just wanted to say hey."

Heading back up north to our area, Ron resumes commenting on my situation. "The captain sure as hell doesn't need you to burn any-one on the fried chicken caper. Yeah, if you'd a said you were there the whole time, and it didn't happen, then breaking you would be neces-sary to burn Morales. But you were up front, telling him it very well could have happened when you were going around the chicken stand and trying to get over the fence. Then there's the shit that went on back in the jail. He didn't even ask you 'bout that 'cause he sure as hell doesn't want to go there. Of course it won't be that difficult for him to sweep the whole thing under the rug, either. But if you had quit, that would have made it easy for him to blame the whole mess on you while making himself look like a strong disciplinarian, upholding the highest standards of the LAPD."

Ron readjusts his position, using his left arm on the window for leverage. "You put a little hitch in his giddyup when you didn't go along with the program. He was sure you'd cop out. When you not only didn't cop out, but refused to resign, I can only imagine how pissed he got. Wish I'd been there." Ron is smiling as he glances my way. "The captain's a fuck'n idiot. But even that dumb shit realizes he can't fire a probee for poor observational skills on his third night in the street. That's why you are still here. Of course, now you're on his shit list for sure."

"So you're saying since Captain Wilks is the one who decides if I make probation, I'm just wasting my time?"

"Wasting your time? Who said anything about wasting your time? If you think what we are doing is wasting time, then I guess you are wasting your time. But me, I happen to think what I do, my decisions out here in the real fucking world, make a difference. But if this is just a paycheck to you, then you still aren't wasting your time. Are you? Staying for as long as you can means getting as many paychecks as you can. Either way, I'm not advising you to quit. Hell no. From everything I've seen, you've got the makings of a good street cop. And there isn't anything more noble, or less appreciated in this whole fucking world."

"So what do you think I should do now?"

Ron looks at me. "Your job."

32

THE NEXT WEEK I do my best to just concentrate on doing the job. When we are racing from call to call, there isn't time to worry about being on the captain's shit list. Up to this point in the shift, I haven't wasted a single moment thinking about Captain Wilks.

The heavy call load in the metropolitan area is reflected in the official dispatch policy. Downtown, they rarely broadcast loud party complaints, and then only in the five-oh-seven format, the equivalent of *FYI, there is loud party at...*After being broadcast as a five-oh-seven a couple of times, Communications Division upgrades an incident and assigns it to us. The address is in one of the swankiest parts of the Silver Lake district.

There isn't even enough room for sidewalks on the narrow streets that service the custom homes that dot the steep hillsides. It's always precarious squeezing around the parked cars on these narrow roads. Tonight, the closer we get to the address, the worse things get. Cars, predominately luxury models, are parked haphazardly into every inch of space without regard for parking regulations.

We don't have to search for the address. We just home in on the noise. Ron stops our police car behind a Mercedes parked half-in and half-out of the steep driveway of the party house. "Normally I'd never park right in front," Ron says, throwing it into park. "But these folks aren't likely to come out with guns-a-blazing. I bet there ain't an NRA member among them." Getting out of the car, he says, "The beautiful people hate it when you park a police car within a hundred yards of their place. Shit, they barely tolerate us in the same zip code."

The noise level is extraordinary. No wonder the neighbors have been so persistent in calling. Nearing the top of the flagstone stairway, I can see some of the guests through a large picture window. Our blue suits definitely don't meet the dress code for this soiree. Out of habit, we deploy to either side of the door. My partner pushes the doorbell, even though it is unimaginable that anyone inside can hear the chime, given all the noise.

Ron is about to announce us by smacking his kill light on the varnished hardwood door, when it swings open. An attractive blonde in her midthirties, wearing an expensive cowl-neck sweater dress is startled. Obviously, she opened the door to step outside, not greet guests. Judging by her expression, Jack Torrance would have been a more welcome sight. My partner tells the blond bombshell with her hair in a stylish updo, that we want to speak to the homeowner. With a condescending grimace of a smile, the beauty queen agrees to get him before closing the door with both hands.

We readjust our Sam Brownes a couple of times while waiting on the porch. After a while, it becomes obvious no one is coming to the door. Ron tries the handle. The door is unlocked. Ron pushes it open. I follow him inside.

The partygoers are stunned by two uniformed LAPD officers suddenly entering their upscale sacrosanct world. Following an awkward moment of disbelief there is a collective gasp, like we were used motor oil spilling onto a priceless antique silk rug. The woman we spoke with at the door scurries out of sight, only to return a few seconds later with the owner of the house. The man in his fifties is dressed in an expensive silk sports jacket with an ascot, dress slacks, and penny loafers. His hair is styled like the Sundance Kid.

The man's suntanned face exudes a stern reproach as the three of us step outside. Closing the front door only marginally improves the conditions for verbal communications.

The owner is emphatic. "You had no right to enter my home."

"You want'a make a complaint? I'll get my sergeant out here, and you can explain to him your objections to my handling of the call." With more than enough volume in his voice, Russell adds, "That is…if he can hear you over this racket."

The owner continues trying to put us on the defensive, but passes on my partner's offer to call a supervisor. "You can't just barge into someone's private residence absent a warrant—"

Ron cuts him off. "It's not like we just decided to jog up your stairway and walk into your house on a whim. We're here in response to numerous complaints. For the record, the woman in the sweater dress opened the door. She said she would go get you. Only after you didn't show up at the door, did I form the opinion something must have happened to you…or to the woman. After all, you are a law-abiding citizen, right? Why else would a law-abiding citizen who knows the police are at his door, not answer it?"

"It's not that I object for myself. But you're disturbing my guests—"

"We're disturbing your guests?" Ron's face is wearing the absurdity of the homeowner's remark. "Your guests are disturbing the whole damned city. My partner pivots and heads down the steps toward our car. "Let me call my sergeant. I think we need a couple of more units up here."

"Wait, Officer. There is no need for that." The owner turns to me. "Look, this is a very special occasion—"

I ignore the man who is obviously used to getting his way, and follow my partner down the stairs. I say in a loud voice, "You're right, partner. At least a couple more units."

The owner scampers down the steps ahead of us. Blocking our path, he struggles to appear at least a little deferential. "I appreciate someone called the police. Really. I'll turn down the music." Lifting his chin, he manages to look down his nose at us despite his being on the step below us. "I'm a personal friend of Captain Wilks's. If you just leave now, I'll make sure you don't get called up here again."

Ron glares at the pretentious man. "You are right about one thing. I'm not going to come back here again, because I'm going to handle this situation right here and now. Turn down the noise...not just the sound system, but the whole thing."

"I can lower the volume of the music, but how can I make—"

"That's your problem. It's your party. It's your responsibility."

"OK. OK," the man says, holding up his manicured hand.

Without another word, Ron and I head down the steps, leaving the homeowner still mouthing his condescension. "Thank you for stopping by...just keep going until you hit Fernwood. It'll take you down to Griffith Park Boulevard."

"Like we need fucking directions," Ron says.

A few moments later, the music volume drops significantly. My butt has barely dented the passenger seat before the volume returns to its previous level. Ron stops me from heading back up the flag-stone steps.

"The guy is just jerking us off. Talking to him is a waste of time. Remember I told you parking tickets can be a tool? It's time to use that tool."

Ron makes a show of writing a parking citation to the Mercedes parked half-in and half-out of the driveway. Several guests have come outside and are watching from a distance. Seeing my partner place the parking ticket on the windshield of the Mercedes, they begin shouting to the others. It doesn't take long before the owner of the ticketed car is descending the stairs.

The Mercedes owner yanks the citation off his windshield. Holding it so he can read it in the limited light, he shouts in disbelief, "Blocking the driveway? I'm not blocking the driveway. Your police car is blocking the driveway!"

Ron is across the street citing a Jaguar. He takes his time placing the ticket on the Jag's windshield, then casually strolls back to confront the infuriated Mercedes owner. Standing between our police car and the curb, Ron explains, "A vehicle parked astride the curb line is in violation. You're welcome to contest the citation if you like." Then he adds, "Sir, I am advising you to have this vehicle moved to a legal parking place."

"Fine. Just move your car and I'll move my mine." The guy grabs the door handle of his Mercedes.

"Sir, I advised you to *have this vehicle moved*—not for you to move it. You are obviously too intoxicated to safely operate a motor vehicle. If you get in your car I will have no choice but to arrest you for driving under the influence." The Mercedes owner is losing it.

And Ron isn't backing off. "I feel I should tell you that under the section I cited, impounding is at the officer's discretion." Ron's face wears a wry smile.

"I pay your salary, you fuck'n pig!" A stream of spittle is running out of the corner of the Mercedes owner's mouth.

My partner picks up the microphone hanging out of our passenger window and requests a tow. The livid owner of the Mercedes trips rushing back up the steps. Lifting himself off the flagstone amid a flurry of expletives, he is screaming to everyone that the pigs are about to tow away all their cars. The *bon vivant* guests pour out of the party, trying to get away before we tag their cars. It is as if someone pulled the plug on a bathtub.

I'm just starting a citation on a Fiat Spider blocking a fire hydrant when two chic women from the party approach. "Hey, get away from my car...you Nazi Gestapo bastard!"

When people call me a pig, it really doesn't bother me. The woman's remark suggesting my parents were never married doesn't bother me, either. But being called a Nazi, being called the Gestapo, really pisses me off. Although I know better, for just that fraction of a second my poker face fails me.

Without any of the ladylike pretense I'm sure they manifested at the party, the women tumble into the little convertible. The sound of the engine starting reminds me of my mother's sewing machine. I hear metal grinding as the driver jams the transmission into first gear. Letting out the clutch too fast she nearly stalls the little engine, but after a moment of hesitation, it catches. Both their heads are thrown back as the car accelerates down the narrow street, trailing fumes of unburned hydrocarbons.

Behind me Ron says, "Bitch thinks she got away."

"She did," I say. "I didn't have time to write her."

"Partner, do you really think she didn't realize you were writing her a ticket? Just because she didn't have the decency to wait for her copy of the citation, doesn't mean she skates. You did get the plate didn't you?"

"Yes, sir."

"After you finish with that cite, you can start on the impound report for the Mercedes. OPG (official police garage) will be here pretty quick."

"Yes, sir."

The party is over. It ended when the owner of the Mercedes ran into the house, announcing the cops were towing everyone's cars. The sight of the wrecker hooking up the Mercedes in the driveway convinces even the hard core. By the time OPG has pulled away, tranquility has returned to the neighborhood.

Officer Russell fires up a Marlboro. "Now that's how you handle a four-fifteen party."

En route to the station, I ask him what I do with the violator's copy of the parker I wrote on the Fiat.

"If it were me...I'd just let it blow out the window. Same difference as if the bitch just let it fly off her windshield driving away. But you are on probation, not to mention on the captain's shit list. And I'm your training officer. So, I'm gonna show you the right way, and keep your butt out of trouble. That's my job."

At the station Ron shows me where they keep the number eleven official city business envelopes. It is a simple matter to run the license plate to get the registered owner's name and address. I stuff the citation, together with a courtesy payment envelope, inside the larger official business envelope and drop it into the outgoing mail.

"That's all there is to it." Ron snickers. "Just don't seal the envelope. They check sometimes to be sure what's in the envelope is really official city business."

33

WE'VE BARELY LEFT the station parking lot before we get a code three run to an "ADW (assault with a deadly weapon) in progress." During my three months in the street, this is the first time the use of red lights and siren have been authorized. All the other hotshot calls were only dispatched as code two. Why code three on this one?

Even Ron isn't sure exactly how to get to the call. Based on the hundred block, we know it is somewhere among a tangle of narrow streets in the hills west of Elysian Park. My finger backtracks in my street guide like I'm cheating on a maze in a puzzle book. "It's off Lemoyne." I shout to be heard over the siren. I'm thankful to get my head out of the map book and gather my bearings.

When we get close, Ron shuts down the siren. "No sense telling the bad guys we're coming."

Turning onto the narrow street etched into the hillside we see a fire engine, its red lights flashing and engine running, parked mid-block. So much for the element of surprise.

The call is in one of the bungalows that dot the hillside on our left. Steep concrete steps provide the only access. How far up, and on which side of the steps, there's no way to know. Starting up the stairway, Ron says loudly enough to be heard over the fire engine's idling diesel, "You watch the right side. I'll watch the left."

There are no streetlights and stands of mature trees obscure the ambient light that normally backfills the darkness. Only our flashlights and the red strobe from the fire truck temporarily push back the night. Climbing the stairs, probing the foliage with my flashlight, I realize there could be a boatload of bogeymen a few feet away, and I wouldn't see them. Reaching the landing at the top of the first set of stairs, the sound of my lungs and heartbeat overtake the idling fire truck far below.

About halfway up the second flight of stairs I detect light filtering through the overgrowth. "Open door," I whisper. We extinguish our flashlights and approach. We hasten our steps when we see a firefighter kneeling just inside the door of the bungalow. Reaching the doorway, we find two firemen attending to an unconscious male victim lying on his back.

"Glad to see you guys," one of the firemen says, as he looks up from treating the man who looks to be in his early thirties. The victim is wearing only his boxers. He has slash wounds everywhere, like tiger stripes of raw meat. I can't believe he's still alive with all those gaping wounds.

"Normally we wait for you guys." The firefighter throws his head back, indicating a woman and little girl huddled in the corner of the living room. "But we couldn't ignore their screams. So I grabbed my friend..." he nods to his fire ax leaning against the wall, "and we ran up here."

The atmosphere inside the bungalow is moist with the smell of blood. Feather-like splashes of life's fluid litter the walls, the floor, even the ceiling. It looks as if someone set a spray bottle to stream and spent about an hour randomly squirting the room with the cochineal liquid. The place is a shambles. Must have been a hell of a fight. My eyes are drawn to a bloody machete on the floor. Holy shit! The feather-like blood splatters are from the machete.

The wife is standing in the far corner clutching her young daughter. When we step past them to make our tactical sweep of the bungalow, the little girl turns her head. The tears in her eyes steal my attention. More than anything, I wish we could have been here soon enough to have prevented this, to have prevented the tears in her eyes now, and all the tears to come. But we weren't. I have to look away. No time now. We have to clear the house.

The couple's bedroom is as bloody as the living room. On the floor next to the bed, I see the barrel of a rifle. The butt portion of the wooden stock has been freshly shattered. On the floor just inside the rear door are a couple of broken glass louvers. Obviously this is the point of entry. A path of trampled weeds leads from the rear door to the concrete steps. Not wanting to destroy any evidence, we retrace our steps. In less than a minute we're back in the living room.

Later, while taking the report, we will learn the wife is a TWA stewardess working LAX to Heathrow. Even disheveled, overwrought, and wrapped in a housecoat, I can see this woman meets the high standards insisted on by the airlines for their premier routes. Although the woman has blond hair, and her facial features are more angular, her expression immediately conjures images of Jackie Kennedy that dreadful day in Dallas a decade ago. Her misty azure eyes remain unfocused as she strokes her daughter's hair.

Her daughter has worked one hand free from her mother's embrace and is fingering the pink ribbon on her nightgown. A miniature of her mom, the child is a beautiful living doll crying real tears as she looks up at her mother. "Why were those men hurting Daddy? Why did they come in our house, Mommy?"

"I don't know, honey."

"The police are here now. Right, Mommy?"

"Shussshhh, honey. Just try to be still."

The firemen kneeling in their turnouts are doing all they can, but they're not miracle workers. The victim's chest quivers, and the firefighter's eyes tell me what I already know. It's officially a one-eighty-seven, a murder.

Under other circumstances we would interview the wife alone. But we need the information now and separating the mother from the daughter is unthinkable. The only room not strewn with bloody evidence is the child's bedroom. Her room was added to the bungalow by enclosing a section of the porch. We adjourn to the child's room, and the wife begins by telling us she was awakened when the assailants kicked in the back door.

Standing on her bed with one arm around her mom and the other on the sill of the large picture window that looks into her parents' bedroom, the little girl interrupts. "That was what woke me up, too." Her big blue eyes beg for our attention as she describes seeing her father grab the rifle when one of the men poked the barrel in her daddy's face.

Even my veteran partner cringes. We all would have preferred to think her innocent eyes had somehow been spared witnessing the heinous attack. Throughout the interview, it becomes evident she saw everything. Up to this point this little doll could have been cast in a commercial, the archetype of a carefree child filled with joy and optimism for the future. Tonight her life has been unimaginably transformed. It will never be normal for her again. How can she even go to sleep at night?

In police jargon, the suspects are two male Hispanics, seventeen to nineteen, wearing tan pants and dark jackets. The description is inadequate on every level. In my limited time as a street cop, I have only put out a few crime broadcasts. This isn't one to practice on. Ron hustles down the steps. Units are arriving, but we don't need them here. Combing the area looking for a couple of guys matching the description and covered in blood—that's what we need. Ron's crime broadcast will make it happen.

The smell of blood that hit me when we arrived is still here. But now there is also another smell, the smell of death. While the analytical side of my brain insists my ability to smell blood is logical, it can't abide the cessation of life having an odor. When decomposition sets in, of course there will be a smell, but not at the moment the life force leaves the body. Dismissing the inconsistency as a fleeting apparition would be of some comfort. Unfortunately, such solace is unavailable since the odor of death, like the smell of blood, lingers.

• • •

Decades later the hellacious scene in the bungalow would come back to me quite unexpectedly, triggered by the tears running down my own daughter's face when a gust of wind carried away her helium-filled Mickey Mouse balloon. Ironically, instead of emotionally paralyzing me, the gruesome images from my past summoned an intense feeling of gratitude, making me thankful to be alive and sharing the day with my daughter at Disneyland.

Her mother seized the moment to chastise me. She called me a brute, utterly incapable of compassion. Brusquely interposing herself between me and our child, my wife lambasted me for not gushing disingenuous sobs to salve the "poor child's tragic loss."

Predictably, her mother's criticism of her father did not diminish our little girl's distress. When her mother's insincere platitudes didn't immediately quell our child's outward manifestations of anxiety, my wife resorted to her usual tough love. Of course, reproving the child didn't work any better.

After her mother turned away in disgust, our daughter sought solace with her daddy. Taking my daughter's little hand, walking at a child's pace on the drawbridge of Sleeping Beauty's castle, we marveled together at the scene. Sitting on my haunches, I pointed to the white swans swimming in the black water. As quickly as the gust of wind had absconded with my daughter's balloon, the sadness of its loss flew away, replaced by the joy of sharing the moment with her daddy. Hoisting my daughter to my shoulders, the ugly crime scene completely receded from my consciousness.

Memories from that tragic night in the bungalow, together with so many recollections from my time as a cop, will remain with me all my days. They are the source of the consuming darkness I saw in my training officer's eyes my first night—now and forever, manifest in mine.

34

WHEN IT COMES time for putting in our days-off request, Ron tells me to give mine to the PM watch commander because I'm going to nights next DP. I guess I have a questioning look on my face.

"It's normal," Ron says. "They rotate probationers through all the watches."

"You know which car I'm working on PMs?"

"Still on A-one. They should keep you on the same car until you're off probation."

I tell Ron, "I gotta admit...I've kind of come to like mornings. It's just that I can't get the hang of sleeping during the day."

"You can't have everything." Ron laughs. "I've spent most of my career working AMs. When I get bumped, I always go to nights for a few DPs, then put in for AMs again." He winces. "Anything but day watch. Days are the worst. All the brass around. Fight the traffic getting to work. Fight the traffic at work. Fight the traffic on the way home. Not to mention...sometimes it's hotter than hell, especially during the summer." Ron grabs a cigarette. "Don't forget, partner, for most of my career we had to wear a class A, and there was no air-conditioning in the cars, either. Chief Parker would roll over in his grave if he knew his beloved LAPD had adopted a class C uniform option. Parker hated short-sleeve shirts for cops. And no tie? No fuck'n way! Not with Parker as chief. It was Reddin, the interim chief after Parker died, who pushed through the class C uniform. But it's good for you to get the experience working days, too. And don't you worry...after a few months on PMs, they'll ship your ass to days."

I figure this is as good a time as any to ask the question I really want to ask. "How about my training officers on PMs? Anyone like Morales?"

"No. The P-3s on PMs are both good guys." Ron throws a quick smile my way. "Not as good look'n as me...but good cops. You keep do'n how you been do'n, and ev'rything will be fine."

We get a four-fifteen man call. It's in a two-story apartment in the hills overlooking Sunset Boulevard. As Ron parks the car, I'm thinking the place has to have a great view. Listening at the door, we can hear two men arguing. From what we are overhearing, it is obvious this is yet another domestic dispute involving male homosexual cohabitants.

Before coming on the job, my experience with this segment of society was limited to working around a few gay guys at Disneyland. Just as my experience with the microphones at Disneyland had not prepared me for the complexities of using the police radio, my experience working around those gay guys had not prepared me for dealing with domestic disputes between homosexual partners. As in any family dispute, emotions run high, and there is a tendency for the parties to shift their hostility from each other to the police. When both parties are grown men, the danger is multiplied.

Ron knocks on the door, and we are admitted to the living room of the apartment. Just as I thought, there is a large picture window with a beautiful view of the city lights. I only catch a glimpse. Arbitrating this dispute will require my full attention.

De-escalating a dispute begins by getting the parties talking to you, and not arguing with each other. The standard tactic is to keep the protagonists facing away from each other while we maintain our line of sight. People want to air their grievances, so you have to at least appear sympathetic enough to get them to start telling you their side of the story. But you must also maintain the air of authority and quell their natural tendency to get worked up retelling how they've been mistreated.

Keeping your half talking to you, telling their story and not responding to what the other party is saying, is an art not easily mastered. It requires reading the person's mood and intentions, and then playing his or her vulnerabilities without triggering a violent response. Gauging the person is key. This involves reading subtle cues and adjusting your demeanor as much as your verbal response. Under the best of circumstances, I find myself missing a nuance or not being able to come up with just the right words or tonal inflection. Dealing with two male homosexuals in a partial state of undress, the task is even more difficult, not to mention awkward.

I assume the position of interrogation, facing my half of the dispute, who was in full drag for an evening on the town. Apparently a physical altercation erupted while he was getting undressed. His red evening gown is on the floor along with a platinum blond wig, leaving him wearing only a flesh-colored body suit. A nylon cap completes his ensemble of polyester stretch fabric. A trickle of blood mixed with garish lipstick and pancake makeup is smudged at an angle from his lower lip toward his cheek. I am trying to keep his attention, but he is still directing his remarks over his shoulder toward his lover.

"That motherfucker! I would have never moved in here if I knew the kind of pervert he was."

"Do you have anyplace else you can go tonight?" I ask.

"That faggot! I gave him the best he has ever had, and look how he treats me. No wonder he was living alone when I met him. Uptight motherfucker! I was just having fun." He looks over his shoulder again. "It wasn't like it was just me. I saw that queen grabbing your joint."

His lover responds, "Yeah, so that gave you reason to suck every guy's dick in the club?"

"We're not here to listen to you guys argue!" Ron shouts. "We're giving both of you a chance to work this out without going to jail. You already told me you don't want him here tonight, but if you keep arguing, we will just leave...or book both of you. It doesn't matter to me."

I follow Ron's lead. "Look, we are not here to referee a rehash of what happened at the club. If you had someplace to go tonight, it would solve the problem."

"Just arrest the cocksucker. Look, he busted my lip," the drag queen protests.

"If anyone is going to jail, it is more likely to be you. Those cuts on his face are a lot worse than your busted lip. One thing is for sure... if we arrest him, we would have to arrest you, too. I don't really think taking both of you to jail is what you want us to do. But, if we can't solve this any other way, then what do you think we are going to do?"

With this, the queen calms down and begins telling me his tale of woe. I agree with him that he has been treated unfairly. I suggest it is not healthy for him to stay in an abusive relationship. Eventually he agrees it's in his best interest to leave, at least for tonight. He resets the wig on his head, steps into his dress, and turns around, asking me to zip him up. It's not like I haven't zipped up a woman's dress before, but never with a guy wearing it. My initial inclination is to do it, but something tells me not to.

The other half of the domestic dispute decides he is going to pull his turtleneck sweater over his head. He turns around, asking my partner to help him pull his sweater down.

Ron's response is immediate. "We ain't here to help you fruits get dressed."

"Your partner is zipping up my roommate."

"No, he ain't," Ron insists.

Ron's half of the squabble pokes his head through the turtleneck and sees his roommate still struggling to zip himself up.

When my half gets his dress zipped, I give him his marching orders. "OK. Time to go."

"I have to go to the bathroom and freshen up first," the queen insists.

I block his path. Letting him out of my sight would open a million possibilities—all of them bad. He could arm himself, slash his wrists, or just lock himself in the bathroom. With authority in my voice, I tell him, "You're heading out the front door. Your only choice is whether you go in handcuffs or not."

Either I'm going to get his compliance, or the fight is on. If it gets physical, it's going to be a hell of a brawl. And we won't have a chance to request backup because our lifeline is down a couple of flights of stairs, parked across the street.

Ron keeps his suspect off to the side as I escort my half of this domestic disaster through the door. Ron joins me on the landing. We wait until the drag queen is halfway down the stairs before following suit. When we get to our car, the transvestite is hanging around on the sidewalk.

"How about giving a girl a ride?" the queen queries in his best falsetto. "Just down to Sunset...I can handle it from there."

"We ain't a taxi service," my partner replies.

"It's the least you can do after kicking me out of my place."

"We didn't kick you out," Ron corrects the female impersonator. "I'd just as soon book your ass. And if we have to come back here, that's exactly what we are going to do."

"Fuck'n pigs!" the queen says over his shoulder as he sashays toward the boulevard.

As we get into our car, Ron says, "Fuck'n faggot better not even think about coming back here tonight. I never like coming back to a call. If we have to come back...that cocksucker is definitely going to jail—the hard way."

As Ron pulls from the curb, he goes back to telling me what I can expect next DP. "Got a couple of shit supervisors on PMs. So you'll have to be wearing your hat. I've been pretty lax on teaching you about wearing your hat. Mostly because I'm pretty lax about wearing my hat."

To my way of thinking, Ron has not been lax on anything, including wearing the hat. I have followed his lead and put my hat on whenever the tactical conditions would permit. Ron has frequently talked about how stupid the whole hat thing is. It didn't take much to convince me. Considering all the important stuff you've got to do every time you get out of the car, reaching into the backseat to grab a hat, has always seemed like more of a hazard than a safety enhancement to me.

Still, from the first day in the academy the instructors insisted the uniform hat is an important piece of our safety equipment. They say it readily identifies us as police officers, repeating ad nauseam a story of the homeowner who was going to take a shot at a silhouette in his backyard, but held his fire because he recognized the distinctive shape of the police hat on the shadowy figure. Even if that actually happened, it isn't very persuasive to me.

Such circumstances would have to be incredibly rare, and a far cry from what we are doing most of the time. For instance, on a car stop, the occupants don't need to see our hats to know we're the police. Fumbling to grab a hat could be fatal if someone in the car is grabbing a gun. Tell me the hat is a part of the uniform, and I'll buy that. Tell me it's a safety issue, no way.

Sergeants bark whenever they show up, and someone is without his hat. OK. It's part of the uniform. When Ron tells me there are a couple of sergeants on PMs who will actually write you up for not wearing your hat, I'm not looking forward to that, especially considering I'm on the captain's shit list. I can see it now. "Probationer Stoller fired for being unsafe," and then in the fine print, "failure to wear his hat."

Three tones on the radio get our attention. "Beep...Beep...Beep." The link is simulcasting a code three ambulance shooting call somewhere in South Bureau. Through the link's open mike we hear units reporting en route to the call. One unit is apparently right on top of the call and goes code six almost immediately. Within seconds, we hear, "Code four—N V N N H I."

My partner says, "I haven't heard that in a long time."

Thinking out loud, I say, "I don't remember that acronym from the academy. What does it mean?"

Ron gives me some context. "When I worked south traffic, I used to hear it en route to my ambulance traffic calls quite a bit. The first unit arriving at the scene would check on the occupants of the cars, then put out a code four—N V N N H I."

"So what does it stand for?"

"Nigger Versus Nigger No Human Involved."

"You gotta be shit'n me!"

"Nope, back in the day it was SOP."

The police radio hasn't stopped issuing its static-laced jargon. The sounds of our patrol car treading the asphalt and pushing aside the cold night air have not abated, either. Yet Ron's explanation dulls my senses. It is as if God turned down the volume. The silence is reminiscent of the quiet that descended on me when I saw the suspect reaching for a pistol under the seat cushion.

I'm proud of the badge on my chest. I've been working my ass off just to be sitting in this car wearing this uniform. I actually believe in the LAPD motto, *To Protect and to Serve*. Then there are guys like Morales who wear the same badge. There are guys like Officer Lance at the academy and people like Captain Wilks, for that matter. Still, I'm shocked by what I heard on the radio. Yeah, the bigot was smart enough not to give his call sign before broadcasting his particular brand of code four. While that might mask his identity from me, his existence is undeniable. Those who work his division obviously recognize the voice.

I've heard a lot of talk in the locker room and at coffee. With street cops, ethnic pejoratives are common. I figure a lot of guys are just trying to imitate the Dirty Harry character. But to think this was common radio procedure as recently as Ron's tenure on the department—that is hard to accept. Although muted from my consciousness, my ears are still functioning. The radio wrests me from my contemplation.

"Two-Adam-one, two-Adam-one...Phone the watch commander, code two."

My hand automatically picks up the mic, and I hear my voice acknowledging the transmission.

"Shit!" Ron says. "Only thing worse than call the watch commander, code two, is Go to the watch commander, code two. Those fruits must have pitched a bitch."

Before two-way radio communications, beat officers contacted the station via a system of callboxes strategically located around the city. The antiquated communication instruments inside the boxes have been replaced, but the telephones are still locked in original sturdy brass enclosures made by the Gamewell Company of New York. The manufacturer's name is molded prominently into the face of each box. Hence cops use the terms "callbox" and "Gamewell" interchangeably.

Ron parks our cruiser next to a Gamewell and rocks himself out of the car saying, "Sit tight while I talk to the lieutenant."

35

WHEN MY PARTNER returns and plops into the driver's seat, he says, "It could be worse. We are to meet the FBI. They have a tip on Patty Hearst."

"No shit? The FBI? Patty Hearst?"

"Don't get excited, kid. Trust me. I've worked with these clowns before. It ain't like you see on TV. You've already done more police work and arrested more crooks than these guys do in a career. After tonight, you can make up your own mind about the FBI. Until then, I'm telling you, these guys are CPAs with guns. No fucking tactical sense at all. If we get into anything, we do things our way."

"Yes, sir."

We meet Special Agents Jenkins and McElroy in a supermarket parking lot, a couple of thirty-something bookends wearing business suits and driving a rental car. They flash their credentials. The oft-heard expression about their badges resembling a prize from a box of Cracker Jack is apropos. We lean against our black-and-white, waiting to hear what the agents have to say.

Special Agent Jenkins clears his throat and then twists his arm with a flourish to reveal an expensive timepiece on his wrist. He is try-ing to sound authoritative. "This information is just about an hour old. A confidential informant reports seeing Patty Hearst, accompanied by two male Negroes, enter a safe house after getting out of a van parked on the street—"

Ron cuts to the chase. "What's the address?"

"We don't have an exact address. It's in the Silver Lake area."

"OK. How about the van?" Ron asks.

"It's supposed to be tan in color, panel side, parked on the street."

"And?"

"That's it. That's all we've got. We were going to drive all the streets looking for the van, but examining the map, we realized the streets run every which way. So we called your watch commander."

"OK. Let me get this straight…" Ron's face is scrunched into question mark. "You don't have an address. You don't have a street name. You don't even have a nearby intersection—"

"No. It is supposed to be this side of the lake, west of Glendale Avenue and north of Sunset. That's all the information we have."

"And no license plate on the van. Not even which state?" Ron's normal look of disgust is gaining intensity. "No make? Early or late model?"

Nonplused, the agent hesitates. "Tan in color, no windows on the sides, parked there about an hour ago. That is all the informant could give us."

As if on command, my partner and I stuff our field officer's notebooks back in our breast pockets and fold our arms across our chests. Up this point I was pretty excited about the possibility of finding Patty Hearst. After all, it's only the biggest kidnapping case since Lindbergh. But this is ridiculous. What they have told us hasn't changed the size of the haystack very much.

"OK," Ron says. "We'll canvas the area and report back here when we are done…ah, or earlier…if we find something." My partner can't help but ask one more question. "You got a clothing description on Patty Hearst or the males?"

The FBI agent lifts his chin. "We'll recognize them if we see them. We'll just tag along with you guys as you canvas the area."

"Suit yourself," Ron says. "Hop in the back."

Out of habit, I check the backseat before the agents climb in.

Fumbling around for the seat belt, Jenkins questions me. "What's up with this seat back here? It's not secured."

I look at my partner. When he nods, I put my left arm over the back of the front seat and explain. "You know how it is. We check the backseat before and after transporting. Thataway, if a suspect drops some evidence, or contraband, we can show it was him who ditched it, and no one else. A thorough inspection requires removing the bench seat. As often as we are checking, it doesn't take long before the attaching mechanism doesn't work anymore. So the seat just kind of floats around. You gotta hold it in place with your butt. You'll get the hang of it."

As Ron expertly traverses the area delineated by the agents, McElroy points from the backseat. "There!" he says, excitement in his voice.

"Where?"

"Up there on the right!"

My muscles relax when I see the van the agent is pointing to. "Not exactly tan, and with all that dew...looks like it's been parked there all night."

As we roll slowly by the van, it is obvious the vehicle is actually green in color. I mention the bumper has a couple of semesters' worth of Glendale City College parking decals. Running the plate, the van comes back registered to the address where it is parked. I rip the sheet off our notepad and hand it to the agent in the backseat.

"It's the light," I explain. "These street lights are high-pressure mercury vapor. The light they give off is shifted toward the blue end of the spectrum. Between the lighting and the dew, it can be difficult to distinguish colors."

During the last three months I have spent hours listening to Ron expound on a wide variety of subjects with at least some tangential connection to street police work. One night he explained the different kinds of street lights and how they affect the colors our eyes see. It is obvious Ron is pleased I paid attention, and even more pleased the two Federal Boy Idiots in the backseat are enraptured by my lecture.

I continue espousing. "Downtown they are converting a lot of the streetlights to low-pressure sodium vapor. Those give off a really golden light. Hell, everything is a shade of tan under those things."

• • •

We don't find anything, not even one van matching the description. *So much for finding Patty Hearst.* Ron brings us back to the grocery store parking lot.

When the agents have climbed out of our backseat, they hand us their business cards along with a stern admonishment. "If you come across the van, call us. Don't approach or stop it! Call us, and we'll take it from there."

"Sure thing," Ron says.

Before we are even out of the parking lot, I'm venting. "You're right, partner. Busted my bubble. Those guys couldn't investigate their way out of a paper bag. Still, I can't believe they told us if we see the van, we should wait for them. You gotta be shitting me!" Still incredulous at what I just heard, I interrupt writing in my log and look at Ron. "Don't stop the van? What are we gonna do? Let Patty Hearst drive off into the sunset? Oh yeah. Our other option is to bumper tag the van, waiting for these two clowns to show up and execute a felony car stop in their rental car! If they really didn't have any more info than what they told us, they should have stayed asleep in their hotel room."

Ron is laughing. "Even if that was all they had to go on, they had to do something. If someone ever found out Patty Hearst spent a night in a safe house in the area, and they had been given a tip and didn't do anything, their asses would be hanging in the breeze. I think this was a CYA caper all the way. If they had approached us that a way, I would have appreciated it." He looks at me as he exhales a big cloud of smoke. "At least it got us off the air for a while. And now you can tell your grandkids you helped the FBI solve the kidnapping of the century."

"Jesus, partner. You got me married with kids...and even grand-kids already. You're worse than my mother."

Officer Russell is grinning like the night he met up with his old partner after the foot pursuit. "Good thing you're going to PMs, Max, you're get'n way too salty to be my boot."

36

IT'S MY LAST shift on AMs, my last night working with Ron, and it's my turn to drive. Hauling our stuff to the car, we hear a unit is in foot pursuit. Forgoing all the usual routine, we throw our equipment into the trunk, and ourselves into the front seat. I fire up the engine and back up just enough to clear the car in front of us with its trunk lid raised. Turning the steering wheel to the right, the tires chirp as I drop it into second and hit the gas. The raised trunk prevents me from seeing the door is open on the car in front of us. Fortunately, the officer yanks his door closed just in time.

Our squealing tires add to the chorus as I jockey with the other units heading toward the driveway. I play the suspension through the dip at the exit as we join the line of black-and-whites hauling ass toward the call. Ron's special quesadilla is going to have to wait.

The air unit is setting up a perimeter. My partner tells the RTO we are code six, then he switches to tac-2, telling the observer in the helicopter which corner we are taking. Sitting on the perimeter, Ron remarks, "Pretty fancy driving. Especially getting out of the lower lot. Even the best can't do that too many times without rub'n someth'n. If it had been a help call—I wouldn't say noth'n. But, it was only an assistance call. Remember it only takes one aw shit to erase ninety-nine atta boys."

"Yes, sir."

He takes a long, slow drag on his cigarette. "You think Captain Wilks is gonna pass up the opportunity to fire your ass for ripping the door off a police car...just 'cause you were going to an assistance call?"

"I see your point, sir."

It isn't too long before we hear "Code four—suspects in custody." Ron switches the radio back to base, and we both get out to retrieve our stuff from the trunk. No morning watch units have cleared yet, but the RTO knows a bunch of units are out here. So instead of assigning a call to an outside division, she says, "Any Rampart unit, or any unit in the vicinity, a four-fifteen family dispute, possible gun involved..."

Ron has completed the five-point safety inspection and is loading the shotgun when he announces, "That family dispute is in A-eleven's area. They should pick it up, but if they don't, and they give it to an outside unit, we'll buy it."

"Yes, sir."

We have barely settled back into our seats when the RTO assigns the call to a Hollywood unit. My partner picks up the mic and buys the family dispute. He tells me, "I'd rather hit my taco place right now, but no way in hell I'm gonna feed my face when outside units are getting calls in Rampart."

En route to the call, Ron tells me another war story. "Working south traffic on PMs out of University Division, kind of like tonight, right out of the box, we get a two-eleven silent (robbery alarm with no audible cue to alert the suspects). This particular savings and loan was located close to a freeway on-ramp and had a nasty habit of getting robbed."

The bench seat creaks as Ron leans back, trying to get comfortable. "I was working with my regular partner, Williams...he's work'n Newton now. Anyways...we approach from the alley in the rear. Don't spot a getaway car or a layoff man, so we bail out, leaving our black-and-white where it can't be seen from the bank. As we are snoop'n and poop'n up to the window to have a look-see, a tall light-skinned African-American sergeant, who looks like he spent his entire police career working manuals and orders, pulls up right in front of the place. The geek is doing his best John Wayne, hauling out the tube. Just as my partner takes a peek through the window of the bank... *blam*! What the fuck? Did we miss a layoff man? Did the suspects get out of the bank already? Not sure where the threat is, my partner and I go back-to-back. I look at the sergeant. The guy looks pretty melanin deprived—like he's been locked in the basement all his fuck'n life.

"'What you shooting at?' my partner asks him.

"'Nothing,' the sergeant calls back. 'I just went like this.' The sergeant works the pump action and *wham* another round goes off. I figure the idiot just had his finger on the trigger."

Keeping my eyes scanning outside the car, I can feel Ron looking at me.

"Why am I telling you this?"

Here comes the payoff.

"Because although the sergeant claims he gave the shotgun a five-point safety check, the armorer discovered the firing pin was stuck in the extended position."

It has been drummed into us countless times on the range. "Be sure the firing pin remains recessed," Ron and I recite in unison. "Otherwise, chambering a round—fires a round."

"Obviously the geek didn't preflight the shotgun, but since he was somebody's bun boy, he only wound up with a paper penalty for his two ADs (accidental discharges). Why am I bringing this up?" Ron is in his rhetorical-teaching mode again. "This department has about a gazillion rules. The reality is that the consequences for breaking the rules mostly depends on your rank...and if you got a sponsor. But out here in the real world, there are some rules that have their own consequences. I'd like to be able to tell you don't sweat the department shit, just sweat the real-world shit. But by now I think you know it's more complicated than that. Still, when it comes to firearms, and the shotgun in particular, there just ain't no excuse for taking any shortcuts."

I take my time driving to the family dispute call, figuring the "possible gun involved" comment is just somebody trying to get a quicker response. Soon after our arrival, my suspicions are confirmed. We solve the domestic situation by employing the street cop's best friend, the unpaid traffic ticket.

37

GETTING BACK INTO the car after booking the husband on his traffic warrant, Ron tells me, "You are really lucky."

"How so?" I wonder where he is going with this remark as I pull out of the jail parking lot and head for the freeway.

"Starting on mornings was just right. PMs can be a bit too much when you are first out of the academy. But now, you are definitely ready for the faster pace. Just one thing I regret..."

I expect my TO is going to continue, but he doesn't. My glance doesn't do it, so I prompt him verbally. "What do you regret?"

"Not get'n you into a great big old donnybrook." He winces and smiles at the same time. "Normally it just happens. I don't even have to try. You are the first boot I've had in a long while who I didn't get into a great big brawl before I handed him off to another TO. I'm not sure this is good for my reputation. Guys gonna think I lost my touch."

"Hey, partner. Don't get down on yourself. The night is young."

"I thought for sure we was go'n with those two fruits. Remember, right before the LT gave us chauffeur duty for the FBI? Those two were just about ready to kiss and make up by turning on us."

"Yeah, I thought the same thing—"

An older-model Cadillac blows through the boulevard stop right in front of us. The Caddy accelerates as it slides into the middle lane of Sunset Boulevard.

"What's up with this guy?" I ask out loud, kicking in the four-barrel carburetor to catch up. Pacing the Caddy, the needle on our calibrated speedometer reads sixty-two. The posted limit is thirty-five. Ron checks the hot sheet, then runs the plate. No wants. No warrants.

I get directly behind the Cadillac, activate the reds, and hit the high beams. Nothing changes. I chirp the siren. Still nothing. Approaching a red light, the Caddy slows down, glides into the left turn lane, and stops. *How can this guy not know we are behind him?* The driver hasn't turned his head or even glanced in the rearview mirror. When the light changes the Cadillac creeps into the intersection.

It's a standoff. The cars in the oncoming lanes see our red lights and they're not moving. Neither is the Caddy. My partner switches from siren to PA (public address) and tells the driver to turn left when it is safe, then pull to the curb.

This guy has gotta be deuce. As the Caddy begins to turn I can see the driver's head canted toward us. Just when I'm sure he's going to make a U-turn, the driver cranks the steering wheel all the way to the right and heads toward the sidewalk. The luxury car stops when the right front tire refuses to climb the curb.

I don't want to park too close behind him, but I don't want to stop broadside in the middle of the intersection, either. I split the difference, throw it in park and bail out. Approaching the Coupe de Ville, I can see the violator alternating between trying to open his window, reaching for the glove box, and turning down the sun visor. I tap on the glass. "Open the window!"

The car rocks backward. Shit! It's still in gear! I grab the door handle and yank. The big car is gaining momentum and threatening to drag me backward or cut me off at the shins. Running sideways, I reach inside the driver's compartment and pull up on the gearshift.

There is a loud clank from the bell housing as the parking pawl catches. The Caddy stops, rocking back and forth on its suspension only inches from hitting our cruiser.

I snatch the keys out of the ignition with my right hand and take a step back. Tossing the keys on the hood to free up my gun hand, adrenaline is fueling my voice. "Out of the fucking car!"

The driver, a bespectacled man in his fifties, was already frightened. My yelling doesn't help. Finally gathering his wits, the violator steps out. "I'm sorry, Officer. I was looking for my registration and thought it was in park—"

"Go to my partner over there on the curb!" I point with my flashlight toward my partner on the sidewalk, directing the violator to walk in front of his car. There isn't even enough room for him to squeeze between the rear bumper of his car and the front of ours. *Man, that was close.*

Amazingly enough, the driver has no objective symptoms of alcohol or drugs, only a major case of HUA (head up ass). I write him a ticket for both the stop sign and speeding, explaining I could have booked him for reckless driving. He is sincerely apologetic and happy to be leaving with just a ticket.

After the violator is on his way, while I wait for Ron to finish his log entry, I'm thinking out loud. "There sure are a lot of ways to get in trouble out here."

"Yep, there are an unlimited number of ways for things to go to shit. That guy was the best example of Mr. Mild-Mannered Milquetoast I've seen. He wouldn't intentionally hurt anyone. Certainly not a cop. Still, he almost ran your ass over and crashed into our car. Even if you didn't get hurt, it would have probably ended your LAPD tenure."

Trying to gauge if he is kidding, I ask, "How could they blame me?"

"Easy. In the traffic report the violator would have been Party One, but you would be driver prior of Party Two. The department would have found you guilty of *failing to anticipate*. Wilks would make certain of that. But, none of that happened. You done good."

"Thanks." I mean it, especially since Ron is downright stingy with anything approaching an accolade.

Closing his books, Ron begins another story. "Weird shit happens on car stops more often than people think. I had a caper where I was chasing *the little old lady from Pasadena*. We were just about to announce we were in pursuit when the old lady pulled to the curb. The silver-haired old biddy is watching me in her side view mirror as I approach. Just as I get near her door, she smiles and daintily locks her door with one finger. I tap on her window just like you did. But she just sits there with a smug smile on her face."

"What did you do...call a sergeant?"

"Fuck no! I wasn't going to take a chance the sergeant who showed up might be one of those mealy-mouth types. Anyway...Granny looks up at me, gives me this innocent little wave while mouthing good-bye, and drops it into gear."

"You run back to your car and go in pursuit?"

"Hell no. I smashed her window."

"What? No way! I can't believe you actually broke her window."

"Neither could she. She was so pissed she jammed on the brakes, threw it into park, and screamed at me through the shattered glass—'Young man, what do you think you are doing?'"

"I snatched the keys out of the ignition, just like you did. Then I told her I was doing what she should have done—opening her window. It was funnier than shit. I can still see the old battle-ax yelling at me, 'Young man, I want to speak with your superior, right this instant!'"

Ron lights up a smoke and says, "One of the things to come out of that big ticket-fixing scandal a few years ago was more paperwork for the supervisors canceling cites. So, I figured if I already had the ticket written, even if the sergeant who showed up was a spineless piece of shit, this clever old witch wasn't gonna skate.

"Fortunately the supervisor who responded was old-school. He didn't fall for her soft-soaping. When the biddy told the supervisor how nice the other officers had always been, and how none of them had ever done anything when she waved and drove away...I knew he wasn't gonna let her slide. I guess she realized it, too. She changed up, going on and on about how I didn't have the right to break her window on account of her being an elderly woman with kids and grandkids and shit. But the old sarge just stood there with his thumbs hooked in his Sam Browne, like Matt Dillon on *Gunsmoke*, telling her she had it all bass-akwards."

Ron is reliving the moment. With his cigarette hanging from his mouth, he stuffs his thumbs in his Sam Browne and imitates the old-school supervisor. "Being an old skirt don't give you the right to break the law. Had you been a young buck, no doubt you'd a got your ass beat and be bleeding in the backseat of the officer's car right now. You already got all the slack you gonna get. Sign the ticket or you're go'n to jail. There ain't gonna be no more discussion."

Ron grabs the cigarette, exhaling smoke out the window. "She signed the ticket for the sergeant. Then in her prissiest voice, lifting her chin in defiance, she demanded, 'Young man, I want to know what you are going to do about my broken window.'

"I looked her dead in the eye as I handed back her license and registration. 'What am I gonna do? About your broken window? I'll tell you what I'm gonna do. I'm giving you a warning. You got forty-eight hours to get it fixed. If I see this car on the road with a broken window after forty-eight hours...I'm gonna impound it.'"

Ron flicks his cigarette out the window. "I guess it wasn't the answer she wanted to hear. She dropped her Super Stock into gear and peeled out. Of course that vehicle code section only applies to the windshield, not the side windows. But she didn't know that."

I'm laughing. I never thought I would, but I know I am going to miss working with this cranky old fart. I tell him, "Just about everybody I stop says they know somebody. Mister Mild-Mannered Milquetoast said he works with some city councilman. Usually I figure it is BS, but I actually believed this guy."

Ron doesn't hesitate. "Most the time it is bullshit, but even if it ain't...it don't make me no never-mind. I'd write the chief's best fucking friend. I only got one rule that a way...I never wrote a cop or a fireman. Don't get me wrong. I stopped plenty. I wanted to a couple of times...but never wrote 'em."

I smile. "Actually, if Wilks is gonna fire me on probation, I'd rather it be because I wrote one of his cronies a ticket."

"Don't worry; captains still fix tickets. Thanks to that big scandal, they don't do it like they used to. Nowadays they usually just pay the fine. Captains have a fund for that kind of stuff. So Captain Numb Nuts can't use that excuse to end your cop career."

There is a period of silence before Ron goes back to his original subject. "I really do regret not getting you into an actual altercation. Knocking a drunk to the ground and yanking his arm behind his back don't count. Remember that great big guy we arrested for child molestation? So big we had to use two sets of handcuffs?"

"Yes, sir."

"The guy was bigger than both of us put together. But when I told him to turn around and put his hands behind his back—he did. Know why? On account of the rep. LAPD has got a reputation. The street assholes have all had their asses kicked by LAPD, or they know somebody who has. When an LA cop tells them they are going to jail—they go'n to jail. It ain't like—maybe yes, maybe no. We don't give 'em that choice. How much it hurts...that's up to them. Go along with the program, and it's painless. We just walk 'em through the jailhouse door. Act stupid, and we beat them to a bloody pulp before dragging them into the cell."

Russell's black holes are boring into me. "You've been riding the rep. The assholes we have booked have all gone along with the program. But eventually some asshole is not gonna go along with the program. When that time comes, you gotta kick ass. You gotta do your part to keep up the rep. Don't be the weak link in the chain."

Ron readjusts his bulk in the seat. "Like I said, it can't be *maybe yes, maybe no*. Every street cop is depending on you to keep the rep intact. Don't get me wrong. I'm not a prizefighter trying to win a title. I'm a cop enforcing the law. I'd always just as soon talk a guy to jail. Uniforms are too expensive. But that is exactly why it is so important that I make sure every one of my boots will kick ass when the time comes. Some TOs will take you out your first night and start a fight, just to get that out of the way. Years ago, that 'a been me. Nowadays, I wait. Some asshole always insists on getting his ass beat. When it happens, I find out what I need to know. It's the only way I know for sure...seeing you actually doing it." Ron pauses. "Somehow that didn't happen with you. That's why I regret not getting you into a real fight. Because now I can't be sure."

There isn't anything I can say. Up to this point I felt fortunate to have avoided a serious physical altercation. But at this moment, I wish it had happened. Not only would it have cleared the issue in my mind, but also I really want to prove it to Ron. He is right. I have been riding the rep. I owe a debt to all the street cops who have paid the price.

I also know myself. I have never been a freeloader. I have always insisted on paying my own way. I don't like to ask anyone for anything. The only way I am going to feel good about myself is by doing my part when the time comes. I've never been the "weak link," and I'm not about to start now.

In a bizarre twist, instead of mentally advocating for a night without encountering a serious physical threat, I spend the rest of the shift actually hoping fate brings trouble. Officer Russell has worked hard mentoring me. I feel like this is my last opportunity to repay him.

• • •

In the years to come, I will develop a much greater appreciation for just how much I am in Officer Russell's debt. I will repay that debt with compound interest, by devoting myself, and by inculcating other LA cops with the same common sense and dedication to duty. The LAPD's rep won't suffer on my account, either.

• • •

At EOW, as we are emptying out our car, Ron gives me his final piece of advice. "Reserve judgment," he says as he grabs his helmet bag out of the trunk.

I look at him quizzically.

"Wait a little before you decide which cops are assholes. There's no hurry. You've got plenty of time to hate 'em later."

38

MY FIRST SHIFT working PMs, I'm amazed at the number of guys in roll call. There isn't enough room for all the sergeants to sit at the watch commander's desk. A couple of the three-stripers stand alongside the wall. One stays busy handing out subpoenas. I sign the court book for my subpoenas when the sergeant comes to me.

The boss is Lieutenant Garcia, a square-jawed Don-Juan type, about half as old as Lieutenant Price. Just like on AMs, the LT reads the rotator after giving out the assignments. After roll call, the line to check out equipment is longer, but otherwise, the routine is the same. Still, it feels strange going outside to be greeted by sunshine and the daytime clamor of the city. When I toss my helmet bag in the trunk, in addition to my partner's helmet bag, I see a stout portable file box with "Shepards E. J." stenciled on all four sides. My new TO is walking around the car with the vehicle damage log open in his hands. His reddish-brown hair doesn't even budge as he leans over to examine the driver's side front quarter panel.

"Found a few new scratches," he says. "Don't want to get blamed for them."

As I am putting the shotgun in the rack I notice my partner's notebook on the front seat along with his hat. I throw my hat in the backseat, and write the shop number and starting mileage in my log.

My new TO climbs behind the wheel and introduces himself, "Shepards, senior P-3 on PMs." He offers his hand.

"Stoller, sir." I shake his hand.

He rattles off his serial number before telling me, "We got two calls already. A death notification and a four-five-nine report that day watch said they couldn't get to." He hands me the information, fires up the car, and glances at the seat between us. "I brought my books, too. Sometimes boots don't have everything, but that's not the only reason I brought my notebook. We get a ton of reports on nights, sometimes as many as four or five in a shift. Putting them all on one guy doesn't make any sense, and it takes too long. So if we get swamped, I'll help you out. Oh, and keep your hat up front. Sergeant Speer is a stickler on hats."

"Yes, sir." I retrieve my hat from the backseat.

En route to the call, he inquires, "Ever handle a death notification before?"

"No, sir."

"OK. Well, you don't just drop it on 'em like a bomb. You try to get them to say it to you. Just follow my lead. You gotta be careful though. Some people get real emotional and want to kill the messenger. The only time I ever put out a help call was on a death notification working the south end." He shakes his head. "The whole family turned on us."

The call is in an older quiet residential neighborhood. My partner and I step up onto the porch and deploy to either side of the front door. A slightly frumpy woman in her fifties wearing a housedress opens the door and inquires through the screen, "What's the trouble, Officers? I didn't call."

It's obvious she was not expecting visitors. She isn't wearing any makeup, and her hair is in the tousled remains of a flip.

"Mrs. Jones? Adrian Jones? Daughter of Arletta Jones of Dubuque, Iowa?" Shepards inquires.

"Ah, yes...last name is Sturgeon now." A worried look comes over her.

"Could we come in for a moment, ma'am? Is there anyone else here? A friend or relative?"

"No, just me."

As Mrs. Sturgeon opens the screen door, I notice a woman coming out onto the porch of the house next door. I make eye contact with Mrs. Sturgeon and point. "Ma'am, how about your neighbor? Are you on good terms?"

"Yes. Gracious me, that's Phyllis."

I linger on the porch for a moment and call to the neighbor, "Phyllis, would you come over to Mrs. Sturgeon's house for a moment, please?" It is obvious Phyllis is anxious to be the first to know the particulars of this washline news.

In the living room, my partner continues, "You might want to have a seat, ma'am."

I hold open the screen door for the neighbor.

"What's this all about?" the neighbor asks, out of breath.

My partner announces, "I'm afraid we have some bad news."

"Oh my God." Phyllis puts her hands to her open mouth.

Adrian looks up from the sofa. "Is it about my momma?"

"Yes, ma'am, I'm sorry to say it is."

"My momma's dead, isn't she?"

"Yes, ma'am."

Adrian's whimpers turn to sobs. She puts her head in her hands and begins to cry.

Sitting on the edge of the sofa, softly patting Adrian's shoulder, Phyllis purrs. "Now, now, child. It's gonna be OK."

"Mrs. Sturgeon, do you have a phone here?" my partner inquires.

The bereaved woman waves her hand toward the kitchen. My partner finds the phone on the wall, records the number off the dial, and then calls the station to tell the watch commander we have completed our task. We leave a piece of paper with the numbers for Adrian to contact in Iowa, as well as the number for our Detective Headquarters Division. As we bid Adrian and Phyllis adieu, my mind is mulling things over. This is not what I envisioned being a cop would be like. Yet, this is another part of the job.

There is an intimacy in death, perhaps because it is one experience we all share. Standing on an old throw rug in the living room next to her worn floral sofa, I shared an intimate moment with Mrs. Adrian Jones-Sturgeon. It wasn't because she wanted me there. Still, I was there when she learned her mother had passed. It doesn't seem right. I don't know these people. Yet something in my humanity tugs at me. How can I not be emotionally involved in such an intimate moment? I don't have a ready answer to that question. I just know I don't have time to contemplate it right now, and that is fine with me.

En route to our next call, my TO explains, "Residential four-five-nine is our major crime problem. (459 is the California penal code section for burglary) They are mostly day watch occurrences, but most people don't discover they got broken into until they come home from work. By then it is PM's. That's why we get so many report calls on nights."

"I see…makes sense."

"It makes sense to have a lot of cops on days to work on the crime problem, too, but we get stuck taking most of the reports. I'm just shy of eight years on the job. My goal is to make sergeant before I earn my *short*. (At ten years of service, officers earn an additional week of paid vacation, and are permitted to take vacation in two, nonconsecutive deployment periods. In the parlance of the department, the second vacation is referred to as your short vacation.)

"I'm pretty much by the book," Shep says. "It can be a pain trying to follow all the rules. But it comes in handy sometimes, too. The guys on day watch said they couldn't get to this burglary report. Officially, it requires a supervisor's approval to pass it on to the next watch. Most guys would have just taken the call and not said anything. But,

I made them get a sergeant's blessing before passing it on to us. Before I started doing that, day watch thought nothing of handing off three report calls."

"Yes, sir."

My new TO's stern look grows more pronounced. "Some guys will do anything to avoid taking a report. And if they gotta take one... they just do the minimum. They do just enough to get the sergeant to sign it. That is a bad habit you won't into get working with me. We are going to investigate. And our reports are going to detail our investigations."

Lieutenant Garcia was singing the same tune. "Be an investigator—not a report taker." This slogan comes right out of a *Training Bulletin* they handed out at roll call. LAPD *Training Bulletins* feature illustrations of clumsy cartoon caricatures of cops. The drawings are condescending, clearly reflecting management's view that street cops are a bunch of Elmer-Fudd-like buffoons. I don't like being treated like an idiot, but I'm on board with the concept behind the slogan. A report call shouldn't be about generating a piece of paper for a supervisor to sign. It should be about describing what happened and getting on the trail of who done it.

Arriving at the scene we find it is a generic break-in. It wouldn't make good TV. The suspect(s) just kicked in the back door. They didn't even try anything else. There is not much to discover, but we make a first-class effort. We even knock on a few neighbors' doors. No one saw anything, not that they'd admit to anyway. I get as thorough a description of the stolen property as the victim can give before having him sign the report. Back in the car, Shepards looks it over, making certain it reflects our efforts as much as our findings.

I'm glad I learned to handle the radio working morning watch. With all these cars out here, radio traffic is incessant. You have to be patient waiting for an opportunity to broadcast, and then quick to jump in when it comes. As quickly as I jump in and announce we are clear, we get an ambulance shooting call at a liquor store. It's a code two call. Officially that means we are to respond without undue delay, yet obey all traffic laws, including the speed limit. Working AMs, code two meant "haul ass." Shepards doesn't violate the rules driving to the call. But to be fair, with rush-hour traffic, there really isn't much opportunity to push it.

The RA (rescue ambulance) is already on scene. The firefighters have the victim on the gurney pushing him toward the back doors of the ambulance.

"What we got?" my partner asks.

"Gunshot wound...transporting to Queens," the fireman says, as he aligns the gurney with the open doors at the rear of the ambulance.

"He gonna make it?" my TO asks over the ratcheting sounds of the gurney's legs retracting as the patient is loaded into the RA.

"Only hit in the arm, but he's kind of out of it. Maybe it is just shock. But, we can't wait around for you to talk to him. If that's what you're thinking."

If it looks like a victim might die, policy says one officer rides in the ambulance as a witness in case the victim makes a "dying declaration." We would like to get a statement from the victim before we put out a crime broadcast, but that's not going to happen. Of course none of this is up to me. It's Shepards's call. He decides we'll investigate here at the scene and then follow up at the hospital.

The RA takes off, and I head inside the liquor store. A middle-aged Asian clerk is busy ringing up customers. I ask the man at the register, "You the one who called?"

"Yep."

"What happened?"

"The guy come back in...say he's been shot. He bleeding on my floor." The man behind the counter points to some drips of blood that have been tracked through by a bunch of customers already.

"You said the victim 'come back in.' Is that because he is a regular customer, or what? Why did you say he came back in?"

"Oh yeah. He regular. He come in a buy two packs of Benson & Hedges menthol. Stuff both packs in his shirt pocket. Walk out store."

"This was before he got shot?"

"Maybe minute later I hear loud pop. Then he come back in saying he been shot. He bleeding on my floor."

"Did you see who shot him?"

"No. I working. Just like now. Take care of customers. Not see any-body shoot anybody. Just hear the pop."

"Any other customers see what happened?"

"Don't know."

"Well, any other customers, regulars, come in just before or after the guy got shot?"

"Hard to remember. Customer come and go. So many, so fast."

"Yeah, I can see that. But you don't have customers shot right out-side your door every day."

The owner of the store looks up at me from behind the cash reg-ister and blinks. "Not my probrem."

"Maybe you're right." I drill him with my eyes. "Still, it can't be too good for business."

I block the path of a teenybopper heading to the counter with a soda and bag of chips. "We had a shooting here a few minutes ago." I point to the trampled blood on the floor. "Your purchase will have to wait while we interview the witnesses and complete our investigation."

I turn back to the pan-faced man behind the counter and lean in to emphasize my point. "This could take a while."

The proprietor looks up at me again. This time he doesn't blink. "OK. OK. Regular. Old lady name Mabel. She run in saying two guys with rifle shooting. She scared."

• • •

When we step through the automatic doors of the emergency room, an attractive brunette wearing a white hospital uniform gives me the once-over before tossing her head back and asking my partner, "Which one you guys here for?"

She directs us to the portion of the ER where we can find our victim. Only thing is, the spot is empty, our victim is not there. My partner turns on his heels.

"Stay here. I'll go check."

I'm thinking to myself, *she is too old for me anyway.* Before Shep returns, an orderly and a nurse wheel our victim back into the room. The nurse pulls me aside and gives me the particulars. She makes it clear she is not blaming the fireman for not seeing the second wound. The ER staff only realized what happened when they removed the guy's shirt. The bullet that hit him in the arm exited his arm, only to reenter his thorax. The difficulties the patient is experiencing are from the chest wound.

The nurse tells me I can talk to him while they are prepping him for surgery and developing the X-rays. She isn't wasting any time. I know I shouldn't, either.

Thomas "Tommy" Henderson is frightened and in pain, but responsive. I get his identifying information including his DOB (date of birth). He is my age. Two hours ago he probably looked it. He doesn't now. He is sweating and has the shakes. His eyes are bleary. He just looks bad all the way around. I ask him what happened.

"My mom asked me to go down to the liquor store and get her a couple of packs of cancer sticks."

"What brand?"

"My mom smokes Benson and Hedges menthol."

I didn't want to interrupt him, but I had to know. The store clerk even remembered the brand of cigarettes. "OK. I'm sorry. Go ahead."

"I don't smoke. I just stuffed the cigarettes in my shirt pocket so's not to have to hold them as I walked back home. I seen some, you know...cholos before I went into the store. They hang out around there a lot, so I don't think nothing of it when I come out of the store and see these two. One got on a big old trench coat. I figured he had to be hot wearing that thing. Anyways, these guys step out onto the sidewalk right in front of me. I'm about to say excuse me, when the one without the coat demands I give him a cigarette. Out of habit, I tell 'm I don't smoke."

"The cholo says, 'Fuck you!' What's that in your pocket?"

"I looked down at my shirt pocket. When I look up, the guy in the trench coat is raising a rifle. I guess that was why he was wearing that big old long coat. Anyway, he fires. I knew I got hit, but I still couldn't believe it. The cholos started running away, and I went back into the liquor store for help."

They start wheeling Tommy to surgery. The nurse tells me, like it or not, my interview is over.

Shep and I are waiting for word on Tommy's condition when a doctor introduces himself in the hallway. He ushers us into a consultation room, closes the door, slaps a large X-ray on a viewer, and turns on the backlight. I've seen X-rays before. Regardless of how clear the medical professionals say they are, the significance of the slight variations in the smoky images has always eluded me. This time is different. The pristine profile of a bullet in Tommy's abdomen is unmistakable.

All the medical jargon notwithstanding, the doctor's meaning is clear. The .22-caliber long rifle round is nasty. Instead of shattering the bone, or simply chewing up the muscle before heading downrange, this capricious little monster bent itself around the humerus bone and reentered Tommy's chest, still carrying most of its kinetic energy. The spinning projectile expended every bit of its evil as it zigzagged through the poor kid's upper torso. The bullet tore up his internal organs so badly the doctors can't save him. My partner calls the watch commander and tells him to roll a homicide team.

39

I CAN'T BELIEVE two deployment periods on PMs have gone by already. Ron was right. I'm getting lots of experience handling radio calls, and my training officers are both good cops. To say Shep is by the book is an understatement. It can be uncomfortable at times, but I'm thankful he takes training me as seriously as he takes everything else. Still, he has about as much personality as a rock. But like Ron says, you can't have everything.

During an average career, a big-city street cop will write enough to fill the shelves of the average municipal library. It looks like tonight we'll be pushing that statistic. Right out of roll call we get three report calls. Although I'm driving, Shep is still the car commander. He says we'll handle the calls in the order they gave them to us. That's what the book says, absent a reason to deviate, handle the calls in the order received.

I steer our black-and-white to our first call. The address is typical of the upscale neighborhood. It is a well-maintained, single-story wooden home, painted light blue. As we approach on foot, we see the curtains move in the house across the street.

"I'm keeping books," Shepards says, "but it looks like you are going to get your fair share of writing tonight, too."

"No sweat, partner. I got this one."

Even though this is a report call, we position ourselves to either side of the door to listen for a few moments before ringing the bell. A woman in her midthirties draws the door open slightly. A woman with her features should look gorgeous. Somehow, she doesn't. Her frosted blond hair isn't a bad dye job. Actually, it looks like it cost her a bundle. Her makeup is perfect, too. Something much deeper is detracting from her natural beauty. When she steps back and opens the door wider, I see she is wearing a navy-blue business suit with high heels. It fits her. I'm not talking about the tailoring.

"I called almost an hour ago." From her tone and the expression on her face, it is obvious she is convinced we were delayed by a long line at the doughnut shop.

"May we come in?" my partner asks.

"I think you should."

Once in the living room there is an awkward silence. Looking to break the ice, I introduce myself. "I'm Officer Stoller, ma'am. We got a call saying there was a burglary?"

She looks past me, directing her remarks to my partner. "They took my television set, among other things. I've been waiting almost an hour."

Shep explains, "Ma'am, we just came on duty. We got three report calls to start our shift. This is our first stop."

Looking at my watch, I say, "We arrived on scene about seven minutes after getting the call. Mind if we look around?"

We take her silence as assent and quickly clear the interior. Arriving back in the living room within a minute, I make eye contact again. "I agree with you, ma'am. No one should have to wait for the police." I give her my best smile. "Actually you are lucky. Can you imagine if we had handled those other two calls first?"

Her dour expression takes on more intensity.

"Where did they get in?" Shep asks.

"Isn't that your job?" she snipes.

"Yes, ma'am. But usually the homeowner steers us in the right direction. It speeds up our investigation. Like my partner said, we have two more report calls to handle after we're finished here."

We follow the woman to the kitchen. She indicates the back door. "It was open when I got home."

Sometimes an open door only tells you how the suspect(s) left, but three of the louvers have been removed from the window in the door. It's a common MO (modus operandi). The burglar removes a few of the panels of glass, and then reaches in to unlock the door. My partner and I step into the rear yard. The businesswoman follows close behind us.

As I am checking the recesses of the yard, her impatience shows. "What are you doing?"

"Just checking, ma'am."

"Checking for what?"

"I don't mean to alarm you. It happens sometimes...the suspects are hiding on the premises. But, mostly we are looking to see if they stashed any of the booty in the backyard. It happens a lot, especially when large items like a television are taken."

A quick walk around the exterior of the house brings us back to our victim who is standing with her arms crossed, balancing on one foot, the toe of her other high-fashion high heel pointing skyward. "Look, I have a lot of other things to do," she snarls. "You already know how they got in, so why are you wasting time looking at all the windows?"

"That's a good question. The detectives always want to know if there were multiple attempts at entry. Checking only takes a minute or two." I gesture with my hand toward the interior of the house. "We can go inside now and I'll scratch out the report. If you have a driver's license, that will speed things up a little. Then it will be a matter of listing the property taken."

The woman hands me her driver's license, and I take a seat on the sofa. She also hands me the paperwork from when she bought the TV and the stereo. Unlike in most cases, I have a full description including model and serial numbers on the electronics. She verbally describes the missing fine jewelry in detail. She also mentions a single piece of costume jewelry, a pewter-colored brooch with a nonprecious blue stone in the center. I record the details of items taken before getting her signature on the report.

We bid our surly victim a good afternoon and head out to knock on a few of the neighbors' doors. Shep and I both know which house will be our first stop. Walking across the street, my TO tells me I did a good job, not only on the investigation, but also on handling the difficult victim. "She wasn't gonna be happy no matter what," Shep says. "That's why I like to handle things by the book."

We see a bulky woman watching us from behind the curtains in a house across the street. When we reach the sidewalk she disappears. There is no response the first time I ring the bell. I look at my partner on the other side of the door and push the button again.

The woman calls through the door, as if she doesn't know it is the cops, "Who is it?"

"Police officers, ma'am. No reason to be frightened. We just want to talk to you for a moment."

The heavyset woman pulls the door open, letting it stop against the security chain. She makes a show of removing the security device before opening the door completely. Brushing away a few strands of oily, yellowish-brown hair with the back of her hand, she sighs. "You can't be too careful nowadays."

"Yes, ma'am. We know that better than anyone. Your neighbor's house was burglarized today. We were wondering if you noticed anything out of the ordinary."

"My heavens. I saw the police car and just knew something happened. It wasn't one of the usual guys."

"Excuse me?"

"It wasn't one of the men who visits."

"You saw him?"

"No, I didn't actually see him. The car, I saw the car. It wasn't one of the cars I've seen before." In a conspiratorial whisper she says, "She has more than one male friend, you know."

"Who?"

"Miss Delaney, my neighbor. You know, the one who got broken into. Not that it is any of my business. But this was a different car."

"What kind of car?"

"I'm not that good on cars. It was sky blue, if that helps. Had a shiny strip of metal. Chrome. You know. A real thin strip. And it had my birthday."

"Excuse me?"

"My birthday. You know. March nineteenth. The license plate—it was three-nineteen. There were some letters, too, but they didn't match my birthday, just the three-nineteen."

Shepards and I exchange incredulous glances. We follow up this revelation, trying to ascertain if the car had California plates. Our witness can't be sure about that. The only thing she is sure about is the numbers were three-one-nine.

The suspicious car arrived after *The Edge of Night* began, and was gone before *General Hospital* started. For the report, that means between 1430 and 1500 hours. It looks like Ms. Delaney came dangerously close to actually needing a rapid police response.

• • •

En route to the next report call, I see a car on a side street jam on the brakes. Probably nothing. But, then again...I make a U-turn.

"I saw a car back there...light blue, Ford, I think. The driver hit the brakes as we passed by." Not only do good tactics dictate that I articulate my observations and rationale, with Shepards, I know I better have a reason for deviating while en route to a call.

"I didn't see it," Shep says, his head now on a swivel.

The car never made it to the major, so I expect to see it when I turn onto the side street. But the car is nowhere in sight. "He was right about here when I saw him."

"He couldn't have gone far," Shep says.

In a couple hundred feet, the roadway Ts into another narrow residential street that parallels the major. I look left at the intersection, but don't see any sign of the blue car.

Shepards is looking right. "There he is! Blue Ford!"

There isn't enough room for me to turn. I put the car in reverse and hit the gas. The tires issue an audible yelp at the sudden change in direction. Dropping the gearshift into drive, I crank the wheel hard right and hit the gas.

The suspect's car has disappeared around a bend in the narrow street, but as soon as we get past the bend we can see him. I keep my foot on the accelerator, but lose sight of him when the road swerves again. As we make the second bend, the Ford is hard on the brakes to avoid broadsiding a full size Chevrolet backing out of a driveway. The Ford skids to a stop a few feet short of a collision, and we are on top of the Ford before either driver can maneuver.

"You see the plate, partner!" I say as I activate the reds, jam it in park, and fling open my door. Shepards put us code six on a possible 459 vehicle, so I know he heard me. I fill my hand with my .38 but keep it down by my leg as I approach the '62 Ford Falcon. A male Caucasian wearing a plaid long-sleeve shirt is the only occupant.

I can't believe it. Some articles of clothing hastily thrown over the bulky item wedged into the rear seat are ineffective at disguising the TV set. I thought this kind of thing only happened in the movies. Without taking my eyes off the driver, I signal my partner to look in the backseat. Committed now to the approach, I bring my weapon up to a two-hand low ready and order the driver to put his hands on the windshield.

The driver plasters his hands on the inside of the glass, turns his head and makes eye contact with me. "She saw me, didn't she? As I was driving off." He is shaking his head as he mutters to himself, "Shit! I just knew this was gonna be a bad day."

I order him out of the car into the felony kneeling position, with his legs crossed and his hands behind his head. The handcuffing is routine. Walking him back to our car, Shepards admonishes me to get my hat before a sergeant shows up. No sooner have I grabbed my hat, than Sergeant Speer pulls up along with a backup unit.

Shepards is talking to the sergeant while I get an FI on our suspect in the backseat. The supervisor surveys the situation and tells us the plan. The other unit will transport our suspect to the station. Shepards will drive the suspect's car, and I will stay right on his tail. Sergeant Speer will follow behind both of us. We'll do the inventory and impound report of the suspect's car at the station.

At the station we all park in the upstairs lot. We rendezvous with the transporting officers in the report-writing area. "Sully" Sullivan, one of the transporting officers, hands me my handcuffs and tells me our suspect is in the number two holding tank. "The asshole wouldn't shut up. Kept bitching he was having a bad day."

Brushing his wiry mustache by spreading his thumb and forefinger, Sully summarizes the suspect's story. The hype-burglar's regular fence got busted. Since his heroin connection only takes cash, he was trying to find the house where he had sold some stolen stuff before, but he got lost in the hills.

Sully lights up a smoke and looks at Shep and me. "Your suspect says he would have got away from you guys except for some old man wearing huge black sunglasses. Says the old guy's car looked like a big white steamship blocking the whole damned street."

We are all laughing. I never thought of a crook having a bad day. Bad luck for the bad guy, or good luck for the good guy—I guess it just depends on your point of view. The one who was really lucky today...was Ms. Delaney. But something tells me she isn't going to see it that way.

I've already made substantial progress on the arrest report when Shep walks in the report-writing room. He looks like a kid on the first day of summer vacation. "The serial numbers match on the TV and the stereo. The necklaces and jewelry match, too. The only thing I didn't find was that pewter brooch. I looked everywhere. I found a man's gold wristwatch not listed on the report. I asked our suspect about it and he copped out. Said it was in one of the dresser drawers. He didn't remember anything about a brooch. The gold necklaces and earrings were in her jewelry box. Sarge says we can give everything back to the victim tonight."

"That's great. The victim will get her stuff back, and we don't have to book it!"

Shep grabs the face sheet of the crime report, puts his finger on the victim's phone number, and starts dialing. "I'm gonna call her and give her the good news. See how long it will take for her to get down here."

I hear Shepards's side of the conversation.

"Ms. Delaney, this is Officer Shepards. I'm one of the officers who was at your home this afternoon."

...

"No, ma'am. No, this is official police business."

...

"No, ma'am. I am not trying to—"

...

"Ms. Delaney, I am calling to tell you we have made an arrest and recovered your property..."

40

THE NEXT DAY after roll call, Lieutenant Garcia takes Sergeant Speer aside. "Pretty good pinch your guys made on that residential four fifty-nine suspect yesterday."

"Yeah. They had a partial plate from a neighbor. But that wasn't what first put them on to the guy. They was just driving to their next call when they seen a car on a side street slam on the brakes. Actually it was the boot who seen the car first."

"Pretty good obs (observation) for a boot," the LT remarks.

"Yeah. He's sharp, but the cap'n don't like him none. The old man made it clear he wants me to cut paper on him if he fucks up. So I been keeping a pretty close eye, but he's been pretty good. Never caught him without his hat, yet."

Lieutenant Garcia uses a more formal tone. "Well, Sergeant, I don't care who it is. You don't write paper on anybody for not wearing a hat without checking with me first."

"Sure, LT. I'd check with you. You know I'd always check with you first."

Lapsing back into a more relaxed voice, the LT cheers his subordinate. "I like seeing my sergeants on top of things. You made a real good call when you told the officers to bring the suspect's car to the station. Much better to deal with the car and the property here at the station rather than out in the street. Safer, too."

"Yeah, when I seen the TV and stereo in the car, I thought we were gonna have to haul all that heavy stuff to the police cars. Then it hit me. Why should we load up the police cruisers with all that stuff when it was already loaded in the crook's car? Why not just drive it to station?"

"Smart move. Did you get a chance to talk to the victim, Ms. Delaney?"

"I talked to her when she came to pick up her stuff." Sergeant Speer lights up a smoke. "Wished I hadn't. I couldn't fuck'n believe it. Most people would be happier than a pig in shit to get even one thing back. She got everything back and was still bitching. She told me her stuff was taken from her house, so the least the cops could do was bring it back to her house."

"Did she really say that?"

"Yeah. I tried to explain it's not like on TV. I was telling her all the stuff the arresting officers have to do. But she didn't want to hear it. Instead of listening to what I had to say, she went off. Said she waited almost two hours for the cops to show up. She said she timed it, and the officers arrived exactly one hour and fifty-eight minutes after she called in."

"She gave you exact times?"

"No. She didn't say the times. She said how long it was from when she called to when the officers showed up. Hell, Shepards and Stoller had only been out of roll call about forty minutes when they made the arrest. They had already been to her house, taken the report, and talked to the neighbors. So if there was a delay, it was a day watch problem."

"Did you check to see what time the call came in?"

"No. Like I said, if there was a two-hour delay, it wasn't a PM watch problem. It couldn't be. And hell, LT, you know as well as I do, a two-hour ETA on a report call is not uncommon. She didn't stop at complaining about the delay. Shit no! She kept saying stuff like the officers were cav-el-air—"

"Cavalier?"

"Yeah. That's it. Said they weren't taking the whole thing seriously."

"OK. I get the picture. But she did get *all* her stuff back?"

"Yeah, everything except a piece of costume jewelry. It's in the report."

"That's why I'm asking. I was off yesterday. Reading the report, I noticed it said the pewter brooch was the only item not recovered. I just want to be sure I have my ducks in a row before I call her back. I get the feeling Ms. Delaney is going be trouble."

"No shit, LT. Better you talk'n to her than me."

Lieutenant Garcia puts his hand on the sergeant's shoulder. "This is what I need you to do. Go down to the glass house and talk to the suspect. He was plenty talkative yesterday, even after being advised and waiving Miranda. But you don't have to worry about Miranda for your little chat. This is strictly administrative. Just see what he remembers about the stuff he took. But we are really only interested in the brooch. Try to pin him down as best you can. Then on the way back, drop by the OPG and search the car from top to bottom. See me as soon as you get back."

41

SITTING AT THE counter in the report-writing room, I sense a presence. I put down my pencil, turn my head, and see Lieutenant Garcia standing behind me. I get up and face him all in one motion.

Before I can say anything, he begins, "Sergeant Speer filled me in on your arrest yesterday. Nice work."

"Thank you, sir."

The corners of his mouth and the edges of his mustache are curling down. "You know, Captain Wilks says you are not going to make probation."

"Yes, sir. He told me that my first DP here."

I want to pull away when the lieutenant puts his arm on my shoulder, but I notice the corners of his mustache turning upward.

His face brightens revealing perfect teeth. "Relax. Captain Wilks has been trying to get rid of my Mexican ass since he got here. But, he's not God...just thinks he is." The LT's face gets serious again. He lets his arm fall away. "I'm a rarity for a lieutenant. I've spent my whole career in uniform. You could always count on me for backup when I was a policeman. Unlike most guys, making rank hasn't changed that. I know all about what happened the night you were working with Sticktime. And I've been watching you these past two months. Just keep up the good work, and you don't have to worry about making probation. I'll handle the captain." The LT offers his hand.

I return his firm grip. "Thank you, sir."

42

THE NEXT DAY after roll call, Lieutenant Garcia again pulls Sergeant Speer aside. "I see what you mean about that Delaney woman."

Sergeant Speer shakes his head. "Better you talk'n to her than me."

"I really appreciate your interviewing the suspect yesterday and searching the car at the OPG. But I'm afraid it's your turn to speak with the lovely Ms. Delaney today."

"Aw, come on, LT. Don't make me to have to talk to her again. You know she's not gonna say noth'n nice. And 'sides, I know you gonna make me write down what she says. After talking to the hype at JD (Jail Division) yesterday and searching his car, it took me the rest of the shift to put all that shit down on paper."

"You're right. She's never going say anything good…not about the officers…not about you…and not about me, either." The LT smiles. "That is why it is so important to write down everything she says."

"That don't make sense. You know she's only gonna say bad stuff, but you still want me to write it all down?"

"Yep. It's good practice."

"Good practice? Good practice for what?"

"For when the officers are dirty. And solid documentation is always a good practice. Especially to CYA."

43

A COUPLE OF days later, Sergeant Speer corners us after roll call. Shaking his head, he says, "I have to interview both of you on the Delaney case. The LT says I gotta do a formal one-eight-one. It don't make no sense. The LT knows you guys didn't take it. I know you guys didn't take it. And God damn it, that bitch knows you guys didn't take it. Still, I gotta do this frigging complaint as if you did. The LT even made me go back out to her house and ask if I could look around in her bedroom, just in case the brooch fell on the floor… got kicked under the bed or something. She wouldn't have any part of it. She said I was there trying to pick her up, or say she was a lousy housekeeper."

Sergeant Speer takes us into the interview room one at a time and asks all the questions. He gives us the usual admonition not to discuss the case among ourselves.

My by-the-book partner is so pissed off, even he can't help himself. We aren't out of the parking lot before Shepards starts. "OK. I get it. There are lots of people like her. Lots of folks who just refuse to be happy about anything." Shep's face is turning red. "If she wants to be miserable, it's OK with me. But to say we took her crappy little piece of costume jewelry. To say we stole it!" Shep's face is glowing. "That is…just—"

Shep is about the least profane street cop I have ever met. His reticence to curse is severely taxing his ability to express his personal outrage, and I'm afraid this self-imposed limitation might cause him to explode. While I'm no Russell, I'm no saint, either. So I finish his sentence for him. "It's *fucked up.* Major-league fucked up."

Shep jumps on my metaphor. "Not just major league—All-Star— *World Series*! It's bad enough drunks are always saying cops took their money. That's expected. Everybody knows it. That's why we don't carry our wallets in the field. Just a five-dollar bill in our pocket along with our driver's license and police ID. When a drunk says the cops took a hundred bucks off him, the sergeant can search the officers, knowing the most he will find is five dollars. But this is worse."

"I agree. The whole thing makes no sense. What would we do with a piece of costume jewelry? Even the burglar says he doesn't take that kind of stuff."

"Yeah, when I talked to him about the pewter brooch he asked me, 'What color is it?' When I told him pewter is gray, he said unless it looks like gold, he does not bother with it. He told me even if it's sterling silver he never gets any real money for it. So if it doesn't look like real gold, he leaves it alone." Shep is shaking his head. "I just can't believe it. This is the kind of beef that can damage your career. If it keeps me from making sergeant—"

"Yeah, well as bad as that might be for you, it's worse for me. I'm on probation."

"I didn't even think of that. But, you didn't inventory the car. The closest you came to the car was when you ordered the suspect out at gunpoint."

"That won't stop Captain Wilks."

"Yeah. Now that you mention it, when you first came to PMs the LT told me Captain Wilks had it in for you for some reason. But, you're about the best probationer I ever had. I kind of forgot about it."

"Yeah, well I hope the captain forgot about it, but I kind of doubt it."

44

SERGEANT STODDARD, THE captain's adjutant, walks across the hall to the watch commander's office, pleased to find Lieutenant Garcia sitting at his desk. "The boss wants to see you. It is about that personnel complaint you've been working on."

"Tell him I'll be in to see him shortly."

Uncomfortably shifting his weight, Stoddard implores, "Ah, he kind'a wants to see you *right now.*"

"Well, *Sergeant,* he can kind'a want in one hand—" The LT stops himself. Stoddard is a kiss ass, but it is Wilks, not his adjutant, who is the real problem. "OK. I'll be there directly."

Before Stoddard has even made it to the hallway, the LT picks up the receiver of what looks like a light blue desk telephone. Instead of a dial on the face, there are knurled nobs like the ones on the radios in the cars. At the first lull in air traffic, the LT depresses the bar on the handle and speaks into the receiver.

"Two-L-ten, have L-thirty come to the watch commander, code two."

The RTO comes right back. "Two-L-thirty, two-L-thirty, go to the watch commander, code two."

Listening to the radio for Sergeant Speer to acknowledge, the LT unlocks his desk and pulls out a large manila envelope.

• • •

Sergeant Stoddard is the only one in the outer office when the LT walks in with Sergeant Speer in tow. The captain's inner office door is closed. Stoddard hits the buzzer, letting the captain know the LT has arrived. Evelyn has gone home for the day. Sergeant Speer collapses into Evelyn's chair. Garcia continues standing.

Sergeant Stoddard breaks the long, awkward silence. "The captain is on an important phone call. I'm sure he will be with you momentarily."

A knowing smile crosses Lieutenant Garcia's handsome face as he glances at the telephone on Evelyn's desk. None of the buttons on the phone is lit. Eventually the LT looks at his watch, and then at Stoddard. "I have an *important* phone call in *my* office."

Before Stoddard can utter an objection, the LT has disappeared into the hallway. As the LT steps through the door to the watch commander's office, he hears one of the desk officers shout, "Communications is on the inside line. Wanna talk to the watch commander."

"I'll take it," Garcia announces in a loud voice and grabs the phone on his desk. "Lieutenant Garcia here."

"Hey, Gene. How's it going?" The LT at Communications Division and Garcia are old friends.

"Fine, Don. How 'bout you?"

"Still living," he says. "Last time I checked, anyway." His voice turns more serious. "Rampart is getting pretty backed up. I'm going have to start assigning calls to outside divisions. If you got some guys hanging around the station? If you could get them to clear in the next few minutes—"

"I know a couple of units are going to be tied up for a while. But, there ought'a be somebody I can shake loose. I'll see what I can do."

"Thanks."

"No. Thank you!" Garcia says. "That info you gave me the other day, it's going to come in real handy. I'll fill you in later."

45

AS USUAL, THE captain has overplayed his hand. Of course nobody other than Lieutenant Garcia would have walked out. The recalcitrant watch commander has just left when Stoddard hits the buzzer twice in rapid succession, so it almost sounds like just one buzz.

This is the signal. Captain Wilks pushes himself up out of his cushy swivel chair and saunters to the door. Swinging it open, he expects to surprise his nemesis, but the surprise is on him. Bewilderment turns to anger. Pointing his fat finger at Sergeant Speer, slouching in Evelyn's chair, Wilks demands, "What's *he* doing here?"

"Lieutenant Garcia brought him," Stoddard answers.

"Where the hell is Garcia?"

"He stepped across the hall—"

"God damn it. Go get him. I haven't got all night."

The captain's shouting lifts Sergeant Speer to his feet. Although he is pretty sure the captain's order wasn't meant for him, Speer welcomes the opportunity to get away. When he and Stoddard logjam at the door, Wilks foils Sergeant Speer's escape.

"Stoddard will get Garcia. Come on into my office. Let's just you and me have a little chat first."

"Yes, sir, Cap'n."

• • •

When Stoddard doesn't find Garcia sitting at his desk in the watch commander's office, it never occurs to him the LT could be scouring the station looking for cops to send into the field. He assumes Garcia is dodging him. Stoddard struts rapidly down the hall toward the back stairwell, thinking, *He's probably downstairs in the locker room pushing weights.*

• • •

Sergeant Speer slinks into one the chairs facing the captain's desk. Before the commanding officer's oversize butt has landed in his overstuffed executive chair, he is already denigrating the sergeant's immediate superior. "Lieutenant Garcia is a problem child. Tries to confuse things with his self-righteousness. Thinks he's running the show." Wilks grabs the pack of cigarettes off his desk and shakes it until a couple of smokes are sticking out. He leans forward, offering one to Sergeant Speer.

The sergeant takes a smoke while fishing for his disposable lighter. He flicks his Bic and lights the captain's cigarette, then his own.

Wilks leans back and exhales a cloud of smoke. "This isn't NASA. We aren't trying to land men on the moon. All cops gotta do is follow orders. Do as you are told, and everything works out the way it's supposed to. It's simple as that."

"Yes, sir."

"I'm a captain, so I got two bars on my collar. Garcia is only a lieutenant, so he only has one. Two bars are greater than one. That stupid wetback doesn't get it. I guess they don't teach that kind of advanced math in Mexico."

Speer and Wilks share a good laugh.

• • •

After sweeping the station, looking for officers to send into the field, Garcia returns to the captain's office. He is surprised Stoddard isn't at his usual post. When the lieutenant approaches the door to the inner office, he hears Wilks calling him a wetback and giving Sergeant Speer a math lesson. Garcia's mustache droops lower. Mathematically speaking, "two is greater than one" is known as an "expression of inequality." Garcia realizes it is true, both in the mathematical world and the LAPD.

The captain's giggle fest with Sergeant Speer ends when Lieutenant Garcia steps through the door. There is an awkward moment of silence as the captain crushes his cigarette in the ashtray. Pointing his pudgy finger, the captain sneers, "Have a seat! When I send word I want to see you in my office, I want to see *you*, not Sergeant Speer or anyone else."

"Your adjutant said you wanted to see me about the Delaney case. This is about the Delaney case, isn't it?"

"Yeah, so what does that have to do about it?"

"Sergeant Speer has been involved in this matter from the very beginning. Likely you are going to ask me something about this case I don't know."

"So?" The captain is glaring at the LT.

"So, chances are...what I don't know...Sergeant Speer does."

"OK. OK." Wilks loosens his tie. "You both know I am a strict disciplinarian. Still, when I have to hand out punishment, I only do it because it's my job. It's not because I like hurting anyone. I'm just duty bound to keep this the best police department in the world. And part of being the best police department is being the most honest." The captain lights another cigarette. "You both know I'm a fair and honest man who never lets personal feelings, or things like that, color my decisions."

Garcia bristles at this pompous bigot's self-portrayal as an egalitarian police administrator. Considering his personal experience with Captain Wilks, Lieutenant Garcia cannot completely stifle his reaction, but he keeps his mouth shut.

Wilks smirks. "Now, of all the things that can bring disrepute to the police department, thievery is one of the worst. I won't tolerate it. Police officers must be beyond reproach in everything they do. So as much as I hate to have to discipline these men, as their commanding officer here at Rampart, I will not shirk my duty. I will not turn a blind eye to misconduct, and I will not allow my supervisors to do so, either. Is there anything I have to do to make that any clearer?"

Captain Wilks wants a draw on his cigarette, but a pause might invite a response from Garcia, a response the captain doesn't want to hear. "The facts in this case are as regrettable as they are clear." Wilks takes a drag on his cigarette. Exhaling a cloud of smoke, he continues, "The complaining party is a fine upstanding citizen. She is a professional woman who works downtown at the prestigious accounting firm of Arthur Andersen. She reported, among other things, the burglar took a brooch." Wilks puts both his palms on his desk and leans forward. "Even the burglar admits he did not have time to dispose of any of the stuff before getting arrested. That only leaves Officer Stoller and his TO."

Pleased with himself and certain he has made his case, the captain gives Lieutenant Garcia his instructions. "I want the complaint finished and on my desk when I come in to work Friday morning. I want it to be thorough." The captain takes a couple of quick puffs before crushing his smoke in the ashtray. "And most importantly, I want it written in such a way that sustaining allegations of theft against these officers is a foregone conclusion. I know both of you share my dedication to maintaining the fine reputation of the Los Angeles Police Department."

He rises from his chair, wiggling his flabby neck as he rebuttons his shirt. "I know you will do your duty. I just always feel better discussing these matters, in an abundance of fairness, and to be sure we are all on the same page."

Sergeant Speer is already up from his chair. He slides past Garcia and is out the door before the LT even stands up.

Instead of following Sergeant Speer, Lieutenant Garcia squares his shoulders to the captain. "I just want to know which one?"

Captain Wilks's bloated face turns quizzical, but with just a hint of the Cheshire cat. "I think I made it perfectly clear."

"Not to me." Garcia's eyes are on fire. "See, Captain, I'm just a 'stupid wetback.' Your words! Remember? I'm just asking to be sure I understand exactly what you want...a thorough investigation? Or a railroad job?"

Captain Wilks's already bloated face expands with the rush of blood. The broken capillaries near the surface of his skin are practically glowing. "Goddamn it! You know exactly what I want, you insolent son of a bitch. Now get out of my office before I relieve you of duty for insubordination." As Garcia reaches the hallway, the captain shouts, "And that one-eighty-one better be on my desk when I come in on Friday morning."

The last place Sergeant Speer wants to be is stuck in the middle. But that is precisely where he is, between a rock and a hard place, between the CO (commanding officer) and the WC (watch commander). No matter what he puts in this complaint, he knows instead of calming things down, it is only going to add to the shit storm swirling around him. Writing has always been his biggest shortcoming anyway. Standing in the watch commander's office, the Oklahoma native is doing his best Texas two-step trying to skulk out of his predicament.

"Lieutenant, you know I was happier than most guys when I made sergeant 'cause I really hate to write reports. Hell, I didn't even pass the written test for sergeant. I only got an interview because when Jacobs came in...they had to add ten bonus points to the written exam to get enough guys." Speer shrugs his shoulders. "It was those ten bonus points and my seniority that got me an interview. Shit man. They made every swinging dick on the list. That's the only reason I got these three stripes."

Sergeant Speer continues pleading, "Maybe you could give this to Sergeant Wilson. He's the beef sergeant. He's good at it. The only

beefs I've done were for guys not wearing their hats. I never did anything more complicated than that. This thing is way over my head. It's
got more twists and turns than Mister Toad's Wild Ride."

Ignoring Sergeant Speer's whining, Lieutenant Garcia grabs
a folder from his desk drawer. As the LT locks his desk he tells the
AWC, "Sam, you got the helm. I'll be back in detectives working on
this beef, and unless the world is coming to an end...I don't want to
be disturbed."

The assistant watch commander acknowledges with a nod.

Sergeant Speer follows the lieutenant's quick steps down the hall
toward detectives, continuing his campaign to escape responsibility.
"Stoller admitted he didn't have his hat on when they first stopped
the burglar. We could burn him for not wearing his hat. That might
make the old man happy. Or we could say it was Stoller who invento-
ried the car—"

Garcia struts into an empty interview room and yanks the door
closed. The sergeant has to turn sideways to avoid getting smacked
by the slamming door. Only inches from his subordinate's face,
Lieutenant Garcia pronounces his words carefully. "Over my dead
body!" Taking a seat and indicating Sergeant Speer do likewise,
Lieutenant Garcia continues, "I don't subscribe to the *just do as you
are told theory* so prevalent on the LAPD, even though I know mine
is a *minority opinion.*" The humor and double meaning are lost on
the dimwitted sergeant. "You and I are going to work together to
be certain our report is thorough, fair, and impartial. That's our job. I
needn't remind you it is also our sworn obligation."

46

WHEN LIEUTENANT GARCIA comes to work Monday afternoon he isn't surprised to hear the old man wants to see him ASAP. This time the LT isn't going to get ambushed like a few months back when he walked into the captain's office feeling proud his investigation had uncovered the truth, completely debunking a particularly ugly allegation against a tenured African-American officer.

On that day, the lieutenant was expecting a pat on the back for his fine work. Instead he found himself facing a one-man firing squad. Not this time. Forewarned is forearmed. Lieutenant Garcia is locked and cocked entering the beast's lair.

"Hi, Gene, what's happen'n?" Evelyn's greeting is upbeat as usual.

"You, foxy lady." The LT flashes his bright smile as he leans closer, taking in her perfumed scent. He lets his eyes linger on her partially exposed bosom. "What you say we handle this thing. Just you and me?"

"Works for me, big guy, but I don't think *El Capitan* is going to go for it." Her smile dips as her eyes move to what the LT has in his hand. "That one of those IA (Internal Affairs) briefcases?"

"Yep."

Sergeant Stoddard interrupts, coldly instructing the lieutenant to have a seat, as he buzzes the captain. It's forty-five minutes before Garcia is admitted to Wilks's inner office.

Dutifully taking a seat facing the captain, Garcia puts the black briefcase down by his side.

The captain leans back in his chair, smirking at his charge. "You didn't learn your lesson the last time...did you?"

"What do you mean?"

"Last time you got Jefferson off using your fancy words. Figured you'd do it again this time, despite my having told you exactly what I wanted." Leaning forward, Wilks's hand shakes a little as he picks up the thick stack of papers that constitutes the completed complaint. "Sergeant Speer didn't do this. You did. Didn't you?"

"We worked on it together."

"Bull Shit! You really think I'd buy that? It's obvious that illiterate hillbilly didn't do this investigation. You can't hide behind him and get away with it...not with me, you can't."

"I'm not hiding behind Sergeant Speer or anyone else. I take full responsibility for the investigation *and* the report. I mentored my subordinate in both the conduct of the investigation and the preparation of the report. If the sentence structure, grammar, and spelling in the report are better than you expected from Sergeant Speer, I'm pleased. That is in keeping with my philosophy of working together to do things better."

Captain Wilks takes a last draw on his cigarette before punching it out in the ashtray. "I don't give a damn about your philosophy! There is only one LAPD philosophy, and it is my philosophy—subordinates shall follow orders. In other words, Do *what* I tell you. *How* I tell you. *When* I tell you. *Period.*"

The lieutenant is not backing down. "You said you wanted a thorough investigation, Captain. And that is precisely what I gave you. If you don't like the facts, don't blame me."

"It's not the facts I don't like. It's you." Wilks throws the sheaf of papers at Garcia. "Take all your paraphrasing out of this complaint!"

"I can't do that, Captain."

"Can't? Or won't?" Wilks sneers at Garcia, then yells through the door. "*Stoddard, get in here!*"

Sergeant Stoddard steps just inside the door.

"The lieutenant was just refusing my direct order." Wilks clears his throat. "I want you as a witness to his insubordination."

Surprised at his own calm, the LT's voice is almost a monotone. "The only statements made directly to me, and paraphrased by me, are Ms. Delaney's allegations against the officers. If I take out those statements, there won't be any complaint, especially considering the investigation did not uncover any evidence the officers did anything wrong." Defiance modulating in his voice, Lieutenant Garcia adds, "So you see, Captain, I'm not being insubordinate. This stupid wetback just doesn't know how to write up a complaint without including the allegations from the complaining party."

"All right, smart ass. I'm going to teach you." The captain's caret-shaped eyebrows sharpen. "To begin with, remove all the bullshit slandering Ms. Delaney. Take out all that crap about how long it took the officers to get to her place. That is not at issue here."

"OK, Captain. I'll take out Ms. Delaney's statements to Sergeant Speer about waiting *exactly* and hour and fifty-eight minutes for the cops to show up. And, I'll take out the time-stamped tickets from Communications Division showing she is a liar."

"Everybody complains about response time. She exaggerated a little. So what?" Shaking his head, Wilks insists, "You can't run her down for saying the officers were *nonchalant*, either. She is entitled to her opinion."

"Actually, I believe she told Sergeant Speer the officers were *cavalier* in their handling of the call. Again, that comment goes to her veracity. Considering the officers arrested the burglar minutes after

taking the report, it seems particularly relevant to me. If all our officers were so cavalier, we'd damn near be out of business. But if you
insist, I'll take that out, too."

"You are damned right I insist." Wilks lights another cigarette.
There is a hint of the Cheshire cat on his bloated face. "And take out
the crook's statement saying he didn't take the brooch. Since when
do we give weight to statements from jailbirds?"

"Good question, Captain. It's just that the only way the officers
can be responsible for that fifty-cent piece of costume jewelry...is if
we believe the burglar lied when he denied stealing it...yet believe
he told the truth when he said he didn't get rid of anything before he
got caught."

"Just leave out his denials. Crooks always claim they are innocent.
Everybody knows that."

"Yeah, but in this case the crook didn't deny stealing. He admitted
to taking everything, except the brooch. He even rode around with
the detectives pointing out twenty-six other places he had burglarized, telling them how he broke in and what he took. They cleared a
whole bunch of DR numbers (case numbers) on this guy, all based on
his own admissions."

"So what? None of those cases have anything to do with this
complaint."

"On the contrary, Captain...the suspect told Officer Shepards,
Sergeant Speer, Detectives Ryan and Smith—when it comes to jewelry, he never takes anything but gold. Look at those twenty-six
reports. In every case the only jewelry items taken were gold, only
gold. The brooch Ms. Delaney says was taken is pewter. No way in hell
the crook could have mistaken pewter for gold."

"What he did or didn't take in any of those other cases has no rele-
vance to this case. I'm telling you to take out the detectives' follow-up
report, along with all those other crime reports. They have no bear-
ing on this complaint." Wilks hesitates, and then sneers. "Oh yeah.
I almost forgot...take out that stuff about Ms. Delaney not letting

Sergeant Speer into her house to look for the brooch. She does not have to submit to a search. Sergeant Speer should have gotten a warrant if he wanted to search her house. He should know better."

"That was my idea, Captain. He was acting on my orders. I thought the brooch might have fallen on the floor, gotten kicked under the bed or something. Sergeant Speer wasn't looking for contraband or evidence of a crime. The police don't need a search warrant to help someone find something they lost. Besides, he never intended to search without her permission, and permission nullifies the need for a court order. It's her refusal that is curious. It's pretty obvious the brooch was never taken."

"There you go again with your theories and philosophies," Wilks says, pushing himself back in his overstuffed chair.

"Her refusal to let Sergeant Speer into her house is not a theory or philosophy. It is a fact."

"I'm telling you none of that belongs in this complaint."

"OK, Captain. Her saying the brooch was taken, and the crook saying he did not get rid of anything before the officers arrested him. Those are the only statements you want in the complaint?"

"Precisely." Wilks gloats. "Those are the only statements that count." His Cheshire cat face is in full bloom. "See, Lieutenant, you *can* learn, after all."

"If we are only going to include the allegations, why bother doing the investigation? I thought the goal was to learn what really happened. Isn't that what we are always telling the troops? Be an investigator, not a report taker."

"There you go again. Just when I think I'm making progress with you." Wilks is shaking his head, the flab on his jowls and neck rolling back and forth. "When are you going get it through your thick skull. I'm the commanding officer. I look at the allegations, then I decide. As the commanding officer, I adjudicate the complaints. *Me!*" Wilks takes a last draw on his smoke before snuffing it out among a bunch of others in the huge glass ashtray on his desk.

The LT can't prevent a hint of a smile as he asks, "Suppose Ms. Delaney said she was mistaken? Suppose she said the brooch was never taken? Would you say that should go in the report?"

"Oh no you don't! I'm not letting you get away with that. I know you. You'll go out there and bamboozle her with some of your fancy jargon and flash your smile, then come back here and say she isn't sure the brooch was taken. I'm giving you a direct order, Lieutenant. You are not to have any further contact with Ms. Delaney. *Is that clear?*"

"Yes, sir. That suits me just fine. For the record, it wasn't me she said it to anyway."

"She didn't say any such thing to anyone. And for the record, I wouldn't believe you if you swore on a stack of Bibles."

Lieutenant Garcia hefts the black briefcase to his lap and opens it, revealing a cassette player/recorder encased in foam. He remarks in a low voice, "It took me a while. But, I finally got it. Just picked up a couple of copies at SID (Scientific Investigation Division) on my way in today."

Stoddard is still standing just inside the door. He and the Wilks lean forward cocking their heads like the terrier, Nipper, in the iconic RCA logo.

Lieutenant Garcia says, "This call came in to Communications Division just about the same time Shepards and Stoller were arresting the burglar." He presses "play" to start the tape.

The voice of an officer working the complaint board is heard. "Los Angeles Police Department, operator two-twelve. Is this an emergency?"

"No, not an emergency," the woman caller says. "I want you to send them back."

"Who do you want me to send back?"

"The officers who took the report. They just left. They can't be far."

"Why do you need the officers, ma'am?"

"I found one of the items I told them was missing, and I forgot to tell them about an expensive men's wrist watch. Have them come back. They just drove off a few minutes ago."

"It happens all the time, ma'am. It's not a problem. You can make out a supplemental property loss form—"

"I don't want to make out any form. I just want them to come back here so I can add the watch to the report, and tell them the other thing wasn't really missing. How long will it take for them to get back here?"

"I can't say, ma'am. It's really busy tonight—"

"I'm tired of hearing how busy you cops are. I'm busy, too, you know! You should be ashamed of yourselves, all of you. First you let them break into my house, and then you take your damn sweet time getting here. Now you are giving me the runaround just trying to make a couple of changes to the report."

"You don't need the officers to make those changes to the report, ma'am. You can make those changes right over the phone. Just tell me where you live and I'll give you the phone number for the detectives handling your case."

"I don't want to have to call again, talk to the detectives, or anything else. I'll just tell you now."

"Ma'am, it doesn't work that way."

"Why not? Why can't I just tell you right now?"

"What's your address, ma'am?"

The sound of the slamming phone ends the tape.

Captain Wilks is choking on his rage. Looking like he has a glob of cheese lodged in his windpipe, he gestures wildly toward the door.

Is he pointing at Stoddard? Garcia and Stoddard exchange quizzical looks, neither sure of the meaning behind the captain's animated gestures.

The captain's meaning becomes clear to everyone in the station when he gulps enough air to verbalize. "Out! Get the fuck out!"

Lieutenant Garcia closes the briefcase and slides it off his lap. He hands the one-eighty-one to Stoddard as he steps out the door.

In the hallway Evelyn is returning on tiptoes from her latest round of gallivanting. The LT smiles at Evelyn. "It looks like El Capitan should have let you and me handle this thing after all."

47

I GET THE word. Next DP, I am heading to days. I'd just as soon continue on PMs or go back to mornings. It really isn't day watch I want to avoid as much as Captain Wilks.

Tonight has been a typical shift on PMs. We have been chasing the radio all night. When we finish booking our body at JD, it's almost End Of Watch. Shep jumps on the freeway heading back to Rampart. In this situation, most guys would take their time, or at least hold off telling the RTO we are available for calls. Milking your last call near shift change is called "engineering End Of Watch." Shep being Shep, he never engineers EOW. As soon as we have crossed the invisible line putting us back in the division, he tells me to clear. Obviously no other Rampart units are available. The RTO immediately gives us three calls.

I recognize the address of the first call as a multistory brick flophouse in the MacArthur Park district. I've been there a number of times. About a month ago I was in the same shit hole for a death investigation. A wino with an ulcerated digestive track bled out sitting on the crapper. This was the first time I saw a dead body perched on a toilet filled with coagulated blood. I thought it was a unique occurrence. Experience would teach me otherwise.

On the DB (dead body) call we were stuck in the disgusting place for hours, first waiting for the K-car, and then waiting for the coroner. Normally the DHD detectives kick you loose pretty quickly, but because this place is the proverbial den of iniquity, the lone K-car detective asked us to stick around. I am glad tonight's call is a neighbor dispute. I just want to handle it and get on to the next one as fast as possible.

We work overtime almost every night. Generally we only work about forty-five minutes extra. Unless you work more than an hour, the rule is you don't submit an OT slip. Usually working extra does not bother me. Not getting compensated doesn't bother me, either. It's just that I've been in court the last two days. I'm coming down with something, and since I have to be back in court again tomorrow, I need all the sleep I can get tonight.

It's well after one in the morning when I drag myself into my apartment. Maybe it's my imagination, but it feels like my condition deteriorated driving home. Barely through the door, I peel off my clothes, throw them on the floor, and fall into bed.

Five hours later, when my alarm tells me it is time to wake up, the urge to turn it off and go back to sleep is almost irresistible. But I'm still on probation, and probationers don't call in sick. I get showered and dressed for court. A pair of polyester trousers, a herringbone sport coat, a perma-press dress shirt, and a cheap tie puts me in compliance with the department regulations regarding court attire.

The orange juice burns my throat, but I figure it is good for me. I can't taste the cereal. I am only spooning the milky concoction into my mouth because I know I have to eat something. Thank God I live in Glendale. *How early would I have to leave if I moved back to Orange County?*

Arriving downtown, I join the line of cars entering the underground parking at the Music Center. It is several blocks away from the criminal court building at 210 West Temple, but this is where we are supposed to park. With a police ID and a subpoena, you don't have to pay. Ron showed me an underground tunnel that runs from the Music Center almost all the way to the courthouse. It's a great way to go when it is raining. It hasn't started yet, but it looks like it could start at any moment.

Just walking to the courthouse, I feel fatigued. Normally I take the stairs to the check-in on the seventh floor. Not today. When the elevator doors open on the seventh floor, I join the line of officers that stretches into the hallway. Eventually it is my turn to insert my subpoena in the time clock and give the court liaison officer my name. I actually have two cases, one that has been trailing for a couple of days, and fresh one. Both are in Division Forty.

I can either wait in the officers' waiting room or in the courtroom. Although the liaison officer is supposed to regularly update the officers' waiting room, in practice it doesn't work that way. The waiting room is more comfortable, but today I want to get out of here as soon as possible, so I opt for sitting in court.

While my subpoena reads 8:30 a.m., the courtroom won't actually open until at least 9:30 a.m. I head down to the cafeteria for something to warm me up. They are out of hot chocolate, so I pull the handle on the huge stainless steel coffee server. At least it's hot. I dilute the steaming black liquid with sugar and cream to take away the bitterness. It proves an unnecessary precaution. My taste buds aren't working.

Finished with my coffee, I head back upstairs and wait in the crowded hallway. The benches lining the hallways are full. When the bailiff unlocks the doors to the court, I file inside and find a spot in the seating reserved for cops.

It is almost ten o'clock before the bailiff gives his spiel. "All rise. Division Forty is now in session, the Honorable..." After we're seated, the bailiff rattles off the rules. "No talking while the court is in session. Chewing gum is prohibited..."

During first call a few cases are dispo'd when the defendant takes a plea in return for time served. A few others get sent out to a trial court. Most of the docket, including both of my cases, hang on for second call. At second call, both sides announce ready on one of my cases. "All parties and witnesses in the Greenwood case report to Division..."

I recognize my victim, Mrs. Littleton, as she files out of the courtroom.

She is waiting for me in the hallway. "You're Officer Stoller, aren't you?"

"Yes, ma'am."

"I thought that was you. You look different out of uniform. When you stood up to leave the same time as me, I was pretty sure it was you." She turns her head to the side a little. "You don't look so good. You feeling all right?"

"I'm afraid I'm a little under the weather."

"More than a little," she says under her breath. "I was running a little late getting here. Then I couldn't find a place to park. This whole thing is so upsetting. Actually I'm glad you're here. It's kind of like that day. There I was watching that man run away with my purse, and out of nowhere, there you were. They say there's never a cop around when you need one, but that's not true."

• • •

It's been less than two weeks since the arrest. Funny how fast the weather can change. That day had been a real scorcher. Even though the afternoon shadows were lengthening, it was still plenty hot as Mrs. Littleton put her purse on the front seat of her car. She lowered all the windows to let the interior cool off as she loaded her groceries in the trunk. The crook must have been staking out the parking lot. He approached while she was loading her groceries, grabbed her purse, and ran.

I was working with John Cicarelli, my other training officer on PMs. We were coming to a stop several cars back from a red light when I saw the suspect running full tilt boogie carrying a woman's handbag. A Sherlock Holmes deduction wasn't necessary. I bolted out of the car after the suspect.

Seeing me coming, the asshole turned on the jets. He dropped the purse and kept going when the parking lot ended, running into the street despite the heavy afternoon traffic. Drivers were standing on their brakes. Somehow the idiot didn't get hit. I grabbed the lady's purse off the pavement and scampered across the street after the suspect. My only close call was with a driver who had taken his foot off the brake when he turned his head to watch the suspect running past him. I slapped my free hand on the hood of the guy's Mustang as it idled forward like I was fending off a big tight end.

The adrenalin that fueled the suspect's initial sprint was gone. I was close enough when the crook turned onto a residential street to see him dodge between two apartment buildings. His path blocked by a ten-foot-high wrought iron security fence, the exhausted purse snatcher gave up without a fight.

• • •

The trial court is in session when we get there. I take a seat in the first row adjacent to the bailiff's desk. My victim settles into an empty spot a few rows back. Watching the witness trying to answer the prosecutor's questions between objections by the defense, Ron's words play in my head. *There ain't no reason for cops to be ordered to appear in a calendar court.* He had said it more than once. At the time, I sloughed it off as the bellyaching of a sleep-deprived veteran street cop. Now I realize he was right. I also realize I'm not going to get out of court before lunch, and that means I'm not going to be able to get home in time to get any rest before reporting to duty. Sure enough, when the court breaks for lunch we are all instructed to report back at 1:30 p.m.

After lunch, Mrs. Littleton approaches me in the hallway and starts to chitchat. "That man told me the boy who took my purse has never been in trouble before. He also said these things can drag on for a long time."

"What man?"

Mrs. Littleton points to the public defender.

"Mrs. Littleton, that is the attorney representing the man who stole your purse. Don't believe a thing he says."

She puts her hands to her mouth. "Oh dear. He seemed like such a nice man. He told me the boy who grabbed my purse was just trying to get something to eat. He said the boy would never do anything like that again."

"Don't listen to what he says. You don't have to talk to him, and if I were you—I wouldn't."

The first time I was in court, Ron told me it's best not to talk to the defense attorneys unless the prosecutor is also present. A favorite tactic of unscrupulous defense attorneys is to engage you in conversation outside of the court, and then relay a very different version of the conversation in front of the court. Ron put it this way: Miranda says we have to advise a suspect of his right to counsel and his right to remain silent. It ought'a require defense attorneys warn everyone else the same way.

It's 1:45 p.m. before the bailiff opens the door to let people back inside the courtroom. The public defender (PD) representing our purse snatcher requests his client be released OR, on his own recognizance. The defense attorney insists his client has never been arrested. The deputy district attorney (DA) counters by noting that the defendant had only turned eighteen five days before the arrest. Without giving specifics, the deputy DA makes it clear the defendant has "seen the inside of a chamber much like this many times before." Of course the judge grants the request.

After the judge releases the defendant on his own recognizance, the defense counsel immediately makes a motion for a continuance.

The public defender and the deputy DA haggle before agreeing on a trial date about a month out. The judge mentions he is out of town that week. He is quick to add that the court will not go dark. The wily defense attorney has deftly played everyone, and he isn't through. He effuses compliments on the court and insists this jurist hear the matter. Negotiations go back to square one. Finally prosecution and the defense decide on a date eleven weeks into the future. The judge releases everyone saying the court will resubpoena.

Mrs. Littleton can't wait until we are out of the courtroom. "Officer, what just happened?"

"Shss." I put my finger to my lips. "Wait till we're outside."

As soon as we are through the first set of doors, before we even reach the hallway, Mrs. Littleton is talking. "In the other courtroom, both sides said they were ready to go to trial. Now, they say it's going be almost three months? I don't understand."

At the risk of appearing pedantic, I explain, "The bad guy has been in jail since we arrested him. Today, the judge let him go free until the trial. The longer the crook can postpone the trial, the longer he stays out of jail."

"I see. Very clever." Mrs. Littleton is walking right behind me as I head toward the court liaison to check out. "They could have done that before lunch. Why did they make us all come back after lunch? That's just rude."

"You are right, Mrs. Littleton." I turn around to face her. "Just remember, if anyone ever asks…you said it, not me."

"They didn't even ask what date was good for me. Come to think of it, they didn't ask you, either. Shouldn't they have at least asked us?"

"I think you know the answer."

48

IT LOOKS AND feels like it's going to start raining any second. Walking from the parking lot to the back door of the station, I can feel my fever. Just putting on my uniform in the locker room is a chore.

Both the LT and AWC are off tonight. Sergeant Speer is running roll call. I was supposed to work with Cicarelli, but he called in and got a T/O. That is department lingo for a using accumulated overtime to take a day off. I figure Cicarelli has got the same flu bug as I do. I'm partnered with a guy named Jonston, a P-3 who is normally assigned to A-seventy-nine. I don't immediately place the name to the face, partly because of my fever, and because everyone refers to Jonston by his nickname, Triple.

I don't think anything of it at first, but when I'm writing his serial number in the log it occurs to me he has almost as much time as Russell. I'm certain he is senior to Clarke, the other P-3 on A-seventy-nine. Shouldn't they have left the most senior man on the basic car and put the junior P-3 with me?

My partner for the night doesn't say a word to me until we are about to pull out of the station. "I'm Jimmy Jack Jonston. How long you been out the academy?"

"Six months, sir."

"Six months or six minutes…it's all the same to me. You're still a boot in my book."

When I reach for the mic to tell the RTO we are clear, Jonston says, "Boy, I'll tell you when to clear. I'll tell you when to piss. Just sit there and do as you're told. Your job is to back me up—period."

"Yes, sir."

Most guys who work the southern portion of the division automatically take the Benton Way exit and head south. I'm surprised when Officer Jonston turns north out of the parking lot. But Triple's northbound direction of travel only continues as far as the Hollywood Freeway. He's driving like a mad man entering the on-ramp toward downtown. Debris is flying everywhere as he passes three cars on the right shoulder. Barely ahead of the third car, he cuts left, accelerating across two lanes before braking hard and diving back to the right. Our police car is inches from the guardrail as we transition to the southbound Harbor Freeway.

There is nothing happening on the radio. He can't be chasing a violator. Why is he driving like we're en route to an officer needs help call?

On the Harbor Freeway, he is does it again, accelerating to the fast lane only to swerve to the right at the last second and catch the westbound Santa Monica Freeway. Exiting at Hoover, he heads up to Washington Boulevard. The insanity ends when he pulls into the parking lot of Juicy Lucy's.

Two other units are already at the window ordering their food. I'm not hungry, but I know I have to eat. When it is my turn, I order a burrito and a shake.

Triple ignores me as he talks with the other cops. Finally he turns to me. "Real cops don't drink milkshakes."

"I got a terrible sore throat. I was hoping a shake might ease it a little."

Triple takes a swig of his large coffee. Giving me the once-over, he says, "Now that you mention it, you do look like a scrawny sharecropper's son after twelve hours of pick'n cotton in the Georgia sun. Yeah...I can see you're feeling puny."

I don't even try to get involved in the conversation as everyone is wolfing down their food off the hood of a police car. The cool ice cream in the milkshake soothes my sore throat enough for me to eat most of my burrito.

When the other cars have left, Triple lights up a cigarette and tells me, "You can clear us now." Cigarette hanging from his lips, his thumbs hooked in his Sam Browne, he surveys the ominous sky. "A good cop never goes hungry or gets wet." He takes a drag on his cigarette. "I've eaten. But I can see it's gonna be hard stay'n dry tonight."

Back in the car, it is obvious Triple has no intention of patroling our assigned beat. After a prolonged silence while patroling the southern end of the division, my partner glances my way and asks, "So where you from, boy?"

"I grew up in Anaheim."

"I didn't ask you where you grew up." Jonston gives me a scornful look. "You're not the sharpest tool in the shed...are ya?" He shakes his head. "Hell. No one...excepting maybe Father JOON-ip-O'sera's folks and a few happy Apaches are from around here. Everyone else is a transplant. You don't look like no Mexican...no Injun, neither. So where's your people from?"

"Chicago."

"They got a whole lot a PO-locks in Shy-Town. Sure your name ain't Stolski?"

I'm tempted to tell this moron to go fuck himself. But it hurts too much to talk, and all I want to do is make it to EOW. I decide to let him think he has me figured out. "Don't tell anyone."

"Don't worry, Ski, your secret is safe with me."

A car on a side street starts to roll through a stop sign, entering the major. The driver jams on the brakes when he sees us.

"There's my ticket," Jonston says.

Technically it's a violation. The vehicle was over the limit line by several feet. Had we not been there, the driver wouldn't have stopped. Still, it's a chickenshit ticket, in my opinion. I don't say anything when my partner stops the car and issues a citation.

Maybe it's because of my fever, or maybe it's just the way my mind works. Suddenly I remember the story. Jimmy Jack Jonston had been known as JJ most of his life, but when he came to Rampart his nickname had to be modified to avoid confusion with the JJ who was already here. Some had started calling him Three J's, but it didn't stick. For a little while they called him Triple J, but that is too long and a bit of a tongue twister. So they dropped the J and his nickname became just plain Triple. To me it's an apt nickname. It's going to be three times as difficult to coax my ailing body through the shift working with him tonight.

The time and temperature sign on the Security Pacific Bank says fifty-nine degrees, definitely a cool late afternoon by Los Angeles standards. The combination of the high humidity and my fever makes it feel even colder. The wind from the open windows feels downright frigid.

Except during a pursuit, LAPD doctrine requires we keep the windows open. It isn't a matter of comfort. It's a matter of safety. Believe it or not, sounds coming through the open windows greatly increase situational awareness. That is why even on the hottest days we keep the windows open while running the air-conditioning on the desert only setting. And in winter, when early morning temps dip into the low forties, LAPD patrol cars cruise through the streets with their windows rolled down and their heaters cranked up.

I ask Jonston to turn on the heater.

He looks at me. "Got the chills, do ya?"

"Yeah."

Instead of putting on the heater, Jonston turns the selector to desert only, pushes the lever to cold, and switches the fan on high.

Ron's last piece of advice is running through my mind. "Reserve judgment. Wait awhile before you decide which cops are assholes." I've
waited long enough. Jonston is an asshole.

To make things worse, it starts to rain. Despite the rain, every
chance he gets, Jonston is hauling ass on the freeway. He tells me in
the years before the LAPD relinquished the freeways to the California
Highway Patrol, he worked the Freeway Flyer detail. Without question, Officer Jonston laments the demise of the unit. He also tells
me how much he admires our captain. He says about a year ago he
caught a serious beef. While he is very circumspect on the details, he
credits Wilks with saving his job. Despite my feverish brain, things are
starting to make sense.

Shivering and coughing in fits, my body is one big ache. If I could
see down my throat, I'm sure it would look like the cracked mud that
forms on the bottom of a dried lakebed. I just want this night to end.

49

STANDING IN HIS office facing the window, Deputy Chief Callahan is oblivious to the wind-driven rain pelting the glass. In his mind, the gray-haired commanding officer of Operation Central Bureau (OCB) is on the thirteenth tee at Torrey Pines. His imaginary round of golf is interrupted when his adjutant, Lukas Gustafson, knocks on the open door. Without waiting for the customary nod of approval, his adjutant steps through the doorway.

Gustafson's voice is subdued, but carries urgency. "The chief of staff is on line one. Chief Davis wants a word."

Callahan slips into his executive chair, picks up the receiver, and punches line one. The phone clicks, and the chief of police comes on the line. "Congratulations, Jack. I heard your son got into USC (University of Southern California)."

"Yes, sir. My wife and I really appreciate your help, sir."

"It was my pleasure. Any chance of him coming on the department after he graduates?"

Callahan's eyes focus on the photo of his son under the clear plastic blotter. "As much as I'd like to see Ian follow in my footsteps, I don't see that happening. He takes after his mother, you know."

"Well, I'm sure he'll make you both proud no matter where he ends up. But that's not why I called. It seems Captain Wilks over at

Rampart has done it again." The chief of police clears his throat. "You know how I like to stay ahead of things, and how I rely on my command staff to keep me up to speed. Rampart Division is in your chain of command. Besides, you and William go back a ways."

The lines in Callahan's face sharpen. He fights the tension in his chest to take a shallow breath.

The chief continues, "I need you to get a handle on this as quickly as possible. I'm sending my chief of staff down to your office right now. The two of you will work together on this...Jack, you need to make this go away."

"Yes, sir. I will give it my full attention, sir."

"Be sure to give my best to Margaret." The line goes dead before Callahan can respond.

When Chief Davis said *now*, he meant it. His chief of staff, Lieutenant Bart Strauss, is at the OCB office before Callahan even finishes briefing Lieutenant Gustafson. The brash chief of staff doesn't wait to be invited into Callahan's inner office.

Deputy Chief Jack Callahan normally wouldn't put up with such brazen impertinence, but this handsome six-footer with wavy dark hair, endless energy, and a reputation for cutting through the crap, is the chief's right-hand man. Callahan offers Lieutenant Strauss a seat while signaling his adjutant to close the door.

Lieutenant Strauss hasn't fully settled in his chair before he begins. "We've been getting calls alleging minorities are being persecuted in Rampart Division: Chicano rights organizations, B'nai B'rith, the mayor's office, a couple of city council members, and of course the ACLU." He holds up his hand. "OK. In and of itself, complaints about mistreatment at the hands of the police aren't all that unusual. But in this case, Captain Wilks is being specifically cited as the culprit."

Callahan feels the cold, windy weather creeping into his office. Twenty years earlier, when Jack Callahan first made sergeant, he was reassigned from his staff position at the Projects Unit at Personnel Division to a uniform billet at Central Division to serve his obligatory six months as a uniform field supervisor. That was where he first met William "Billy Club" Wilks. The reckless racist was one of the policemen Callahan supervised.

What made it worse was the Central Division captain had taken a shine to the young officer with the well-deserved nickname. Consequently, Callahan spent nearly all his time as a probationary supervisor writing "fact sheets" to keep the captain's boy out of trouble, officially at least. Although Callahan frequently counseled the young policeman, he was never able to convince Wilks that beating handcuffed prisoners wasn't sporting, not to mention illegal. Callahan had thought he had at least impressed upon Wilks the need to avoid doing such things in front of witnesses. Perhaps Callahan had been too optimistic.

Lieutenant Strauss continues, "Wilks's reputation could be at play here. We thought so at first." The chief of staff looks down at his notes. "There is a one-eighty—"

Callahan's voice cuts him off like an ax on a sapling. "A formal complaint naming Wilks?" Callahan throws a menacing glance at this adjutant. But the look on Gustafson's face confirms he is as surprised as his boss.

"No. The complaint doesn't name Wilks. It's against a P-3 and his probationer."

"Excessive force?" Callahan queries.

"No. Theft."

Callahan's core temperature drops a few more degrees as he contemplates a couple of Wilks's boys getting caught in a shakedown, and the captain being somehow personally involved. Callahan wants to know if Officer Jonston is named on the complaint, but he stops himself, asking instead, "Who are the officers?"

Lieutenant Strauss looks down at his legal pad. "The allegations are against Shepards and Stoller. I got the names off the face sheet of the complaint at IAD (Internal Affairs Division). Of course there are a bunch of witness officers—"

"Who's handling the complaint?" Callahan interrupts.

"It's at the division." Lieutenant Strauss again consults his notes. "Sergeant Speer is handling."

Callahan stands up and announces in his deputy chief's voice, "OK. The one-eighty-one is our starting point, but I'm going to have to speak to Captain Wilks to find out what is really going on." He glances at Gustafson before he settles his eyes on Strauss. "Getting candor from Mr. Wilks can be difficult under the best of circumstances. In this case...well let's just say, having the chief of staff in the room wouldn't make things any easier."

Lieutenant Strauss rises slowly from his chair as Callahan comes out from behind his desk. The commanding officer of OCB briefly touches the chief of staff's shoulder as he escorts him to the hallway. "You can assure the old man I've got everything under control."

Lieutenant Strauss's eyes linger on Callahan a moment too long. "Be certain to keep me informed."

Lieutenant Strauss hasn't made it to the elevator before Callahan is back behind his desk dialing the number for the CO's office at Rampart. When Wilks comes on the line, Callahan doesn't offer any pleasantries. Speaking through gritted teeth, he says, "I don't know what the hell is going on over there, but I'm going to find out. I want to see you in my office in ten minutes. Bring everything you've got on the Delaney beef."

Captain Wilks is already dodging. "Chief, in rush-hour traffic it's going to take me longer than ten minutes just driving. Who knows how long it will take my adjutant to gather up all the—"

"I am not discussing this with you on the phone. I'm not asking you—I'm telling you. I don't give a damn if you take Mary Poppins's umbrella, or hitch a ride on the broomstick of the Wicked Witch of the West. Have your ass in my office in ten minutes." Callahan slams the phone into its cradle and begins to pace.

Callahan stops pacing and makes eye contact with his adjutant. "Wilks is going to lie like the proverbial rug. When he gets here, you keep his ass glued in a chair. Keep him guessing about where I am, what I'm doing, and who I might be talking to. Take your time looking over the complaint. We have got to make him stew in his own juices for a while." Callahan goes back to pacing. "The last thing I need is the chief of police on my back. And I damn well don't need his chief of staff looking up my asshole."

Callahan's career has been intertwined with Wilks since their paths first crossed at Central Division. When the captain of Central Division was reassigned as the commanding officer of PRD (Planning and Research Division), he took then Sergeant Callahan and Officer Wilks with him.

Assignment to PRD virtually ensures promotion. It boosted Jack Callahan's already impressive career on an even higher trajectory. Working PRD, even Wilks was able to climb the LAPD ladder.

Because he has the goods on him, and because Callahan knows the pathetically incompetent Wilks could never mount a serious challenge to him, Callahan lent Wilks a helping hand on several occasions. Callahan thought, if he should ever need a scapegoat...The deputy chief rocks back in his executive chair. This might be the time.

50

FORTY-FIVE MINUTES AFTER being summoned by his boss, Captain Wilks waddles through the back door of Parker Center. He skulks into the men's room to spruce up before presenting himself to the commanding officer of Operations Central Bureau (OCB). Placing the manila folder on the stainless steel shelf above the sink, he buttons his coat in front of the mirror. He tugs at the bottom of his suit jacket with both hands to keep it from bunching up on his corpulent torso. He pops a couple of sticks of gum in his mouth and runs a comb through his thinning hair. Lifting his arms to comb his hair has caused his jacket to ride up again. Once again he straightens his coat. Then, being careful not to lift his arms too high, he grabs the folder from the shelf above the sink.

As soon as Wilks steps into the OCB office, Lieutenant Lukas Gustafson reaches for the folder. "Is that everything on the Delaney complaint?"

"Yep," Wilks lies, handing over the folder.

Rifling through the folder's modest contents, Gustafson glances at Wilks. "Have a seat, Captain."

The lieutenant is marking up the paperwork before the overweight captain even settles into a chair.

Wilks can't help but wonder...why so much fuss over a simple personnel complaint? All this urgency is unnerving. Fuck it! Gustafson might be the chief's adjutant, but he is still only a lieutenant.

Wilks says abruptly, "When Jack called, he made it clear he wanted to see me on a matter of some importance. You'd better let him know I'm waiting."

"*Captain,* I was with *the chief* when he spoke to you on the phone, and I heard his words conveying the urgency of the matter. I also heard him telling you to bring *everything* on Delaney." The chief's adjutant stares at the captain. He waits for Wilks to break eye contact before he returns to reading the complaint.

When Callahan's door eventually opens, Wilks stands up, anticipating being called into Callahan's inner office, but the chief dips his index finger. "Have a seat. I'm not ready for you yet."

Wilks settles back in the chair and watches Gustafson cross the room to lock the door leading to the hallway before disappearing into the Callahan's inner office.

What the fuck is going on? Must be something big. Can't be about the Delaney complaint. Nobody really gives a shit about personnel complaints. Nobody except the officer who the complaint is against. Still, the chief did tell him to bring the Delaney file. Wilks reassures himself Callahan only mentioned it in passing. After all, it isn't anywhere near overdue. On the other hand, maybe that Delaney bitch is the chief's concubine or something. *Good thing I didn't unfound the damn thing like Garcia wanted. Imagine explaining that to Callahan.*

As comforting as the thought is, Wilks can't believe this is about the Delaney complaint. It has to be something else. *Could someone have squealed on his own little skimming operation? Does it involve sex? Everyone knows there's a ready supply of whores in Rampart. What am I supposed to do? Call Callahan and offer sloppy seconds every time one of my boys sets me up? So what if I get a head job every now and again from my secretary. Big fucking deal. Somewhere along the way, Evelyn has probably had Callahan's dick in her mouth, too.*

Wilks removes his smokes from his jacket. Shit! Only four left. In his haste to get to Parker Center he forgot to grab another pack.

51

CALLAHAN WAS CERTAIN after his adjutant got his hands on the complaint they would be well on the way to putting this problem to rest. But nothing makes sense. The complaint stems from a burglary arrest. The burglar is a white guy, and he isn't the one making the allegations. It's the victim who is complaining, and she isn't a minority, either. Based on the arrest report, there should be a commendation not a complaint.

Callahan lets Wilks stew in his outer office while he and Gustafson strategize. When the deputy chief figures the captain has had enough, Callahan opens the door.

Wilks saunters into Callahan's office plops into the chair facing the chief's desk, and fishes inside his jacket for a smoke. After lighting his last cigarette Wilks looks up, surprised to see Callahan still standing behind his desk.

Callahan's eyes remain unfocused as he pushes his chair against his desk and begins to pad back and forth behind his desk. The patter of raindrops on the glass grows louder as the tension mounts.

Finally Wilks can't stand it any longer. He exhales a lung full of smoke and declares in a loud voice, "Of all the things that can bring disrepute to the police department, thievery is one of the worst. I won't tolerate it."

Wilk's inane outburst brings Callahan's pacing to a halt and his eyes into sharp focus. Like the turret of a tank, the chief's head rotates until it is aiming directly at Wilks. "What the hell are you babbling about?"

"I know they stole the jewelry," Wilks asserts.

"What jewelry are we talking about?" Callahan's mind is spinning with visions of diamond-encrusted treasures.

"The brooch," Wilks says flatly.

Callahan turns to his adjutant. Gustafson cannot mask his disgust as he leafs through the complaint. He offers a page for his boss to see. It only takes a few seconds for Callahan to read the highlighted description of the brooch. "Why should anyone give a damn about a buck's worth of costume jewelry?"

"It's the principle of the thing." Wilks lifts his fat chin.

Callahan is trying to maintain his composure, but Wilks's obfuscation laying claim to morality is too much. "Principle? You and I both know you don't have any principles. Save that shit for the promotion board!"

It is almost inconceivable, but Wilks continues jabbering. "SID says voice identification from tapes of phone conversations is impossible."

Callahan is certain this is another smoke screen. Getting the truth out of Wilks is probably going to take all night, maybe longer. Callahan turns to Gustafson. "Who did the complaint?"

Wilks stops prattling.

Gustafson looks at the paperwork. "Sergeant Speer, sir."

The chief's attention returns to the suddenly silent Captain Wilks. Canting his head ever so slightly, the deputy chief looks the pudgy captain up and down. A light flickers in Callahan's eyes. "I told you to bring everything you had on the Delaney complaint."

Wilks recoils deeper into his seat and alibis himself. "You told me to be here in ten minutes. I told you it would take longer than that for my adjutant to get everything together."

Callahan whispers in his adjutant's ear. Lieutenant Gustafson smiles and nods his head in the affirmative. The deputy chief picks up the phone and dials the extension for the CO's office at Rampart. Sergeant Stoddard answers and immediately recognizes the chief's voice.

Callahan is reassuring. "Don't worry, Sergeant. Your boss made it down here just fine. That's not why I'm calling. In his haste to get here, he neglected to bring everything related to the Delaney complaint."

...

"No. No. I'll send my adjutant to your office."

...

"Yeah, everything—log entries, interview notes, tapes, the whole ball of wax."

Wilks lifts himself out of his chair and reaches for the phone. Callahan, switches the receiver to his right hand, using his left hand to gesture Wilks back into his seat.

"So, you have the completed one-eighty-one as originally submitted by Lieutenant Garcia?"

...

"Outstanding! You know my adjutant, Lukas Gustafson?"

...

"He'll be there in a few minutes."

...

"No copies! We want the originals of everything."

...

"Of course not the Communications tape—just a copy of that."

...

"You don't even have a copy?"

...

"I see."

...

"Excellent!"

...

"It's under your name?"

...

"No problem. I'll have Lieutenant Gustafson pick it up for you."

...

"Thank you, Sergeant."

Callahan turns to his adjutant. "Stoddard says he has everything ready for you, everything except a copy of a Communications tape. He had to order copies, and they are in Will Call under his name. On the way back, stop by SID and pick them up."

"Yes, sir. I won't be long."

The chief crosses his arms on his chest. "No hurry. Captain Wilks and I have a lot to talk about."

52

WILKS STANDS UP and starts for the door. "I'm out of cigarettes. I'll be right back—"

Callahan's voice is like blue steel. "You're not going anywhere until Lukas is back. Might as well make yourself comfortable." When Wilks doesn't immediately return to his seat, Callahan snarls, "*Sit the fuck down.*"

Wilks pouts as he drops his plump posterior back into the chair.

The moment Garcia's name was mentioned, Callahan knew the dynamic at play. The deputy chief rolls his executive's chair back from his desk. Sliding into the chair, he adopts an even tone. "I don't micromanage any of my COs. You got a copper who's disrespecting you... go ahead and slap him. That's what the discipline system is for." He leans back. "I know some other deputy chiefs have lost all their hair trying to control everything and everyone in their command. Not me. We have to cross the t's and dot the i's, but when it comes to disciplining blue suits, I've never say no to any of my COs."

Wilks thinks he has an opening. "We can't just let *them* take over. We can't let *them* run the LAPD."

"No doubt race plays a role in your vendetta with Lieutenant Garcia." Callahan picks up the stack of papers, shakes it, and then throws it back down on his desk. "And probably with the coppers named in this complaint." Callahan leans forward and takes a long slow deep breath. "But, that is not what is driving you now. It's your ego. It's being bested by Garcia. That's what's got you so torqued."

"Garcia's a menace." Wilks smirks. "He continually undermines my authority—"

"So beef Garcia. That's simple enough."

"That's what I'm trying to do."

"No, it isn't. In the Jefferson case you bragged you were going to 'purify' your division, get rid of the only African-American cop in Rampart. When Garcia proved the allegations were bullshit, you got pissed at Garcia. You're still pissed at him. And now you're playing catch up."

"I'm just maintaining discipline over the officers in my command. I was waiting to beef Garcia. This dropped in my lap, and it looked like the perfect opportunity to hammer that greaser. Getting the movie-star-lookalike Jew-boy was just icing on the cake."

"How does the Jewish kid fit in all this?" Callahan knows he is on the right track.

"I was going for a twofer. The Hebe probee is one of the arresting officers. Right after he came to Rampart he 'lied and denied' seeing his partner beating a defenseless juvenile lying on the ground. Got away with it by playing deaf, dumb and blind."

There is no way Captain Wilks's animus toward the probationer stems from the kid's silence on a police beating. But Callahan can't afford to get sidetracked. He must stay focused on uncovering what Wilks has done to stir up the political hornet's nest. Callahan needs Wilks to keep talking.

For Wilks's part, he is glad to keep the conversation on the Delaney beef. Walking his boss through the complaint would be a lot easier if he had a cigarette, better yet a pack of smokes and a bottle of scotch, but he doesn't. He takes a deep breath. "It started when Louise struts her stuff into my office—"

"Who is Louise?"

"Louise Delaney. The one whose house got broken into? You know...the one making the complaint." Wilks's voice is a little more derisive than he intended.

"You are on a first-name basis with her?"

"I'd like to be more than that." Wilks gets a lecherous look on his face. "Ooh. She's a looker. Has that air about her that turns me on. You know. Hard to get...but worth the effort. Prudish...but slutty at the same time."

"I get the picture. Go on."

"She sashays into my office about noon really bent out of shape. Says she has left three messages for Lieutenant Garcia, and he is not returning her calls. I figure I finally got Garcia by the balls. But in talking to her, I realize she left the messages earlier in the morning. Garcia hasn't even come to work yet. So it's not a done deal. She's complaining about everything. It was hard for me to concentrate. She kept crossing and uncrossing her legs, biting her fingernail, and..." Wilks is babbling, obviously reliving the moment. He loosens his tie as he yammers incomplete sentences. "...she says she never got broken into when she lived in San Francisco...no excuse in LA...almost an hour before the cops showed up...officers wasting time wandering around her backyard...had to drive to the station to get her stuff back—"

Callahan stops Wilks's desultory mutterings with a leading question. "I take it Garcia returned Delaney's call?"

"Yeah."

"So you couldn't charge him with failing to return her call."

"No. So, I switched up. I figured I would get Garcia for not initiating a personnel complaint. The only problem was, nothing Delaney was complaining about rose to the level of misconduct—"

"That's where the theft allegation comes in?"

"Exactly!" Wilks gloats. "The crook said he didn't have time to get rid of any stuff before getting arrested. Since the brooch was still listed on the report as property taken, I had the officers in a vice. I told Louise to allege the arresting officers either stole it or lost it. It was brilliant!"

With the origin of this canard revealed, Callahan cuts to the chase. "But when the delectable Ms. Delaney made the ridiculous theft allegation, Lieutenant Garcia didn't dismiss it. Instead, he followed policy and initiated a formal complaint, foiling your plans again."

"Yeah...pretty much." Wilks dips his head.

"OK. You knew you had a losing hand, but instead of folding, you thought you'd bluff—"

"I wasn't bluffing. I had enough cards in my hand to at least get rid of the probationer. I was going to teach Garcia a lesson, too. I figured he would fight me on the complaint, and if he pushed too hard, I'd get him on insubordination."

"Jesus Christ, Bill! We don't charge anyone with insubordination. It makes you look weak and smacks of persecution." The word has just left his mouth when he makes the connection. The whole thing is coming into focus.

Wilks is still in the dark about his boss's concerns. He can't stand the suspense any longer. Wilks looks at the deputy chief. "What do you want, Jack?"

Callahan is once again out of his chair and pacing, but it's no longer rhythmic. It's syncopated, disjointed. "What I want?" He stops midstride. He turns his head toward his subordinate. "What I want is...things to go smooth. I don't want to clean up after you anymore. Bore sighting the captain he says, "It would be bad enough if they were harassing me. But *no*! These assholes are making a stink to the chief of police! Bill, when are you going to learn to let shit like this go? What do you care? That south-of-the-border lieutenant isn't going any further north in the LAPD command structure. And as for this Jewish kid you are so worked up about, if he really fucks up during probation, I'll personally ensure he gets fired. And even if he doesn't get fired, after probation I'll wheel his butt to the jail. I bet he quits. And if he lasts through his tour in the jail, he'll be working the south end for the rest of his career. The Negroes down there will eat him alive. All the rest of this is bullshit. Unnecessary bullshit. Hell, the fucking ACLU is pushing the legislature to pass a Police Officer's Bill of Rights—"

Lieutenant Gustafson's entrance stops Callahan from getting any more worked up. The tirade stops, and Wilks doesn't ask, nor wait for permission. He is out the door.

Gustafson closes the door behind Wilks, and immediately gives his boss the straight scoop. "The arresting officers didn't take anything. They didn't lose anything, either. Lieutenant Garcia and some Jewish probationer named Stoller have frustrated Wilks before. So Wilks came up with a little ploy to say the officers either stole or lost a piece of costume jewelry that was actually never missing. It would have worked except Garcia somehow came up with this." He puts the cassette tape in the portable player, closes the lid and presses play.

...

After the tape ends, Callahan breathes a sigh of relief. "OK. No problem. I was thinking this was going to be much worse. Of course the complaint is going to have to go by the wayside. I can't trust Wilks to do it, so we are going to take over." Callahan smiles at Gustafson. "Of course when I say we, you know I'm talking about you."

"Yes, sir."

"You can open the door now. I'll handle Wilks when he gets back, and we'll get out of here."

Callahan is leaning back in his chair with his fingers interlaced behind his head when Wilks returns. "Have a seat, Bill. You have a chat with Stoddard?"

"I just called to tell him we would not need him anymore tonight."

"OK. So I don't have to play this tape again?"

"Boss, they can't prove the voice on the tape is Delaney. I've checked with SID. An expert who works in the sound lab says voice identification from tapes of phone conversations is impossible—"

Callahan tries to stop Wilks's narration. "Bill—"

Wilks continues unabated. "The SID guy says with all the background noise, and without a known sample—"

"*Bill, shut up!*"

The captain reluctantly resigns himself to silence and grabs a cigarette.

"Listen. For once in your life, *just listen*! We are taking over this complaint, and we are going to unfound it."

Wilks is feeling confident now that he knows his other nefarious activities are not being targeted. "Just because some commie groups are bitch'n about civil rights? Shit, man!" Smoke and spittle accompany his outburst. "Cops don't have any civil rights."

"You're right, Bill. Not yet anyway...You know they don't, and I know they don't. But somebody has convinced a lot of people they do, and those same folks are trying to pass a state law saying they do, and I'm not going to give them any more ammunition."

"I told you Garcia was dangerous." Wilks smirks.

"Yeah. A little too smart for his own good though. He can't go public with any of this because he would be violating the confidentiality of everyone involved. But he sure got a lot of people's blood pressure up. That is why the complaint has to go away. The tenured officer on this thing could demand a trial board, and then the whole damn thing would go public. I'm telling you right now...that is not going to happen. As of this moment, you are out of it."

"Caving in to these creeps is a mistake," Wilks mutters.

Callahan springs forward in his chair. "No, Bill. I'm not caving in. And I'm not the one who made a mistake! *The only one who fucked up here is you!* Now, I'm giving you a direct order. You are not to have any further involvement in this matter. You are not to discuss it with anyone. Have I made myself perfectly clear?"

Wilks is defiant. "I can't believe you are going to let *them* get away with it."

"I'm not letting *them* get away with *anything.*" Callahan is reaching his boiling point. "There wasn't any truth to this thing to start out with. And I'm going to administratively transfer Garcia's ass to Communications Division—he's done. And even if the probee makes probation, he's done. So help me, Bill, you're like the blind man who kills his Seeing Eye dog for barking at danger. Now get the fuck out of here before I lose my temper."

After Wilks is gone, Lieutenant Gustafson tells his boss he'll lock up. The deputy chief is anxious to call it a day. He grabs his umbrella and heads out the door. The cold and damp surround him the moment he pushes open the heavy steel door leading to the lower-level parking lot. Callahan walks gingerly across the wet, oily sheen on the pavement and gets into his brand-new take-home car.

Callahan stops at the driveway to wait for a patrol car coming northbound on San Pedro Street. As the black-and-white turns into the jail parking lot, the deputy chief heads for the freeway and switches the windshield wipers on high. He curses under his breath, "If it wasn't for that idiot Wilks, I'd have been home before the rain even started. This would be the easiest job in the world if it weren't for assholes like him."

53

TRIPLE STILL HAS the A/C on full blast. But I'm not sure the air coming through the vents is any colder than the air coming in through the open window. I'm consumed by a single thought. After tonight I'm off for three. I just have to make it to EOW. I swear I'm going to sleep seventy-two hours straight.

I can barely talk. Fortunately, my verbal chores are restricted to cryptic radio communications. Jonston is doing all the talking, boasting his way through every call. The cold rain intensifies as we near the end of our shift. Although it is contrary to policy, we are sitting in the station parking lot waiting for morning watch to relieve us. If there is anything good about working with Jonston tonight, it's sitting here waiting for change of watch.

When the back door to the station finally swings open, someone clues in the RTO, and she broadcasts, "Rampart units, mornings are down." Knowing mornings are out of roll call, the RTO broadcasts the call she is holding. "Any unit in the vicinity, an ambulance traffic, Sunset and Alvarado, handle code two."

Jonston puts to rest any lingering doubt about his character. "That call is in our area," he says and floors it. Heading out of the parking lot, he grabs the microphone and tells the RTO, "Two-Adam-one will handle the ambulance traffic, Sunset and Alvarado."

"Verify, that's two-A-one of the morning watch?" the RTO asks.

"Negative, that's two-A-one of the PM watch," Officer Jonston tells the incredulous RTO.

A traffic car comes on the air and tells the RTO to cancel the patrol unit and show them handling. I could kiss those guys. But Jonston is not going to be denied. He tells Communications to have the T unit disregard, insisting we will handle the traffic accident.

When we get to the scene, Jonston pulls in the parking lot of a closed business. Leaning back in the seat, he lights up a smoke. "I told you a good policeman never goes hungry or gets wet. I ain't get'n wet." Disdain coloring his face, he says, "Get out there and handle it."

I venture into the street with a box of road flares. The fireman on the scene help me set the flare pattern. My rain gear notwithstanding, I'm soaked. Jonston never gets out of the car. Each time I come back to the car, he sends me back to pace off another measurement or get some other piece of information. Eventually I get everything handled at the scene. I don't remember writing the report or driving home.

54

THIS IS MY second DP on the day shift. Working day watch is definitely different. Actually all three watches have their own unique feel, and it goes beyond the time of day. It's the people. Different types of cops gravitate to the different shifts. But it's not just the cops. At the city limits the signs proclaim the population of Los Angeles at two point eight million. It is estimated that during the typical workday that number swells upward of seven million. Interacting with the multitudes who ingress and egress to earn a living during the day, is very different from our contacts with the indigenous criminal element who stalk during the hours of darkness.

Of course not everyone working days is here because they want to be. I'm not. Still, the majority of cops are here by choice. While I am still relegated to the front of the roll call room, there are plenty of cops in the front row with less time than me. In fact, today is some guy's first day out of the academy. As much as I want to think my face never looked like his, it probably did.

In the parlance of the LAPD, the cops who gravitate to days are derisively referred to as *day-watch-drones*. It is another example of the police vernacular on point.

"Drone | drōn | *noun* — a male bee in a colony of social bees, which does no work but can fertilize a queen."

Of course day-watch-drones come in several subcategories. Some are burned out vets. Some are climbers. The greatest common denominator is they each have their own agenda, and it's not police work. By noon it's rare to find a unit clear. I've learned day-watch-drones start engineering EOW shortly after roll call.

There is only one P-3 on the car, Friedrich "Fritz" Hoffman. He has his twenty years in. In other words, he is vested. Even if he gets indicted and sent to prison, he will collect a pension for the rest of his life, at least the amount not going to his ex-wives. He is twice divorced and convinced that working nights was largely responsible for his first two marriages failing.

The other guy on the car is a tenured P-2, Buford Ambrose Tidwell. No one calls him Buford; they call him Tidwell or use his nick-name, Bat, a play on his initials. He hails from Fayetteville, Arkansas, the home of the Razorbacks, a fact he interjects into almost every conversation. His southern dialect immediately conjures images of mature magnolia trees shading a plantation house.

The boss is Lieutenant Horacio Hollingsworth, the archetypal pencil-neck geek. Born and reared in Massachusetts, he attended a prestigious prep school before matriculating to a small private liberal arts college in upstate Vermont. Behind his back, even the other supervisors refer to him as Hollingsworthless or just plain Worthless. He doesn't look old enough to be wearing sergeant's stripes, much less lieutenant's bars. His oft-verbalized desire to become the youngest captain on the LAPD does nothing to abrogate the natural dislike he engenders.

Even by squint standards the guy stretches credulity. He actually stands up to read *Special Orders*. The word "shall" is always bold-faced in the department manual. Worthless adds his own brand of emphasis.

I am trying unsuccessfully to get the attention of the boot sitting next to me. The kid is actually taking notes as Worthless delivers the LAPD scripture to the congregation of cops. I hope for the kids' sake none of the veterans notice his stenography.

After reading the last *Special Order*, the lieutenant continues his sermon of the LAPD gospel: "I cannot stress enough the importance of bringing these orders with you into the field. Not having this essential information at your fingertips is inexcusable. Just as ignorance of the law is not a defense to a criminal charge, not keeping abreast of the latest departmental regulations is no excuse, either. The LAPD does not tolerate mistakes." He pauses for effect. "And I assure you, I do not tolerate mistakes."

This brings a few snickers and groans from the back of the room. The derisive sounds intensify as Worthless continues, "Even one mistake could cost you. It could result in a kickback, a comment card, a negative log entry, a notice to correct deficiencies, a less than exemplary rating report, or even a one-eighty-one. I don't need to remind you how these actions will adversely impact your ability to promote."

Cognitive dissonance overloads the neural pathways in my brain, shutting out the lieutenant's nonsensical remarks. It isn't defiance— it's an act of self-defense. This idiot actually believes having a copy of a *Special Order* tucked in a notebook is going to help a street cop avoid a critical mistake.

While roll call is officially forty-five minutes long, most watch commanders talk no more than thirty minutes, allowing at least fifteen minutes for guys to check out their equipment and get to their cars. I have personally overheard tenured supervisors explaining these realities to Worthless. Still, the Boy Wonder continues to hold the troops to the last minute.

Everybody is antsy. I can feel the station parking lot is full of morning watch coppers waiting to go EOW. But Worthless continues his monologue. "All right, settle down. We still have a couple of minutes, and I have a commendation here for Officer Stoller."

I wish he had done this earlier. I don't want to be culpable in any way for us getting out of roll call late. Of course there isn't anything I can do. I'm certain the "attaboy" stems from two GTA arrests Bat and I made last week. It was a pretty good caper. We went into pursuit of two stolen cars at the same time and were able to recover both cars and capture both suspects.

I'm replaying the events in my head as the LT begins to read the commendation. My reverie is interrupted by the realization that the attaboy isn't for police work. It's for a Neighborhood Watch meeting. I was embarrassed just getting singled out in roll call. When I realize the commendation is for talking to a bunch of old ladies at a BCP meeting, I want to do a Houdini and disappear. The analog clock on the wall reads seven forty-eight. We're three minutes over.

The derisive catcalls from the back row are cut short when a mob of morning watch coppers angrily yank open the bulletproof door and pour into the hallway across from the roll call room. Their appearance prompts a couple of guys from the back row to get up and start heading out. The voice of the LT dismissing us is almost inaudible over the sound of guys gathering their stuff and shuffling out the door. I sign for the commendation and stuff the "flimsy" copy into my notebook.

I see Ron in the hallway. As I approach him he is dangling the keys to the police car. "Worthless ought'a know...some guys on mornings are about ready to frag his ass." Ron's black holes focus on mine as he emphasizes his point. "I'm serious as a heart attack."

Grabbing the keys from Ron's hands, I tell him, "That's fine with me."

Both Fritz and Bat are off today, so I'm working with a tenured P-2, Fernando Ortiz, the "Macho Man." As we toss our stuff in the trunk and preflight the equipment, the Macho Man is giving me the needle. "It's been a while since my last attaboy. Let me see it."

I try to shine him on, but he insists. Finally, I fish the flimsy copy out of my notebook and hand it to him.

Macho holds the onionskin paper above his head with both hands, studying it like a suspected counterfeit note. He lowers the piece of paper and sighs dramatically before handing it back to me. "I thought they only gave out commendations for police work. The boxes for the arrestee's name and booking number are blank. Then again...maybe I'm mistaken. It looks real enough."

I pretend to be seriously scouring the commendation for a few seconds before stuffing it back into my notebook. I sidle close to the Macho Man and whisper, "Don't tell'm down at the doughnut shop. I heard they'll give me a free cup of coffee for a *real* one of these."

My partner starts cracking up. "You're all right, Stoller. I don't care what Worthless says about you." He gives me his signature line, "Stick with me—I'll set you free."

While I was clowning around with Macho, pretending to be closely examining my commendation, I did notice something. The name in the commanding officer's box wasn't familiar. It definitely wasn't Wilks. I open my notebook and sneak a peek—Captain McNair.

"Who the hell is McNair?" I ask.

My partner glances at me, trying to figure out if I'm serious. When we stop for a red light he turns toward me, "He's our new captain. El Jefe. You know the head mutha-fucker what's in charge."

"What about Wilks?" I ask.

"He got promoted to commander...working Valley Bureau, I think. Why? You miss him?"

"Hell no! If he is gone, that's fine with me."

The pace on days is almost glacial compared to nights, especially at the beginning of the shift. Right out of roll call there is usually a spate of alarm calls as places open for business. Occasionally a patrol unit will get a traffic accident when the number of crashing commuters overwhelms the T car deployment. Day watch normally begins with only a trickle of activity.

We have already picked up our uniforms from the dry cleaners, and taken care of Macho's shopping. We are clear. My partner keeps looking at his watch while he slowly cruises on Beverly Boulevard. As soon as he turns onto a side street, he works his way back to Beverly.

Finally I ask, "What are we doing?"

"Extra patrol." Macho smiles.

Not likely. *Extra patrol* is a PR tool. If somebody calls the desk with a chronic complaint that doesn't warrant dispatching a unit, the officer will frequently try to placate the complaining party by saying he will have the car in the area drive by, give them a little extra patrol. Not surprisingly management realized the utility of the concept and formalized it. If the somebody complaining is important, or if the person complains to somebody who is important, the request will be placed in the rotator. It will get read at roll call, and a supervisor will tell the car in the area to log it when they drive by. My partner's extra patrol rationale becomes clear when a stream of young women pour onto the sidewalk on their morning coffee break.

What makes a man and a woman connect? Is it the clothes she wears? The way she does her hair? I think it is more the way she holds herself and the way she walks. There is something else, too. It's in the eyes.

"See anything you like?" Macho inquires.

"Yeah. Auburn hair…pleated skirt…we just passed her."

Macho makes a right on the next side street. He takes a parallel residential street back toward where we last saw her. My partner's timing is perfect. Approaching Beverly Boulevard, the attractive young woman is framed perfectly in my open window. This time our eye contact is prolonged. When she is just a few feet away, Macho leans over toward my open window.

"Miss, could you please give my partner your phone number? He made me drive all the way around the block just to get another look at you."

She takes her eyes off me for an instant to look at my partner, but only for an instant. Macho rips a sheet off the notepad we use to write our calls and hands it to me. I relay it to her.

Immediately after she hands the paper back, Macho apologizes to the young woman. "We have to go now. Duty calls."

I carefully fold the paper with Amber's number and slide it into my breast pocket as Macho accelerates away on Beverly.

"I told you, Max. Stick with me—I'll set you free."

Of course this little escapade violates department regulations. It's called "attempting to convert an on-duty contact to an off-duty relationship." It falls under the catchall category of CUBO (conduct unbecoming an officer). This particular phrase shows up frequently in the "department rap sheet," the report on internal discipline. The problem only arises if the woman complains.

55

IT'S MY LAST DP on probation. With Captain Wilks out of the picture, I feel pretty confident. It isn't just the job that is on the upswing. I've been out with Amber several times, and that has been great, too. The only downside is her living with her uncle and aunt in Signal Hill about thirty miles from my apartment. But as much as I drive for work, a little more windshield time for the pleasure of her company is fine with me. As Freddie Prinze says in *Chico and the Man*, things are "looking good."

Worthless has settled into the watch commander's chair and begins reading the assignments. He announces Hoffmann and Thompson are working A-one. *Who the hell is Thompson?* The brand-new boot, sitting off to my left answers up. When the lieutenant reads off my name, I learn I'm working X-9 with a guy named Levy. Not likely he's a raging anti-Semite. The only time I can recall seeing him outside of roll call, he was on a traffic stop selling a ticket.

My partner introduces himself in the hallway after roll call. "Nathan Levy," he says and offers his hand.

"Max Stoller."

He disappears after shaking my hand. While I'm standing in line to check out our equipment, Sergeant Green tells me to see him before heading out.

Sergeant Green is talking to Nathan in the parking lot. As soon as I hand my new partner his keys, he takes off.

"What's up, Sarge?" I ask.

"Somehow we wound up with three Team 22 probationers on day watch. That's why we assigned you to X-9. Besides, you don't really need a training officer anymore...and you'll officially be a P-2 before the DP ends anyway."

"Yes, sir."

"I just wanted you to know what happened. Team policing is FUBAR. Used to be each lieutenant ran a watch. Now we got an LT for each team. But the brass still want a lieutenant on each watch, too. So now the lieutenants are left balancing between the needs of their team and the needs of the watch."

"I appreciate the explanation, Sarge...and the confidence."

"I'm glad you're good with it." Sergeant Green nods toward my new partner. "Nathan isn't. Putting you with him is definitely going to cramp the guy's style. But a sergeant's job isn't making cops happy."

I drop my helmet bag in the trunk. It is alone among the boxes of road flares. I find Nathan primping himself in the rearview mirror. Nothing distracts him from perfecting his coiffure. As I kneel on the front seat to secure the shotgun, my partner doesn't take his eyes off the mirror, even when he has to move his leg to let me secure the shotgun in the rack.

Finished flicking his hair with a pick-type comb, Nathan returns the rearview mirror to its normal position, asking, "So you're a P-2 now?"

"Not yet. I got a couple of more weeks on probation."

"I don't know why they sent so many boots to Team Twenty-Two. I would have thought they would have spread them around a little more. Not that it matters to me. I'm a P-2."

"I just go where they send me," I say.

My new partner explains, "They asked me to work on A-one along with Fritz. They told me working on an A car and training boots would give me a leg up making P-3...but I don't want to be a training officer. It's not that I hate working with boots...I just prefer working alone." He studies my face. "I was in West LA for five years. Most of that time I worked an XL car on middays. I loved it."

At least I understand where my partner is coming from. Obviously Sergeant Green has already explained to Nathan this isn't my doing. Still, I hope to ameliorate things a bit. "Well, you won't have to put up with me for long. I've already told them I want to go back to nights next DP."

My pretty-boy partner heads to a coffee spot. Standing outside our police car with our morning joe, Nathan breaks the awkward silence. "This job is great for meeting women. You married?"

"No, sir. Since I've been on the job, lots of guys have said the same thing, but compared to where I used to work...well, not so much." Watching Nathan inspecting his fingernails, it's obvious his number one concern is chasing skirts, not criminals. "I take it you aren't married?"

"Me?" My partner straightens his back and adopts his best Bob Bitch'n pose. "Not in a million. No reason to get married if you're a cop in LA. There are way too many women in this town who just love a man in uniform." Nathan looks me up and down. "You're not an ugly guy. With a little coaching from somebody like me, you might find this job is just the ticket for you."

"I'm not really on the job to meet chicks. Besides, I recently met a young lady and everything is groovy between us." From the expression on Nathan's face, that wasn't the answer he wanted to hear.

After coffee, Nathan is staying on the main streets. He tells me, "I write a lot of tickets. The expectation for cops working patrol is about fifteen to twenty a DP. I average between forty and fifty. So supervision pretty much leaves me alone. I figured it out once. The city actually makes more money on my citations than they pay me."

I pretend to believe this patently false statement. Adding up the bail on the cites and comparing it to his salary, his assertion might appear to have some merit; but that's hardly the whole story. In truth, the benefits package significantly increases the actual salary cost to the city, and only a fraction of traffic fines collected by the courts are redirected to the city. Just the notion of the police department as a moneymaking enterprise is an anathema to me.

My partner continues, "Another reason I like working an L car is that policy says you shall go code six on everything, even routine traffic stops. So I don't spend a lot of time clear. Since dispute calls can't be dispatched to a one-man unit, I don't end up handling a ton of ridiculous, jacked-up radio calls."

"Sounds like you have the system down pretty good."

• • •

We've made several traffic stops. Nathan has warned a couple and written a couple. He is getting his tickets. Even though we are a two-man car, and our stops have all been on single women drivers, he always insists we go code six.

Right in front of us, a guy in an old fender-side pickup truck passes on the right, almost taking out a pedestrian in the crosswalk. "I'll take that one!"

"What?" Nathan is oblivious.

"Number two lane...the brown pickup truck. He almost creamed the ped in the crosswalk!"

Nathan maneuvers behind the pickup and hits the reds. Coming back to our car with the guy's license and registration, Nathan says he has decided to write him.

I look at him in disbelief. "Hey, partner, I'm up. Besides, you didn't even see the violation."

"I thought you weren't that interested in writing tickets," he says with irritation in his voice.

"I'm not. But a good ticket is a good ticket. And writing tickets is part of the job."

I think to myself, Sergeant Green was right. I'm cramping this guy's style.

• • •

Nathan insists we take our code seven at the station. As soon as we get "OK Seven," he disappears, saying he has a few calls to make. After lunch we get a found property call. The PR is a prissy woman in her late fifties wearing heavy makeup and garish red lipstick that only accentuates her sagging, blanched complexion.

She unlocks a huge padlock and opens her garage to show us a bicycle lying on the floor. Leaning forward as she gestures toward the kid's bike, the gray roots below her bouffant hairdo are apparent. Her disingenuous eyes focus on my partner as she insists she doesn't know who the bike belongs to. "I just had to lock it up in my garage for safekeeping," she says.

I'm sure if we knocked on a few doors we could find out who the bike belongs to. But Nathan puts the bike in our trunk. He says, "Booking this into property will be our End of Watcher. We'll go out to the station about two hours early. Just take your time doing the paperwork."

I can't wait until this DP ends. Not only will I be off probation, but next DP I won't have to work with Nathan. It is not doing the paperwork required to book the bicycle that bothers me. It isn't his engineering EOW that sticks in my craw, either. It is Nathan's wittingly aiding the old biddy in her battle with the neighborhood. Some kid is going to be without his bike. More than that, I am convinced Nathan is using his official position to stop lone female drivers in furtherance of his prurient ambitions. Of course I do not have any proof. Nonetheless, I'm convinced that's what he is doing, and it bugs me.

Still, I can't help but feel hypocritical. After all, I met Amber on duty. If push came to shove, I'm sure the department wouldn't see any distinction between my actions and Nathan's. There is no denying

I was working in uniform when I met Amber. But I didn't pull her over. If she had just looked the other way and walked away, that would have been the end of it. Shouldn't I give the same benefit of the doubt to Nathan?

When I was working PMs almost every night near EOW, there would be a spate of prowler complaint calls. A surprisingly large number of these calls were cop groupies requesting stud service. The callers were typically divorcées in their late thirties. A lot of the women were pretty blatant, asking for a little company to help them "feel safe during the night." Some of them were fairly attractive. While the women typically went for the older-looking guys, a couple of times they came on to me, but women about my mom's age don't turn me on. These liaisons violate policy, too. Still, I don't begrudge any of the cops who followed up on those invitations, and I don't regret meeting Amber.

56

ROLL CALL THE next morning brings another surprise. Bat is on a regular day off. Hoffman banged in for a T/O, so they need someone to work with the new boot on A-one. Nathan gets elected, and he's not happy about it. It's fine with me, because it means I don't have to work with Nathan. But holy shit! It also means I'm working an L car. I'm going out by myself.

Even the familiar process of preflighting the car feels novel. My nervousness reminds me of my first night in the field. Maybe it's because my mind is replaying that first night, or maybe it is just habit. I fumble my first radio transmission. "Two-Adam-one...ah correction...Two-X-Ray-Lincoln-nine, clear." It is going to take conscious effort to remember my new call sign.

The RTO gives me two calls as I am driving in traffic, and I realize just how much having a passenger officer eases the load on the driver. At least this car has a cheater. Hearing the other officers talking to the RTO helps both my situational awareness, and makes it easier to avoid stepping on someone, especially when I am trying to broadcast and drive at the same time.

A guy runs a red light right in front of me. I take off after him. Just as I grab the mic to run the plate, the violator makes a quick right. I almost wrap the cord around the steering wheel. At the last second, I let the mic fall into my lap. That was what Ron said to do if I found myself driving solo.

The violator's two quick turns don't shake me. I'm right on his ass when he yanks it to the curb. I didn't have a chance to run the plate before the stop, so I give the license plate to the RTO as I am going code six. There is still no return on the plate as I approach.

I ask the bushy-haired college kid behind the wheel for his license and registration. The smart mouth insists he didn't run the light. Why am I not surprised? Before heading back to my car to write the ticket, the RTO comes back with "no wants, no warrants." Before scratching out the ticket I run the violator anyway, hoping he has at least an unpaid parking ticket. He doesn't.

Back at the driver's door, the nineteen-year-old looks up at me and says, "You wrote the wrong guy, pig. I wasn't even at that intersection. I was here on this side street the whole time. You can't make me sign noth'n."

"You are right about one thing…I can't make you sign the citation. Your signature is not an admission of guilt. It's simply your promise to appear in court. If you refuse to sign, you are refusing to promise to appear." My voice turns to hardened steel. "Without your signed promise to appear, I can't let you go—I have to book you, and that's fine with me."

I don't understand why this guy is being such a dick. A number of people have initially said they wouldn't sign, but no one has actually refused. After all that blustering, he takes the pen and signs the ticket. Before he pulls away, he looks up at me and says, "That's a fucked-up intersection. It changes red way too fast."

As soon as I clear, the RTO gives me a business dispute call in the southern portion of the division. They jointly assign the call to L-thirty and me. After handling the call with Sergeant Green, I take my time meandering through the business district back toward my beat. No sense rushing; they don't assign a supervisor to a call unless there are no other units clear. No doubt I'll get another call soon, and likely as not, it won't be in my area.

Sandwiched in traffic, stopped at a red light, I hear through the cheater, "Officer needs help, shots fired in the bank parking lot…"

Holy shit! I didn't hear a unit designation, and I don't recognize the voice of the officer requesting help, but whoever he is, he is really close. There are cars in front of me, behind me, and to the left of me. I can't just sit here with a cop in a gun battle only a few blocks away. *Fuck it!* I turn into the curb and step one wheel at a time onto the sidewalk. I flip on the reds, reach down and squelch the siren. Pedestrians are scattering out of the way—a mixture of fright and disbelief in their faces. A wobbly wino, almost immobilized by alcohol, is in my path. His eyes swell like in a cartoon. There is no way the drunk can scamper off the sidewalk. Somehow he plasters himself against the building. God bless him!

Reaching the corner, I drive off the curb. *Bam!* The undercarriage slams into the pavement as the suspension maxes out. Heavy on the gas, the rear end starts to fishtail. I back off the throttle just enough to keep control. With only two blocks to go, my foot is back to the floor. I slide to a stop at the edge of the bank parking lot. From here I can see the entire parking lot and the door to the bank. *What the fuck?* I don't see any marked units, or uniformed officers.

As I grab the mic, my eyes are scanning for plain cars. I don't see any detectives, either. "Two-XL-nine is code six on the help call. I don't see the officers. Have you got a better location?"

I want to get out the shotgun, but it is locked. Looking for anything out of the ordinary, I grab the extra set of keys from my belt. My hands feel for the right key.

Why isn't there a commotion in the parking lot? People are just going about their business. *Could the officers be inside the bank?*

The link has taken over for the RTO. He acknowledges my code six, and then broadcasts: "Unit requesting help, come in to control and identify."

After a prolonged silence, I hear through the cheater, "Two-L-thirty, can you phone the bank to verify if there is a two eleven (robbery)?" The sound of Sergeant Green's siren in the background is clearly audible through the radio. Although only one unit is authorized to respond code three, on a help call, everyone goes balls to the wall.

"Roger L-thirty, we are doing that now." The link continues trying to raise the unit. "Unit requesting help—code one—come in to control and identify."

I hazard a glance to insert the key in the lock on the shotgun rack. With my eyes once again looking outside the car, I turn the key and open the latch. I pull the tube from its mount and exit the driver's door in one motion. With the shotgun at port arms, I take cover behind the engine compartment of my cruiser and continue scanning the parking lot.

The reflection off the bank's glass doors prevents me from seeing inside. When the door swings open, I see a middle-aged woman wearing a full skirt and heels exit the bank nonplussed.

Sirens are coming from all directions. A motor officer is coming in at light speed. Hard on the brakes, the rear tire skids and the heavy motorcycle yaws sideways. I'm sure he is going to drop it, but somehow he keeps the shiny side up. Jumping off his motor, he must think I'm the unit that put out the help call. When I tell him I'm just the first unit to go code six, he joins me, using my car for cover.

Police cars are pouring in now, both marked and unmarked units. There might not have been any units clear, but that doesn't mean there aren't a lot of cops out here. Sergeant Green pulls up behind me. Despite the feedback in his radio, I can hear his broadcast.

"Two-L-thirty, show a code four on the help call. Sufficient units at this time. Let's do a roll call."

This is the procedure when the identity of a unit cannot be determined. Communications goes through the call sign of every unit, asking them to respond. Before the link can begin the roll call, two-Charlie-fifteen comes on the air. Charlie is the radio designation for the parking enforcement units. Although most who work parking enforcement are women, there are a couple of males. The civilian parking checker working two-Charlie-fifteen today is a man.

"Two-Charlie-fifteen, it was me…ah, I heard what I thought were gunshots, but now I think it was probably…ah…a car backfiring."

The agitation in the link's voice is apparent. "All units code four on the help call in Rampart. No shots fired. No officer needs help. All units resume normal patrol."

The motor cop who damn near dropped his bike yanks off his helmet. "Jesus Fucking Christ! Just when I thought I'd seen everything. A fuck'n Charlie unit putting out a fucking bullshit help call."

I want to shout, "Amen, brother." But I don't. Instead, I look at Sergeant Green. "Do you know what I did to get here?"

Sergeant Green's eyes bore into mine. "Unless you hit something, I don't think I want to know."

I smile at my sergeant. "There might be a wino with a load in his pants, but I didn't hit anything."

"Good."

With that, he makes his way back to his cruiser. As he is driving away, I hear him on the radio. "Two-L-thirty, have two-Charlie-fifteen meet me at the watch commander's office—code two. And show me out to Rampart."

I don't want to admit it. But I'm not certain if in the excitement I jacked a round into the chamber. I'm not taking any chances. Before I return the shotgun to its rack, I unload the magazine and work the action. The chamber is empty. Still, I feel better knowing for certain.

When I heard the voice on the cheater reporting shots fired and requesting help at the bank, I was convinced an officer was in a firefight. No other possibility even crossed my mind. I am really lucky I didn't hit something, or *someone* getting to the scene. Ron is right. There are an unlimited number of ways for things to go to shit out here. He was also right when he said, "Experience is a hell of a teacher."

As soon as I clear from the bank, the RTO gives me another call. "Two-XL-nine, two-X-Ray-Lincoln-nine, See the woman, a four-five-nine report—correction—a four-five-nine investigation at…"

• • •

The Orwellian LAPD has issued an edict. The word "investigation" shall be substituted for the word "report" in every possible situation. Poags at PAB have been scouring thousands of pages of manuals and procedures to discover every instance where the word "report" appears. Untold man-hours have been wasted debating the perfect derivative of the word "investigate" to be utilized in its place.

It is not simply a matter of grammar or syntax. For the bureaucrats, this newspeak is critical. The issue elevates simmering administrative skirmishes into full-blown turf wars. Barrages of intradepartmental correspondence are exchanged as the debate rages. The movement grows, and for a while, the term "detective" is replaced with "investigator," even on the badges.

• • •

The address of my burglary investigation is a dingy single-family residence of wooden shiplap construction. The front door is open as I make my approach. Through the screen door I see a woman about thirty years old wearing a tie-dyed top and a midi-length floral skirt with a macramé belt. Her reddish-brown hair is frizzed out à la Janis Joplin.

Turning at the waist, she uses her hand to indicate the stuff strewn on the floor. "I came home and found the place trashed. The back door was wide open."

"Yes, ma'am." I expect her to push open the screen door, or to do something to invite me in, but she doesn't.

It's obvious she would just as soon I do my investigation standing on the porch. After more than a few awkward moments, she says, "I guess you have to come in."

"Yes, ma'am." A quick check of the interior shows the whole place has been pretty well ransacked. I ask her the normal questions. During the conversation she mentions her boyfriend left last night for Cincinnati on business.

I ask, "Anyone else know he was leaving?"

"Not that I know of."

"Do you leave and come home about the same time every day?"

"No. I don't work. I'm in and out a lot during the day."

Walking around the outside of the residence, I notice a window screen has been bent and removed, and there are fresh tool marks at the bottom of the window sash, but this is not the point of entry. The window is still locked. The window hasn't been opened since the last time it was painted. The point of entry is definitely the back door. The suspect(s) pried at the doorjamb near the striker plate until they were able to force the door open. A deadbolt would have stopped this effort. I am beginning to think the suspect(s) have not broken into a lot of places before. Juveniles in the neighborhood are the probable culprits. I question the victim in this regard, but she begs off answering my questions.

I sit down in the living room to scratch out the report, and I can see the victim is getting agitated. "Why are you asking me so many questions?"

"I'm just trying to find out what happened."

"I got broken into. Isn't that all you need to know?"

"Not quite. It's my job to try to find who took your stuff."

"You don't ever actually catch anyone, do you?"

"Not too often, but sometimes. The detectives will get this report and follow up from their end."

"Well, if you did…catch someone…if you found out who broke in? What would you do?"

"I'd arrest them—put them in jail."

"Oh, my God. No! I don't want that. Whoever did this is probably strung out...needs drugs really bad. I wouldn't want anyone to go to jail. I just want a number...you know, for my insurance company. Just give me a number. That's all I want."

"It doesn't work that way. I do the preliminary investigation, write the report, and then it gets assigned a number afterward. The report automatically goes to the detectives. The whole process is designed to identify the perpetrators and bring them to justice."

I already have all the boxes filled in on the face sheet. With as many burglary reports as I have written, the narrative isn't going to take long. But, I smell trouble. "Are you telling me you won't sign this report?"

"I'm not going to be responsible for someone going to jail. If signing means someone might go to jail...then, the answer is no. No way!" She is shaking her head from side to side so hard I'm afraid it might fall off.

I don't want her to accuse me of "kissing off" the call, so I stuff the nearly completed report back in my binder and pull out my field officer's notebook. I write her name, the date and time, followed by the simple statement: "I refuse to make a report at this time." She signs my notebook, and I'm out the door.

57

I LEFT MY apartment early, thinking I would have plenty of time to pick up Amber in Signal Hill and get back to the academy for my "probation party." It feels more like I'm piloting a skiff on a river than driving a car on a highway. With the downpour overloading the freeway drainage system, the markings on the roadway are little more than wavering illusions. I might not be late picking up Amber, but getting back to the academy is another matter. Like it or not, it looks like tonight the Stoller Man is going to be fashionably late.

Traffic is slogging along at about twenty knots with arcs of water squirting from everyone's tires. As cars plow into pools of water, they create rooster tails that easily vault the center divider. Likewise, tsunamis launched from the other side descend without warning. When a wave of water lands on your car, instead of splashing, it sounds like a skip loader dropping a bucket of gravel. The loud rattling on the sheet metal coupled with the sudden obstruction of vision is disorienting.

Careening into the deep water is as treacherous as getting hammered by the waterfalls coming from the other side. Even at moderate speeds running into these pools can yank the steering wheel from your hands. It is hard to resist hitting the brakes. But I know slamming on the brakes is the worst thing to do. So I'm avoiding the center lane, keeping a firm grip on the wheel, and maintaining a lot of distance from the car ahead me.

After I transition to the southbound Long Beach Freeway, the inevitable happens. Somewhere in front of me a driver hits the brakes and spins out. Coming up on the scene, I see a VW Bug resting perpendicular to the flow of traffic, its front bumper flush against the center divider, its rear bumper protruding into the fast lane.

A dark blue Suburban pulls to the center divider short of the accident. I stop behind the SUV and get out with my umbrella. In these conditions my chrome and cloth contraption doesn't provide much shelter. It is a struggle to light road flares while holding the umbrella. Still, I manage to put down a couple before joining the man from the Suburban who has approached the driver's door of the VW.

The young woman behind the wheel is sobbing, literally shaking from the experience.

"You can't stay here, Miss," the guy from the Suburban says. "It's too dangerous...somebody's going to hit you."

He turns to me. "Let's get her to my vehicle. My wife can look after her there."

Escorting the shaken girl to the SUV, my umbrella is more symbolic than sheltering.

The man's wife rolls down her window enough for us to hear her directions. "Put her in the backseat." The wife reaches back and unlocks the door. As the young woman is climbing in the back of the Suburban, the wife tells her husband. "Get the blanket in the back. Poor thing. She's shivering."

After doing as he was told, the burly man rejoins me at the VW. The sooner we can get the girl's car out of the fast lane, the better. But the spin killed the engine, and now the little car doesn't want to start. Another vehicle pulls over and parks in front of the accident, a safer choice for sure. The driver gets out and jogs toward us. It is clear the VW doesn't want to start.

We are all of one mind. "The hell with it!"

We each grab the rear bumper and yank in unison. The relatively light car bounces on its suspension as we lift and pull it toward the guard rail. After a few repeats of this strategy the VW is hugging the center divider, pointed in the right direction, and out of traffic.

The guys who parked in front of the accident says, "I gotta go, or I'll be late for roll call. I work Torrance PD."

"Thanks for your help," I say.

"No sweat!" the off-duty Torrance cop shouts back over his shoulder as he heads back to his car.

Heading back toward our cars, the driver of the Suburban says, "I'm with the Secret Service."

"LAPD," I respond.

He tells me, "My wife and I will take care of the girl until the Highway Patrol gets here."

I acknowledge him with a thumbs-up and jog back to my car. I don't have to kick the flares out of the roadway. The rain has drowned them. Back behind the wheel I take a quick glance in the mirror. I'm a wet mess.

Again headed toward Amber's place, I can't help but contemplate what just happened. Three people stopped to help the accident victim in the rain. It's easy to know why most people don't stop. *What makes some people stop? Why did I stop?*

I am preoccupied with a more immediate concern. *What will Amber say when she sees my sorry, soggy self?*

After Amber hears what happened, she isn't angry. "That could have been me crashed on the freeway," she says. "You and those other cops stopping to help her out—I think that's wonderful." She laughs and grabs my arm as we head to the car. Playfully wiping at my shirt she chides me, "But you *do* look like you took a shower with your clothes on."

• • •

By the time we get to the academy the rain has moderated and my umbrella does a good job keeping Amber dry as we walk to the Academy Lounge. I'm folding my umbrella under the overhang just outside the entrance when the door opens. Although he has shaved off his mustache and is dressed in civilian clothes, I recognize him immediately.

"Officer Robles! I didn't expect to see you here." I quickly hang my umbrella on rail of the landing and introduce my girlfriend.

"You don't have to call me Officer Robles anymore. It's Ray. Just call me Ray," he says, nodding to Amber.

"Let me buy you a beer." I say.

Ray gives me a funny look. "I'm just here because the brass 'encourages' us to make an appearance at these things. I've done my duty, and now I'm out of here, but..." He jots his home address and phone number on the back of his business card. "Call me tomorrow. I'll throw some steaks on the barbecue and we'll have that beer. Bring your girl, too. I'm sure both of you will hit it off with my wife." He gives me one of his flashbulb smiles. "She's a *Jap*."

What? Why would I care that his wife is Asian? And why would he be so crude as to call her a Jap?

As he heads down the stairs, he says over his shoulder, "And bring bathing suits and a change of clothes tomorrow—like you should have tonight."

58

WALKING INTO THE Academy Lounge, the first person I spot is Sean Edwards. As big as he is, he is hard to miss. As soon as Sean sees us, he grabs his wife by the hand and pulls her in our direction. I alibi my appearance as I am introducing Amber. I remember Sean's wife from the graduation party, but at this moment, I can't remember her name. Recognizing my dilemma, Sean helps me out and mentions his wife's name is Suzanne.

It isn't long before Grissom and his wife, Bonnie, join us. Bonnie looks like she is going to give birth to their second child before the night is out. Although Rutherford's wife is enthralled in an animated conversation with several other wives, that doesn't dissuade the Crazy Scot from dragging her to our group.

It's only been eight months, but in some ways it feels like years since we were recruits. Seeing the guys I used to eat lunch with every day on the stone wall in front of the academy, I almost expect to see Silverstein. He was a genuinely good guy. *Why am I thinking of him like he died?*

There is another classmate who shouldn't be hard to spot if he is here. I saw his name on the transfer, so I know he made probation. Scanning the room for Booker, I see a much less welcome sight heading our way. Arm in arm with his platinum-blond wife, Logan strolls up to our group. Like a politician he glad-hands his way around our circle.

Maybe it's because I'm still soggy. Whatever reason, Logan doesn't recognize me immediately. When he does, the competition between dismay and surprise are evident. Dismay wins.

"Stoller? You made it?"

"Yeah. Looks like it."

Logan can't pull his hand away quickly enough as he hurries to the next introduction. The self-impressed couple lingers only long enough for his wife to gloat that her husband is working CRO (community relations office). As soon as the pair are out of earshot, Sean gives voice to what we all are thinking.

"Logan has always been a dick. He's just sore 'cause Tafolli has him beat."

Tafolli is one of our classmates who subscribed to Logan's credo—scam everyone. But Tafolli ran under the radar much more effectively. All I remember of him in the academy is a bad vibe. Tonight I learn my feeling is shared by everyone in the group.

"What do you mean Tafolli has him beat?" I ask.

"Tafolli spent most of his probation working in the captain's office in Wilshire Division."

"I thought you had to work the street when you're on probation, unless you're on the Buy Team." The Buy Team is an undercover narcotics assignment. Instead of going to patrol after the academy, a few officers who can pass for teenagers are assigned to work uncover, posing as high school students. They purchase illegal drugs to make cases against the pushers, hence the name, Buy Team.

"Yeah, I thought that, too. But somehow Tafolli became the captain's bun boy and wormed his way out of patrol. He made LAPD history. He's the only guy ever to go from P-1 to P-3. Not even a single day as a P-2."

"No shit? When I saw his name on the transfer I thought it was a typo."

Sean changes the subject and starts talking about his experiences working Club Dev in the valley. "I gotta admit the academy was pretty tough. But it was worth it. This is the best job I ever had...getting paid to sleep." He is laughing as he throws back his drink before announcing, "I'm gonna work morning watch the rest of my career. Hell, half of our shifts are three liners."

"Three liners?" Rutherford asks.

"You know, roll call—code seven—EOW, a three-line log." Sean can't believe we don't all understand.

"Maybe working Devonshire Division. That's the reason they call it Club Dev. But downtown? No way! Working Rampage our logs are usually two pages, front and back. Shit, one night I only avoided a third sheet of paper by putting EOW in the remarks. It was crazy. We spent half the night handling calls in Hollywood Division."

"I think I know the night you mean," Grissom says. "I was working mornings in Hollywood. Right out of roll call there was an OIS (officer-involved shooting). After the OIS went down, there was a two-eleven-one-eighty-seven (robbery-murder) at a gas station. Man, that was a bad scene."

He takes a long draw on his beer before launching into his street cop description of the events. "John Q Public pulls his Buick up to the far pump of the only station selling gas at that hour. While the citizen is walking toward the pay window, he sees the suspect come out of the shadows pulling a ski mask over his face...and a *big-ass automatic* out of his waistband. The bad guy is between the citizen and his Rivy. So, figuring discretion is the better part of valor, John Q books up. But when John Q gets across the street he notices the suspect isn't paying any attention to him. So he does what he is supposed to do..." Grissom pauses for a sip of beer. "He drops a dime. He is watching the whole thing go down from the phone booth across the street. He sees the gas station attendants give up the cash. He sees the suspect order both employees to get on their knees. The poor citizen is still on the pay phone, hearing for the umpteenth time, 'You have reached the emergency number for the Los Angeles Police Department. All our operators are currently busy...please stand by...' when he sees the suspect shoot the kneeling victims in the head."

It's like the referee blew his whistle. Suddenly we all stop and look around. But, the girls have since slipped away and are in a circle of their own.

Sean interrupts, asking, "They give out the poop on that caper at roll call?"

"Yeah, the watch commander mentioned it the next night, but it wasn't news to me. We were the primary unit on the call."

"That had to be a good code three run. Were you driving?"

"Me driving? Hell no. This went down my first or second DP. But, it wasn't a code three ride. It came out as a 'four-fifteen man with a gun, code two.'"

"Somebody at communications fucked up on that one."

"I don't know, but I'm going to find out pretty quick. I'm being wheeled to Communications Division next DP," Grissom says, and empties his beer.

"They got me on the wheel too," I tell everyone. "I'm going to the jail."

Rutherford crows, "Man, I hear both are fucked-up assignments. That's why they have to wheel guys there."

"No shit, Sherlock."

By now our circle has expanded. Actually, it has morphed into an amoeba-like glob of guys telling war stories. Maybe that's another meaning to the term *bull session*—it's just the guys.

Inevitably the topic turns to everyone's first few nights in the street. All my classmates who broke in working the South End tell similar stories. One of my classmates who did his probation in Seventy-Seventh Division, recounts his first night. "My TO had hash marks all down his arm. He was a serious old salt with a one-zero number. As soon as we pull out of the station, he tells me he's gonna stop the first dirt bag he sees. 'After I pat him down, you got exactly eight point two seconds to choke his ass out.'"

Somebody says, "Shit man, at least my TO didn't give me a time limit."

"Yeah, well mine said, 'Twelve months on probation gives the department eight months after the academy to decide if you have what it takes.' Then he says, 'Work'n the street, you gotta think a lot quick'n than that. Me, I only need eight point two seconds.'"

• • •

It is as if the intervening eight months were just a dream. Just as a dream ends, suddenly the party is over, and it is time to go.

A light rain is still falling as we head to my car. I have my left arm around Amber's slim waist. The warmth between us is delightful. I'd wrap my right arm around her, too, except I have to use it to hold the umbrella.

As we approach the car I apologize for my inattention during the evening. "I hope you weren't too bored."

Her aquamarine eyes twinkle as she replies, "I'm glad you invited me. Talking with the other cops' wives, I got a better sense of what it's like."

I don't want to let her go, not even for a second. But I can't hold the umbrella and open the door without letting go. After she slides into the passenger seat, I hurry to the driver's side. Quickly stashing the wet umbrella on the rear floorboard, I jump into the driver's seat. Out of reflex my right hand inserts the key in the ignition even as my left hand pulls my door closed.

Amber gently tugs at my right arm. When I turn toward her she surprises me with a passionate wet kiss. When we come up for air, she murmurs, "I don't want you to have to drive me all the way back to Signal Hill. It doesn't make any sense when your apartment is just a couple of miles from here."

My lips linger on hers for as long as I dare before turning the ignition. When the big V-8 comes to life, I slide the selector to defrost and put the fan on high. The energy flows between us as we wait for the windshield to clear.

59

THE ADDRESS OFFICER Robles wrote on the back of his business card is in Arcadia. I've never even heard of Arcadia. Looking up the street in my Thomas Guide, I envision a working-class neighborhood. I never imagined the street would be shaded by mature trees and feature custom homes on large lots.

I pull to the curb in front of adobe-style house and check the numbers against the address on the business card. *Yeah. This is it.* The architecture and construction tell me the place was built in the twenties. Although it is not as large as some of the other homes in the neighborhood, there is no question it costs way more than a policeman can afford.

I take Amber's hand as we approach the double doors inside the arched entryway. In my other hand is a bottle of Chardonnay. The clerk at the spirit shop said it was a good vintage. When Amber presses the doorbell, we hear the elegant chime through the solid oak doors. In less than a minute Ray ushers us into his "hacienda." He relieves me of the bottle of wine as he introduces his wife, Rachel.

I'm surprised. She doesn't look Asian. *Why did he tell me she was a Jap?*

As his wife shows Amber the house, Ray leads me into the back-yard. He grabs both of us a beer from a small refrigerator built into the flagstone cooking station that overlooks the pool. I'm not usually much for beer, but this stuff tastes terrific.

It's a beautiful day, just the way I like it. The skies are clear, the sun is warm, and the air is crisp and clean. When the light breeze brushes the placid surface of the pool the clear blue water sparkles. I take another drink from the malty brew in the green bottle. This is the way to live. I have a million questions for Ray.

Before I can ask any of them, Ray says, "My wife's an attorney. Corporate. She does really well. And of course, we're DINKs."

"Dinks?" My eyebrows arch.

"You know. Double Income—No Kids."

"I've never heard that before."

After a sip of his Heineken, Ray asks, "So how did things go at Rampart?"

"For a while I wasn't sure I was going to make probation." I savor another sip of elixir. "I almost came up to the academy to ask your advice—"

Ray interrupts. "Had a little go-round with Wilks, did you?"

"A little go-round?" I shake my head. "No. I got ambushed."

I give him the CliffsNotes version of the chicken stand caper.

When I get to the part where Wilks called me into his office, Ray interrupts again, "Let me guess. He told you he'd forget all about your previous statement."

"Exactly. How did you know?"

"It's common practice." He drains his beer and rests his eyes on mine. "Actually, I'm surprised you didn't fall for it."

"Thanks for the vote of confidence."

"I wouldn't have made you a squad leader in the academy if I doubted your ability to survive in the street." Ray laughs. "But, your

John Boy naiveté concerned me." He lights the burner on the BBQ, and then resets his attention on me. "Honestly, it still does."

"What do you mean?"

"Let's get real. As long as there are guys like Wilks in charge, there are going to be guys like Sticktime. That is why good cops have more to worry about than the crooks on the street. But there is way more to it than that—"

I interrupt him. "I'm not completely out to lunch. I know there are still some real jerks on the department." I'm about to tell him I heard a cop saying NVNNHI on the radio, but I don't get the chance.

Ray announces, "The LAPD is like a battleship. Even a slight correction in course takes time. Any serious change of direction requires a lot of time and a lot of ocean...not to mention an experienced hand at the helm." He looks at me with genuine surprise. "Did you really think that because there was a little diversity at the academy, that the LAPD wasn't still just a good ole boy's club?"

"I knew guys who look like Booker were going to have it rough, but why me?"

"Why you? Do you think 'If you're white you're all right, if you're brown stick around, and if you're black get back' tells the whole story? Shit, man! You should understand better than most. Did you think anti-Semitism stopped when the Allies liberated Dachau? My wife's a JAP, Jewish American Princess. She grew up in America, went to the best schools, and has a terrific job, but she knows. How is it you don't get it?"

This isn't what I expected when my old squad adviser invited us for a "nice afternoon." I put down my beer and snap, "I'm not that stupid. I know some people just—"

"Do you really think no one knows?" Ray looks at me in disbelief as the realization hits him.

"Knows what?"

"That you're Jewish?"

I'm completely taken aback. "What?" I stammer, "Amber doesn't even know."

Ray chuckles. "If your girlfriend didn't know before, she does now. I'm sure my wife has brought it up already."

I take a deep breath and start to explain, saying, "My parents changed our last name just before we moved to California. We assiduously avoided any reference to our ancestry or any connection with Judaism. My mom insisted we attend a Lutheran church. We did Christmas and everything. How could anyone think of me as Jewish now? I don't even look Jewish. I can't even remember ever being inside a synagogue."

Ray laughs. "That's it. Isn't it? All this time you thought no one knew." Ray grabs both of us another beer and shakes his head. He puts his hand on my shoulder as he offers me the fresh one. "So it is OK for people to hate on you if you went to a synagogue instead of a church? Would that make it justified? Would it make it right?"

I've been both blind and stupid. A lot of things were hidden, but mostly I just chose not to look at things I didn't want to see. I feel guilty and ashamed, realizing that I've been willfully complicit in bigotry. Tipping back the fresh beer helps me avoid eye contact with my mentor.

"What is the most dangerous type of call a cop can get?" Ray asks.

Without hesitation I answer, "A family dispute." I want to tell him about the family dispute call where I almost shot the guy reaching for a gun, but again Ray doesn't give me a chance.

"Why are family disputes so dangerous?"

"Because when people get all emotional, you don't know what they are going to do."

"Exactly." Ray uses a set of tongs to place the steaks on the grill. His eyes shift from the grill to me. "It is even worse when the person you're dealing with seems to be rational and then suddenly does something crazy. That's the problem with bigotry." He takes a swig from his beer and gives me the same look he did the day he handed me the squad leader insignias. "It is dangerous enough when you know the person you're dealing with has crazy hatred inside his or her head. When you don't know—it's much worse. It's what you don't see that kills you. As a LA cop, you can't afford not to see.

The End

Thank you for reading *False Negatives*.
Please visit us on the web at www.goodguypublishinghouse.com

Registering on the website makes you eligible to win cool stuff, including a free copy of *Black and White*, the upcoming sequel to *False Negatives*. You won't want to miss Officer Stoller coming into his own as he literally fights his way through his next assignment at the jail. *Black and White* is more than an action-packed cop drama that reunites Stoller and Booker policing the city's toughest neighborhood. It is a first-rate political thriller that makes the internal politics of the LAPD look like child's play.